CONNIE

- - - -

MEG

Robert Silverberg

WITH A FOREWORD BY THE AUTHOR

Stark House Press • Eureka California

CONNIE / MEG

Published by Stark House Press
1315 H Street
Eureka, CA 95501, USA
griffinskye3@sbcglobal.net
www.starkhousepress.com

ISBN: 978-1-951473-32-7

Cover design by Jeff Vorzimmer, ¡caliente!design, Austin, Texas
Text design by Mark Shepard, shepgraphics.com
Proofreading by Bill Kelly
Cover art by Paul Rader

First Stark House Press Edition: May 2021

CONNIE

Teenage Connie has her life all mapped out. She and John will go steady until she joins him at college. Then after graduation, they will be married. John will begin law school, and there will be three children, a pretty little home on Long Island and a trip to Europe… but all that changes the night she is kidnapped by a gang of young toughs, taken to an old warehouse, and repeatedly raped. Connie's dreams are shattered—nothing is the same. John is hesitant and uncomfortable with her. Her parents only want to send her away to live with her grandparents for a while. With nothing left to lose, Connie decides to start getting even with the world.

MEG

The night Meg loses her virginity she sees her Idaho life mapped out for her: marriage to a farmer, a bunch of kids, old before her time. But Meg has bigger dreams than that. She knows the power her body has over men. So she hops a bus for New York City and discovers a talent agent named Max Bonaventura who is so impressed by her bounteous figure that he decides to throw all his efforts into making her a star. Sure, she might have to strip in front of total strangers… she might have to sleep with a few guys to get there… but it'll be worth it. Max knows what he's doing, and Meg knows that anything is better than going back to Idaho. Or is it?

Contents

FOREWORD

You will note from the copyright notice that these books were written more than sixty years ago. The world has changed quite a bit in the past sixty years, and I ask you not to hold me to account for having failed, in 1959, to have my characters live up to the moral standards now being set forth by the inhabitants of 2021, who were not even born when I wrote these stories. I have written, among other things, a great deal of science fiction, but these two were not science fiction books and I made no attempt to predict the future in them. They are novels of their time. Please read them as that.

Robert Silverberg

CONNIE

- - - -

Robert Silverberg

writing as Loren Beauchamp

One

On the evening which was to see the neat fabric of her young life shattered forever, Connie Barrett had spent more than an hour writing a letter to the boy who would soon be her fiancé. The letter, like any other of the dozens she had been sent, began and ended with fervent protestations of love, with a long, rambling, chatty account of local doings in between. His name was John Ludwig; he was eighteen, a year older than Connie; he was a freshman at Syracuse University. Connie had been dating him since her fifteenth birthday. When she became sixteen, her parents allowed her to accept John's suggestion that they go steady.

Connie had the future all mapped out neatly in her mind. She and John would go steady for the next year, while she was stuck in Brooklyn finishing high school. Then, after next summer, she would join him at Syracuse. By that time he would be a fraternity member, and they could be "pinned"—the formal prelude to engagement. The ring would follow, the year after, and upon John's graduation they would be married. That would be June of 1963, in Connie's orderly plan. John would begin law school that fall, while she completed her four years of college. After that, in unflagging succession, there would be three children, a pretty little home somewhere on Long Island or in Westchester, a trip to Europe when they could afford it—

Connie's favorite amusement was planning her future, month by month, extending the groundwork as far ahead as she could. Such planning helped to fill up the loneliness. It was hard to believe that John had been away at college only three weeks. It seemed like as many months. And he probably wouldn't be home until Thanksgiving, though she would see him before that, going up there some time in October for one of the football weekends. That, too, she had planned long in advance.

She finished her letter, signing it with a florid little phrase of affection. After she had sealed the pink, faintly-scented envelope, she held it to her full lips, imprinting a kiss on its flap. She smiled at herself; sealing a letter with a kiss was a silly, high-school-girlish sort of thing to do. But, she told herself, she was still entitled to act like a high-school girl.

She addressed the letter with care and stuck a stamp on it. Then she glanced at her watch. It was five minutes after ten. The final mail pickup, she knew, was 10:21. In her methodical way, she had made a point of finding that out. If she made the last collection, she thought, the letter would be aboard a train by dawn, and would reach Syracuse some time late tomorrow, to be delivered the first thing Saturday. But if she waited until the morning to mail the letter, it might not reach Syracuse until late Saturday, and would not be delivered before Monday.

She slipped into a light jacket and straightened her hair. She was a tall girl, looking older than her seventeen years, with long curving legs, ripely mature out-thrusting breasts, wide shoulders, broad hips. Her face still had a trace, but only a trace, of little-girl poutiness. John would tell her that she had sexy eyes. "Bedroom eyes," he called them.

"I'll bet you've got bedroom thighs, too," he would say.

"Wouldn't you like to find out?"

"I will, some day."

"June 1963, not before. Think you can hold out till then?"

"It seems like a long time."

"It is a long time. But don't you think I'm worth waiting for?"

"Sure you are, Connie," John would say, and then he would kiss her and fondle her tenderly.

That was one thing Connie was adamant about: they were going to wait until their wedding night before they had any sex with each other. It was—well, the *right* thing to do, Connie insisted, and, because he loved her, John agreed with her.

It wasn't always easy to keep from being carried away, either, Connie knew. After all, she had been dating John for two years now, and after that much time he was entitled to take certain liberties with her. There had been at least five or six occasions when they had almost lost control of themselves. Connie remembered the last one

The night before John was supposed to leave for Syracuse, it had been. They had gone downtown to see a double feature at the Fox, and on the way home they had stopped for a while, on a dark side-road in Prospect Park, to make parting warmer. They were parked off the road, sheltered by a giant horse-chestnut tree; they were in the front seat of John's father's car, borrowed for the evening, and she was cuddled against him, her head leaning on his shoulder, trying to pretend that he would still be near her the next day, instead of on a train to Syracuse. His hand had slipped down to touch her breasts. That was a liberty she granted him, now; he could touch, from outside her clothing.

But suddenly his hand dove into the collar of her blouse. Connie's alarm-system set off signals at once, but before she had a chance to remove his hand, the questing fingers had crept under the fabric of her bra and had reached her nipple.

There was no room for both her breast and his hand within the confine of the tight bra. Thinking only that he was about to rip it, that she would be coming home with a torn bra, she automatically reached around behind and unsnapped the hooks. The bra fell away from her breasts.

Taking that as an invitation, John quickly unbuttoned her blouse. The bra hung loosely, revealing the full, pale globes of her breasts. He bent, hungrily sucking at them, his tongue flicking over the suddenly erect nipples, his lips compressing the firm flesh.

"Johnny," she murmured. "No—darling—"

But the fury had taken hold of her, too. Her hands gripped his body tightly. She clamped her knees together, but he forced them apart, slid his hand under her skirt. His hand was cool against the warmth of her thighs. She felt him groping at the elastic waistband of her panties, felt the eager fingers roaming downward. Her body seemed on fire. In another moment he would possess her, and there would be nothing she could do to stop him.

And then she broke the spell. Perhaps it was a distant cough that pulled her back to reality, perhaps a footstep on the path. She was never able to remember, afterward. But she sat up, suddenly, pulling his head away from her breasts, taking his hand from under her skirt. Like two strangers they faced each other in the car. The only sound for a long moment was that of their passion-stirred breathing.

With trembling fingers Connie hooked her bra, buttoned her blouse, straightened her skirt.

She laughed nervously. "We almost lost our heads, didn't we?"

"Connie, I'm sorry—I didn't know what I was doing, honey—"

"Neither did I. But we came to our senses in time, and that's what matters."

John shook his head. "This has happened before, and it's going to happen again. How many times? Don't you realize that it's four years till we can get married? *Four years.*"

Connie realized that. But part of her plan was to have a wedding night with all the trimmings, and no matter what the cost she intended to stay virgin until that night. Her own body cried out for love as much as John's did, but she told herself she must not give in.

Must not.

So they had driven home from the park, not speaking much to each other. Connie's breasts were sore and throbbing from the stimulation they had received, and she ached with unsatisfied desire.

She had no doubt that it had been wise to cause the interruption before matters got any more serious. But John had raised a disturbing point. They had four years to go, three of them to be spent together on the same college campus, far from home, far from restraint. Could they hold out? Connie had no answer to that. It was the one variable in her otherwise smoothly constructed blueprint of the future.

Now, John had been away at college three weeks. He had written every day; so had she. But she had the feeling that he wrote his letters at arm's length. The words were there, the expressions of love, the chatter of courses and professor and classmates. But something vital seemed missing. Love? Maybe, she thought, and a chill gripped her. Maybe he had met some other girl up there already. Maybe he had already gone to bed with her. Maybe....

Maybe I better mail this letter and stop inventing jealousies for myself, she thought sternly.

She turned out the light in the room, walked to the head of the stairs, and knocked at her parents' door. They were watching television. Her father came to the door, wearing his bathrobe.

"What is it, Con?"

"Just wanted to tell you I was going out to the corner to mail a letter, Dad."

"Going out now? It's after ten."

"The last pickup is at ten twenty-one."

Her father glanced at the imprint of the kiss on the back of the letter she held, and smiled. "How can you find anything new to tell that boy day after day?"

"I tell him the same things, Dad. They're good enough each time."

"Well, don't stay out long. The streets aren't so safe these days, you know. Especially for a sexy dish like you."

She chuckled. "I'll hurry back. Thanks, Dad."

He returned to the television set. Connie went skipping down the front stairs and out of the house. It was a pleasant late-September night, with some of the lingering warmth of the summer that had just ended. A light breeze was blowing. The moon was only a sliver, and the streets were dark.

As she walked down the street toward the mailbox, she wondered why her father was so cautious. It wasn't as if she were going out at two in the morning, after all. It was only ten at night—and yet he had warned her, "*The streets aren't so safe these days.*" Connie shrugged. She was a citizen with every right to walk down to the mailbox after dark. This wasn't the middle ages. Nothing was going to happen to her.

True, there had been some muggings in the neighborhood during the summer. But Connie had a complacent feeling that nothing would happen to *her*. Muggings, murders, robberies, these things happened to *other* people, the people you read about in the morning papers. It was as though there were a special breed of people born destined for calamity, a breed to which she did not belong.

The neighborhood had changed a little lately, though. There was no denying that. It was still a respectable middle-class Brooklyn neighborhood, mostly two-family houses with one or two six-story apartment buildings on each block, and the people who lived there were peaceful and law-abiding sorts.

But there was encroachment on all sides from various undesirable sections. An Irish section, an Italian section, a Negro section, a Puerto Rican section, had all sprung up around them. And there was constant turmoil there, the Negroes quarrelling with the Puerto Ricans, the Irish with the Italians, and all four groups with each other. Occasionally an innocent bystander got caught in the middle.

But it was foolish to live in constant terror, Connie thought. The mailbox was only a hundred feet from her house. She reached it now, pulled the red-white-and-blue lid down, and dropped the letter to John in. In her careful way, she pulled the lid back a second time, to make sure the letter had actually fallen into the box. It had. She checked her watch. Twelve past ten. In a little while the post office truck would come trundling up, the man in the blue uniform would get out, open the box, take the letter, start it on its way to Syracuse.

By that time, though, Connie would be back in her own room, getting into her pajamas, getting ready to comb out her auburn hair. She turned to go back up the street, thinking pleasantly that she had cheated the dark terrors of the night, that she had mailed the letter and nothing had hap—

Her way was blocked.

There was at least a dozen of them. They had congealed from the shadows, without a footstep. They had her hemmed in, bordering her in a loose semi-circle. They stood between her and the way to her house.

By the dim light of the streetlamp across the way, she saw their faces. Dull, ugly, acne-pocked faces, with little gleaming lustful eyes and grinning predatory thin-lipped mouths. They were clad in a uniform: black leather jackets with olive-drab gloves thrust insolently through a shoulder-loop, and identical khaki pants. They were all in their teens, with thick, greasy hair piled up high on their heads.

For an instant Connie thought they were simply playing some grim game with her, that they were on their way home from a movie or a gang-fight or something, and that they were merely amusing themselves by causing a bit of momentary panic in the mind of a girl they had happened to meet. She refused to let herself panic. Because they were blocking the entire street, she stepped off the curb, thinking to step around them and continue on her way. It was only a hundred feet to home

But as she stepped off the curb two of the gang boys did the same. Her way was still blocked.

She came to the abrupt realization that their intentions were much more sinister than simple baiting. The panic reaction flooded her brain with fear. She wanted to cry out, to rouse the neighborhood to her defense. Her heart pounded furiously; and, deep within, her brain still ticked with the quiet conviction that all this was unreal, that it could be happening only to some member of that breed of trouble-prone people whose faces are always on the front pages, and not to Constance Barrett of 1381 Mortimer Avenue, Brooklyn 28, New York.

She opened her mouth and before a sound came out a powerful hand was clamped over it. She tried to bite it, but the hand was skillfully placed so that none of the fingers were actually over her teeth; her lips were clamped shut by pressure from above and below. Connie clawed out wildly, kicking and scratching. Her arms were caught and pinioned to her sides. Like so many dark insects, the gang boys clustered tight around her, hiding her from view, and she found herself being hustled into an automobile parked across the street. It was a new car, shiny, probably stolen. They piled in, five of them cramming themselves in the front seat, the other six and Connie packing into the rear. They sat all about her, hiding her from view, practically crushing her with their bodies. The hand remained clamped to her mouth. Connie smelled the sour flavor of beer. She could not see where they were taking her. Her mind still had not fully accepted this.

Sitting hunched on the floor in the back, pressed in on all sides by knees, her mouth held tight shut, Connie began to quiver with fear. *They're going to rape me, she thought. They were out cruising, looking for a girl, and now they're going to rape me.*

She thought of the house a hundred feet from the mailbox, of her mother and father peacefully watching television and beginning to wonder, just about this time, what was taking Connie so long to mail that letter. She thought of John, hundreds of miles away, and of the virginity she had with such difficulty managed to preserve for their wedding night.

She thought of all the plans, college, getting pinned, engagement, marriage, honeymoon, three children, house on Long Island, trip to Europe. All the carefully-docketed events of her future whirled dizzyingly in tumultuous confusion now. All, all lost.

She heard her captors laughing above her, poking and congratulating each other on their luck. She was sick with the reek of beer and of their unclean bodies and of the breath of a dozen people jammed into one car, and with the fear that possessed her.

A hand reached down from somewhere behind her and roughly squeezed her breasts, first one, then the other. "Boy, what a pair of tits!" somebody snickered. "Real ones, too! We gonna have ourselves a ball!"

Connie felt numbness invading her brain. Her mind refused to accept the situation. It couldn't be happening. They weren't going to rape her. They weren't. They weren't. They weren't.

The car came to an abrupt jerking halt.

Two

They had her gripped tightly under the arms, and his hand was still over her face, as she was propelled out of the car. They all came boiling out, like the clowns at the circus. Only this wasn't any circus.

It was a neighborhood Connie didn't recognize. There was only one streetlight on the whole block, and it was three quarters of a block away. She saw some garages and a couple of low houses and a glass-fronted store. It was a dead neighborhood, no pedestrians out walking and no cars whizzing past and hardly any cars even parked in the street. There was a vacant lot, heaped high with junk and overgrown with straggly weeds, and there was what looked like a watchman's shack in the middle of the lot, and they were pushing her toward the shack.

Her legs were wobbly. She felt the sharp pressure of fingers gripping the soft flesh of her arms, and tasted the acrid taste of sweat rolling off the hand plastered over her mouth.

They opened the door of the shack and crowded her inside, slamming and bolting the door. Someone lit a match. A moment later, there was a candle burning.

The shack was empty except for a big pile of baling straw, excelsior, pushed together in one corner. By the flickering light of the candle Connie saw the lust-expectant faces of her kidnappers. She had seen boys like this before, in her high school. They kept to themselves, mostly, roaming like wolf-packs, huddling in the corridors to grab a quick smoke. And now they had grabbed her.

The hand over her mouth was taken away. Instantly, hysterically, Connie started to scream, but the scream was no more than half a second old when a thick hand slapped her in the mouth.

Her voice died away. She felt blood trickle into her mouth from the place where her lip had split.

"Keep your mouth shut. Screaming won't do you no good here anyway. But we don't like noise. Got that? You scream again and we'll cut your tits off."

Connie heard a clicking sound. Candlelight glimmered off the surface of a switchblade knife inches from her face. She nodded stiffly.

"What—what are you going to do to me?"

The boys chuckled. They couldn't be any older than seventeen, Connie thought. Some of them looked about fourteen. And their mouths were watering.

The biggest boy, the one who seemed to be the leader, said, "Get her clothes off. Let's have a look at her and see what we got."

Two of the others advanced toward her. Connie backed away. "No—no—keep away—"

Again she was shown the switchblade knife. "You just keep shut and don't make trouble, or we'll mark you. We'll carve our initials all over you. You wouldn't want that, would you?"

Connie did not answer. All she wanted to do was shut her brain off and blot out whatever was going to happen to her now.

Two of them held her hands while a third pulled her jacket off. She felt stubby fingers fumbling at her blouse; too impatient to bother with the buttons, the gang boy simply ripped. The buttons sprayed clatteringly on the shack floor. They pulled her blouse from her in two chunks. A hand inserted itself between her shoulder-blades and tugged at the straps of her bra. The straps broke, with a little popping sound. The brassiere fluttered to the ground. Her breasts, high and round and full, were exposed to view. Whistles went up from the gang.

"Looka those knobs!"

"What a handful, huh?"

"Lemme at them knockers!"

The disrobing process continued. Numb now, Connie did not even make token resistance. The inexorable hand ripped open the button at her waist, pulled down on the zipper. Her skirt dropped to her ankles. Cold hands tore her filmy panties apart. She was naked, wearing only white bobby-socks, standing in the ruins of her clothing. She was shivering. She was vaguely conscious of eleven pairs of eyes looking at her body, but now she was hardly aware of what was happening.

The gang chieftain stepped forward. He squeezed her breasts as though he were buying melons at a market. He nodded at her flat belly. He grasped her shoulder and spun her around, and she felt cold hands squeezing her silk-skinned globular buttocks, in that humiliating way that turned her into so much feminine merchandise.

"We really hit it this time," the gang leader said. There were approving comments. Suddenly he caught her by the shoulders and pushed her down, onto the heap of excelsior. She felt the rough straw scratching her skin, but she made no attempt to rise. The gang boys were passing a bottle around. The place smelled of cheap liquor.

"Choose for your turns," the gang leader ordered. "I'm gonna be first. Anybody argue with that?"

"You got the right," somebody said. "It was your idea, so you go first."

The boy stepped forward, looking down at Connie. She was covered with gooseflesh. Only a tiny corner of her brain seemed to be working, now. She knew that everything was to be shattered now, all her plans. The impeccable castle of her body was about to be invaded. It was too incredible for her mind to accept it.

She heard the harsh sound of an opening zipper. She glanced up, and what she saw terrified her, so she closed her eyes. Something crazy ran through her head. She had been at a party with John (John? How many million years ago had she known somebody named John?) and there was this inevitable game of charades, and when it had come her turn they had given her a slip of paper that said, *"If rape is inevitable, lie back and enjoy it."* It was one of the standard charades gags, but she couldn't figure out a good way of acting it out, and though she gave it a try she couldn't get it across to her partners. And now the phrase chased itself round and round in her fear-shocked brain. *If rape is inevitable, lie back and enjoy it. If rape is inevitable, lie back and enjoy it. If rape is inevitable—*

It was. The gang boy hadn't even bothered to take his clothes off. He was lying down on top of her now. She felt the raspiness of his khaki trousers against the soft flesh of her thighs, felt the cold sleekness of his black leather jacket touching her breasts.

Connie moaned and with what little part of her brain was still functioning she recorded the trickle of her own blood warmly over her thighs, and she knew she had been taken, that she had given up unwillingly what she might have given in love to John that night in Prospect Park.

The world disappeared and the only thing that continued to exist was the bright, hot ball of pain. Dimly she perceived that the gang boy was finished, that his weight no longer pressed stiflingly down on her.

She heard a voice a thousand miles away say in tones of wonder, "For Christ's sake, you know what? She still had her cherry!"

There were loud guffaws.

"Not anymore, she don't!" somebody said.

"You get all the lousy luck," somebody else complained.

"Who's next? Let's get on with it."

Connie lay crumpled on the straw, feeling the wash of pain slowly subside, feeling suddenly a new weight on her, a new pair of hands kneading her breasts. And then it was happening all over again, a new invasion of the castle of her body, but this time there was less pain, less agony, less regret. What was done could not be undone, what was opened could not be sealed again.

After the fourth one, Connie lost track. She could no longer detect the interval between one assault and the next. She felt that she was lying in a bottomless pit, falling endlessly with no sensation of falling, and all about her were bright blazing flares of light, and pain, pain, pain....

And suddenly pleasure. It burst over her like a bombshell. The tenth or perhaps the eleventh of her attackers had taken possession of her, and now she felt a strange tingling, a throbbing that began somewhere deep in her belly and grew until it filled the entire universe, a great reverberating boom of ecstasy, and the pain melted from her and her body seemed to be on fire. A low, fierce moan escaped from her contorted lips. Her body, which had lain limply, passively, puppet-like beneath her various attackers, writhed suddenly as though an electric wire had been touched to her skin.

She clawed fiercely at the faceless body above her, and for an instant she thought her brain would explode, and then release came, and her head fell back on the straw, mouth lolling open, and the idiot phrase danced behind the walls of her skull. *If rape is inevitable, lie back and enjoy it....*

Finally the orgy was over. Eyes shut, mind numbed, Connie somehow could hear them talking.

".... what a hell of an evening ...."

".... crazy thing, the way she came alive every once in a while...."

".... can't tell what a girl will do...."

".... getting close to morning. We better clear out before the sun comes up...."

".... just leave her here?"

".... what the hell else can we do? Keep her around as a mascot....?"

".... shame to let her go...."

".... dangerous to try anything like that. Just clear out and leave her. When the cops find her she'll be too shell-shocked to tell 'em anything...."

There was more, much more, but Connie had lost touch with the world again. She sensed nothing until the moment when the cool night breezes, blowing across her naked body, awakened her.

They had gone, leaving the door of the shack ajar, and the brisk winds of early morning had blown it open. Connie sat up, and the effort sent darts of pain through her body. Gradually, she began to remember. They had forced her into the car, and brought her here, and ripped her clothes off. And after that? She could not remember. But she could guess. She looked down, at the soiled and bloodstained excelsior, and she knew what they had done to her, and a shiver of self-revulsion went through her. Soiled. Fouled. The castle of her body forever breached. Shamed. Raped.

Raped.

Her clothes lay in a tattered heap across the room.

The pale light of early dawn showed a guttered, nearly-consumed candle mounted on a rickety table. She remembered that she had gone to mail a letter....

A letter to John. John? John was in Syracuse. Her parents had been watching television. The mail was collected at ten twenty-one. Isolated facts crept into her mind as the numbness receded.

The pain was terrible. It was like fire in her loins, and her breasts were bruised and aching. How many of them had there been? About a dozen, she remembered. About a dozen.

She had to get out of here, had to find the police, had to tell her parents she was still alive. Rising uncertainly to one knee, she balanced there a moment, collecting the strength to rise further. Every movement sent new pain through her body. She got to her feet; began to fall, tottered forward, and caught the edge of the table, holding herself upright. The morning wind, blowing against her nakedness, chilled her.

There were her clothes, lying over there. But they were all ripped to shreds. She couldn't put them on, they were too badly torn. But she couldn't leave the shack without any clothes. That would be indecent. That would be....

She shook her head. It didn't matter now, decency and all the rest of it. She had been defiled. She could walk through the streets naked now without feeling humiliation. What further humiliation was there left to feel?

Taking a hesitant step, she reached the entrance of the shack and clung for support to the door, standing there naked in the doorway. The sky was pearly grey, with the first straggling wisps of sunlight breaking through. The streets were empty, absolutely empty. It could have been not later than five or five-thirty in the morning.

Suddenly she was violently sick, emptying out what little there was in her stomach, gagging and retching, and in her exertions she nearly fell face-forward into the vomit. Catching the door, she managed to remain upright.

Got to find a policeman, she told herself. Parents will be worried. Searching all night.

She took a single step downward, out of the shack, into the vacant lot. The neighborhood looked bleak, desolate—another empty lot across the street, and a run-down auto repair shop, and three little shabby one-family houses clustered one against the other as if for protection. Connie put one foot after the other. She was five steps from the shack now, seven, ten....

Only twenty-four hours before, she would no sooner have thought of walking naked through the streets, at any hour of the day or night, than she would have of flying to the Moon. But now nothing mattered anymore. She had been raped.

The ugly word seemed to hang in the air before her. Raped.

Her mind, beginning to function again, visualized headlines, police inquiries, hysterical parents, her older sister rushing home from college, John coming in from *his* college, and the shame, the shame, never to be obliterated....

And then, in the rush of thoughts and ideas, the mocking phrase danced into her mind once again.

If rape is inevitable, lie back and enjoy it.

She had done just that. After the pain, after the shock had been blanked out, her brain turned off, her body had taken command. And some primeval force deep in her body had responded. She remembered that clearly, now. Most of the rest of that night was a fog, but there was no escaping the damning fact that she had, incredibly, derived some pleasure during that hellish experience.

She stopped short, halfway out of the empty lot. Her legs, growing steadily weaker, refused to support her any longer. She swayed, toppled, reached out to find something to hang on to, found nothing, and fell. She stretched full length on the ground, staring idiotically at a rusty tin can inches from her face. She lay face down, her aching breasts pressed against the cold ground. The morning dew, glistening on the weeds beneath her body, made her shudder with its wetness. She sobbed gaspingly and cried out feebly to be found, to be helped. If only the clock could be set back, she thought. If only she could take back her decision to mail that letter in time for the ten twenty-one pickup.

But the clock could not be set back. What had happened was irrevocably embedded in the fabric of space and time. It could never be undone.

Connie closed her eyes. She felt a dull throbbing behind the front of her skull. She tried to rise, succeeded in lifting herself six inches off the ground, and fell back, exhausted, drained, unconscious.

Three

Without opening her eyes, Connie put out her hands and rubbed them slowly along whatever it was she was lying on. It felt like a bedsheet. Good; she was in a bed. Home in bed? No, this bed did not feel like her bed at home. In the hospital, then? Perhaps. She opened her eyes.

The room was about twelve by fifteen, walls painted a light green, and a flood of sunlight was coming in through a picture-window partly screened by thin drapes. It was a hospital room, a private room. Her nostrils brought her the characteristic smell of a hospital. She was lying on her back. Someone had dressed her in a white hospital gown. There were people in the room.

Connie took them all in at a quick glance. Her father was sitting in the extreme right-hand corner, his face very pale, his lips clamped tight together and twitching a little. Next to him sat her mother, eyes black-bordered, red-rimmed, hair unkempt and disarrayed. A woman in a white uniform stood smiling beamingly; a nurse, no doubt. Connie smiled back. Then she remembered. The smile vanished; a slow shivering wave of sadness crept up over her, and she felt her eyes grow moist.

"How long have I been here?" she asked in a rusty-sounding voice.

"Since the day before last, dear," the nurse said. "You've been under sedation all this time."

"I— feel hungry," she said. Speaking was an effort, and a slow throbbing began somewhere within her. And she remembered again, remembered them pawing and feeling her and she shuddered.

Her parents were looking at her strangely. They didn't seem to know what to say. They began to fumble for words, but no words came. Her mother burst into abrupt convulsive sobs. The nurse came quickly over and said in warm, tender tones, "We don't want to get the poor girl all upset, now, do we? Why don't you and Mr. Barrett wait outside for a while, and let Dr. Janssen have a talk with your daughter and see how she feels."

Efficiently, the nurse ushered Connie's parents from the room. They had not spoken one word to her while they were present, and they said nothing as they left, simply staring back over their shoulders at her.

The doctor entered. He was a stocky, red-faced man with an amiable smile and stiff white hair worn in a crew-cut. He pulled up a seat at the side of the bed, leaned forward, smiled at Connie, and signalled the nurse to leave the room.

"How do you feel, Connie? Any pain?"

"A little. Sort of—an ache. Doctor, do my parents know what happened to me?"

"They know as much as any of us do."

"Which is?"

"You were found naked and unconscious in an empty lot a good many miles from your home, day before last. You were in a state of shock. Police had been searching for you since the previous night. An examination here showed that you had been sexually violated upwards of twenty times."

"You told them all that?" Connie asked in a whisper.

"Of course."

Connie felt isolated on an island of misery. The doctor's soft voice seemed to be reaching her from across the waters of a vast ocean.

"What's been happening to me here?" she asked.

The doctor smiled. "We've had you under sedation, mostly. There was a certain amount of physical damage, and we've treated you for it."

"Do you think—think I might become pregnant?" Connie asked. She was calm now. She felt detached from the universe.

Shrugging, the doctor said, "We've done everything we could to make sure nothing like that happened. There's a certain element of chance, but I don't think you need to worry much about it. In a couple of days you'll be discharged, without any physical aftereffects."

He had faintly stressed the word *physical*. Connie closed her eyes briefly. "What about mental aftereffects, doctor?"

"You've been through a hellish experience, child. I don't doubt it'll leave some mark on you. The extent of the psychological effects will depend on your own strength, Connie, and on the attitudes of those who love you." He stood up. "There's someone here from the police who wants to ask you some questions. Whenever you get tired of talking to him, ring for the nurse. I'll send your parents back to you after you've seen the policeman."

But instead of one policeman, there were two, one to ask questions and the other to take notes. The question-asker was very tall, very solemn-looking; his stenographer seemed much younger.

"You left your house shortly after ten o'clock Thursday night, and you weren't seen again until early Friday morning. Can you tell us something of what happened in between?"

Connie moistened her lips. "I went downstairs to mail a letter. I had just finished mailing it when these boys—eleven of them—came out of nowhere. They had black leather jackets. They pushed me into their car—it was a big car, it looked new and stolen."

"Do you know the make?"

"No. Anyway, they drove. I don't know how long we were driving. I couldn't see out of the car. Finally we stopped, in front of this empty lot with the watchman's shack. And they took me into the shack and ripped my clothes off and—and—" Connie stopped. "They raped me. Over and over again."

"Yes. I've seen the medical report."

"And then when they got tired of that, they left me there. I went outside and collapsed, and next thing I knew I was here." She was surprised at her own calmness; she had told the horrible story unflinchingly. It was as if her mind were held in some kind of freeze that kept her from going into the hysterics she wanted to go into. But she knew the reaction was on its way.

"Can you describe any of the boys?"

"No."

"Not at all?"

Connie shrugged tiredly. "They had black leather jackets, that's all I remember. I was too frightened to get a good look at any of them. And it was too dark for me to see them."

"Did you catch any names?"

"No."

"None at all, Miss Barrett? Not even a nickname?"

Connie wrinkled her brow, knowing she had heard one or two of them refer to each other by nicknames. But her mind yielded nothing. "I can't give you any of that kind of information," she said. "I just don't know it."

"They were complete strangers, then. You couldn't identify them if you saw them in the police station, could you?"

Her face drained of blood. "God, you aren't going to make me go down there and—" She realized she was almost shrieking. "I don't want to see any of them! Even if they are the ones! I couldn't look them over! I—"

"Easy, Miss Barrett," the policeman said soothingly, and Connie noticed that the nurse had glided back into the room at the first sound of shouting. "We won't insist on your coming down to the station, if you don't want to. But we're always picking these kids up, you see, and we figured if you came down and identified a few as the ones who had attacked you, we'd be able to press charges against them and—"

"What good would that do?" Connie asked, slumping back tiredly against her pillow. "Would arresting them cancel what was done to me?"

"It might save some other girl from having it done to her."

"But that can't help me either," Connie insisted loudly. She realized she was being selfish and stupid, but her nerves were beginning to fray. The nurse saw that, too, for she quickly interposed herself between Connie and the policemen and said, "You'd better not question her anymore now. Why don't you come back tomorrow? She's only been awake a short while, now, and you'll get her all worked up and bothered."

The nurse's word was law, and the policemen knew it. They thanked Connie for allowing them to talk to her, promised that every effort would be made to bring her assaulters to justice, and made their exit.

"You'd better rest a while, dear," the nurse said. "And then I think your parents will want to have a little talk with you."

The drapes were drawn, the room darkened, and Connie was left alone, supposedly to sleep. But no sleep came. She was fully awake now, fully conscious of her position. At the moment she felt no lingering shock effects from Thursday night's violence, but she suspected there was hysteria not very far ahead for her. And beyond the hysteria there would be far-reaching implications. She would never be allowed to forget what happened to her that night. In the eyes of her parents, her relatives, her friends, her neighbors (if the story had hit the papers, and nine chances out of nine that it had) she would forever be That Unfortunate Girl. They would never let her forget, because they would forever go out of their way to be gentle to her, and in their downcast eyes and soft tones would be eternal reminders of the night of hell. The pool would widen. Everyone she came in contact with would, sooner or later, discover that at one time in her past she had been taken to a watchman's shack and forcibly raped by a pack of juvenile delinquents, and that would color their relationship with her.

It would be an incident forever fresh in her mind. The only way she could eradicate it would be in a total change, a leaving behind of Constance Barrett. Only by getting out of this environment, away from parents, friends, relatives, neighbors, Brooklyn in general, could she shake from her memory that nightmare come real. So her entire life would be changed, changed forever, by the events of Thursday night.

Nothing would ever be the same again. All the elaborate plans she had spun in her fancies were shattered now.

She rang for the nurse. "I can't sleep. You might as well send my parents in."

They entered, pale, uncertain. The nurse glanced inquiringly at them and slipped out of the room again. Connie's parents pulled up two chairs close to the bed.

"She's very kind, that nurse," Connie's mother said. "Mrs. Henrichs, her name is. So tactful."

Connie looked at her parents. They still seemed tongue-tied.

Her father said in a low, wobbly voice, "This is a terrible thing. What happens in this city is shameful. The police—"

"My little girl!" her mother broke in, sobbing.

Connie twisted uncomfortably beneath the bedclothes. She had her own emotions penned in so severely that this despairing display of emotionality distressed her. To break it up she said, "Was the story—about me—in the papers?"

"All of them," her father said. "We wanted to keep it out, but they wouldn't hear of it."

"My name?"

"Everything."

Connie nodded bleakly. That was what she had feared. Now she would become That Unfortunate Girl, and all eyes would turn toward her on the street, in school, everywhere, eyes of people curious to see what the victim of a mass rape looks like, whether she still can smile, whether she is still like other unraped human beings.

Her parents were fidgeting. No doubt it was as hard for them to believe the circumstances of their daughter's abrupt and violent devirginizing as it was for her herself to realize it.

Her father said, "You mustn't let this leave a mark on you, darling. Pretend it was all a bad dream, something that never really happened."

"Yes—a bad dream," her mother echoed.

"But it wasn't a dream," Connie said bitterly. "It happened. And I'll have to live with the fact that it happened for the rest of my life." She felt her control starting to give way; in another moment, she knew, she would be screaming at the top of her lungs. Biting her lip, she compelled herself to calm down again, and said quickly, "Have—have you told John?"

"He called yesterday, and we told him."

"Everything?"

"He had seen it in the papers," her father said tonelessly.

"Oh. What did he say?"

"He's coming in today. He took the morning train out of Syracuse, and he'll be here later. He sounded very upset."

That was small surprise, Connie thought. Who wouldn't be upset at learning that his unstained pre-fiancée has just been debauched by a flock of J.D.s?

Leaning forward impulsively, her father grabbed her hand and said, "Don't let this thing get you all shaken up, Connie. It's over with, and everything's going to be okay. I phoned Grandma in Arizona and told her you were going to come out there for a little while. A few weeks resting up out there and you'll be in fine shape."

Connie's father's parents had retired to Phoenix, Arizona, and had been urging for visits from their children and grandchildren ever since. Hoarsely Connie said, "You didn't tell them—what had happened to me—?"

"No. We just said you were coming out for a little rest. That you'd been working too hard in school, or something, and needed a vacation."

The nurse reappeared just as Connie was saying, "I guess I ought to get away. The change of scene—it'll do me good."

"There's a Mr. John Ludwig outside to see you," the nurse announced.

Connie paled. She wanted to cry out, screaming her rage at the world that had allowed such a deed to be done to her, but her iron control held. Stammering, she said, "S-send him in."

John entered, looking solemn, smiling in a jerky way at the parents of his intended. He seemed tall and gawky and very ill-at-ease. Connie's father nudged his wife, murmuring something about "leaving the two of them alone," and they left the room.

John sank into a chair, as though he could no longer stay on his feet. He cradled his head in his hands, not looking at Connie. In a hollow voice he said, "I read about it in the paper up there. You know, just out of curiosity. I see the headline, GIRL FOUND IN EMPTY LOT, and I start to read, and I see the name, and—oh, God! I called your folks right up! But maybe I shouldn't be talking about this."

"It's all right. I'm pretty calm now."

"It must have been hell."

Connie shrugged. "I hardly knew what was going on. I was numb, like."

She peered closely at him. He was not meeting her eyes, but stared at a point behind her left shoulder. She wished she could read his mind. That last night in the parked car had been so silly, she thought. She had kept him from taking her virginity, only to surrender it violently to a band of barbarians.

"How—how do you like college?" she asked gamely.

"It's okay."

"Nice social life?"

He stared at his shoes. "You know how I feel about you, Connie. I haven't been seeing anybody else up there. I wouldn't even think of it."

"And everything's still okay between you and me—after what happened?" she asked.

There was a split instant of hesitation, a fatal moment of hesitation so far as Connie was concerned. Then he said, "Sure, everything's still okay. We just gotta pretend it never happened. We—"

"I wouldn't want you to think you had to be nice to me, John. The whole situation's different now. I'm not—pure—anymore."

He was very pale. "It's crazy to try to talk about this now, here in the hospital room and all. When you get out, we can figure out where we go from here."

So he was beginning to persuade himself that maybe some adjustments in the plan would have to be made, Connie thought. She said, "I'm going to spend a couple of weeks with my grandparents in Arizona right after I get out of the hospital. I'll write you from there."

"Okay. Okay, Connie. And remember—everything's going to work out all right."

He left the room, promising to stop by for another visit tomorrow before returning to college.

Connie stared at the pale walls of her room for a long, moment. Everything was becoming clear to her now. The events of Thursday night had transformed her from an innocent girl to an unclean woman, now. At the moment, everyone was simply being sympathetic. But her parents were unable to speak frankly with her; she was like a person diseased, now, and the best thing they could think of was to ship her off to Arizona, where they wouldn't have to see her and constantly console her.

As for John, he was making standard responses of bedside sympathy too, just now. But as the shock wore off, so too would his sympathy, and he would ponder the desirability of marrying a girl who had been through such an experience. He would tell himself that she would be unstable, subject to hysterics; besides, she would no longer be pure. He would reconsider the whole notion of shackling himself to her and thus losing out on much of the social life of college. And, inevitably, he would come to the conclusion that marrying her was no longer to be considered.

Connie sat quietly in her quiet hospital room while waves of panic beat against the inside of her skull. The girl who had been Connie Barrett was dead, and the new person who would wear that name had not yet emerged. But she would be different, Connie knew—harder, colder, more cruel, less innocent. It was an inevitable consequence of the night in the watchman's shack. The brutality of the world had been demonstrated in an unforgettable fashion, and she would never again be the child she was.

Suddenly the restraining walls of her self-control gave way. She uttered a loud wail of hysteria and the world went spinning. The nurse came rushing in; Connie was given a pill, acid-tasting; she felt the insistent undertow of sleep. Still sobbing, whimpering fitfully, Connie let sleep take her.

Four

Four days later, Connie was discharged from the hospital. Her father picked her up in his car and drove her home in mid-morning. Connie was glad of the odd hour; there would be no neighbors around to bother her.

She had not had many visitors in the hospital. Her parents had come every day, and John, as he had promised, had paid her a second visit, during which few words were exchanged. But at Connie's orders no one else came. She did not want to see any classmates or teachers, did not want to see aunts and uncles, did not want to see cousins and friends. She just wanted to be left alone. Her older sister, a senior at Michigan State, had made hurried plans to fly home, but Connie had told her over the phone not to bother.

After the one outburst in the hospital, there had been no further trouble with hysteria. The steely band round her emotions had gone back in place, but Connie knew there might be an explosion at any time. Eventually, she would no longer feel the direct effects of her experience, but the marks would remain on her soul.

She was not pregnant. That much was confirmed the day she left the hospital, and it was a major consolation. Another was that there would be no permanent damage to her body; the bruises had already begun to heal, the torn flesh to grow whole.

But the other damage, the damage to her soul, to her integrity as a woman, as a human being—that damage could not be repaired so easily.

She left for Arizona the day after her hospital discharge. Two bulky suitcases accompanied her, containing her best clothes, and some textbooks as well, so she would be not too far behind when she returned to school. Connie quietly shuddered at the thought of returning to school, of being whispered at in the corridors ("There's that girl who was raped by a kid gang") and of being stared at in her classes. But she said nothing to her parents about that. They seemed happy to get rid of her, and she was equally happy to be breaking loose from an environment in which she could no longer remain.

Her father drove her to Idlewild Airport. She had never flown before, and he kept telling her not to be nervous about it. She was not nervous. She told herself the best thing that could happen to her now would be to die quickly in a plane crash. That way she would not have to drag about the burden of her humiliation for decades and decades. But she did not tell her father that. She tried to act cheerful, to keep her spirits buoyant. It was almost as though the calamity had befallen not her but her parents, and, in a way, she thought, perhaps it had.

Waving goodbye, she boarded the plane, nestled down in the seat they gave her, waited for takeoff.

It was a quiet flight. Connie's seat-partner was a frowning businessman who, blessedly, made no attempt at conversation, but spent the entire trip busily studying some important-looking document. Connie relaxed, staring out the window at the fleecy shelf of clouds that blotted out the earth below.

The plane stopped at Chicago, unloaded a few people, took some on. From there it headed on a sharp line across the southwest, over incredibly bare and parched deserts, and by late evening, New York time, it landed in Tucson. It was only mid-afternoon there. The temperature was sizzling; it was at least 90, nearly double what it had been in New York. After a short stop at Tucson the plane took off once again, and, less than half an hour later, Connie emerged into the shimmering heat of Phoenix. An enormous cactus plant, twelve or fifteen feet high, was her first sight as she left the plane. Hurrying into the air-conditioned waiting-room, she found her grandparents waiting, both of them looking tanned and leathery and spry.

She hugged them and they made a fuss over her and asked her a hundred questions about home, and all the time Connie concealed from them the real reason for her trip westward. "My nerves," she explained a couple of times. "Doctor says I'm too strung up, need some relaxation." There was no need to trouble them in their twilight years with details of their granddaughter's humiliation.

Her grandfather drove at a serene thirty miles an hour through streets lined with huge palms and pulled up finally at a neat little one-story house ten minutes' drive from central Phoenix. It was an attractive little place, with its coral-colored walls and its little garden of exotic-looking desert plants out in front. The old people had four rooms, which was one more than they absolutely needed, but they had bought the place with malice aforethought, hoping to lure their children from the east out for prolonged stays. At last they had succeeded. Connie established herself in the little guest bedroom.

On the fifth day after her arrival, she got the letter from John.

Up till then everything had gone pleasantly enough. The temperature had hovered between seventy and eighty-five and Connie liked the long hours of sun and the dry, clear air. She had been swimming, she had gone horseback riding, she had been introduced to some of the local teenage boys and girls. She had written a couple of letters, one to her parents, one to John, telling them both approximately the same thing: that the rest was doing her good, that her nerves were less jangled out here, that she expected to be as good as new when she came back to New York. Her parents replied quickly, but it was a vague letter full of platitudes. They seemed glad to have her so far away from them.

And then, on the fifth day, there came the letter from John.

Connie didn't see it until nearly sundown. She had been out all day with some of her new friends. It was Saturday, and they had wanted to give her a full day of fun, so she had been swimming at a public pool, then was taken on a drive through the desert, and finally out to Scottsdale for a look at the homes built by the millionaires out there. It was half past six when Connie returned to her grandparents' house, tired, sun-reddened, and, in the bargain, happy. She had had a good day. None of her new friends knew what had happened to her, and she had almost begun to forget herself, in her new environment, in the company of these friendly, uncomplicated openhearted westerners.

Her grandmother had greeted her at the door with a hug, a cheery smile, and the words, "There's a letter for you from home. From that boyfriend of yours, I think."

Connie began to tremble. The sudden reminder of the existence of the world on the other side of the Mississippi shattered the mood she had been building all day.

"Give it to me! Where is it?"

"Good Lord, girl, it's bad for your nerves and mine for you to rush about like that! There it is, right on the table in front of you."

Connie snatched it up, started to rip it open, then changed her mind on a sudden impulse and carried the letter into her room. There, alone, the door shut, she stared for a long moment at the envelope, imprinting on her brain the design of the blue airmail stamp, studying the neatly typed return address and the little Syracuse banner he had pasted on the envelope. Then she tore it open.

It wasn't a very long letter.

Dear Connie:

Thanks very much for writing. I'm glad you seem to be having a relaxing time out west.

As you might expect I've been doing a lot of thinking about Us since I got back to school, and I guess you've been doing the same. I wonder if it isn't a little smarter for both of us if we postpone going steady for a while. What I mean is, we both don't have a very good perspective on the world yet, and if we went on seeing other people for a while longer it might help us to understand each other better. At our ages we can't really be sure we're right for each other. I think if you saw some other fellows and I went out with other girls during this year that we must be separated, it would be a healthy thing. And if by so doing we were to break up, well, that would simply mean we weren't really in love with each other in the first place.

Please don't think that this has any connection with the recent terrible event. I hope we will both forget about that soon. But I think we should reconsider some of our other plans before we go rushing into something as serious as engagement and marriage.

Yours ever,
John

When she had read the letter, Connie ripped it into four parts, shriveled the fragments, and dropped them into the wastebasket. Her face was an icy mask.

She knew what the letter meant. Translated, it said, *"Let's call the whole thing off. Everything is changed by the fact that you were raped. Besides, there are some girls here I'd like to date."*

It was understandable enough. He figured, rightly, that she would never fully recover from the effects of the raping. Maybe it would affect her sex response in marriage, maybe it would change her entire personality. No virgin girl could be submitted to such an experience without coming out of it wearing psychological scars. She was no longer the girl he had fallen in love with, and he wanted out. Well, he could have what he wanted. When a couple of weeks went by without his receiving any reply, he could draw his own conclusions.

"Connie? Supper's almost ready!"

Connie opened the door. "I'm not very hungry, Gram. I'll just take a little walk, I think. Some fresh air—"

"Why, how pale you are! Was there some bad news in that letter?"

"Letter? Oh, no, that was nothing important."

"Come in then, and put some food into you, girl."

She toyed with her supper, eating little of it. But the old people, having been warned about the delicate state of their granddaughter's nerves, made no attempt to nag her into eating. After supper she announced she was taking a walk by herself, for a little while. It was a mild evening. Before she had gone half a block, she realized wryly that it was by taking a little walk by herself that all the trouble had begun. But Phoenix was not New York City; no gangs lurked in these open streets. She walked on.

Her heart felt like a cold lump of lead. Her parents had packed her away; John had taken the first steps toward breaking off with her. Like ships drifting off in the night, the segments of her old life were vanishing.

She wondered what lay ahead. Marriage? With whom? She felt befouled. Her body had been profaned. She had no right to offer herself to another man in marriage. For all the years of her adolescence she had come to regard sex as something almost sacred; you saved yourself for your husband, who was the only man ever to know your body intimately. But that was impossible now. Eleven teenage hoodlums had possessed her. Perhaps she could hide her past from her husband, but never from herself.

Her life had suddenly lost all direction. Her goals could no longer be attained.

She felt the change coming over her. She was no longer the "good" girl, Connie Barrett. Through an action not of her own making, she was an outcast from society. Her throat felt suddenly dry. She realized her nerves were jangling terribly. A drink, she thought. She needed a drink.

Neon signs blinked at her. THE MOJAVE HOTEL—COCKTAIL LOUNGE. The Mojave was more of a motel than hotel, a long, flat, green-walled affair laid out snaking around a central swimming pool.

Connie passed through the sleek glass doors and into the dark cocktail lounge. Waitresses in sexy dresses scuttled back and forth, fetching drinks for the patrons. Connie settled down at the bar. She had never in her life ordered a drink at a bar before, but this was as good a time to begin as any.

She tried to make her voice sound husky. "Dry martini, please."

"Sure thing, Miss." No questioning glance, no request to see a birth certificate. Either they weren't particular about serving teenagers, or else they thought she was older than she was. The drink came; Connie surrendered eighty cents, and sipped it. It was cold, bitter-tasting. She realized she had never had a martini before, either. But she felt the warm glow of intoxication almost before she had finished it. As she nibbled the olive she said to the bartender, "I'll have a refill, please."

He stirred the drink for her. As she was drawing a dollar from her billfold, a pleasant western voice said, "Mind if I pay for that drink, Miss?"

Turning, Connie saw a tanned, solid-looking man of about thirty smile at her and put a silver dollar down on the bar. Recklessly, Connie decided to accept his offer. "Thanks very kindly, Mr.— Mr.—"

"Streeter. Ted Streeter, of Dallas. And thanks to you for allowing me."

She smiled at him, and he ordered a drink for himself, and they clinked and drank. Connie's heart began to race. Streeter was handsome, in a rugged sort of way, and he had undeniable charm. Connie felt her face beginning to grow flushed. *I'm getting drunk*, she thought, and gulped down her second martini.

Streeter bought her a third, and another for himself. They talked, mostly about him. He was a car-rental man in Dallas, and had flown up to Phoenix this day to talk over a deal for taking over the local car-rental agency. He had a wife and two children, missed them all dearly, and also had more money than he could conveniently spend.

"And what brings you to this part of the world?" he asked finally, when he had said all he wanted to say about himself. "I detect an eastern ring in your voice. New York City?"

"Right you are."

"You're a long way from home."

Connie shrugged, hoping it looked sophisticated. "Call it a vacation. I came out here to have a look at the wide open spaces."

"What do you do in New York?"

"I'm in advertising," Connie improvised.

Streeter smiled knowingly. "Madison Avenue and all that stuff, heh? Well well well. And you're out here all by yourself?"

"That's right."

"You're kind of young to be making such a big trip."

Connie reddened. "How old do you think I am, anyway?"

"Oh, twenty-two, twenty-three."

Connie chuckled and said, "Right the second time. Isn't that old enough to be travelling alone?"

"Guess it is, guess it is. Care for another drink?"

Connie did, and got one. She was amused to think that Streeter had been five or six years off in guessing her age. Evidently she looked a good deal older than seventeen. She wondered how much she had aged in the past three weeks.

Streeter kept edging closer to her at the bar, finally putting his arm around her. After the fourth martini, Connie decided she had done enough drinking. She and Streeter left the bar, hand in hand now, and strolled through the motel, out of the air-conditioned coolness briefly, past the floodlit swimming pool, and into the far section where Streeter's room was. No formal proposition had been made. He was simply taking her to his room, and Connie was following. Within her haze of drunkenness, she was still capable of being surprised at what she was doing, but she brushed all objections away. She had no virginity left to lose. Why not have some fun? Besides, she wanted to prove to herself that the rape had not left her permanently numb sexually.

She followed him into his room. He had plenty of alcohol in him too, and he kept telling her how much she reminded him of his wife.

"Diane's twenty-seven, but she looks a lot younger. You'd never know she'd had two kids. People think she's twenty, y'know? Looks a lot like you—tall, good figure—"

He locked the door of the room, pulled her easily to him, ran his hands down the length of her body, over her breasts, her thighs, her hips. His fingers worked at the buttons of her blouse. He removed blouse and bra, gently kissed her stiffening nipples, and then, as desire became more urgent in him, fumbled open the zipper of her skirt, hastily peeled down her panties, tugging them past the full globes of her buttocks. He undressed in a moment himself and dragged her down on the bed. His hands roved her body, caressing the silken skin, cupping the heavy breasts, toying with the nipples, lightly brushing the soft skin between her thighs, until she began to gasp with pleasure. This was so different, she thought, from the brutality of the night in the shack. He was so loving, so kind. Her body tingled with lust; she could feel currents of air drifting past her erect nipples, stimulating them.

"Now," she muttered thickly. "Now!"

Connie lay by his side, slowly sobering, slowly letting the passion ebb from her. She knew now how complete was the change that had been worked in her. She had given herself to a complete stranger, without guilt, without pain. And she had derived pleasure from it.

Rising from the bed, she showered in his bathroom, and surveyed herself critically in the mirror, eyeing the full spheres of her breasts with the tip-tilted nipples resting upon them, eyeing the supple flaring curve of her hips and the sleek, flawless line of her legs. She knew she was an attractive woman. And she felt strangely free of all the shackles of society. Society—as represented by her parents and by John—regarded her now as a Fallen Woman, though her fall had been none of her own fault. Well, to hell with society, then, Connie thought.

She dressed quietly. Streeter was still sleeping. She took his wallet from his trousers and riffled through it, finding a photo of a sullen-looking heavy-breasted woman holding two lumpy babies. There was also a thick wad of bills. Connie took ten dollars for herself, as payment for her night's services, putting the rest back. Tiptoeing from the room, she closed the door carefully and left, feeling no remorse. Outside the motel, she hailed a taxi. It was shortly after ten o'clock when she reached her grandparents' place. They were still up, watching television in the front room.

"You really took yourself some walk," her grandmother said. "Three hours' worth, it was."

"I met a couple of people I knew and went for some sodas," Connie said glibly.

"Feel better now? You were in an awful bad mood at supper time."

"I feel fine," Connie said, and went on into her room, closing the door behind her. She undressed, got into bed, and read for a while. At eleven o'clock she turned out the light, closed her eyes, and fell almost immediately into a deep, dreamless sleep.

Five

She woke in the morning with a cottony taste in her mouth and an annoying throb back of her forehead. Not surprising, she thought; after all those martinis it was logical to expect a hangover. It was the first genuine hangover she had ever had, and despite the ache in her skull she managed to smile about it.

But it won't be the last, she thought.

After a quick shower and some breakfast, she felt a good deal better. She was cheerful, and had a pleasant idle conversation with her grandparents. She felt no guilt about her affair with Streeter.

That part of it surprised her a little. Deep down within, the *old* Connie Barrett was a little upset by the lighthearted way she had sold her body. But it didn't bother her very much. She had enjoyed the encounter; and she had made a profit on the evening. It was the first step in repaying herself for the precious thing that had been taken so violently from her. Connie wondered only if she had underpriced herself. Streeter probably wouldn't have minded if she had taken twenty or thirty dollars, instead of ten. Well, no matter now. The next time she would be cleverer about it.

She had no doubt there *would* be a next time.

During the next few days Connie spent a lot of time alone, swimming, cantering on horseback, walking through the streets of Phoenix. She wanted to think things out. She was getting her mental balance back, she knew—but now she was a new person.

One thing was certain: she wasn't going to go back to New York. That episode in her life was finished. She wanted nothing more to do with her family or with anyone she had ever known. She was going to make a fresh start.

What about money? she asked herself.

The answer came quickly enough. Her body was her capital. Why not, she wondered? There weren't any degrees of non-virginity. Either you were, or you weren't. And as long as you're not, why not go the whole hog and capitalize on your body? She had read some articles in the New York papers about prostitution. A high-class call girl was able to make anywhere from twenty to fifty thousand dollars a year. Connie smiled. She had a body, and she had breeding. All she lacked was experience, and she could acquire that as she went along. With the right contacts, she, too, could be making $500 or $600 a week before long. And a few years like that could give her a nest egg for life, if she took care of her money and invested it wisely.

Once the decision was reached, Connie felt that she was on an even keel once again. She was happiest when she could map her future out, and now she could make an entirely new set of plans. Five or six years of prostitution; she would still be in her mid-twenties. Then a life of genteel retirement, travel, maybe a movie stint or a novel or two. Then, possibly, a stint as a millionaire's mistress. Her new future began to come vividly to life. It was bizarrely different from her old plans, but she was adjusting rapidly to the change. The night of the rape formed a boundary line in her life; the goals of the years before that night were the goals of an entirely different person, she told herself, and the new Connie Barrett was not going to be bound by them.

At the end of the week came another airmail letter from John. It was long and rambling, and repeated itself half a dozen times. It started off, *"Connie, darling, did my last letter offend you in any way? I can't understand why else you haven't written. Perhaps you read something into my words that wasn't there. Please write to me. I want to know how you feel, when you'll be coming home, and everything else. I also would like to know your reaction to the suggestion I made in my last letter, about us not going steady for a while. If you feel...."*

Connie's answer was short, but not very sweet. She scribbled it on half a sheet of notepaper.

"Dear John:

"Your last letter didn't offend me at all. I couldn't have cared less. For your information, I don't intend to come back east at all. I'm going to stay out here and try to start a new life for myself. Consider yourself free to date anyone you like. Kindly don't write to me again."

Connie.

She sent the letter by ordinary mail instead of airmail. John could wait; let him sweat a little. Besides, he was likely to get in touch with her parents the minute he read the letter, and Connie wanted to contact them herself, first.

She wrote to them that afternoon, by airmail. Connie told them that she had incurred a few expenses, and would they please send her $400 by return airmail? Ordinarily she knew, she stood about as much chance of prying that kind of money out of her parents as she did of winning the Irish Sweepstakes. But the situation was unusual now. They would want to coddle her, to please her. They wouldn't want to deny her anything at this point.

She was right. Three days later she had her check—$400, along with a note hoping she wasn't spending money rashly in Phoenix.

"Not at all," Connie murmured, smiling slyly.

She had close to $500, now. That was enough to start on, at least. The following Monday, after breakfast, she strolled into downtown Phoenix, identified herself at the Valley National Bank as the granddaughter of Lester Barrett, and converted her money into $20 traveler's checks. The next stop was at a travel agency. There, she turned in her paid return-trip airplane ticket to New York, had her reservation cancelled, and got a one-way ticket to San Francisco on a plane leaving two days hence. There was a good-sized cash refund involved as well. Connie added the money to her slim supply of capital. Everything was arranged, now. All very neat.

That night she told her grandparents she was leaving. "I've been here a couple of weeks," she said. "It's been grand, staying here with you, but I really can't stay on any longer. I'm probably hopelessly behind in school as it is. And since my nerves have improved so much, I think it's time to go home."

The old people were visibly disappointed that she was cutting her visit short. But there was no denying that she ought to get back to school, and certainly there had been a 500 per cent improvement in her condition while she had been in Arizona.

On the day of the flight, her grandparents drove Connie out to the airport. She parked them in the waiting-room while she checked in at the flight desk. If they happened to notice that she was checking in for a flight to San Francisco instead of New York, there might be some trouble.

But everything went smoothly. By half past one she was filing across the broiling field toward the big DC-6, and waving goodbye to the two elderly people standing at the loading desk. Fifteen minutes later she was airborne, heading swiftly northwest, over the parched stretches of the Mojave Desert, past Death Valley, above the snow-topped heights of the Sierra Nevada.

By mid-afternoon she was in San Francisco International Airport, where she sent a telegram to her parents while waiting for her luggage to be unloaded:

MR AND MRS D B BARRETT, 1381 MORTIMER AVE BKLYN NY:
HAVE GONE TO WEST COAST TO START NEW LIFE STOP DO
NOT WORRY LOVE ALWAYS

CONNIE

She handed the blank to the girl at the Western Union desk, and then went red; what if the girl realized she was a runaway and called the police? Connie held her breath while the girl mechanically scanned the message, nodded as though she had not understood one word of it, and told Connie how much it would be.

Connie's hand shook a little as she paid for the wire.

"W-when will that reach them?" she asked.

"First thing in the morning, most likely, Miss. It won't get delivered tonight on account of the time difference."

"I see. Thank you."

Connie made her way to the baggage pickup desk. Her two suitcases were waiting there. She hailed a porter and had him carry the grips outside to the place where the city-bound airport coach was loading. On her way out, Connie bought a small booklet containing a city map and a guide to San Francisco, Berkeley, and Oakland.

The airport coach made its first stop about half an hour later, in front of the Sir Francis Drake Hotel on Powell Street. Her guidebook listed the Drake as a luxury hotel, which probably meant that it was in the $15-$25 a day price range, well beyond her means. Connie left the coach anyway, and paused in front of the Drake to check through her guidebook again. It listed a number of inexpensive hotels clustered on Geary Street. Her map showed that they were only three or four blocks from where she was now, and she didn't want to invest any of her limited cash in a taxi ride, so she picked up the suitcases and started to walk south along Powell toward Geary.

Or rather, started to stagger. The suitcases weighed about thirty pounds each. She carried them a quarter of a block, felt herself starting to get dizzy, and hastily put them down. Resting a moment, she picked them up again and managed to get across Post Street before the light changed. She was on the verge of fainting, and her arms felt like they were being ripped from their sockets. It was impossible to go on. But it was only another block to Geary, she thought, then perhaps a block or a block and a half to the hotel she had picked out. She hefted the bags again and tottered another few yards. Then she stopped.

It was silly to take a taxi two blocks, she told herself. But it was even sillier to break her back lugging these valises, just to save a pitiful fifty cents. She saw a cab half a block away and started to raise her hand to signal him, but he had shot past before she made up her mind.

Then a man's voice said, "Pardon me, Miss, but I couldn't help but see you struggling with those big suitcases. How would it be if I gave you a hand?"

Connie's old self automatically sent up the warnings: *Don't accept favors from strangers*. But she brushed caution away. The man was about thirty-five or forty, well dressed, with slick black hair and a pleasantly unhandsome face. Connie smiled and said, "Oh, would you? I'm only going to the Hotel Tennyson, around the corner on Geary, and I guess I'm not going to be able to make it by myself."

Nodding, he scooped up the suitcases as easily as though they were empty, and they started off at a rapid pace toward the hotel. Glancing at the airline baggage checks tied to the suitcase handles, he said, "Come from Phoenix, do you?"

"I—just stopped off there briefly to visit some friends," Connie said. "I'm really from New York."

"New York, heh? Out here for a vacation?"

"No, I've come to stay," Connie said. "I'm only going to bunk at the Tennyson till I've found myself an apartment somewhere around here."

"Better go across the bay to Berkeley," the man I advised. "Lot more apartments over there."

"Maybe I'll do just that," Connie said. "First I'll need a couple of days to shop around. I've never been out here before, you see."

"No? Well, let me tell you, you'll love it!"

"Are you a native San Franciscan?"

"Me? No, I'm from L.A. But I got out of Southern Cal right after the war, when they started building those damn freeways. Been here ten years, and wouldn't live any other place on earth. What's your line of work, Miss—Miss—"

"Thornton," Connie invented. "Connie Thornton. I was in advertising in New York, but I don't want to get back into that rat-race out here. I figure I'll try something new, but I'm not sure what." She was impressed with the glibness with which she reeled off these fantasies. "How about you?"

He chuckled. "I'm an announcer for KGFG and KGFG-TV out here. Good hours, easy work, can't complain about the pay. Enough to handle my alimony and still let me live the way I like to live."

"Oh—you've been divorced," Connie said immediately.

"Smart little gal, aren't you? Yes, I've been happily unwed for three years now. The wife is in Glendale with the kiddies, and I send a nice fat check off to her every month. But I guess you don't want to hear my troubles. Here's your hotel, anyway."

The Tennyson had probably once been a very fashionable hotel, but now it merely looked seedy. The lobby was long and narrow, with fraying broadloom carpeting and a desk at the far end. A pudgy bellhop jumped forward immediately to take Connie's bags.

She turned to face her new friend. "You know, you never even told me your name—"

"Tyler—Nick Tyler."

"Thanks for helping me, Mr. Tyler—Nick—I never would have made it here alone."

"A pleasure, Miss Thornton. Connie." He smiled. "After you've checked in—have you any plans for dinner? If you're a stranger here, that is, you might not know your way around too well—"

Connie smiled warmly. She remembered her new role in life. Tyler made good money, he was divorced, he obviously had a yen for women. He was certainly good for a fancy dinner, and perhaps afterwards Connie could supply him with some entertainment—entertainment for which he would have to pay.

A little tingle of excitement went through her at the thought of deliberately selling herself. It hardly seemed wicked at all. It was simply a way of getting vengeance against the society that had permitted her disaster. Now she had license to break all of society's rules.

"I appreciate that very much, Nick. Matter of fact, I really didn't know *what* I was doing for dinner tonight. Or with whom."

"Suppose I pick you up here at seven, then," Tyler said. "Do you like seafood?"

"Love it."

"Fine. No better way to introduce you to San Francisco than to take you down to Fisherman's Wharf for dinner. I'll make reservations for two at Tarantino's. See you at seven."

"See you at seven," Connie repeated.

She checked in at the desk. They had a room for her, nine dollars a day, on the eleventh floor. She signed in, registering as Constance Thornton and giving a nonexistent Manhattan address, just in case her parents tried to trace her.

The bellhop showed her to her room. It was nothing fancy, but not as dingy as the hotel lobby had promised. At least the carpeting was fresh and the walls freshly painted.

She tipped the boy a quarter and locked the door after him. Then she undressed rapidly and surveyed her body in the mirror. There was no denying that she was attractive. Her breasts, high and full, pale white with just the faintest traces of blue veins, would send any man afire. She decided to ask $25 for her services tonight. Nick Tyler was going to be surprised—he certainly wasn't expecting her to be a pro—but she had a hunch he would pay, and pay willingly, for her.

Six

Connie took a long, slow, cool shower to wash away the sweat and grime of her trip from Phoenix. There was a sensuous thrill in turning the tap to ice-cold, and standing under the frigid water as long as she could stand it, with the coldness coursing down her breasts and belly, her flanks and her buttocks, and the breath escaping from her clenched lips in little hisses of pleasure.

After the shower she dressed, putting on a tight blue sheath that had always annoyed her parents because it was so revealing. It clung practically to her skin, outlining every curve of hip and thigh, and the neckline plunged daringly to reveal the creamy globes of her breasts. A specially engineered bra went with the dress; for a daring moment she considered meeting Tyler without any bra at all, but changed her mind. From what she had heard about San Francisco's surface morality, that kind of display would be considered far too risqué. Only in Los Angeles was near-nudity commonplace.

She was ready at five minutes to seven, but she sat down to smoke a cigarette until ten after. Let Tyler wait, she thought. Let him think he's getting something special tonight.

Connie had no feeling of affection for Tyler, even though he had helped her. He was a man—and men were crude panting beasts who had only one use for a woman, and took it violently if they couldn't have it for love or money. Connie didn't intend to give it up for love, but she was determined to get the money. Men would pay for what those teenage animals had done to her.

She rode downstairs. Tyler was waiting in the lobby. He had changed his clothes, put on a fresh shirt, shaved. He smelled agreeably of men's cologne.

"Hi," Connie said. "Sorry I'm late."

"Late? Compared with most girls, you're half an hour early! All set to go?"

Outside, he said, "It would be quicker if we took a taxicab. But since this is your first night in San Francisco, we'll do it the traditional way—via cable car. Let's go over to Powell Street."

They walked across to Powell and joined a group of people waiting in the middle of the street. Soon, the cable car came along, an ancient-looking green trolley clanging its bells and making a tremendous amount of noise. They climbed on—the car was open along the sides— and off they went with a clang and a roar, up one incredibly steep hill and down into the valley, then up the hill again. Connie giggled. The cable car ride was fun.

It came to rest, finally, on a turntable at the foot of Mason Street. The salt air was bracing and fresh. Tyler guided her briskly through the streets, crowded with souvenir stands, and, toward the restaurant.

Fisherman's Wharf was alive and swarming with tourist traps, places where cheap pennants could be bought, or fresh crabs, or gifts and curios.

The restaurant was superb. Connie let Tyler buy her a champagne cocktail; he had a martini. Then they ordered. Connie treated herself to broiled swordfish. The price was astronomical, but Connie didn't care. This wasn't a date with some budget-conscious college freshman.

They had shrimp cocktail before the main course. The shrimps were miniatures, unlike any Connie had seen in New York. There were at least fifty of them in the dish, and they were newly caught and delicious.

The meal was extra good, too. Connie and Tyler lingered over it, making idle small talk. From the way Tyler's eyes came to rest on the cleft of her bosom from time to time, Connie knew he was hooked, but good. She wondered if she should raise the ante to $50. She decided against it. $25 was good enough for now; she could start charging higher prices later, when she would be worth it, when she had learned a few specialties and tricks of the trade. The check was for $19. Connie knew that was a good sign. No man would spend $19 for dinner with some girl he had just met unless he planned to get something from her in return. And Tyler, if he was geared for sex this evening, would probably be willing to pay.

After dinner they strolled along the wharf for a while. "San Francisco's a fascinating town," Tyler said. "You ought to take in the North Beach area, up above Grant Avenue near Telegraph Hill—that's where our Beatniks hang out. The bohemian crowd. It's the Greenwich Village of San Francisco. Phony, of course, but it's worth a look. And then there's Chinatown, of course, and you ought to get out to Golden Gate Park if you go for trees and flowers and zoos and stuff like that. I sometimes go there when I'm through at the studio, just to stroll around. And we have a pretty good opera company in town, too. Do you like opera, Connie?"

"Very much," she said. "I used to go to the Metropolitan pretty often." It was a lie—John had never been able to afford tickets—but she thought it would impress Tyler.

It did. "I'm a bug on opera myself. It's swell that you go for it too. Maybe we can take in a few performances this year—I want to see *Boris* again, and maybe *Butterfly* or *Boheme*. Schmaltz, but good schmaltz."

They strolled on a little further. "And then you want to take a ride across the bay to Muir Woods, and have a look at the redwood trees. It does something to your soul to see trees as old as the Pyramids and as tall as a thirty-story building. At least, it does something to my soul."

"I'd love to see them," Connie said. "They must be magnificent."

"That they are. So you see, this is a pretty good little city. It's got just about everything New York has, except snow in the winter and heat waves in the summer—and it's a damn sight friendlier and prettier than New York. S.F. is kind of wonderful. And—you know, I think you are too, Connie."

Tyler slipped his arm around her shoulders and under her light jacket in such a way that his hand just barely touched the side of her right breast. She made no attempt to remove the hand. Tyler hugged her a little. He was hooked, all right.

He went on, talking about the beauties of the Bay Area, and interspersing his Chamber-of-Commerce talk with a few increasingly warm and affectionate personal remarks. And finally, when they grew tired of walking, he suggested that they got up to the Top of the Mark for cocktails.

They took a cab. The Hotel Mark Hopkins was at California and Mason. There was a brief wait in the lobby; then, as space became available, they rode upstairs to the window-walled cocktail lounge on the uppermost floor.

It was nearly ten o'clock, and darkness covered the city. Fog had wrapped itself around the downtown area, spoiling the view, but that didn't matter much. They sat at a table near one window, holding hands and drinking brandy, and Tyler said, "You don't have any early-morning appointments tomorrow, do you, Connie?"

"No. Why?"

"I was just wondering. It's the middle of the week and all that, and I wouldn't want to keep you up late if you had to be up early."

She smiled. "I can sleep all day tomorrow."

"Good. Then, look—just suppose the two of us went over to my place for a little while? I'm not too far from here—on Sacramento near Van Ness. I've got a pretty cozy place, and we can listen to music, and I've got some drinkable liquor there. There's no sense paying these thieves a buck-and-a-quarter for a pony of brandy when there's a fifth of Courvoisier VSOP cognac sitting on my shelf at home, is there?"

"Of course not," Connie said.

"Finish your drink and let's go, then, huh?"

This was the time to spring it on him, Connie thought. She felt a twinge of nervousness. How did you go about telling a man that he had been dating a prostitute?

She said in a low voice, "There's just one thing you ought to know before we go over there."

"Oh? What's that?"

"You want to go to bed with me, don't you?"

Tyler reddened beneath his tan, and looked confused and embarrassed. "Why—that is—"

"Don't play around, Nick. You aren't inviting me up to your apartment to listen to your opera records, and both of us know it. I just want to get everything straight before we go over there, so there aren't any misunderstandings later."

Tyler shook his head, grinning. "You New Yorkers—you drive straight to the point right away, don't you? Well, if you pin me down to a confession, I'll have to admit that I *do* have some slight designs on your virtue. Is the whole thing off now?"

"Not at all. I told you, I just wanted to get everything straight. This way it saves a lot of uncertainty and guessing around."

"You amaze me," Tyler said.

"I still haven't told you the one thing you ought to know."

"Which is?"

"I'm perfectly willing to go over to your apartment and sleep with you. The catch is that I'm not in the habit of doing it for the fun of it. If you want to give me a roll in the hay, it'll cost you twenty-five bucks. Otherwise I might as well go back to my hotel right now."

Tyler's jaw dropped. He started so violently that he almost knocked Connie's drink over. The expression on his face was half one of anger, half one of bewilderment and surprise.

"Well, I'll be a pie-eyed emu!" he whispered incredulously. "Christ almighty, so you play for pay? And here you were giving me this scared-little-stranger-in-town routine all night?"

Connie forced herself to keep a mask of toughness on her face. Within, she was quaking. "I *am* a stranger in town. And you were very helpful with the suitcases. It's been a wonderful evening all around. But I've only got one trade and I can't afford to give away free samples."

"What about the advertising business?" Tyler was smiling now at his own earlier gullibility.

"Phony," Connie said. "I just thought I needed a change of air, is all. So I packed up and went west, young girl, like it says in the books. So you happened to pick me up half an hour after I hit town. That was swell of you—but I still won't play any games with you for free."

"Then I took you out under false pretenses," Tyler said. "I thought you were a sweet, demure little thing who could be swayed by much booze and soft talk into submitting to my lusts—and instead I find I've been dating a chippie! A smooth and slick one, to boot." He stood up. "Okay, honey. Let's go."

"Where to?"

"Over to my place."

"On my terms?" Connie asked.

"What else? I've got a yen for you now. Had it all evening. If it's going to cost me a quarter of a bill to satisfy it, I'll just have to grin and bear it. Come on."

Fifteen minutes later they were at his apartment. It was a neat little three-roomer, expensively furnished in excellent taste. There were Picasso prints on the wall, a big hi-fi set, a handsome bar. Tyler put some music on the phonograph and mixed a couple of drinks. They sat and listened for a while, neither of them saying much. Tyler still seemed stunned by the news that she was a professional; Connie herself was fascinated by the extent of the change in her personality, and by the smooth way she had delivered her little speech. Her heart pounded. She hadn't thought she had the guts to put over anything quite so bold.

In the middle of his drink, Tyler put it down and said, "Come here."

Connie went to him. He put his arms around her, cupped one hand over her breasts, drew down the zipper of her dress with the other. He slipped it off her. A moment later he had undone her bra as well. Connie waited passively as he undressed her. When she wore only a garter belt and stockings, the excitement began to thunder in her. His hands skimmed gently over the cool flesh of her buttocks, rested for a moment on her thighs. Then he removed the garter belt and she was naked.

He undressed quickly. His body was lean and in good condition. They stood in the middle of the floor, embracing, body against body, thigh against thigh. Then he drew her down to the bed and they began to make love.

It' was a slow, careful procedure. His hands travelled over her body, cupping her breasts, stroking her buttocks, tightening on the flesh of her thighs. He kissed her in a dozen places. Her breath began to come hard. She squirmed and writhed and panted. It was the same wildness that had seized her that other night, that hideous night in the watchman's shack. She could think of nothing but the knot of desire in her belly.

He gripped her tightly and their bodies clung together. She felt his heart thumping—or was it her own?

"Christ," he muttered. "Christ!"

It was over.

The room was very silent. Connie felt his weight upon her. She could hear the thumping of hearts and the distinct ticking of his wristwatch. He rolled over to lie at her side, cupping one of her breasts limply, fondly in his hand.

Connie smiled in the darkness. She felt wonderfully relaxed, wonderfully good. And she felt even better for knowing that a man had not only given her this pleasure but would pay for it. *Men. Pigs!*

After a while she rose from the bed and went into the bathroom to clean herself up. While she was in there, she heard the sound of music coming from the other room. When she returned, she saw Tyler standing by the phonograph, having just put a chamber music record on. He was wearing a silk dressing gown, and was smiling at her.

"What time is it?" Connie asked.

"A little past midnight."

"I guess I'll go home now," she said. "It was a swell evening. There's just the little matter of my bill to settle."

Tyler chuckled. "You're pretty new at this game, aren't you, kid?"

"What do you mean?"

"How old are you, anyway? Nineteen? Twenty?"

"None of your business," Connie snapped.

Shrugging, Tyler said, "Okay, you're right. But I can still tell you're new. Maybe *brand* new."

"How can you tell that?"

"A lot of ways. For one thing, you enjoyed it too much. You weren't faking it. I can tell by your eyes. No hustler can get that much pleasure out of it. Maybe you can at the start, but after a while it becomes just another routine to you. So you're new to hustling. I'm willing to bet you were a virgin up till less than a year ago, too. You didn't make love like an expert. Don't get me wrong, you were damned good—but you didn't have the poise and polish that an experienced woman has. You probably haven't made love more than a dozen times. Am I right or am I right?"

Connie glared at him. The truth stung. In a low voice she said, "I don't want to be psychoanalyzed. Give me my money and let me go."

"That's another thing, honey-bun. A professional *always* gets paid before she delivers the goods. That's the first rule of the business. It's ten times easier to collect from a john before you've satisfied him than afterward. Remember that the next time you try this routine."

Connie was close to tears. Calmly and methodically Tyler had shredded her apart and exposed her, for the rank amateur she was.

He reached into the pocket of his dressing gown drew out three ten-dollar bills, and handed them over. "Here. Keep the change as a tip." He smiled. "I don't know what a cute kid like you thinks she's gaining by peddling her lily-white body. You'd do a lot better to find some rich bastard and marry him. Not me, mind you—I've been there once, and I'm not getting married anymore. But with your looks you could grab someone good."

"I'm not interested in getting married. I want my freedom, and this is the easiest way I can have it without depending on anybody else."

Tyler shrugged. "If that's your philosophy, good luck to you. Will I see you again?"

"It'll cost you. The price may even go up."

"I'll take it off my income tax. Give me a ring when you get permanently settled, eh?" Tyler said. "I'd like to keep in touch. I might even be able to find some clients for you. A lot of my friends are willing to pay good cash for a high-priced lay who likes opera."

"Don't do me any favors," Connie said acidly. In another moment, she knew, she would be weeping. Looking away from him, she dressed rapidly and left without saying goodbye.

Seven

By the time she reached her hotel, Connie no longer felt the sting of Tyler's remarks. He had been cutting and sarcastic, but only because he was annoyed at having the price-tag sprung on him. Connie had to admit that everything he had said was true.

She was still an amateur. She had only the foggiest idea of the way members of her new profession worked. That bit about collecting in advance—it seemed coarse and grasping to her. But what the hell: prostitution was a coarse and grasping business. Payment in advance made a lot of sense, now that she thought about it. So did the other things Tyler had said. She refused to let his harsh words discourage her.

Connie smiled ironically. Breaking into high-class whoredom was like breaking into any profession. You had to learn the ropes, pick up the special skills, establish a reputation, make contacts. She didn't want to be a mere streetwalker, parading around looking for quick five-dollar encounters. She pictured herself more as a classy courtesan, drawing a hundred dollars or so for a night's services. That was more dignified. Also more profitable, and easier on the feet.

In the morning she bought a copy of the *Chronicle* at the hotel newsstand, and read the apartments-for-rent section with care. Picking out half a dozen likely ads, she armed herself with her street-map and set out to go apartment-hunting.

The first place on her list was rented already. The second was not open for single girls. (*Does it show on my face already?* Connie wondered. *Or are they just generally nervous?*) The third place, though, turned out to be just about what she wanted—two and a half furnished rooms in a small apartment building on Mission Street. It was a quiet, peaceful neighborhood with broad streets and narrow two-story frame buildings, mostly. The rent was $125 a month, which was a bit more than Connie wanted to pay, but not exorbitantly high. The furniture was far from modern, but it was clean and in reasonably good repair. The renting agent told Connie she had the option of surrendering the furniture and furnishing the place herself, at her own expense; the rent would drop accordingly. Connie nodded. As soon as she had enough cash, she would do just that.

She checked out of the hotel, found a bus that went toward Mission Street, and by late afternoon was settled in her new apartment. The previous occupant had left a telephone there, which was handy.

She telephoned Nick Tyler. "Why aren't you out looking for a pick-up?" she asked when he came to the phone.

Tyler laughed. "I'm an old man of almost forty, remember? I've *had* my sex for this month. Maybe for the rest of the year. What's doing with you?"

"Got myself a telephone number, and an apartment to go with it. Interested?"

"Maybe."

She gave him the number and the address, and he wrote them down.

"Doing anything tonight?" she asked.

"Recuperating from last night, mostly. I figure on a quiet evening alone with some Bach and a can of ravioli. My budget can't stand a $50 date every night."

"How about your friends?"

"Lord, you *are* a hustler, aren't you!"

"I'm free tonight, that's all," Connie said. "You wouldn't want me to have to go out and walk the streets for my night's pay, would you?"

"Perish the thought. But I don't have any clients for you tonight, kiddo. Now that you've got your own pad, I'll spread the word around. What's my rake-off?"

Connie didn't know whether he was serious or not. "Give me a big build-up with your friends and I'll let you have some fun on the house every once in a while," she said.

"Good enough. How about tonight for a starter?"

Connie laughed into the phone. "I don't extend credit anymore. You taught me that last night, and I learn fast. Good night, Daddy."

She hung up. For a moment the gay mood of the phone conversation remained with her. Then she remembered that she was just another whore without a night's work ahead of her. A surge of bitterness went through her. She clenched her fists and reminded herself that she was still new at her trade, that gradually her reputation would grow until she was in demand every night. She couldn't miss. She had brains and looks, and brainy call girls weren't found everywhere.

Checking through her finances, she found she had close to $300 left, even after paying a month's rent in advance. For the next few weeks things would be touch and go, she realized; $300 could melt away awfully fast if no income was coming in. But if she could get through the rest of this month okay, everything would be going smoothly from then on.

It was six o'clock; time for dinner. She found a restaurant on Valencia Street and invested a dollar in hamburgers, french fries, and coffee. No point tossing her own money away on a fancy dinner when she could get her clients to wine and dine her. After dinner, she strolled up Valencia coward Market Street. It was a nice night, typical late-autumn weather for San Francisco, with the temperature near sixty and a mild breeze blowing in from the Bay.

She stopped at a bookstore on Market Street and, after browsing through two shelves of marriage manuals, finally picked out a fat volume called *Sex Life in Marriage*, marked down from eight-fifty to six dollars. The price was still steep, but a quick skim through the book indicated that it would be more than worth her while to study it carefully. It was intended to guide people contemplating marriage, but there was nothing printed on the jacket that said it couldn't also be used by a young would-be call girl to get some pointers about her trade.

Connie blushed shyly as she brought the book up the desk to pay for it. The clerk was in his early twenties, and he glanced quickly at Connie's hands, probably looking for a wedding ring. She was wearing an imitation ruby ring that might be taken for an engagement ring. As the clerk wrapped the book he said, "This is a fine year for getting married."

"Yes, isn't it?" Connie chattered.

"I'm getting married next month myself. My girl and I have both read this book. It's really detailed."

Connie smiled nervously. So he mistook her for someone's soon-to-be-bride. Well, let him delude himself. Connie wondered what he would say if she told him that for twenty-five dollars she would sleep with him this very night. He would probably have a fainting fit, she decided. Anyway, twenty-five bucks was probably half his week's pay. She took her package and, still smiling, left the store.

On her way back to the apartment she passed a package store, and, on a sudden impulse, went in and bought a fifth of cognac, the same kind Nick Tyler had given her the night before. She winced when the clerk told her the price—nearly ten dollars—but she had already committed herself, and didn't want to back out now. She bought the bottle.

Returning quickly to her apartment, she unwrapped her book and her cognac, and set them both on the little night table in her bedroom. Then, sitting down at her desk, she began compiling a list of the things she would have to buy in the next few days. Food, for one thing—it was senseless to eat at restaurants when she could be cooking for herself. A couple of sexy negligees might be in order, too. And she needed some liquor, in case she did any entertaining here—gin, scotch, rye, and vermouth to begin with, other things later as her income increased. But she would have to be careful about inviting men up here to drink with her. A john with a hollow leg might use up five or six dollars' worth of her liquor in an evening. Maybe she would add the cost of any liquor served to the cost of her body. That seemed fair enough, she thought.

When she had completed her shopping list, she undressed and showered, and spent fifteen minutes doing setting-up exercises. (*My body is my capital*, she told herself. *Mustn't let it get out of trim.*) Then she poured herself half a glass of brandy and climbed into bed to read the marriage manual.

She skipped quickly through the parts about choosing a mate, about love and tenderness, and all the rest. She didn't want to think about those things. Love and marriage were things of the past for her, things that had been forever locked away in a compartment of her mind that she didn't care to open again. All that mattered now was earning a living with her body. Making the male sex pay for what had been done to her.

She read for about an hour, until the alcohol started to blur her eyes. Then she closed the book with a slam. She knew all sorts of things she hadn't even dreamed of before. A dozen different positions. Ways of prolonging the sex act. Stimulating a tired partner.

Smiling, Connie looked across the room at the little bookcase where she had put her textbooks. American History. Trigonometry. Economics.

High school seemed to be a billion years behind her, on some other world. She padded across the room and put the sex manual into the shelf next to the Eco book. Sex was one subject that wasn't on the high school curriculum. She laughed.

She walked to the window. The blind was open, and anyone who looked up from the street would have an eye-opening view of her upthrusting breasts and white belly and thighs. She realized she didn't care. She hoped half a million people were down there looking at her. Giggling, she stretched, still standing in the window, raising her arms to make her breasts thrust forward and her nipples rise outward like little buttons. She realized she was a little bit drunk. She wriggled her hips voluptuously, holding her breasts from underneath and extending them forward toward the silent street. Finally, she blew a kiss to any audience there might be out there, and pulled down the blind. She snapped off the light and climbed into bed.

Sleep was a long time coming. Bitter thoughts kept wandering through her mind. It didn't need to be this way, she told herself. She didn't have to be living in a furnished apartment three thousand miles from home, with her parents probably half crazy with worry about her, this way. She didn't need to angle around for men willing to pay $25 for the privilege of sleeping with her. If only she hadn't gone downstairs to mail that letter, she thought. Everything would be so different. She would still have her room at home, with the teddy-bear on the dresser that she had had since she was five, with John courting her from Syracuse, with college ahead of her, and marriage, and kids, and the little house in West-chester, or maybe Long Island.

To hell with all that crap, she thought sharply. No teddy-bear, no John, no college, no wedding, no kids, no little suburban split-level. Just money. Lots of it. Money and drink and sex.

She rose unsteadily from the bed, tottered across the room, put the cognac bottle to her lips, and gulped down as much as she could hold. The fiery stuff burned her throat and made her eyes water, but it numbed the reproachful furies in her skull. She just about made it back to bed. Before she knew it, she was asleep.

Next thing she knew, sunlight was streaming into her room. Eleven-fifteen, her watch said. So she had slept more than thirteen hours.

She washed and dressed quickly, and breakfasted at a nearby luncheonette. Then she did her shopping, enough to keep her from having to eat out for the rest of the week. It was about one in the afternoon when she got back to her apartment. She put the groceries away and flopped down limply on the unmade bed.

Afternoon of a call girl. The long hours stretched ahead into the future. She felt bored and a little disgusted with life. What did a call girl do when nobody called her? Connie shrugged. She couldn't depend on just one contact to scare up business for her. The thing to do was to dress up seductively and head over to one of the fancy convention hotels, the Fairmont or the Sheraton-Palace or the St. Francis. It couldn't be too hard to pick up some prosperous junior executive in town without his wife for the annual Nut and Bolt Manufacturers' Convention, or whatever was going on at the moment.

But not yet. During the afternoon there would be formal sessions going on, most likely. The time to go over was about four-thirty, just before the cocktail break.

As it turned out, though, she did not need to work the hotel route that night. About three that afternoon, as she lay curled up reading the marriage manual, the telephone rang. She snatched it up.

"Yes?"

"Miss Thornton?"

"That's right." The voice was deep, rich, startlingly masculine.

"This is Mr.—uh—Smith, calling. I'm a friend of Nick Tyler's."

Instantly Connie was all business. Her pulse raced. "Yes, Mr. Smith. Can I—ah—be of any help to you?"

"I was just wondering," "Smith" said, "whether you might be free tonight. I've got a couple of tickets to the musical at the Curran, and my escort was—ah—suddenly taken ill. I'd hate to see the tickets go to waste."

"Of course, Mr. Smith."

"And Nick suggested you might be available. I'm in rather a depressed mood, and I—ah—could use some cheering up."

"I'd be happy to oblige."

"How about meeting me for drinks and dinner, first? Then we can take in the show. What about the corner of Geary and Mason, at five? Nick described you well enough so I'll recognize you, I think."

They agreed to meet there. Connie was excited, as excited as if this were her first date—which, in a sense, it was. That first encounter in Phoenix, with the man from Dallas, had been strictly a quick pick-up; the other night, with Tyler, she had practically bludgeoned him into paying her. But now someone had phoned *her*, with the unspoken understanding that she would be paid for her troubles.

She dressed in the same low-necked dress she had worn when going out with Tyler, and took a cab downtown. At five sharp she was at the corner of Geary and Mason, in the heart of San Francisco's department-store and office-building neighborhood.

"Miss Thornton?" a deep voice said. "I'm Mr. Smith."

He was very tall—six feet three, at least—and older than Connie had expected, close to forty-five. Old enough to be my father, Connie realized with some surprise. His appearance matched his voice in suave distinction: he was expensively dressed, and there were streaks of gray in his wavy black hair.

And by the way his eyes lit up, Connie knew he was impressed with her.

They ate at Marsalli's, a French restaurant on Geary Street. "Smith"— who soon identified himself as being actually named Henrichs—started pouring out his troubles over cocktails, and continued right on through the cherrystone clams and the filet mignon. He was part owner of a large cosmetics firm that advertised on the station where Nick Tyler worked, and he knew Nick well. Henrichs had been married twice, divorced twice. His current light-of-love was a girl who lived in Berkeley. She was married, but had promised to divorce her husband and marry him. Yesterday, though, Henrichs had gotten the bad news: she and her husband were being reconciled, there would be no divorce, and hence no marriage with Henrichs.

Henrichs was disconsolate. He had built all kinds of plans around this new affair, and now, unexpectedly, his plans were shattered. Connie listened attentively, making sympathetic comments from time to time. She was being paid to be sympathetic, and she intended to earn her pay.

"I don't think I was ever really in love before," the big man was saying. "This girl had everything, though—looks, poise, intelligence, passion. And, unfortunately, a husband. But she said she was leaving him. Why did she have to change her mind like that?"

"It must have been a terrible shock to you," Connie said, properly consoling.

When Henrichs grew tired of talking about himself, the conversation took a more general turn—current events, new books, plays, music. Connie did her best to keep up, bluffing where she was out of her depth. Henrichs did not appear to notice. He seemed very pleased with her.

They finished the meal off with liqueurs, and strolled down the block to the theater. The show was a hit musical in New York; this was the road company, playing to sellouts on the west coast. Henrichs had orchestra seats. Connie had never been this close to the stage before.

After the show, they stopped for more drinks, then taxied to Henrichs' home in the wealthy Marina district along the city's north shore. It was at least a $50,000 home, Connie estimated.

"Do make yourself comfortable," Henrichs said courteously. "You will be able to stay the whole night, won't you?"

"If that's what you want, yes."

"I hate rushing things," he said. He smiled a little awkwardly. "Perhaps it's crass to descend to the commercial level, but I'd like you to have this, in thanks of the pleasant evening you've given me—and for what's to come." He handed her a sealed envelope and excused himself. While he was gone, Connie ripped the envelope open and peered inside. It contained two fifty-dollar bills. She made a mental note to thank Nick Tyler *very* generously for having given Henrichs her phone number.

Eight

A moment after she had slipped the money into her purse Henrichs returned, bringing with him a tray of drinks. Connie was already a bit dizzy from the liquor she had consumed, but she graciously accepted the drink, then sipped it as slowly as she could.

Henrichs was in no rush to go to bed. He showed her around the house, demonstrating his automatic kitchen equipment and his stereophonic hi-fi and his wine cellar and his library, while Connie made properly appreciative noises. He also showed her photographs—of his first wife, looking harsh and 1930ish in the faded sepia print; of his second wife, wearing her hair long in the style of the war years, her face greedy-looking and showing the signs of self-indulgence. He showed Connie a photo he had taken of his Berkeley mistress, the one who had refused to divorce her husband for him. To Connie's surprise, the picture, a glossy eight-by-ten color print, showed her in the nude. She was about thirty, with short blonde hair and a lush, overripe body. She was lying sprawled on the rug of Henrichs' living-room. Her breasts were heavy, almost pendulous, and her hips were fleshy. She looked like something out of a Rubens painting.

"She loved to pose for me in the nude," Henrichs said dreamily. "Isn't she beautiful? I have hundreds of photos of her. Some of them are very personal, you understand." He sighed. "And that's all I have left of her— memories and photographs." The nude photo seemed to put Henrichs in an amorous mood. He led Connie into a bedroom, undressed her, stood a few feet away and studied her.

"You're beautiful," he said finally. "Your breasts are even lovelier than *hers*. I like a woman to have big breasts. My first wife had practically none. My second was on the flat-chested side, too. I'll never make that mistake again. If I ever marry, I'll marry someone built like you. Would you mind very much if I photograph you—just as you are right now?"

The request took Connie by surprise, but after thinking it over for a second or two she readily agreed. Henrichs was the client, and if it amused him to photograph her, she had no objections. Besides, a few photos of her in the nude, passed around to Henrichs' wealthy friends, would effectively advertise her wares a lot better than any mere word-of-mouth could do.

Henrichs set up his camera and took a dozen shots of her in various positions. When he decided he had enough, he thanked Connie profusely. "I'll send you prints," he said. "I develop them myself. Photography's one of my hobbies."

Then they went to bed. Connie had been looking forward to trying out some of the new things she had learned from the marriage manual, but Henrichs didn't give her a chance. He was abysmally inept as a lover. He embraced her quickly, and was finished in less than a minute, just when Connie was beginning to feel the first tingles of passion. She began to understand at least one of the reasons why Henrichs' Berkeley sweetheart might have decided to stay with her husband after all.

But Connie had already acquired enough professional poise to know better than to seem critical of the big man's performance. She smiled the smile of a satisfied woman, and he kissed her tenderly and nestled down to sleep with his head tucked between her breasts. Just a big overgrown baby, she thought, half with affection, and half with cold contempt, as he snuggled up in her bosom and rapidly fell asleep. Connie curled up on her side and soon was asleep too.

In the middle of the night she was awakened; Henrichs was passionately kissing her breasts, and her nipples had sprung to erectness. They made love again, with exactly the same result as before, and after that slept until morning.

An alarm went off. Connie kept her eyes shut. She was dimly aware that Henrichs was getting out of bed. She dozed off, and awakened again when she felt his big hands slip under the covers to cup the firm mounds of her breasts. She opened her eyes.

"It's half past eight," Henrichs said. "I've made some breakfast."

He was fully dressed and shaved. They ate in his chrome-lined $10,000 kitchen, and at his request Connie wore only her panties. Henrichs' eyes hardly left her breasts during the entire meal.

"I usually take a cab to my office," he said. "Care to ride downtown with me?"

She smiled and shook her head. "If it's all the same, I'd rather not. I was thinking of going to Golden Gate Park for the morning."

"Have a good time." He kissed her tenderly. "Thanks for a swell time. I'll be calling you again."

Connie spent the morning at the park, wandering through the Japanese Garden and the aquarium, and returned to her apartment at lunchtime. She was in a very good mood. She had had a splendid dinner, had been taken to a hit show, and had earned $100 to boot. It was a soft way to get rich, and what did it matter that Henrichs was a flop in bed? *He* was satisfied, and that was all that counted.

It wasn't long before Connie was on her way to becoming one of the most popular free-lance call girls in San Francisco. Her reputation spread like a chain reaction. Henrichs gave her number to a choice selection of his friends, top businessmen and executives all. By the end of the first week, she was getting more phone-calls than she could easily handle.

She never had to mention price. It was understood that she commanded $100 for a night's services, and that she liked to be taken to expensive restaurants and hit shows before getting down to the main business of the night.

The secret of her appeal was simple. She had the fresh, almost virginal look of a teen-ager—and the morals of an experienced whore. She was never coarse, never vulgar. Of course not; hadn't she been brought up in a cultured middle-class home? She could discuss the arts with growing familiarity, especially after she started spending her days improving her mind. In short, she was the perfect companion, witty, pretty, and accessible. Unlike a wife, she never denied her favors. Also unlike a wife, she could be had whenever necessary, and forgotten the rest of the time.

The next of her clients was a man named Jacobs, a buyer from Chicago. Henrichs was trying to persuade the Chicago man to place a big order with him, and, accordingly, Connie was hired to visit Jacobs in his suite at the Sheraton-Palace.

He met her at the door with a broad grin. "Ah—you're that friend of Paul Henrichs', aren't you? Connie Thornton?"

"That's right. He asked me to make sure you had a good time while you were in San Francisco."

Jacobs was a short, stocky man in his early fifties. He wasted little time with preliminaries, and he gave Connie a strenuous workout. She got little sleep that night; every time she drowsed off, Jacobs clawed her into wakefulness again. He seemed insatiable. He had the fierce energy of a demon. But he was obviously pleased with Connie's performance. The next afternoon, about four, her telephone rang. She had been dozing.

It was Henrichs. "Jacobs just left my office," he said. "He placed an order big enough to start sounding like the National Debt. And he was particularly impressed with you. Thanks ever so much, Connie."

"Glad to have been of help," she said.

"He'll be coming to San Francisco again on a buying trip in the spring—third, fourth, fifth of April. And he told me four or five times to make sure that you were available for those three nights. Will you reserve them for him?"

Connie laughed. "That's months from now!"

"I know. But he's very insistent about it. Be sure to keep those nights open. Speaking of which, are you free tomorrow?"

"Sorry, I'm not. How about Tuesday?"

"That'll have to do, I guess," Henrichs said. "I'll send you your check for Jacobs right now. I developed those pictures I took of you, but I guess I won't bother to mail them out. You can have them on Tuesday."

The next morning there was a check for $125 from Henrichs, with a note explaining that the $25 was a bonus for having impressed the Chicago buyer so deeply. Connie deposited the check in the Bank of America branch near her house. Her account was beginning to grow.

That night she saw Nick Tyler—on the house, she told him in advance. He had directly or indirectly supplied her with nearly a thousand dollars' worth of business in the past two weeks.

"From what I hear, you're really setting this old town on fire," Tyler said. They were in his apartment, sipping rum collinses.

"I'm doing all right," Connie said quietly.

"All right? To hear Henrichs talk, you practically landed him a six-figure contract single-handed. Six big figures. And he says you're in hot demand with a lot of important people. How come you can afford to donate a night to a peon like me?"

Connie smiled warmly. "I treated you pretty shabbily that first night. You weren't expecting to have a price-tag put on the night's entertainment. Well, I'll even things up now. Help yourself to a hundred dollars' worth of fun."

Tyler didn't need a second invitation. He made love to her lingeringly, passionately. Connie shivered as his hands tightened over her breasts, as his lips travelled up and down her body. Already, in only a couple of weeks, she had come to regard her clients with contempt, and she rarely felt any real passion for them. The ecstasy she displayed in their arms was mostly an act. But she felt differently tonight. She was not charging for her favors. There was a certain illicit thrill in that, just as, at first, there had been a thrill in making love for money.

It was a wonderful evening. The next night, though, she was dated by Tyler's boss, Jim Felks, the head announcer at KGFG. Felks was a slick, hard-drinking, hard-driving bachelor with plenty of money. He drove Connie out to Point Lobos in his bright red Mercedes-Benz 300 SL sports car, and they necked by the Pacific for a while. Then he headed for Sutro Forest, right in the center of San Francisco, and they made love outdoors. "I like doing it outdoors," he explained. "It adds zest to it."

Felks was an expert at making love. He handled Connie's body the way he handled his $13,000 car—with precision and complete control. But Connie had to fake her response again. She remained outside her own skull, as it were, looking down objectively on the two naked bodies twisting and moaning on the grass. All of Felks' sex virtuosity could not conceal the fact that he was just another client, paying for the use of her body.

Felks sensed it too, apparently. He said very little as he drove her home, and there was no mention of a second date.

The next day Nick Tyler called. "Hey, my boss was complaining about you, Connie."

"Complaining?"

"Uh-huh. He said I sold him a bill of goods. I guaranteed that you'd be one hundred percent responsive, but he claims you were just putting on an act. What goes? Starting to get the professional blasé attitude?"

"I— I don't know what went wrong, Nick. He handled me perfectly, but I just couldn't get the fire lit. I was hoping I'd fooled him."

Tyler laughed harshly. "Jim Felks can't be fooled, kid. But looky here—your big selling point so far is that you're just like the girl next door, only you can be had. If you're going to turn into just another frigid call girl, you won't have such an easy time as you've been having up till now. Bedroom actresses can be found anywhere. But someone who really *responds*—that's what guys like Felks want."

Connie tried her best. But some nights she had it, some nights she didn't. Some nights she was a panting, urgently demanding, torrid creature; others, she was just a high-priced lay going through a standard routine. She couldn't help it. Five nights a week of her trade was giving her a gloss of professionalism, and it couldn't be avoided.

Most of her clients either didn't notice or didn't care. Henrichs' friends, and *their* friends, were mostly pudgy middle-aged businessmen who weren't fussy about their partners, so long as the girls weren't vulgar. Connie was anything but vulgar.

Sometimes a younger man would date her—a playboy friend of Tyler's, usually. Some of these saw through Connie's pretenses, others didn't. And with some, there was no need for pretense. One date with a handsome young Sloat Boulevard millionaire worked out that way. He took her to his private suite at the Milford Country Club, and just the touch of his hand against her stiffened nipples sent her into a fever of lust.

She had his clothes off in a second and practically raped him. For the rest of the night their bodies were joined almost continuously. A raging fire burned inside her; she held him prisoner between her thighs, exhausting him with her passion.

"I've never slept with anyone like you," he told her wearily in the morning. "Christ! It was like going to bed with a tornado!" But he was pleased. He gave her double her usual rate, and made a date with her for her first open night, ten days hence.

Things didn't work out so well that night, though. Connie couldn't kindle the flame again. Her lovemaking was restrained and mechanical, and he was obviously disappointed. There was no bonus that night. And, though he said he would phone her for another date, he never did.

At the end of her first month in San Francisco, Connie took a week off, and took stock of herself. She had worked every night since her first date with Henrichs, five nights a week, generally taking Sundays and Mondays off. She had never earned less than $100 a night cash, plus dinner, shows, gifts, things like that. She had refurnished her apartment, had built up a library of books and phonograph records, had set up a collection of liquor as well. And she had almost $1000 in the bank, and was making daily deposits.

Not bad at all for a girl who hadn't yet reached her eighteenth birthday, she thought. Of course, she told everyone she was twenty-two. She planned to stay twenty-two for a long time.

Her datebook showed a week's dates already scheduled, and she knew the phone would be ringing constantly. Henrichs had already reserved two nights a month with her for himself, mostly for the purpose of taking pornographic photos of her. Nick Tyler had asked to have one night a month, paying for it, and Connie privately resolved to let him have a night free at least once a month, besides.

And there were so many others. Executives, playboys, visiting buyers from out of town. San Francisco had a little elite of call girls, some of them syndicated and some free-lance, who were used to impress visitors from out of town. Connie had rapidly climbed her way into the top ranks of that group. The number of men willing to pay $100 for a night in bed with a pretty, bosomy young girl amazed her.

She never wrote home, and hardly ever thought about it. Once she picked up a copy of the *New York Times* on a newsstand, and glanced at the "public notices" column in the back. There was a little ad that said, "CONNIE, PLEASE COME HOME, WHEREVER YOU ARE. WE LOVE YOU AND WANT TO HELP YOU. MOTHER AND DAD."

She smiled at that. Obviously they had given up attempting to trace her. Pretty soon, they would just blot her from their minds.

Connie asked herself if she were happy. Happy? Why not? She had an income, a kind of fame, a life of ease and luxury. But she realized that she was far from being happy. She was doing a lot of drinking, and then doing a lot of exercising to keep from getting puffy and fat. The bitterness was getting the upper hand. Sex was just a mechanical thing for her, now; she looked up at the ceiling, closed her eyes, and went through a pattern of groans and gasps for the delight of her client. She felt nothing, no pleasure at all, five times out of six. The early rapture was gone. Now it was just a business, and a sordid one at that.

She was bored with it. Her clients disgusted her, most of them. Henrichs with his filthy photos (it turned out he had a collection of photos of both his wives, as well as the Berkeley girl, and he insisted on showing them all to Connie) was not as bad as some of the others, dirty old men with revolting habits. Connie stood as much as she could. And still the money poured in—five, six hundred dollars a week.

Two months passed, and a third. By now she was booked up for ten days in advance as a regular thing, and, if she cared to, she could have doubled her income by adding a daytime shift. She drew the line there. During the day she rested, read, amused herself. The night was for business.

But she began to look around for some variety.

Nine

It wasn't until the following spring that Connie found the change-of-pace she was looking for. It had been a pretty hectic five months in between, with work almost every night, unexpected Christmas bonuses from Henrichs and another of her regulars, and a steady inflow of cash from her eager patrons.

She was more bored than ever. After six months of full-time work as a call girl, her interest in sex was dulled by satiety, and now that money came to her so rapidly she no longer had much interest in acquiring things. She had $10,000 in the bank and was looking around for a good stock-broker to help her with an investment program. Life had become just a businesslike routine for her. Rise at noon, read and shop till three, nap till five or six, meet the customer of the night for cocktails and dinner, go to a show, perhaps, and finish up the evening in bed. She had been to just about every night-club and fancy restaurant in the entire Bay Area, had seen every worthwhile show and movie at least once.

She needed a change of pace. So she asked a few subtle questions and found out what she wanted to know. It wasn't hard for her to get information about such things.

And on a mild night in mid-April she put on black toreador pants and a tight white sweater and headed toward the Telegraph Hill area, just north of Chinatown—the home of San Francisco's Beat Generation.

The place she was looking for was on one of the tiny streetlets in the triangle formed by Montgomery Street, Columbus Avenue, and Bay Street. She had been told it was an upstairs loft, above an avant-garde bookstore.

The sound of drumming half a block away told her she was going in the right direction. She found the bookstore, a tiny hole-in-the-wall with a stock of paperbound books and arty magazines. Peering through the window, Connie saw three young men with beards clustered around a portable phonograph, listening intently to something, while from the second floor came the pounding of drums and the wailing of voices.

The only entrance to the upstairs club was through the bookstore. Connie walked in. None of the three bearded ones paid any attention to her.

The music they were listening to was harsh, dissonant, ultra-modern. Connie waited a moment, wondering what to do. They were all staring at the spinning phonograph record as though hypnotized.

"Excuse me—" Connie finally said.

Two of the men glared at her. "Don't drown the music, sister," said one with a wispy red beard.

"I'm looking for the entrance to the club upstairs," Connie said.

"Around back. Behind that shelf."

They returned their attention to the music. Shrugging, Connie walked to the back of the little store, peered behind the indicated shelf, and found a staircase. She went up. A closed door at the top of the stairs bore a crayoned card that said, PRIVATE CLUB. MEMBERS ONLY.

Connie knocked. The door opened and a boy of about eighteen, wearing a blindingly bright turquoise shirt and, as though to protect his eyes from it, an enormous pair of dark sunglasses, peered out.

"Well?"

Connie smiled. "I'd like to come in."

"Private club, members only. It's because of the license laws. You want to come in, you'll have to buy a membership."

"How much is that?"

"Three-fifty. It's good for six months. All it entitles you to is to come in. Drinks are extra."

Connie gave him a five-dollar bill. In return she got a handful of quarters and a small blue mimeographed membership card. She stepped inside.

It was a long, low-ceilinged room, about twice as long as it was wide. The only lights were a couple of dim bulbs dangling from the ceiling. A mobile twirled slowly between them. The walls were covered with paintings, most of them unframed and very abstract.

At the far end of the room, an improvised bar had been set up. Tables circled the outer fringes of the place, and in the center there was room for dancing. Just behind Connie a three-piece band was providing the music—a bongo drummer, a guitarist, and a saxophone. It was a weird-sounding combination.

About forty people were in the room. Half a dozen couples were dancing, moving about the center of the room in a slow rhythmless slouch, bodies pressed tightly together. The rest were seated at the table. About two-thirds of the club's patrons were girls, sitting in groups of two or three at the tables. Nobody in the room looked much older than twenty-five or thirty. At least half of the men wore beards or long hairdos, or both. Connie repressed the urge to smile. This place had "phony" written all over it.

She found a table in the corner and sat down. The bongo drummer, a muscular Negro stripped to the waist, was thumping away wildly, and Connie watched him for a few minutes, while the rhythm of his pounding soaked into her mind.

She was aware that she was getting a lot of attention from the regulars. This was probably a tight, closed clique of arty kids, and any stranger was news.

After perhaps five minutes, a tall, spidery-looking boy came over to her table and stared owlishly down at her. "Dance?"

Connie shook her head. "No."

"Split a bottle of chianti with me?"

"Not interested."

"Play it your own way, if you like." He shuffled back to his own table, where he had been sitting with two other boys.

Connie waited. Nothing much happened. Finally she got up and walked the length of the room, down to the bar. "Two glasses of red wine," she told the boy who was tending bar.

"That'll be seventy."

She paid him and returned to her table, putting the extra glass of wine in front of the seat next to her. It was supposed to be the signal for action, according to her informant.

Her information was right. Within two minutes a girl came sauntering over. She was short, no more than five feet two. She wore a black turtleneck sweater, much too tight, through which her breasts jutted like ripe melons. Her dark hair was combed straight back along the top of her head and ended in a long ponytail. She wasn't wearing any makeup, and even by the dim light Connie could see that her skin was blotchy and poorly taken care of.

In decent clothes, with her face washed and her lips reddened, she might have been sensationally attractive. As it was she just looked untidy. She was about nineteen, Connie figured.

She stood gripping the back of the vacant chair, and nodded her head meaningfully toward the glass of wine.

"Anybody sitting there?"

"Not right now," Connie said.

"Anybody using that wine?"

"It's yours if you want it."

The pony-tailed girl slipped into the seat next to Connie's. She picked up the wine without thanks and took a deep pull. After a moment she said, "You're new around here."

Connie shrugged. "I'm from New York."

"Greenwich Village?"

Connie nodded. The bongo drummer seemed to be going wild. At the table across the aisle, a burly, shaggy-bearded man was loudly reading poetry to two companions who weren't listening. At the next table, two pony-tailed girls were openly fondling each other's breasts. Quite a place, Connie thought.

"I'm Eileen," the girl said. "You?"

"Connie."

They finished their wine and sat with the empty glasses in their hands. About five minutes ticked by. Then Eileen slipped her right hand below the table and placed it experimentally on Connie's knee. Connie did not react. She remained motionless as the hand advanced up her thigh. Her breath began to come in little irregular snorts.

Eileen withdrew the hand. Connie seized it and put it back, and gripped it tightly with her own.

Eileen said, "You dig the scene up here?"

"It's okay."

"Like I mean, we could take off and go over to my pad for a while. Not so crowded there, you follow? It isn't too far. Over on Margrave."

Connie shrugged. "All right. Let's go."

They rose and walked toward the door. The boy in the loud turquoise shirt said nothing to them as they left the club. Downstairs, the three beards were still inclined reverently over the phonograph. Connie and Eileen went past them, past the tottering stacks of old paperbacks, and out into the street.

The streets had a quiet, deserted look about them. Before they had walked half a block, Eileen moved very close to Connie, so close that their hips touched, and put her arm around her. Connie responded, circling Eileen's shoulders self-consciously. Eileen seized Connie's hand, drew it down to her hip, and inserted it in the side pocket of her blue jeans.

To Connie's surprise, she found that the pocket had been cut away. And Eileen was wearing nothing under the jeans. Connie's hand touched the soft, firm flesh of the bohemian girl's belly.

They walked along that way for four blocks without speaking. Then Eileen said, "This is it."

They were in front of a narrow building four stories high and about twenty-five feet wide. Eileen pushed the front door open. The stink of uncollected garbage and stale beer was powerful in the lobby.

There was no elevator. They climbed narrow stairs to the top floor. Eileen pushed an unlocked door open, but locked it behind her after Connie had entered.

It was a single good-sized room. Heaps of books and clothes and dirty laundry lay everywhere. There was no bed, just a soiled mattress lying on the floor. The window was shut tight, and the room had a stale odor of perspiration and cigarette smoke. What furniture there was looked like it had come from the Salvation Army.

"Drink?" Eileen said.

Connie nodded. Eileen rummaged around in the debris and produced a wine-bottle and two soiled glasses. She poured a full glass for each of them.

It was sauterne, cheap, sickly-sweet, and unchilled. Eileen gulped hers like fruit juice. Connie drank more slowly, forcing the stuff down her gullet. She was beginning to regret this whole idea.

Eileen looked at her carefully. "If you don't want to make it, say so now so I can go back to the place and pick somebody else up."

Connie smiled. "You don't need to do that."

"You're just out for an experience, aren't you?" Eileen said. "You a tourist?"

"No"

"Have you ever made it with a woman before?"

Connie debated for a moment. "No," she said.

"How about with a man? You still got your cherry?"

"Afraid not," Connie said.

Eileen giggled. "Neither do I. Lost it when I was fourteen. Haven't slept with a man since I was seventeen. Three years ago. You still haven't told me why you want to go to bed with me."

"Call it variety," Connie said. "I'm a little tired of sleeping with men."

"Been sleeping with a lot of them?"

"You might say that."

"You don't look it. You look pure and innocent, like."

"You'd be surprised," Connie said.

Eileen finished her drink, poured herself a second, and filled up Connie's nearly empty glass. Connie winced, but obediently drank some more.

Suddenly Eileen stood up and took off her sweater. She wore nothing underneath. Her breasts were startling sights. They rose from her chest like twin grapefruits, big and round, double globes tipped with red erect nipples. Her breasts were bigger even than Connie's, and they stood up as if by magic, not drooping at all.

With a second motion Eileen pulled open her jeans and stepped out of them. Her body was softly rounded, with full hips and rounded buttocks that quivered gently as she moved. Connie drained the rest of her glass and set it down.

"Come over to me," Eileen ordered.

Connie obeyed. Eileen drew Connie's sweater over her head, unbuttoned the toreador pants and rolled them down her hips, opened her bra, pulled her panties off. Connie felt her skin flushing. The close contact with another nude girl was disturbing.

They stood together in the middle of the floor. Eileen put her hands on Connie's buttocks and drew Connie toward her, until their breasts met, nipple touching nipple. Then Eileen began to dance without music. Her body writhed rhythmically against Connie, grinding her belly against Connie's, pressing her stiffened nipples into Connie's. It was a warm night, practically stifling in the room with its windows closed. Soon their bodies were perspiring freely. Sweat oiled their skins, making breasts and thigh gleam in the dim light.

When they had danced long enough, Eileen gently drew Connie down onto the mattress. They lay side by side, very close to each other. Eileen gripped Connie's breasts gently and began to toy with them, running her fingertips over the out-thrusting nipple-mounds. Connie took Eileen's breasts as well, heavy globes that filled her entire hands, with plenty left over.

"Kiss me," Eileen said.

Their lips came close and abruptly Eileen's tongue was inside Connie's mouth. They clung that way for perhaps a minute. Then the bohemian girl broke away and kissed each of Connie's nipples, caressing them lightly with the tip of her tongue. Her kisses moved lower on Connie's body. She kissed her everywhere.

The fire was lit. Connie's nervousness vanished. Her body throbbed with the rich, heady force of sheer animal lust. The same lust that could come to unexpected life in the midst of a sadistic rape awakened now under Eileen's skilled ministrations.

It was different, doing it with another girl, Connie thought in a moment of pause. Eileen's body was soft and curved, not hard and muscular; her skin was tender, not rough and abrasive. And she knew exactly where to touch, where to kiss. A man could only guess at the most responsive parts of a woman's body. Eileen *knew*.

Connie was utterly spent. She lay with her head on Eileen's soft breasts, dripping with sweat, letting her heart slow down.

There was the long moment of descent from the peaks of passion. And then, like high tide rolling in over the beach, came the swift, sharp flood of revulsion. Connie felt sick. The cheap wine, the sour smell of sweat, the sordid apartment, above all the vileness of the act she had just performed, all seemed to make her gorge rise at once.

She knew she had to get out of here.

She rolled over. Eileen, who had been dozing, woke immediately and grasped Connie's thigh.

"Wait a while. We'll rest half an hour and then we'll do it again."

"No. I don't want to do it again."

"But you enjoyed it. I know you did."

Connie shook her head. "That doesn't matter. Once is enough for me. Where are my clothes?"

She found them, scattered every which way, and donned her panties. Eileen came up behind her, pressing the points of her breasts into Connie's bare back, and slipped her hands under the elastic waistband in front. Connie stepped away.

"I told you I had enough."

"You enjoyed it," Eileen repeated reproachfully. "You were great. I never made it so good with anyone else before. Both of us, coming off at the same time the way we did—"

Connie slipped into her sweater and buttoned her pants. "Sorry. I've had it."

Eileen blocked her from the door. The other girl no longer looked attractive to Connie; she was just another naked girl now, with big breasts bobbing up and down as she moved. Connie couldn't imagine how she had ever been able to feel desire for this girl.

"Listen," Eileen said desperately, "You were something special. Stay here all night with me."

"No."

"I'll give you five bucks if you do. Honest!"

Connie laughed out loud, sharply, scornfully. The expression on Eileen's face changed from a pleading one to an angry one.

"What's so funny?" she demanded,

"You offering me five dollars," Connie said. She laughed again. "I'm flattered, I suppose. Women as well as men bid for my services."

"I don't dig you."

"Well, dig this," Connie said. "When I'm not slumming up here in North Beach, I earn my living as a whore. I'm a hundred-buck-a-night call girl.

Surprised? I thought you would be. Thanks for the entertainment."

And she pushed her way past the astonished lesbian and went on out into the hall.

There, the nauseating stench of garbage made her retch. She nearly threw up in the hall. But somehow she made it all the way out to the street.

There, she lost her supper and all of the cheap wine she had consumed. She felt filthy all over, as filthy as she had felt the night of the rape. She had fouled herself.

Walking rapidly toward Montgomery Street, she hailed a cab and was home in less than half an hour. She took a scaldingly hot shower, trying to erase even the feel of Eileen's lips and fingers from her skin. Then she poured herself a stiff nightcap of rye, gulped it down, and went straight to sleep.

Ten

By the next morning, she was busily trying to forget what she had done in the dingy pad on Margrave.

It had been an interlude, Connie told herself. A fling. An experience. But it made her feel sick and filthy and degraded. It was worse than selling herself to men—a thousand times worse.

The fact remained to nag her: she had enjoyed it. But that didn't matter. She had known moments of pleasure during that nightmarish rape, too. It was just some weird twist of her character that allowed her to derive pleasure in such unusual circumstances. One raping had been enough, though, and also one sordid little interlude in North Beach. She had tried it, and it had revolted her. She didn't want any more of it.

She went back to her former routine. Within a few days, she had practically forgotten the dark-haired girl with breasts like melons, the girl who had pleaded so desperately with Connie to be loved.

The weather, which had been mild all winter, now grew warmer. The summer fog started to cover San Francisco most of the time. Connie's services were in heavy demand. Henrichs used her two or three times each month. He now had a thick album full of nude photographs of her. Sometimes he asked her to move in with him and become his mistress, but Connie refused him. She preferred the life of a free-lance operator.

There were occasional phone-calls from Nick Tyler, but Connie didn't see him much. He was romancing a girl from his office, a bosomy redhead half his age, who gave him what he wanted for nothing. He saw her just about every night of the week. The line he had given her was that he had pull with television producers, and could get her acting roles if she would only string along with him for a while. Well, she was stringing. Sooner or later Tyler would get bored with her, but right now he was living it up.

It was just as well, thought Connie, that she didn't see Tyler often. She liked him, and she didn't want to find herself liking men. Men were the enemy. Men had seized her by force. Men had raped her.

The last thing Connie expected to have happen was for her to fall in love. But she did—and not with Nick Tyler. Nor with Henrichs.

His name was Dan Garfield, and he was president of the Garfield Electronics Corporation, a Los Angeles outfit that manufactured computer elements for guided missiles. Garfield Electronics had received several juicy government contracts, and was rolling in money.

Garfield came to San Francisco at the end of June, to see about arranging a loan with some of the finance moguls on lower Montgomery Street. He was staying at the Sir Francis Drake and he wanted to be entertained. He was a friend of a friend of Paul Henrichs, and that was how he got Connie's phone number.

He rang her up on a Friday afternoon, as she was dressing for a date she had that night with an advertising executive from New York, and said, "My name is Dan Garfield of Garfield Electronics. Bill Clyde gave me your number. Are you free this weekend?"

He spoke in a staccato, rapid-fire, high-pressure voice. Connie was irritated. "Bill Clyde should have told you that I'm booked pretty far in advance. Anyway, I usually take weekends off. How long are you planning to be in town?"

"Through next Wednesday, but that isn't the point. I want company this weekend. Is it worth your while to spend Saturday and Sunday with me for $500?"

Connie hesitated. She valued her leisure—but still, that was a tremendous lot of cash.

Garfield took her silence for dissatisfaction with his offer. "Well, $600, then," he said before she could speak. "What the hell—it goes right on the expense account."

"All right," Connie said. "$600 it is."

She showed up at the Drake at five o'clock Saturday afternoon. They had arranged to have cocktails, dinner in Garfield's suite, then visit a night-club before retiring for the night.

The moment Connie saw Dan Garfield she was fascinated by him. He was about forty, and not very tall, no bigger than five-ten. But he radiated energy and drive and purposefulness. His dark eyes gleamed like beacons in his lean, tense face. They had almost a hypnotic effect. Instants after Connie had entered his suite, she was yearning to go to bed with him, to find out what it would be like to have that dynamic strength burrowing into her body. She felt almost dizzy.

"You're lovelier than Bill said you were. How about a martini?"

"Fine," Connie said. She followed him into the suite's living-room. He walked as though he were at least ten feet tall. It was an imperious stride. He was the most lordly man Connie had ever seen.

His broad shoulders and confident walk made him seem much taller than he really was. And when he sat down across the coffee-table from Connie, he seemed like a giant. His eyes took her all in at once.

"For half an hour after I hung up the phone yesterday I told myself I was an idiot for throwing away so much money on a woman," he said. "But now I don't regret it at all. You're a dazzler, Connie."

She smiled and sipped her drink without saying anything. She knew that if she opened her mouth, she'd start gushing schoolgirl talk.

Garfield's eyes seemed to be boring through her clothing. After a moment he said, "You must have had an early start. You can't be more than nineteen."

"Twenty-two," she said.

Garfield shrugged. "Okay, twenty-two, if that's the age you prefer to call yourself. It isn't very often that you find a woman *adding* to her age." He chuckled. "I still think you're nineteen, though. I can tell by the texture of your cheeks. That light golden fuzz—it's nineteen-year-old fuzz, not twenty-two-year-old."

"Are you an expert on complexions?"

Garfield took a deep sip of his drink. "I'm an expert on everything, Connie. That was how I got to be worth a million by the time I was twenty-five. You don't do it with luck. How old were you when you first slept with a man?"

The sudden question jarred her. "S-seventeen," she said. "And I didn't do it willingly. A gang of teenagers grabbed me in the street."

"Oh. Christ, that must have been awful. You poor kid!" His sympathy didn't sound insincere.

"I survived it," Connie said. "But it influenced my choice of profession, you might say."

"Interesting. You know, I've got a daughter who's seventeen now. I'd hate like hell to have something like that happen to her."

"You—have a seventeen-year-old daughter?"

"Why are you so surprised?"

"Because—well—you look so young!"

Garfield grinned. "How old do you think I am? Go on—now it's your turn to do some age-guessing."

"You're about thirty-five."

"I'm thirty-eight. I got married when I was twenty. My daughter was born ten months later. I've got a son, too. He's eleven. I just celebrated my eighteenth anniversary last month."

"You sound happily married," Connie said. "How come you need a girl for the weekend?"

Garfield stared off into the distance. "When I'm in L.A., I'm faithful to my wife. But I can't go two days without a woman, and Esther won't travel around with me. So I have to hire somebody. Simple?"

"I guess so. It makes a kind of sense."

Garfield refilled her glass. The martinis were ice-cold and delicious. Connie felt her pulse racing. She had never reacted toward a man like this before. She was drawn to Garfield by a magnetic force. He was married, had a daughter practically her own age, cheated his wife regularly, was probably a grade-A louse in his business dealings. And yet she loved him.

It wasn't possible, Connie thought. There wasn't room in her heart for love. And it was crazy, anyway. A call girl wasn't supposed to develop crushes on her clients.

"You look preoccupied with something," Garfield said. "Everything all right?"

"I was just thinking how good these drinks are," Connie improvised. "They're the best martinis I've ever had."

Garfield showed two rows of perfect white teeth. "I'm glad you like them. I mixed them myself. They wanted to mix them downstairs, but I wouldn't let them." He stood up. "How about my having dinner sent up now?"

"Are you going to cook *that* yourself too?"

"Uh-uh. I could if I wanted to, but I have better things to busy myself with now."

The meal was a sumptuous one—the fifty-dollar special, at least, complete with three kinds of vintage wines and champagne. Connie's head began to swim. Usually before each date she loaded herself up with caffeine tablets, which helped her stay sober. But she was getting very woozy, despite the pills.

Garfield kept up a running monologue while they ate. He might have seemed to be bragging, but he was simply stating the truth about himself. He was worth fifty or sixty million dollars, and had every intention of parlaying that into a billion by the time he was sixty. He had a fleet of Rolls-Royces and Cadillacs, as well as sports cars to fit other moods, and when anything went wrong with a car he, and not a mechanic, made the repairs. He was superbly competent at anything he turned his hand to.

He was not happy with his wife. That much was obvious. He showed Connie her picture. She was rather a plain, domestic-looking woman. He had married her on the one rash impulse of his life, and he had been regretting it quietly ever since.

Connie listened avidly to every word he said. She was mesmerized by him. The emotion she felt bewildered her, but she could not fight it.

They finished eating about eight. After Room Service had cleared the trays away, Garfield said, "Well? I've got a table reserved at the Gay Nineties. Should I phone for a cab?"

Connie shrugged. "If it's all the same to you, I'd just as soon skip it. I mean—I'd rather stay here."

Puzzled, Garfield said, "I thought you were a gal who liked to be taken out to the hot spots. Did they give me the wrong info on you?"

"No, I usually like night-clubs. But somehow I feel different tonight. I'd just like to stay here—with you—" Connie shook her head. "Oh, this is terrible! I've never acted this way before."

Garfield strode toward her. His strong fingers gripped her shoulders. "What's wrong? Are you sick, Connie?"

"No— I'm fine. I'm messing things up, though. You want to go out and have a good time."

"We can have a good time right here," Garfield said. "I'm not much of a night-club man. The only reason I made reservations was that you were supposed to like going out."

She lifted her head and stared straight into his deep, hypnotic eyes.

"Let's just stay here," she said.

She was wearing a dress with peek-a-boo front. He circled around behind her and slipped his hands down over her shoulders, into the front of her dress, caressing her breasts. Connie shivered. Her lips parted and her breath became choppy.

Turning, she melted into his arms. He kissed her, pressing her tight against him. Connie realized dimly that this was the time to collect her cash for the night, that she never let matters get beyond this stage without making sure of her money. But tonight she didn't care if she got paid or not. She would do it with Dan Garfield for nothing. If she had to, she thought, she would pay him.

He undressed her slowly, remaining fully dressed himself, and when she stood nude before him he stepped back to admire her body the way a connoisseur might admire a fine Arab steed or a piece of sculptured jade.

"Isn't this the time when you're supposed to ask for money?"

"That can wait, Dan," Connie moaned. "Love me. Love me now."

He was out of his clothes in a moment. Through slitted lids Connie looked at him. There wasn't an ounce of fat on his body. It was all lean, powerful, with long flat muscles and little cords standing out on his arms and shoulders. He had an athlete's body.

He carried her to the enormous bed inside, and they began to make love.

Then he slapped her.

The harsh impact of his palm against her cheek dragged her abruptly back from her dreams. Eyes open, she stared up at his face, saw it contorted with lust, the nostrils flaring wide, the mouth amped tight.

Her cheek stung. "Why—"

"Sorry," he murmured. "I have to."

He slapped her again, harder this time, and before she could say anything he was gripping her tightly, bearing down on her with all his weight, and she felt him shudder and knew that the long act of love had reached its end. The tension went out of him and he slumped relaxedly down, his head buried in the pillow with his cheek against the one he had slapped.

"I'm sorry if I hurt you," Garfield said in a muffled voice. "It's the way I have to do it, right at the end, you see."

Connie nodded. She had slept with enough men to know the wide range of individual quirks many of them had. There was one industrialist who could make love to her only of she continued to wear her garter-belt and nylon stockings during the act. Another insisted on having her bite his shoulder at the crucial moment. And another kept his shoes and socks on.

But it was surprising to find that Garfield—who seemed so flawless in so many ways—was himself bound by some compulsive action like slapping his partner at the climax. Well, she could take it. She had been less injured than astonished when he had hit her.

He rested for a while, and then they made love again. Once again, Connie was satisfied as she had rarely been before. And, once again, he slapped her at the finale.

Afterward they lay arm-in-arm on the bed, neither of them asleep but neither fully awake. Connie pondered what had happened to her this evening.

She said, "Dan? Are you awake?"

"Yes."

"Dan, I've got to tell you this. It's the damndest thing." She felt the tears beginning to crowd into her eyes. "Dan, I'm a whore and you're a whore's client, and that doesn't make either of us very much of anything. But—God help me, Dan—the moment I walked in here tonight, I fell in love with you!"

Eleven

Garfield was silent for a moment. Then he uttered a short, sharp laugh.

"Do you think it's so very funny?" Connie asked in a suddenly bitter voice.

"Yes, it is," Garfield said. "Not for any reason you might think. It's just that—well, dammit, I find myself powerfully attracted to *you*, too."

"Powerfully attracted? That's a roundabout way of saying things!"

"All right, then. I'll say it the way I ought to say it. I love you, Connie."

She shivered. The words had seemingly been wrung from the depths of him, unwillingly but unavoidably. The only other man who had claimed to love her was John. Man? No, not him. And he had said the words only because he felt it was expected of him, because when a girl let you deep-kiss her and touch her breasts you were supposed to respond with affectionate words.

"This is insane," Connie muttered. "I'm for sale and you bought me for the weekend. That's where it began and that's where it ought to end. And instead we're getting ourselves involved in something serious. Maybe I'd better get out of here right now. Let's forget the whole thing. I had a swell time in bed with you and I won't even charge for it."

She rose from the bed. Garfield shot out his hand like a bolt of lightning and clamped it tightly, almost painfully, around her wrist.

"No. Don't go."

Connie sank down again. She realized she had wanted him to do this. Her wrist tingled and throbbed, where he had grabbed her.

"Listen to me," Garfield said quietly. "Are you tied up with any kind of syndicate, or any stuff like that? Do you have an agent?"

"I'm completely free-lance."

"Good. What other ties do you have in San Francisco? Family, leases, stuff like that?"

"I could leave tomorrow, if I had to," Connie said. "The only tie I have is a couple of weeks' of dates ahead of me. And I could break those."

"Damn right you could. You're going to!"

Connie turned to face him. "What are you getting at, Dan? Why should I leave San Francisco?"

"You're going to move down to Los Angeles. I'll set you up at one of the big hotels. A suite at the Beverly-Wilshire, maybe. And at the same time you'll retire from the call girl business. You'll be my mistress for the next few months, until I get my divorce arranged. Then I'll marry you. Eh? How's that?"

The stream of positive statements silenced Connie for several moments. She was amazed by the calm, cool way that Garfield had taken it upon himself to rearrange her future. Mistress? Marriage? Once again all her plans were junked in a moment of swift action. She did not want to be any man's mistress, let alone his wife. Yet she was helpless before Garfield's unstoppable drive.

Lamely she said, "You wouldn't want to marry me. I— I've slept with so many other men—"

"How many? Fifty? A hundred?" Garfield laughed. "What does that matter? Am I any angel? I'm fifteen or twenty years older than you are. I can't count the women I've had. Is it any less of a sin to buy sex than to sell it?"

"But you've got a wife—children—" Connie shook her head. "You can't just abandon them!"

"Why not? My wife hasn't loved me for ten years. The only time she sleeps with me is when I insist on it. And my kids think of me just as the man at the other end of their allowance. No, I'm not worried about them. Esther won't be turned out onto the street. She'll get fifty or sixty or a hundred thousand a year to keep her happy. That's all she wants out of life, anyway."

He put his arms around her. "I knew you were something special the minute you walked in the door. I love you, Connie. I want you. And Dan Garfield always gets what he wants."

"Suppose I make up my mind that this time you're not getting what you want? You're spoiled by success." Connie folded her arms across her breasts. "The answer is no. I won't move to Los Angeles. I won't be your mistress and I won't marry you. So there."

Garfield didn't get angry. He smiled and slid his hands across Connie's shoulders, down under her folded arms, to cup her breasts. He squeezed them gently, gripping her nipples between two fingers of each hand. Connie began to tremble as his powerful hands made slight stroking motions, lifting her breasts and compressing them.

"Well?" His voice was just a murmur. "Will you reconsider? Will you leave San Francisco and come away with me?"

"Yes!" she cried. "Oh, God, yes!"

He caught her and dragged her down next to him on the bed.

For the rest of that weekend they did little but make love, sleeping now and then, pausing to order meals from Room Service. Garfield seemed inexhaustible. He had a definite sadistic streak, Connie was discovering; he took a positive pleasure in slapping and punching her. But she didn't care. Before he hit her, he worked her up to such a height of passion that the blow simply added to her pleasure.

Connie was in a dream-world all weekend. The past seemed to be blotted out. There was only Dan, Dan with his hypnotic eyes and his fantastic self-confidence and his glowing vision of the future the two of them would have. Right after they were married, he promised, he would take a leave of absence from his company and they would go on a round-the-world cruise, anywhere she cared to go. They would see and do everything. And then it would be back to California to live the life of millionaires. Besides his electronics company, he owned a farm in the Imperial Valley and a ranch in Oregon. And he had movie investments, too; if Connie were interested, he could probably get her a good part in some forth-coming film. The world was hers for the asking. And what was she giving up for it? Her independence, yes. But that independence had consisted only of the freedom to be unhappy, the freedom to drink too much and to sell herself to paunchy industrialists for a fancy price. Dan offered much more than that. He offered practically everything but the sun and the moon and the stars. He would make her his queen.

So it was all arranged. Sunday night, when she left him, he gave her a thousand dollars in cash—not as a fee for the weekend's services; that would be degrading—the money was to help her get packed and relocated in Los Angeles. He phoned the Beverly-Wilshire and rented a $40-a-day suite on an indefinite basis, beginning at the end of the week.

Connie spent the next day phoning her clients for the next seven days and letting them know that she would have to break the date. "Unexpected sickness" was the reason she gave, and though some of them were bitterly unhappy they had no choice but to accept the breaking of the date. It was a prostitute's privilege to develop "unexpected sickness" when necessary.

She closed out her bank account—she had nearly $15,000, which seemed like a lot to her, though it was insignificant compared to the money Garfield had. Her lease still had a few months to run, but she bought it up for $200, to save the delay of an argument. She hired a trucker to move her possessions to Los Angeles.

Connie told nobody of her decision, neither Henrichs nor Nick Tyler nor any of the other clients who had reason to think they were special friends of hers. She wanted to make a clean break with San Francisco. For nine months she had earned her living with her body. Now that was all to be blotted out. She was, once again, making a brand new start.

Mrs. Dan Garfield. That sounded just fine, she thought. She wondered whether there would be any trouble about the divorce. Perhaps she might get her picture in the papers as the co-respondent, and that would be strictly no good. If the wire services picked the story up, and it got back to the New York papers

She wondered then about her parents. She hardly thought of them, now. They seemed like dream-images, like remnants of some other existence. Her father, busy, terribly cautious, an ordinary man in every way. Her mother, pale, nervous, jumpy. Her sister Harriet, graduating from Michigan State around this time, perhaps engaged or else bartering her virginity for an engagement ring. Connie had always thought of her older sister as incalculably more mature than she, but from this perspective Harriet looked like a child. She was nothing but a big-breasted bobby-soxer waving a college pennant. She was twenty-two and Connie eighteen, but yet Connie had been through so much more, had had so many experiences her sister had not had and would not ever have.

Probably her parents would carry silent grief for their runaway daughter in their hearts forever. Connie did not care. At the moment when she had needed them most, when she awoke in the hospital, they had failed her. They had looked at her as though she were now horridly deformed, and their only concern had been how fast they could pack her away to Arizona, out of sight and out of mind. Well, to hell with them. To hell with everybody.

To hell with everybody except Dan, Connie corrected. In a cruel and hollow world, he was the one thing that was real and substantial and loving.

At half past eight on Friday morning, the truckers arrived to pick up Connie's furniture and belongings. They carried everything out to the truck with great care. They ought to; Garfield had hired the most expensive truckers in San Francisco to do the job.

"What time can I expect everything to arrive?" Connie asked.

"We'll try for five o'clock this afternoon, Ma'am. If the road's crowded, we may not be there till six or six-thirty. But we'll *be* there. Don't you worry about that."

"It's a long trip, isn't it?"

"Four hundred mile or thereabouts."

Connie nodded. Having spent all her life until last fall in the east, the idea of a state so big that you could drive four hundred miles and still be nowhere near the end of it was incomprehensible to her. She had always thought San Francisco and Los Angeles were practically next door to each other. It was still a little hard to believe that they were as far apart as New York and Pittsburgh were.

The truck roared off, starting on the long, hot journey down Route 101 to L.A. Connie paced around nervously in the bare apartment, peering into closets and cupboards to make sure she was leaving nothing behind. As if it mattered, she thought wryly. Dan could replace anything she might leave here. She tried to get used to the fact that Dan had enough money to buy *anything*, and that in a few short months she would be Dan's wife.

At ten o'clock, after making sure the phone was disconnected, Connie went downstairs, turned in her key to the janitor, and hailed a taxi to take her to the airport. Her reservation was waiting for her—a one-way flight, no baggage. She took a seat by the wing. The plane rose from the ground at eleven. In less than fifteen minutes she was further south than her furniture, which was toiling along the highway far beneath her in the third hour of its journey. Shortly after noon, Connie stepped down onto the concrete field of Los Angeles International Airport.

The climate was different; she sensed that at once. Though it was July, the temperature had been only 60 in San Francisco that morning, and the air had been clear, sharp, with a salty breeze blowing. Down here, the thermometer stood at a balmy 87. And the air was different—hazy, soft, almost shimmering, tending to blur things where the San Francisco atmosphere clarified them.

Dan was waiting for her inside. He swept her into his arms and hugged her until her breath seemed about to leave her.

"Darling! Five whole days without you!"

"It seemed like months. Uh—Dan—"

"Too tight?" He released her from the bearhug. "Sorry, darling. I got carried away. The car's parked out back in the lot."

The car was a sleek, topless Alfa-Romeo roadster. Garfield apologized for having driven it. "The right way to do it would have been to pick you up in the Rolls—that's travelling in style. But the sports car makes better time on the freeways. The Rolls is a honey, but a small car weaves in and out like a needle."

He drove the way he walked and talked and lived—proudly, and with little regard for any obstacle that might be blocking his way. As the open car sped along the freeway at sixty-five miles an hour, the breeze caught Connie's hair and set it fluttering. She relaxed in the sun, feeling the throb of the engine beneath her feet, and feeling the dynamic pull of the man at the wheel. The world seemed to belong all to her at that moment.

They pulled off the freeway and soon entered a wide avenue lined with handsome new buildings of glass and plastic. "Wilshire Boulevard,"

Garfield explained. "This town is too big and sprawling to have one main stem, but Wilshire is *one* of the main stems. You've never been in L.A. before, have you?"

"No, I haven't."

"It'll take you weeks to begin to be able to find your way around here. But don't let that upset you. There are people who've lived here all their lives who couldn't tell you the best way to get to South Gate or Culver City. Anyway, Wilshire starts way the hell downtown, over thataway, and it runs all the way to the Pacific Ocean. It ends up in Santa Monica. I live a little ways north of there, in Pacific Palisades. Right now we're in Beverly Hills. And there's your hotel."

It was a tall, square building, dignified-looking on the outside, splendid within. Connie went to the desk and was greeted with expansive warmth; Garfield had evidently tipped them all well. He waited outside while Connie was taken to her sixth-floor suite, three big air-conditioned rooms with a back view showing tennis courts and a large swimming-pool. After inspecting her rooms, she returned to the front of the hotel, where Garfield was waiting.

"What now?" she said.

"This is a working day for me, remember? I've got to get back at the plant by half past one or so, to take care of the payroll. It's Friday, you know."

"When will I see you?"

"For dinner tonight. My wife thinks I'm eating with somebody big from Washington."

Connie frowned. "Will we have to keep up the pretense long, Dan?"

"Don't worry, chick. It's no strain, is it?"

"I hate to think of you having to tell all sorts of lies to your wife all the time. And I want you whenever I can have you, not just when you've been able to invent some alibi."

He smiled. "Put up with it for a little while. I'll be having a long talk with my lawyer first thing next week, and we'll start getting things arranged. Good enough?"

"I can't wait, Dan."

"Neither can I. See you at six, yes?"

"Right."

He drove away. Connie waved after him until his bright red car was lost in the maelstrom of Los Angeles traffic.

It was only a little after one o'clock. Her clothing and furniture would not be here for hours, yet. Her suite was furnished, but the arrangement was that she would use her own furniture while living in it.

There was nothing she could do until the truck arrived. But the swimming-pool looked inviting. She needed a swimsuit. That was easy; there were swank-looking stores half a block from the hotel. Connie strolled across, and a short time later returned, bearing a brand-new forty-dollar swimsuit.

It was a sleek thing of white plastic that molded itself to her hips and gently embraced the rising swell of her breasts. She took a towel from her room and rode down in the elevator in her swimsuit, thinking how unlikely it would be to find anyone wearing just a bathing suit in the elevator of a large New York hotel.

She signed in at the pool entrance and stepped out onto the pavement. Many people were sunning themselves in deck chairs around the pool; fifteen or twenty were actually swimming. Most of them were tanned youths and pretty girls. But somehow Connie drew everyone's eye as she stood at the edge of the pool.

She made a graceful dive. The water was cool, and invigorating to the skin. Fully conscious of the attention she was attracting, she turned on her back and began to float, giving her audience a good view of her breasts as they jutted above the surface of the water.

They probably think I'm a starlet, Connie told herself. She grinned quietly and swam back and forth. In the crowded pool she occasionally bumped into others; once, some daring swimmer actually put his hand to her breast as she scissored past, but her eyes were closed, and when she opened them she had no idea who had done it. She was more amused than angry by the incident.

After swimming until she was tired, she sunned for a while, returned to her room, stripped off the wet suit, and napped. Awakening about half past four, she began to dress for dinner. The bedroom had an arrangement of two full-length mirrors which allowed her to see herself back and front, head to toes. She surveyed herself critically, as she had done so many times before. There was no sign yet of any dissipation. The line of her thighs was still flawless, her buttocks still retained their youthful firmness, her breasts stood out high and proud, needing no support. She was satisfied.

At five, her truck arrived. The loading and unloading job was accomplished swiftly, and by six, when Dan arrived, she was moved in completely.

"You look lovely," he told her. "How did you spend your afternoon?"

"Swimming and napping. It's a grand life."

"It's going to keep on being a grand life," he said.

They ate at a fabulous restaurant on La Cienega Boulevard, and returned to the hotel about eight.

"I haven't had any sex since Sunday," Garfield said. "I was waiting for you. I'm practically foaming at the mouth."

They had their clothes off in seconds. For the next two hours they lay twined together in the bed. At ten, Garfield rose and dressed, kissed her tenderly, and left. Connie smiled goodbye to him with her eyes half-closed. She felt like purring. She had never known such happiness. She was even grateful for all the misery that had come before, because the misery had led her eventually to Dan.

She fell asleep still smiling.

Twelve

It went along that way for seven weeks—seven weeks of absolute heaven, before Connie began to realize that anything was wrong.

She slept late, each day, getting up around eleven and having breakfast sent up. Then she swam or played tennis until one or two, ate, and either returned to her room or went on shopping trips. Los Angeles was an incredible city, or rather a conglomeration of cities. Garfield arranged to let Connie have the use of one of his old cars during the day. It was parked in the hotel lot, and she used it sparingly, taking trips around to look at Hollywood and Pasadena and the movie lots in Burbank and Glendale. She even drove out to Pacific Palisades, going past one $75,000 house after another, and wondering which one belonged to Dan Garfield.

Twice a week he had lunch with her at the hotel and they made love in her room. On two other days of the week he took her out for dinner. He said his wife didn't see through the arrangement.

During those first seven weeks, he had to take two business trips— one to his ranch in Oregon, and one to San Diego, where he was considering building a second plant. Connie accompanied him as his "secretary." She stayed out of the way, kept herself amused while he was in conference, and shared his bed at night. There was also one trip for the hell of it, a weekend in Las Vegas. They stayed at the Riviera, took in the Minsky show at the Dunes, and played the machines. Fascinated by the slot-machines, Connie fed two dozen silver dollars into one in hopes of a jackpot, but the best haul she made was only five dollars at a time. Garfield, though, had better luck; he took several thousand dollars away from the roulette tables. He seemed to scatter his chips at random, almost without looking, yet with each spin of the wheel his pile of chips invariably increased.

"It's the kind of luck I have," he explained.

Connie nodded. She was fascinated by him. She loved him the way a faithful dog would love a master.

But one thing bothered her. She hardly thought about it at first, but by the seventh week it had grown into a problem of considerable magnitude. It gnawed at her.

Garfield had stopped talking about a divorce.

Connie was sure he still planned to leave his wife. But he grew vague when asked how his lawyer was coming in preparing the papers. "It takes time," was all he would say. "You can't rush into something like a divorce until you know where you're heading. I don't want Esther to bleed me white in the settlement."

There matters rested. Garfield paid the $250-a-week cost of her suite, and gave her $300 a week besides, as spending money. It was nearly as much, altogether, as she had been making in San Francisco as a freelance, and the life was much easier now that she was no longer dependent on the whims of her buyer-for-the-night. Garfield insisted that she buy the best clothes, and not stint herself at all, but even so Connie found it difficult to spend all of her weekly allowance. Quietly, she added $50 or $100 a week to her private bank balance, saying nothing about it to Garfield. She had only to ask, and he would shower her with money—but she maintained her own bank account out of some innate caution she hardly even understood.

It was a good life. Sex four or five times a week, and always satisfying, though Dan got increasingly rough with her, pummeling and slapping her sometimes. One night he came in saying, "I'm in a nasty mood. We just missed a $5,000,000 contract by a whisker. I've got to take it out on someone."

Connie was dressed to go out. But, grinning all the time, Garfield caught her and dragged her down over his knee. He flipped up her dress and yanked down her panties, exposing the firm pink buttocks. Connie giggled, thinking it was a joke, and then his hand descended—five, six, eight, a dozen times, until her skin sizzled with pain and she cried out, "Stop it, Dan! You're hurting me!"

He let her go, then, and she stood up to straighten her clothes, but he shook his head and pointed to the bed. He was aroused, he said, and dinner could wait. There was not even time to undress. He slipped her panties down and had her quickly, brutally almost. The strange savagery of his approach took Connie's breath away. And then, afterward, he rose from her and said, "I feel better now. Let's go out to eat."

He had his strange moments. But Connie could tolerate them, even when he caused her pain, because of the depth of her love for him. She went through one day after the next, swimming, shopping, taking in movies, once even going to see a Dodger baseball game out of a sentimental urge. *We're both transplants from Brooklyn*, she thought. *If things had gone differently, we might both still be there, the Dodgers and I.* But the game bored her, and she left before the sixth inning.

Connie debated whether she ought to ask him about his divorce plans. It was September, now—a year since she had left New York, two months since she had come to Los Angeles as Dan's mistress. She wasn't sure whether or not to bring the matter up. Maybe he was saving the news of his divorce as a surprise for her. Maybe there were legal complications he didn't want to tell her about.

Or, Connie thought, maybe he'd been leading her along for two months, and wasn't planning to get a divorce after all. Did that make any difference, she asked herself? After all, she had no complaints now—she had every material thing she needed, no responsibility, no troubles. Why insist on being Mrs. Dan Garfield?

She knew the answer to that. It was a matter of pride.

She had given up her independence because he had promised to marry her. The fact that life as his mistress was agreeable didn't count. If he ducked out of marrying her, then he would be deceiving her. It would be just another time when the male sex had used her and discarded her callously.

She had to know. If Garfield was only using her, if he had no real intention of marrying her, then she wanted out. True, she loved him, or thought she did—but love or no love, she would not let him play games with her affections.

She decided to put it to him point blank.

Her chance came two days later. It was a Thursday night; they had planned to eat dinner at a Mexican restaurant near Olivera Street. Garfield was meeting her at six, the usual time, and she was supposed to be ready when he got there. But this time she decided not to be ready. When the phone rang, she was wearing nothing but a light robe.

It was Dan, phoning from the lobby. "All set, honeygirl? I'll meet you out front, yes?"

"No."

"No? Something wrong?"

"I'm not ready yet, Dan. You might as well come up and wait while I finish up."

He let himself into the suite with his own key. Connie sat in an armchair, legs crossed, gown dangling half open so he could see she was naked beneath.

Garfield blinked. "Huh? You were supposed to be ready at six. Cesar's holding a table for us for six-thirty, Connie. How come the slow-motion?"

"Sit down, Dan. I want to talk to you seriously before we go anywhere for dinner."

He frowned and folded his arms, and leaned back against the door. "You can talk. I'll stand. What's eating you all of the sudden?"

Refusing to sit was typical, Connie thought. She was at a disadvantage because she had to look upward to talk to him.

She moistened her lips and said, "It's more than two months since you brought me down here from San Francisco. I just happened to be looking at the calendar this afternoon and it reminded me that it was two months and some since I came here with you."

Garfield's eyes were twin needles boring into her face. "So? You were looking at the calendar. What of it?"

"When I agreed to come here, I was told by you that you'd be divorcing Esther in 'a few months' and marrying me. Well, two months is 'a few.' And I don't see you doing anything about that divorce."

Now that he knew what the trouble was, Garfield's stiff manner dropped from him. He smiled good-naturedly and said, "Oh, so *that's* it? Hell, Connie, you shouldn't have got yourself all worked up about *that.* You only had to ask me. I was talking to my lawyer just the other day. It's all being arranged. Just a little while longer, and then I'll pack Esther off and we'll get married the next day. I tell you the papers are being drawn up right now."

Connie shook her head, vowing silently not to let herself be swayed by Garfield's hypnotic charm. "That's not good enough, Dan. 'Just a little while longer' is too vague. I want a timetable. I want to know when you're filing the papers, when you're starting the action, what grounds, who's divorcing whom. And most of all I want to know what day we're getting married."

"Now, look, baby, you mustn't press me like this."

"Why not? These are things I ought to be told!"

"Aren't you happy this way? I've spent thousands on you already. I'm good in bed. I take you to the best restaurants. We had a grand time in Vegas last month, didn't we?"

Connie smiled thinly. "Sure, it's been one long hell of a ball. But I don't want to be tied up here as Dan Garfield's private shack-up. You promised you were going to get a divorce and marry me."

Garfield looked pale, and his eyes shifted back and forth. Connie knew him well enough to be able to figure out the story from his reaction. He *had* lied to her. It was incredible, but he had just been giving her a line.

"Connie, baby, I don't know why you're talking this way," he said soothingly. "You—"

"Don't try the soft-soap, Dan. I'm starting to figure it out now. You never intended to marry me. You were feeding me the old borax up there in San Francisco. Go on, deny it! Tell me I'm wrong!"

Her voice reached a high shrewish shriek. Garfield's face seemed to harden. A slow smile crept over his face and he said in a soft, quiet voice, "Okay, honey-child. I guess this had to come out into the open sooner or later. The answer is yes: I was handing you a line."

"You—aren't getting a divorce?"

"No. I'm not. Why the hell should I? Esther lets me play around all I want. She's a good mother to my kids. And I've lived with her so long she's a habit."

"But—everything you told me—"

"Lies," Garfield said calmly. "You're a cute kid, Connie. I liked you when I saw you walk into my room in San Fran, and I was trying to figure out schemes to get to see you again, because you were such a hot little dish. Then you started coming out with this business about being in love with me. Well, I can adapt. I fed the love-crap back to you, so I could bring you down here and set you up for a few months' fun. You didn't think I was going to marry a hooker, did you? You were just a hobby of mine. Too bad it couldn't go on any longer than it did."

Connie shook her head incredulously. The world was flying to pieces around her. "All—lies? But *why?* How could you do anything so cruel? And all the money you spent on me—!"

"Money comes easy to me, Connie. The amount I spent on you was just the interest on my interest. And as for why I did it—well, part of it was for the fun of having you to myself for a couple of months. But there's more than that. I was waiting for *this* moment, Connie. I wanted to see the look of shock on your face when I gave you the straight scoop. I wanted to see you crumble."

"You're mad!"

"Mad? No—I just like hurting people," Garfield said, still smiling. "I enjoy wielding power. Some of that shows in the way I make love, doesn't it? I had power over you. I turned you into a little puppet that danced any way I cared to pull the strings. And now the fun is over for me. The jig is up. Tonight's the last night I can have you, now that the news is out that there'll be no marriage. Take that robe off and lie down on the bed."

Connie gasped. "You think you're going to make love to me *now?* After what you've said?"

Garfield shrugged. "Why not?"

"I won't! Get out of here!"

He took out his billfold, counted out five one-hundred dollar bills, and handed them to Connie. "Here. You're a whore, aren't you? You ought to be flattered to know that I think a single lay is worth five hundred bucks."

Connie slapped the money out of his hand. The bills fluttered to the floor. Laughing, Garfield said, "So you're going to be independent?"

He unbuckled his belt. Connie watched in horror as he slid the belt out of its loops and advanced toward her. She was too frightened even to cry out.

He reached out, ripping the robe from her, exposing her nakedness. She turned to run into the corner of the room, but the belt licked out, striking with burning fury across one buttock. Connie turned, tried to shield herself. Garfield stood over her, laughing sadistically. He brought the belt down again, and a narrow red line sprang out in relief against her thighs. Another stroke, exploding against the softness of her breasts.

Again and again and again the belt descended, cracking across buttocks and breasts, thighs and belly, while Connie tried futilely to ward off the blows. She huddled down on the floor, turning herself into a little ball, while he rained blows on her shoulders and arms, rolled her over, smashed the belt across her exposed buttocks. He was laughing all the time.

The world turned into a red haze of pain. Connie became aware that he had stopped hitting her. She felt herself being lifted, being carried toward the bed. Her skin was aflame with agony. He dumped her on the bed. She heard a zipper opening.

"No—I won't let you—" she moaned.

But his weight descended on her, bringing new pain to the areas of her skin that were streaked with red. Connie clamped her knees together, but he was too strong for her, and at last she could no longer prevent him from taking her.

It was short and fierce. At the height of it he slapped her, the way he had always done, and the slap same as a trigger. For a wild moment Connie thought she was back in the watchman's shack. Her lips drew back from her teeth and she gasped with mingled pleasure and pain, unable to tell the difference any longer, knowing only that her body was alive with lust and that she had to writhe and twist until it was satisfied.

Which it was, finally. She felt Garfield rising from her. She kept her eyes closed. Her body throbbed with pain.

"So long, Connie. It was swell. Don't bother to get in touch."

Footsteps, retreating.

The sound of a slamming door.

Connie lay sprawled on the bed, exhausted, sick with pain. Every part of her hurt. Once again a man had taken advantage of her, once again had forced entry into the castle of her body.

And what Garfield had done was far worse than the mindless act of the juvenile savages. He had deliberately, almost criminally, led her along—to satisfy his own delight in inflicting pain.

Psychological pain as well as physical, Connie thought bitterly. He had abused her body and he had abused her personality.

She rose uncertainly from the bed, wanting to look in the full-length mirror and see what damage he had done to her. But her legs would not support her. She took two steps and dropped to the carpet.

Reaching out with her hands to steady herself, she touched pieces of paper. She looked at them. They were five one-hundred dollar bills. Connie ignored them. She stretched out flat on the floor and began to laugh, but after a few seconds the laughter turned to hysterical tears.

Thirteen

The weeping stopped, after a while, but Connie remained where she lay for a long time. The world seemed to be standing still.

Dan was gone. He had beaten her, mocked her, raped her, and now he was gone out of her life. The marriage, the trip around the world, the queenly visits to ranch and farm and factory—so much dream-smoke now.

She had not been expecting it, but yet, she knew, she had been a fool to trust him. He had hypnotized her into thinking he was different. But underneath his charm, he was no less a beast than the kid-gang boys.

All men are pigs, she thought. Some of them pretend to be kind and loving, but it's only pretense. Down deep they're all alike.

Connie rose unsteadily and walked over to the full-length mirrors. She pulled them out at an angle so she could examine herself front and back.

The belt-marks crisscrossed her entire body. Swelling red lines puffed against the whiteness of her thighs. Her buttocks were sore and the belt had broken the skin in a few places. Another whiplash had caught her across the cheek, just below her left eye.

Garfield had been like a wild man, intoxicated by the sheer joy of inflicting pain. Connie still saw him vividly, arm upraised, eyes glaring, nostrils wide—and then the belt descended, and she shrieked in pain

She shivered. It was some kind of twisted streak he had, she thought. He had been waiting for two months for the chance to use his belt on her, comforting himself in the meantime with slaps and blows. And then, in the height of his sadistic ecstasy, he had raped her. Connie felt the hot tears crowding into her eyes. She could abide a beating, perhaps. But rape was something different. Rape was the violent seizure of that which no woman should have to give except in love. It robbed a woman of her humanity, turning her into a mere mechanical device for pleasure, to be used without regard for the device's own wishes or protests.

Connie walked toward the dresser on wobbly legs. Half a bottle of bourbon sat there. She and Dan had had a little party in the room one night, and they had not used up all the liquor.

She uncapped it, poured two inches into a drinking glass, and downed it, fast. It hit the bottom of her stomach like a thunderbolt. Some of the pain of the beating and the rape began to subside.

But it wasn't good to drink all this stuff straight. Connie reached out, picked up the house phone, said to the operator in a level, almost toneless voice, "Would you please send some ice-cubes and mixer up here?"

"I'll notify Room Service for you, Ma'am."

Connie let the phone drop back onto its cradle. She wondered if she should order some more liquor. No; the fifth was still half full. If she couldn't get tight enough on that much bourbon to wipe out the sting of her injuries, she would never do it.

Bending, she scooped up the crumpled bills lying on the floor and put them on the dresser. There was a knock at the door. Connie started to answer it; then, remembering she was nude, she called out, "Just a minute," and slipped into her robe. The gauzy fabric was painful against her whip-marks.

She went to the door. A bellhop stood there holding a tray, on which were a pitcher full of ice and half a dozen bottles of ginger ale.

"Just set them down anywhere," Connie told him.

"Yes, Ma'am."

He put the tray down. Connie handed him a bill and said, "Here. This is for you."

The bellhop took the bill, looked at it, looked back at Connie. He gulped.

"You aren't serious, Ma'am?"

"What do you mean. I—"

Then she saw the bill she had given him. It was one of Garfield's hundred-dollar bills. Laughing, she took the bill from his trembling hand. "Careless of me," she said. "Here. Take this one instead."

It was a single. "Thank you, Ma'am."

But instead of leaving he remained at the door, staring peculiarly at Connie. She looked at his eyes and saw that they were focused on her breasts. She closed the door quickly.

Glancing at herself in the mirror, she saw what kind of appearance she had presented to the bellhop. Her gown hung open and her breasts were practically bare. But had he been looking at the breasts, or at the livid whip-marks on her cheek and on her throat and in the valley between her breasts?

No bellhop was going to gape that way just because a pair of knockers was jutting into his face, Connie thought. It was the marks that fascinated him. Between the marks and the hundred-dollar tip and her general woozy behavior, the bellhop was going to have a pretty good story to tell when he got back downstairs.

To hell with him, Connie told herself.

She switched the radio on, picking a station at random. Whining jazz came out.

She fixed herself a drink. One lump of ice, fill the glass one-third of the way with bourbon, the rest of the way with ginger ale. It tasted mellow that way. Connie sat down in the armchair next to the radio, tossing her gown aside. It hurt when she sat down, but it was harder to stay standing.

The drink went down rapidly. She was beginning to feel the effects now. Her face felt fuzzy and the sting of the whip-marks was beginning to recede. She leaned back, closed her eyes, and sealed off her mind to everything but the sound of the music coming over the radio.

After a while she poured herself another drink, the same mixture as before. She made it last half an hour, sipping at it slowly. The next drink went down quickly as did the rest.

Suddenly it was three in the morning, and there was only a half inch of bourbon left in the bottle. Shaking her head sadly, Connie poured it into her glass and dumped the empty into the wastebasket with a loud crash. The ice had long-since melted. She filled up the glass with warm ginger ale and sipped away, slowly. The clock said quarter to four when she finally consumed the last drop. She was wide awake, but very woozy.

She sat in the armchair a long time, thinking things over. She remembered John, that night in the park, and how eager he had been to make love. And then the hell in the watchman's shack. The pickup in Phoenix. Nick Tyler. Henrichs. Jacobs. Dan.

Dan.

What was it all for? Why keep on going through one humiliation after another, selling herself or giving herself away or simply being raped? Was it worth it, waking up morning after morning, shoveling meals into her mouth, climbing into bed and submitting to the sweaty embraces of one man or another? For what? Why go through the long round of minutes and hours, only to have the next day bring new humiliation, new shame, new self-loathing?

Connie shook her head. She was eighteen, and felt like she was thirty. Onto seventeen years of Brooklyn middle-class respectability had been grafted a year of debauchery and sin.

There was no going back to the innocent girl that had been. The road went only in one direction, ahead.

And the picture hardly looked cheerful. She couldn't keep her looks forever. The time would come when she was no longer desirable to men. Perhaps by then she would be wealthy, and would have to pay younger men a stud fee. She shuddered. She would have no family, no children, no memories worth remembering.

Abruptly, in a moment of weird clarity, Connie saw what she had to do. Why live out all those years of boredom and shame when she could cut them off right here?

She stood by the window for a while. Dawn was just coming up, over Los Angeles. It would be so simple, she thought, to open the window and fling herself outward. She would fall six stories and land on the concrete surrounding the swimming pool, and they would find her there in the morning, her nude body no longer young and ripe and appealing, but squashed like a pulpy tomato.

She shook her head. There was always the danger, remote but possible, that she would survive the fall, live on in a twisted, broken body, and have to do it all over again. Or that she would bounce from the parapet four floors below to the pool, and writhe for hours in slow agony. It was a chance she did not want to take.

Instead she went into the bathroom. There was a razor in the medicine cabinet. She remembered having put a new, sharp blade in it only that morning.

Kneeling by the bathtub, Connie carefully unscrewed the razor, set it down on the sink, and took the blade in her hand. She studied the blade a moment. It was single-edged, steel-blue, a lovely instrument of death.

Holding the blade in her right hand, she peered at her left wrist, thin, waxy, with the little network of blue veins just under the skin.

Voices, memory-blurred, echoed in her mind.

John's voice. *"Sure, everything's still okay. We just gotta pretend it never happened. We—"*

Her parents. *"Don't let this thing get you all shaken up, Connie. It's over with, and everything's going to be okay. I phoned Grandma in Arizona and told her you were going to come out there for a little while."*

A leering teenage savage. *"Choose for your turns. I'm gonna be first. Anybody argue with that?"*

Taking a deep breath, Connie held the blade over her left wrist.

She heard Nick Tyler's voice. *"I might even be able to find some clients for you. A lot of my friends are willing to pay good cash for a high-priced lay who likes opera."*

Dan Garfield. *"I enjoying wielding power. Some of that shows in the way I make love, doesn't it? I had power over you. I turned you into a little puppet that danced any way I cared to pull the strings. And now the fun is over for me. Take that robe off and lie down on the bed."*

Connie lowered the blade until it touched her skin lightly.

.... pray for us now and at the hour of our death ....

With a quick down-and-across motion she drew the blade across her wrist. The pain did not begin until she had lifted the blade. A thin red line no wider than the width of the blade sprang up on her pale skin. Then the blood began to well out in driblets. Her left hand started to shake.

Transferring the blade quickly, she slashed her right wrist. It was a less even cut, because her left hand was throbbing already from the open cut.

Holding her wrists up, she extended them over the bathtub so the blood wouldn't make a mess. A great drop of blood rolled down the side of her wrist and splashed on the white porcelain. The blood was darker, more richly purple, than she had expected.

Her hands felt very cold and the fingers were starting to curl up limply. She felt tired, mildly regretful. For one instant she even thought she wanted to rise and telephone down to the desk for help, but she changed her mind; now that it was done, let it be finished. Besides, she was too weak to get up. She slumped forward, her breasts touching the cold porcelain of the tub, her slashed wrists dangling over the tub's rim, her blood trickling in an ever faster flow into the tub, her skin getting colder, her mind growing cloudier.

.... now and at the hour of our death ....

She had no regrets. None at all.

She realized she had forgotten to leave a suicide note. It might have been her chance to strike back one last time at the world, by indicting humanity for all that had been done to her. But it was too late now. Her numbed fingers would never obey her. The writing-desk was two rooms away, anyway. And if she tried to write a note now, she would get blood all over the sheet.

She laughed.

Then she closed her eyes and tipped her head forward, so that her forehead rested against the tub. Her body seemed to be turning to ice. Every vein was throbbing. She could hear her heart pounding out its hammer blows, forcing the life from her with every mighty contraction.

Hell smelled like a hospital room—crisply antiseptic, faintly chemical.

Connie opened her eyes. She was in a bed; a nurse stood watch over her. It was all so very familiar. For an instant she lost contact with time, went back a year, remembered awakening in a hospital that other time, after they had found her in a vacant lot. Her heart sank. Did she have to go through it all again, that year of prostitution and heartbreak?

No, she thought. This was a different room. It was square; the other had been oblong. The furniture was better here. The other nurse had been a middle-aged woman, and this nurse was a hawk-faced blonde in her thirties.

"She's awake, Dr. Reynolds," the nurse said.

Connie watched dully as a vigorous young man of about thirty came striding into the room. He was dressed like a doctor, but he looked more like an undergraduate, with his short red crew cut and his broad grin.

The nurse left the room. Connie glanced up at him and said, "There's nothing more depressing than finding out you've bollixed your own suicide."

Laughing, the doctor sat down at the side of her bed. "You did a pretty good job of it. Another half hour and you wouldn't be here."

"How *did* I get here?"

"The maid came in to clean your rooms, and found you keeled over with the bathtub full of blood. Most maids would have flopped right down and given up the ghost themselves, but this one had enough sense to notify the desk in a hurry. They got a doctor right away. When he came, you had about enough blood left in you to nourish a good-sized snail."

"And what hospital is this?"

"You're in West Hollywood. My name's Jack Reynolds. In case you don't remember, there was five hundred dollars lying on the floor of your hotel room. So the management shipped you to a pretty fair hospital. Do you feel like talking, or should I let you sleep some more?"

"I feel like talking," Connie said. "I'm still getting used to the idea that I'm alive. I feel weak as a kitten."

"You ought to. I pumped a couple gallons of the Red Cross' best blood into you."

"How long have I been here?"

"Three days," the doctor said. "Sleeping like a baby most of it. Your wrists are healing nicely, but they're going to itch like the deuce for a while. I suggest you just grin and bear it. Incidentally, are you still planning to knock yourself off?"

Connie shook her head slowly. All desire for suicide seemed to have left her.

"No. I was—drunk, you see. It was a crazy idea that came over me all at once."

Reynolds nodded. "Try to see that it doesn't come over you again. You'll have round-the-clock nurses to keep an eye on you. And there'll be a psychiatric examination before you can get out of here. It's against the law to try to murder yourself."

Connie grinned faintly. "Don't worry about me. I won't be trying again."

"Care to talk about it?"

"There isn't much of a story. I had a fight with someone I thought I was going to marry. He walked out. I got boozed up and cut my wrists."

"He gave you a pretty good beating, too, didn't he? Or were you trying to whip yourself to death with a belt before you thought of razor-blades?"

"He went a little wild," Connie said softly. "Do I still have the marks?"

"They're going down," Reynolds said. He grinned. "I need some more information about you. The hotel says your name is Constance Thornton."

"That's good enough."

"Where from?"

"New—San Francisco."

"New San Francisco, eh? Where's that?"

Connie laughed despite herself. "I started to say New York. I haven't lived there in over a year. I was living in San Francisco before I came to L.A."

"And you were supposed to get married to somebody, only he backed out. And because you couldn't find an apartment, you were living in a $40-a-day suite at the Beverly-Wilshire while waiting to have him tie the knot. And you left five hundred dollars scattered on the floor. Are you a missing heiress, or something?"

"Are you a doctor or a detective?"

"I get paid for doctoring," Reynolds said. "But I'm always intrigued when pretty girls try to kill themselves under mysterious circumstances. And you are pretty. Even looking like a ghost."

"Thank you."

"I guess you've done enough talking for now," Reynolds said, rising. "And you haven't told me very much of anything. Well, I've got no right to ask, as long as you pay your bills."

"Did I make the newspapers?" Connie asked.

"In this town you can sneeze four times in succession and get into the papers, provided you're well stacked and photogenic. You were on the front pages."

"What did the articles say?"

"Girl slashes self in Bev-Wilshire suite. What else could they say? What else does anyone know?"

"And were there any messages for me?"

"Just one. We got an anonymous thousand-dollar contribution for your medical expenses. Your boyfriend must have a guilty conscience," Reynolds said.

"He ought to."

"I'll be back after lunch. I'll look in on you twice a day, just to see how you're coming along. The friendly approach, it's called. See you later."

He strolled out. Connie let the smile die slowly from her face.

She was alive. After everything, she was alive. She looked down at her wrists. They were heavily taped.

She didn't know whether to be happy or miserable about being alive.

Fourteen

The next day, she was strong enough to get out of bed and walk around the hospital. She spent all afternoon out on a sun porch, feeling the strength flow back into her. It was two days more before she could take more than an hour at a time on her feet.

Reynolds checked on her progress twice each day. They talked; and because Connie insisted on being tight-mouthed about herself, she began to find out things about her doctor. He was twenty-nine, had finished his residency, had begun a small private practice which he supplemented with hospital work. He was unmarried. He thought Connie was the prettiest patient he had ever had.

Every afternoon he examined her bruises. It was somewhat embarrassing for both of them. Connie's body had been viewed by dozens of men and in his line of work Reynolds had handled hundreds of women. Yet he maintained an elaborate pose of professional disinterest while studying the welts on Connie's breasts and buttocks that concealed an obvious unprofessional embarrassment, while Connie felt strangely shameless at letting him look at her body. Neither of them mentioned the phenomenon.

At the end of the week, he decided that Connie could leave the hospital. She was still weak and shaky, but the wrist slashes had healed and the whip marks no longer were painful, and she could do any further recuperation on her own.

The psychiatric test was necessary first. It was administered by a gruff-looking medic in his sixties, who questioned her thoroughly.

Connie stuck to her basic story: she had been deceived by the man she loved, she had had too much to drink, and in a fit of despondency had decided to end it all. No, she had never attempted suicide before. Yes, she felt fine now. No, she would never try to kill herself again.

He signed the release form. "I'm letting you go on probation. Who's your personal doctor?"

"I have none."

"All right, then. I'm appointing Dr. Reynolds to look after you. Report to him by telephone once a week, beginning Wednesday. Visit him personally the first week of every month."

"Suppose I forget?"

"Let me remind you that you've committed what might be considered a serious crime. If you happen to make another attempt to take your own life—"

"I won't."

"*If* you do, and *if* you are again unsuccessful, you'll probably find yourself committed to a state mental institution. And if you forget to report to your probationer, you may wind up there anyway. The State of California doesn't want to encourage suicide."

Later that afternoon they discharged her. Reynolds wished her good luck, and offered to meet her for dinner that night, but Connie turned him down. "Let's keep it a strictly professional relationship," she told him. "I'll phone you on Wednesday."

He shrugged sadly. "Is that final?"

"I'm not exactly anxious to socialize just yet. Let me get used to the idea of being alive, first."

She returned to the hotel. The manager looked at her rather sourly as she came to the desk. He obviously hadn't cared for the publicity the hotel had received as a result of the suicide attempt.

"I'm checking out tomorrow or the day after," she told him. "Just give me time to find myself an apartment."

"Madam does not need to be hasty."

"Madam wants to be hasty. My bank account isn't going to last long if my rent is $40 a day."

They seemed relieved to learn that she was leaving. The elevator operator and the bellhops stared strangely at her as she rode up to her rooms. They eyed her wrists, still lightly bandaged, and nodded to each other. Connie tried to ignore them.

Her suite had been tidied up, the empty liquor bottle removed, the bed made, the furniture—which had been tossed every which way while Dan was beating her—straightened around. Morbidly curious, Connie peeked into the bathroom, fully expecting to find the tub filled with blood. But, of course, they had cleaned up the mess. There was not even a stray drop of red on the tiles to serve as a reminder of her drunken little attempt at self-destruction.

That night, in the suite, she tried to appraise her position—where she stood now, where she was heading. The suicide attempt seemed to have cancelled out the past. There was only the future now—a future empty and enigmatic.

Even after settling the hotel bill, she would still have a couple of hundred dollars in cash. There was close to $20,000 in her bank account, besides. And here in the suite was an enormous conglomeration of clothes and other property, mostly bought with Dan Garfield's money. She could sell some of the surplus gowns and things and be able to live for a year on the proceeds.

She had no idea where to go now. The easiest thing was to pack up and go back to San Francisco and resume her old profession. San Francisco wouldn't have forgotten her in such a short time; within a week, she could be earning big money again. Or, if she preferred, she could accept Paul Henrichs' offer and move in with him as his mistress. San Francisco offered ease and economic security. But it also meant a return to prostitution. Right now she did not find the idea of sleeping with men—or women—at all appealing. She wanted to be alone.

A second alternative was to throw everything up and go home to Brooklyn. But that was impossible. How could she live with her parents, after what she had done, after what she had been through? Any honest relationship was impossible there. It was better to go back to San Francisco and be a whore again than to try to turn the clock back a year and more, Connie told herself.

The third possibility was to stay put—find an apartment in Los Angeles, live off her savings, perhaps get a decent job. Stay away from men and liquor, try to strike a sane balance of living.

In the long run, that sounded like the healthiest idea. She had enough cash to let herself mark time for a while. She had to remind herself that she was only a month past her eighteenth birthday. She felt as though she had lived for centuries.

The next morning, after a light breakfast at the hotel coffee shop, she set out apartment hunting, and by three in the afternoon she had found a place—three rooms in a reasonably attractive apartment house on Sixth Street, a couple of blocks from MacArthur Park. She hired a moving van to cart her stuff over, and, by the following afternoon, she had checked out of the Beverly-Wilshire and was settled in at her new home.

For the first few days the sheer work of getting the place arranged kept her busy from morning till night, and when she was through working in the house she collapsed on her bed and sank instantly into sleep. Wednesday came, and she remembered that she was on probation and had to call Dr. Reynolds.

The number she had been given was his private office's number, on Sherbourne Avenue near the Beverly Hills-Los Angeles border. A receptionist answered in frosty tones, and Connie asked for Dr. Reynolds.

"Hello there," he said immediately. "How has everything been?"

"All right. I moved out of the hotel and got myself an apartment. I've been too busy fixing the place up to have time to worry."

"You shouldn't overexert yourself, Connie. Your body needs time to build up its reserve of strength again. Have you been feeling tired?"

"A little. I sleep a lot."

"But everything's generally okay? No despondent thoughts, or stuff like that?"

"I told you. I've been too busy to worry."

"I suppose that's all right," Reynolds said. "And you sound calm enough. When am I going to see you, Connie?"

"The first week of next month."

"No, I don't mean in my office! When am I going to collect that rain check on the dinner date?"

Connie was silent a moment. "I'm not seeing anyone socially yet, Dr. Reynolds."

"Jack."

"Jack, then. I'm trying to keep away from people and think things through."

"No complaints there," Reynolds said. "But you mustn't make a hermit of yourself. What if I prescribed a date with me as required treatment for your recovery?"

"I might get myself a new doctor," Connie said.

"Umm. Okay, then, dammit. I won't prescribe it. But I would like to get to see you after hours, Connie. If you'll pardon the unprofessional attitude, I'll have to admit that I'm a wee bit interested in you."

But she successfully fended off his agile attempt to make a date, and he had to be satisfied with getting her new phone number and address. After she hung up, Connie sat down heavily on the edge of her bed and stared broodingly at the scabs on her wrists. She wondered why she had been so stubborn about not letting him have a date with her. It wasn't that she was afraid of jeopardizing his reputation—doctors weren't prohibited from dating patients—nor did the story that she Wanted To Be Alone have much substance, she admitted.

The real reason was different.

I'm not worthy of him, she realized.

He was a rising young doctor, a hard worker, cheerful and no doubt good at his trade. He was obviously looking for a wife, now that he had finally begun to earn a living after the long haul of medical school, internship, residency, and perhaps the army. And he had taken a fancy to her.

But, Connie thought, there was no point in wasting his time. Regardless of what he might think of her, she knew he was much too good for her. He didn't deserve an ex-prostitute, a would-be suicide, a victim of a mass rape, as his wife. He was too lighthearted to be stuck with a walking heap of neuroses as his partner. The best thing for both of us, Connie thought, is to keep away from each other. Let it be a strictly professional relationship, no more. And if he persists, she would simply switch doctors. Otherwise he might badger her into something that would only ultimately hurt him.

Two more days passed. The apartment was presentable, now. Connie had come to regard it almost as a shell. She had stocked up with dozens of paperback novels, and now she hardly ever went out of the apartment. Outside was the bustling complexity of the world, with its Dan Garfields and its teenage hoodlums, its call girls and lesbians, and even a few nice people like Jack Reynolds. Connie had ventured into that world and it had all but destroyed her. Now she intended to stay out of trouble as long as she could.

But certain recently-developed habits obsessed her. She had gone without sex for two weeks, now, ever since the night Dan had beaten her. It was the longest spell she had gone since setting up business in San Francisco, and not until now did she realize how necessary sex was to her. The demon of the flesh, once unchained, demands constant sacrifice. Her body burned for love. She lay alone at night, gripping her pillow tightly, remembering what it felt like to have a man's body locked between her thighs, to have a man's hand gripping her breasts.

All the rest, the rapes, the brutality—she could almost overlook those. But she had to have a man.

She had to have a drink, too. She had been drinking more and more, all year, and now she had stopped cold. It was rough on the nerves. More than anything, she wanted a drink.

It was Tuesday night. The next day, she would have to report to Dr. Reynolds again. What could she tell him? That she was in fine shape, except that she was going quietly crazy from lack of sex?

Women weren't supposed to feel pangs of lust. They were supposed to go along for months, years even, living perfectly chaste lives. Connie laughed. For the better part of a year she had spent practically every night making love, and she had made it with some experts. What she was feeling now was far from imaginary. It was the pull of a young, healthy body that was racked by desire.

At half past nine on Tuesday night she finally could resist no longer. She needed a drink. She needed a man. And she needed them both in the worst way.

God help me, she thought. *If I get into trouble, I'll have nobody to blame but myself.*

She dressed in a pair of tight pedal-pushers and in a sweater that clung tight to her skin. There was a bar on the corner opposite hers. She crossed to it, drawn magnetically by the blinking neon lights.

A big sign over the door said, ABSOLUTELY NO ADMISSION TO PERSONS UNDER TWENTY-ONE YEARS OF AGE. Connie smirked at it. No one ever questioned her age out here. Nine months of whoredom does something to a girl's eyes that takes the teenage sheen out of them forever.

The bar was small, dim, air-conditioned. The television set was tuned to an old movie, Jimmy Cagney at age twenty-five or so. About a dozen people were in the bar, half of them staring at the flickering screen and half of them down into the depths of their drinks.

The bartender looked at her blankly as she took a stool. Play it carefully, Connie thought. You don't want to get the barkeep sore and have him run you in for soliciting in his nice little bar.

"Bourbon and ginger ale," she said.

He made the drink, Connie paid for it, and she sat sipping it slowly. Leaning over the bar, the pudgy bartender whispered hoarsely, "Are you expecting to meet a friend of yours here?"

"There's a sign on the front of this place that says Ladies Invited. Can't a thirsty girl come in and buy herself a drink?"

The bartender shrugged. "I ain't implying anything. Except that I can get in trouble for letting hustlers use my place."

"Don't worry," Connie said. "I don't sell it. I *give* it away."

One of the television-watchers, seated three stools down from Connie, looked away from the screen. Evidently he had heard some of the conversation between Connie and the bartender. Shifting ponderously, he slid across until he was sitting next to Connie.

"Pardon me, Miss. You look like someone I once knew in Oxnard. Laura Rotsler, I think the name was. You wouldn't by any chance be—"

"No, I'm not," Connie said. In a lower voice she added, "My apartment is right across the street. Buy me a bottle of bourbon and we can have some fun."

He was about forty, with the bloated, puffy look of a man on a toboggan-slide to nowhere. His voice had been refined-sounding, though. He blinked now and said, "Are you on the level?"

"As level as anybody. Come on!"

He paid for a bottle of Jack Daniels and followed her out of the bar. "You'd better carry the package," he told her. "My hands aren't very steady. I'd hate to drop it, especially considering how much that bartender soaked me for it."

Connie took the bottle from him. She said nothing, led him across to her apartment, walked up the two flights of stairs, shut the door behind him. In the light, she saw that he had once been handsome, maybe ten years and fifty pounds ago. But his sandy hair was thinning, his eyes were dull, his cheeks droopy. He hadn't shaved in a couple of days, and his clothes were shabby.

Connie poured two drinks. He said, "We really should put this on a formal basis. My name is Roy Burkes, and I'm a writer by profession. Was. Praps you've seen some of my films. I did the scripts for *One More Tomorrow, Wings Over Tokyo*, half a dozen more—"

"When was your last film?"

"Five years ago. I've been having it a little rough since then. But my agent says there's a big deal brewing for me. Sid Clifton wants me to script the new *Crime and Punishment* for him. And after that everything will be okay for old Burkesy-boy. I might even be able to get a part for you. You could play Sonia. You know, whore with a heart of gold. Very juicy part. I—"

"Skip it," Connie said curtly. She wasn't interested in this blubbery drunk's tale of decline and fall. Los Angeles was full of has-been script writers, actors, directors, producers.

She pulled her sweater over her head, threw it down, and unsnapped her bra. Burkes stared at her bare young breasts in surprise. Connie felt her nipples stiffening already. Quickly she stripped off pants and underwear.

Burkes was already half undressed. "Christ, you're a pretty one," he mumbled. "Don't know where I get my luck. You—"

She pulled him down on top of her. He tried to go through some fumbling preliminaries, but Connie was already aroused, already on fire. It was a fire that only a man could quench, even a seedy, broken-down man like Burkes.

Then it was over.

Burkes muttered, "You're the hottest thing I've ever known. What the hell are you doing hidden away like this? With your talents you could be a top star. If you sleep with the right people, you—"

"Get off me," Connie said coldly.

"Huh?"

"You heard me. Get up."

Burkes lifted his heavy body from her. Connie rose, standing with her arms folded across her breasts. "Get your clothes on and scram," she snapped.

"Huh? Now, look here, we were just getting to know each other—"

"Out."

"—bust up a beautiful friendship right at the beginning—"

"Want me to call the police and tell them you broke in here and raped me? Get dressed."

Still muttering puzzledly, Burkes found his clothes and clambered into them. "I don't understand you," he said as he stood at the door. "First you pick me, up in a bar, then you practically throw yourself at me, and two minutes later you toss me out—"

"That's right. Out."

He shrugged and left. Connie slammed the door behind him. Then she looked down at her body, still marked lightly with the imprint of Dan Garfield's belt, and she could still feel Burkes' weight on her, still taste his stale taste.

She felt unspeakably filthy. Whatever serenity she had managed to obtain since the suicide attempt deserted her. She had gone out, picked up the first man she had found, and given herself to him. It wasn't possible to sink much lower. She felt vile.

She dropped to the floor and began to sob hysterically.

Fifteen

After a while, the idea of suicide began to tempt her again. What was the use of this life, veering between wild pleasure and bitter self-loathing? The pleasure brought on the loathing. And the loathing spurred her on to renew her quest for numbing pleasure. Round and round and round, and there was no escape from the vicious cycle.

No escape but one.

She grew calm. It would be so easy to take her life, here in this place. No one knew who she was, no one cared. There was still a razor in the bathroom. She had done it once; that qualified her practically as an expert. Flick, flick, two quick slices across the still-healing wrists, and the blood would come bubbling out. There was nothing to be afraid of. The wrist-slicing hurt, just at the start, but the pain was bearable, and soon died away. And after that ... peace. There would be no maid coming in next morning to clean the rooms, who might discover her and call for help in time. There would be no miraculous reawakening in some antiseptic hospital room. There would only be darkness and sleep. It might be days before her body was discovered. It—

Connie shook her head. She struggled to her feet and stood in the middle of the room, breathing deeply, clinging to the world. Suicide was the wrong answer, she told herself. She had tried that once, and had been reprieved. There must be some other way out of the trap of humiliation and pain. Giving up the whole world was too drastic. There were still things she wanted to keep: the smell of summer grass, the tang of champagne, the sound of great music. She was only eighteen. Perhaps things would get better as she grew older.

And suicide was so final.

Connie shambled unsteadily across the room. The bottle of Jack Daniels stood on the dresser, open. Connie and the seedy ex-film writer had had a couple of shots apiece, no more. Most of the bottle's contents were still there. Connie stared at the black label until the white letters blurred and danced.

Once before, a bottle of bourbon had served to numb her conscience long enough to let her try to take the easy way out. Right now the bottle was about as dangerous as a loaded gun. Quickly, she snatched it up, carried it into the kitchen, and upended it over the sink. The bourbon went gurgling out. Connie watched it swirl around the drain with a peculiar fascination. When the bottle was empty, she put it carefully down at the edge of the sink, and sighed in relief.

She felt better. But the suicidal impulse still hung heavy around her. Every time she remembered what she had done this evening, the temptation to take down the razor became a little stronger. She pictured herself going on through life this way, sternly repressing her desires, finally breaking down periodically and indulging them with some seedy drunk, and then pondering suicide afterwards. It was an unpleasant picture. And it would be so very easy to make sure that it never came about. The razor—

She took three steps toward the bathroom, realized where she was going, and stopped short. An armchair presented itself; Connie sank down into it, gripped her knees tightly, and started to shake.

.... help ....

She wanted to cry out. She wanted someone to stand by her, and hold her hand, to grip her shoulders, perhaps, and steady her. Someone to see her through this hellish night.

Who? She didn't know any of her neighbors well enough to ask them to stand vigil over a potential suicide. The only person in all of Los

Angeles that she could say she knew was Dan Garfield, and she had no idea where or how to reach him. Nor did she particularly want Garfield's company right now. The sight of him, Connie thought, might just push her over the brink.

Who, then?

She glanced at her watch. It was five minutes past midnight. Connie smiled. That meant it was Wednesday morning; and on Wednesday, she was supposed to telephone Dr. Jack Reynolds. So it would be legitimate to call him, late as it was. Would he get angry? Suppose he was asleep? Or entertaining a lady friend? That last idea made Connie redden. She walked toward the telephone, stood over it for nearly half a minute, and then began to dial Jack Reynolds' telephone number.

His apartment adjoined his office. Most likely he had separate telephones for apartment and for office, but if he were home he would probably be able to hear the telephone ringing in the office. Connie listened. The phone rang three times, fourth, a fifth. On the eighth ring she debated hanging up. On the tenth, she almost replaced the phone on the hook.

Two more rings, she told herself, then I'll hang up. Eleven, twelve....

"Hello?" a sleepy, irritated voice said.

"Jack! Thank God you answered. I was afraid you were asleep, or at the hospital or someplace like that. And I wanted to talk to you so much!"

"Who's this? Connie?"

"Yes."

"Do you know that it's after midnight, and I have to be at the hospital at six-thirty in the morning?" He sounded grumpy. "I wish you'd wait till a decent hour to call. You—"

"Jack, I was going to kill myself."

He was silent for an instant. "*What?*"

The words came out of her in a bubbling rush. "Everything was going along so nicely, and then yesterday I started to feel in a bad mood, all pent up and repressed, and I just *had* to have a drink. So I went out and had a drink and picked up this filthy old worn-out script writer and brought him here, and then afterward I threw him out and I've been sitting here staring at my toes and wondering if I ought to slit my wrists again. And instead I decided to telephone you. Jack, I'm sorry if I woke you up, but—"

"Forget that. Are you home?"

"Yes, of course."

"Okay. I want you to hang up the phone and sit very quietly where you are. Don't do anything, don't go anywhere, and don't even *think* anything. I'm going to come over to keep you company."

"Jack, you mustn't. Not if you have to be at the hospital at—"

"To hell with the hospital. I don't want to have to give anybody any more emergency transfusions for a while. Will you do as I say? Sit right where you are until I get there. And don't start worrying about things. Do you have any liquor in your place?"

"No. I just spilled a whole bottle of bourbon into the sink."

"Smart girl. Remember, now, I'm going to be right over. Stay calm. Nobody's going to hurt you. Nothing's going to happen to you. See you soon."

"All right, Jack. But—hurry."

"I will. So long, Connie."

"So long."

She let the receiver drop back into place. For the next few minutes she sat perfectly still, as he had ordered her to do. She concentrated on the wall opposite her, trying to see through it into the street. The minutes ticked by.

At last she could sit still no longer. Restlessly, she rose and paced around, wondering how much longer it would be before Reynolds arrived. She thought she could hold out alone. The razor in the bathroom no longer beckoned quite as strongly, now that she had been able to speak to him. But it would be safer all around if he were with her.

Connie realized she was hardly dressed for company. Jack had seen her body often enough, but that was no excuse for greeting him in the nude. She slipped into her light robe.

A few moments more went by. Then she heard the sound of a car pulling up in the quiet street outside. She sprang to the window. A snub-nosed black Volkswagen had parked in front of the house. And there was Reynolds, leaping from the car, sprinting into the building.

Connie opened the door and waited by it. He rushed in, looking flushed, his collar open and his shoelaces untied. He was carrying his little black bag.

"Jack—thank God—"

"Thank yourself for having the brains to call me," he said. "Is everything okay now? Did you have any trouble while waiting for me?"

"No. I just sat here, like you told me to do."

He smiled in relief. Opening the bag, he took out a bottle of orange pills, shook one out, and presented it to her. "Just to make sure," he said, "wrap your stomach around one of these."

"What is it?"

"A tranquilizer pill. It's likely to help keep you from flipping your wig for a while. Go on. Take it. Then I want to talk to you a little."

Connie went into the bathroom, turned on the tap, poured a glass of water. Glancing around, she saw Reynolds watching her.

"Can't a lady have privacy even in her own john?" she asked.

"Not if she's an unstable young lady and the john contains dangerous implements," Reynolds said. He was smiling, but behind the smile was a look of grave concern for her.

Connie swallowed the pill. "I don't feel any different," she reported. "Is a mystic air of tranquility supposed to steal over me now?"

"Don't ask me," he said. "*You're* the patient. I wouldn't touch one of those happy-pills myself. But from what I hear, they're kinda relaxing. Come on inside and sit down on the couch with me. And tighten your belt, while you're at it."

"I thought doctors were unmoved by the sight of feminine flesh."

"That's the legend they tell, all right. And I suppose after thirty years of carving up females, the feminine form becomes just so much meat. But I'm pretty new at this trade. Besides, I'm off duty now. I'm a susceptible young bachelor, and I'm in a young lady's apartment without a chaperone. If you keep on waving your fair young body at me, Hippocrates alone knows what I'm likely to do."

Connie giggled. It was partly the effect of the pill, partly a result of Reynolds' mock-serious bantering manner of conversation.

They sat down chastely at opposite ends of Connie's long modern couch. Reynolds leaned forward, eyes drilling deep into her, arms folded, legs crossed. He said quietly, "Two weeks ago you slit your wrists, and tonight you were on the verge of doing the same thing again. How come you find life so repugnant, Connie?"

"I—I don't know."

"You mean you have a vague and unmotivated compulsion to suicide? If that's the case, I'm going to have you committed tomorrow."

"No. It isn't like that."

"Then what is it? The fact that your well-heeled boyfriend jilted you? Sure, that must have been a blow. But romances get punctured all the time, and it usually isn't an exit cue when your great love affair goes *phht!* So what's eating you? Tell old Doc Reynolds all about it."

"Why don't you just go home?" Connie suggested. "I'm sleepy now. And I'm all right. I don't want to have to pour out the story of my life."

Reynolds slid along the couch until he was less than a foot from her. "Listen to me, sister. You woke me out of the best sleep I had had in weeks, and I came tear-assing over here wondering whether I was going to find you spurting blood all over the bathtub or not. You aren't going to clam up on me now."

"I am if I want to."

Reynolds shook his head. "Connie, I've got more than a professional interest in this thing. You're a hell of a fine kid. I want to help you. I want to see you shake off this suicide thing—and then I want to get to know you a lot better."

"No, you don't," Connie said hollowly. "Suppose you let me give *you* some advice. Leave me that bottle of pills, so I can get through any future fits of depression, and go home and go to sleep and forget all about me. I'm poison, Jack. Don't get mixed up with me."

"Too late for that, Connie. I *am* mixed up with you." He shifted uncomfortably on the couch, crossing his legs beneath him, and pulled a pipe from his jacket pocket. He lit up. "I guess I might as well make a confession, then. I'm pretty hopelessly gone on you."

"Don't be a fool, Jack. You don't know anything about me."

"I know you're beautiful. I know you've got a good little brain back of all that auburn hair. And I know you've been through hell, somehow. I also know I want to help you. You've been keeping me at arm's length so far. Now I want you to let the drawbridge down and start telling me a little about yourself."

"You'd hate me if you knew anything about me."

"There isn't a thing you could possibly tell me would make me hate you, Connie." He turned to face her, and she saw that his face had lost its ironic smile; he was dead serious now. "What if I told you that I love you, Connie?"

"I'd say you were a damn fool."

He took the pipe out of his mouth. "Okay. I'll make a damn fool out of myself. I love you, Connie."

She stared at him. This was what she had been afraid of. His declaration of love was sincere, terribly sincere. She knew that. This was not Dan Garfield, telling her he loved her simply to set her up for a fall. Jack Reynolds was talking from the heart.

Connie said softly, "I appreciate that, Jack. It's always nice to know that somebody loves you. Now that you've told me, would you kindly get up and go home—and forget all about me?"

"Do you really mean that, Connie?"

"I'm afraid I do. I'm no good for you—no good for anybody. Least of all you. You need me the way you need a hole in the head. You say you love me, but that's only because you don't really know me."

"I *want* to know you. You won't let me."

"Let's leave it that way, yes? Go home, Jack. And thanks for everything you've done so far. Don't worry about me. What do I owe you for coming out here tonight?"

"Skip it."

"No. I want to pay."

He shook his head. "I don't charge for errands of mercy. Connie—" he began appealingly.

"No." She forced herself not to weaken. "You've got all the world ahead of you, Jack. Don't try to tie yourself up with someone like me. Go home."

He stood up. "All right," he said in a thin, tight voice. "If that's what you want, I'll leave. I don't want to force myself on you."

He stood up, opened his bag, took out the little bottle of tranquilizers. "Here. Take them three times a day for the rest of the week, then twice a day until you feel really stable again. This bottle ought to be enough to last you through the rest of the month. If you think you need more, call me up and I'll mail you a prescription."

"All right. Won't you let me pay you for the pills, at least?"

"Don't bother. I get them as samples from the drug company."

He walked toward the door. Connie trembled inwardly, but she told herself that this was for the best, that he would only suffer unless he walked out that door and drove away, forgetting her completely. He was too good, too kind, to get himself mixed up with a girl as confused and sick as she was.

Standing at the door, he said, "What I told you before still goes, Connie. I—"

"Don't say it again," she broke in. "It'll only make it hurt that much more for both of us. Will you forget me fast, Jack? Please?"

"That's one thing I can't promise. But take care of yourself, Connie. And—so long."

He was gone. Connie stood by the closed door for a long moment, holding the knob, trying to look through the door and see him. She wondered if he was really gone forever. She hoped so, much as her heart ached for him. It was far better that way.

Only now she was alone again. She had a little bottle of pills, but they were no substitute for love. And she knew that the time would come, somewhere in the dead of the night, when she would no longer be able to stand the loneliness, and she would take the razor down from the cabinet and once again watch, fascinated, as her blood drained from her.

Jack was gone.

Connie stood listening for the sound of his motor starting in the quiet street. She frowned; he should have started the car by now. Timidly, hesitantly, she walked toward the window, expecting to hear the little Volkswagen come to life any moment.

Then she was at the window. She peered through the blinds.

Jack hadn't left. He was standing in the street below, looking up at her window as though debating whether to return. His face, in the light of the street-lamp, was pale, drawn, tense, doubtful.

Suddenly Connie doubted no more. She pulled up the blind, threw open the window, shouted out into the street.

"Jack! Jack, come back here! Please, darling!"

He glanced up, his eyes meeting hers, his face blank with surprise. For a moment they remained that way, eyes locked, bodies frozen.

Then he ran toward the entrance of her building. Connie opened her door, and heard him pounding up the stairs toward her floor.

Sixteen

She had started regretting the "*darling*" the instant the word left her mouth. Now, in the moment just before he entered, Connie knew exactly what she was going to say to him.

He came in. He wasn't smiling. "You told me to go home. Then you yodel for me to come back. Why can't women make up their minds?"

"Come in and sit down, Jack. I decided I had to tell you some things."

"I'm listening."

"It wasn't good, letting you go away like that. It wouldn't solve anything. I knew it the minute you were out the door. You would go on thinking about me, and maybe bothering me with phone calls and visits, and I know I'd keep on wondering about you. So I decided to call you back and let you know everything. That way there'll be a clean break, without any loose ends."

"Cautery," Reynolds said. "Stick a hot iron in the wound to insure antisepsis. Okay—that's what I wanted you to do before you threw me out. Fire when ready, Captain."

"It isn't pretty."

"Life never is. Mind if I smoke?"

"Of course I don't mind."

He lit his pipe. Connie sat opposite him, he on the couch, she on the facing armchair. The only light in the room was a dim lamp. Connie was silent for a long moment, debating now whether or not to go through with this. She decided she had to, now that she had actually called him back.

She said, "How old do you think I am, just for a starter?"

"Twenty-one, twenty-two, in that general region. Maybe twenty-four at the outside."

"I'm eighteen," she said. "Eighteen and a few weeks. I know, I look a lot older."

"You sure had me fooled!"

"I've had you fooled about a lot of things, Jack. Let me start at the beginning, though. The first seventeen years we can skip over pretty fast. Nothing much happened in them except that I grew up, went to school, did all the usual schoolgirl things, had the usual schoolgirl crushes and such. I'd been dating a kid named John Ludwig, from my neighborhood. He's a year older than I am, and I guess he's a sophomore at Syracuse now. We were going steady, talking about getting engaged, the usual high school stuff. All this was in Brooklyn, by the way.

"Well, one night a year ago September I went downstairs to mail a letter. A dozen teenagers grabbed me, stuffed me into a car, drove across town to an abandoned watchman's shack, and raped me. One after another, two or three times apiece. Until that night I'd been a virgin."

Reynolds said nothing. But his forehead wrinkled in a frown, and his lips soundlessly shaped the single word, *"Christ!"*

Connie went on, telling the story in an emotionless, flat voice, practically a monotone. "I woke up in a hospital bed, not remembering too much of what had happened to me. But I remembered enough. And there were my parents, standing around the bedside clucking like a couple of hens, mumbling little phrases of sympathy. But they obviously didn't know how to handle the situation. Here was their nice shiny cellophane-wrapped virgin daughter dragged through the mud by a teenage gang. It shocked them. It shocked them so much they had to get me out of their sight, so they shipped me off to my grandparents' place in Phoenix, Arizona.

"Here's where the kicker comes in, you see. The rape was a pretty brutal thing. But right in the middle of it, I experienced a sexual climax. Ever hear of such a cockeyed thing? It was like catching fire. All those years of carefully saving my virginity for my husband, and then all of a sudden I was losing it on a pile of straw in some old shack.

"So I changed completely. In Phoenix I went into a bar and picked some guy up and let him take me to bed. After he was asleep, I took ten dollars from his wallet, just as an afterthought.

"Then I wired home for money, got it, and took off for San Francisco without telling my parents or grandparents where I was heading. And I set up shop there. I was determined to make as much money out of sex as I could. Right away I had a long list of clients. I was getting $100 a night, plus bonuses."

Reynolds stared at her. "You're making all this up. You *couldn't* have been a call girl!"

"No? Well, maybe I don't look or act the type. But that rape did things to me. It changed my entire personality. You might even say it made me go a little bit out of my head. Anyway, there I was on Mission Street, peddling myself to the highest bidder. And it was a grand life, for a while. But I got tired of it. I started to do a lot of drinking. I even got mixed up with a lesbian one night—just once.

"Okay. And then along comes a wealthy electronics manufacturer. He visits S.F. for the weekend, hires me, and when I show up at his place we click, like that. I fall all over myself in love for him, like the dumb teenager I really am. He hands me a line. Come to Los Angeles, he says. Live at a fancy hotel and wait a couple of months, and then I'll divorce my wife and marry you. So I say okay, and I leave San Francisco and come here and move into the Beverly-Wilshire. Two months go by. No divorce. I start to get impatient. He's showered me with money, but I begin to think he's stringing me along.

"One night I ask him. And he admits the truth—he was just playing a little game with me, because it amuses him to monkey with other people's emotions. He isn't planning to marry me.

"Next think I know, he has his belt off and he's letting me have it. When he gets tired of beating me, he rapes me and leaves. I pick up a bottle of bourbon and spend half the night drinking it. Then I go into the john and slash my wrists. After which, I'm waking up in a hospital for the second time—still alive, despite everything.

"Okay," Connie said. "You know pretty much the rest of it. I set up housekeeping here and lived like a hermit for a little while. Last night everything got too much for me. I went out, picked up a drunk, brought him back here, and let him lay me. Then I threw him out. I wanted to commit suicide. Instead I called you. You came, gave me a pill, started talking about how much you loved me. That's why I called you back. I wanted to give you the whole story, straight and unprettied and uncensored. I wanted you to see just what kind of a girl you were getting mushy about. A rape victim, a whore, a drunk, a potential suicide. Not to mention my night in bed with the lesbian. Lovely, yes? A prime specimen of American womanhood. The girl-next-door sort of girl."

While she had been speaking, Connie had been staring straight off into space, avoiding Reynolds' face. Now she turned to look directly at him. His lips were drawn tight, his eyes were grim. His face bore none of its earlier boyishness.

"Well?" Connie demanded. "Now you've heard the story. I've unburdened my soul, and all that sort of stuff. *Now* tell me what you think of me."

"I love you, Connie," he said gently.

The words had the impact of a blow. Connie jerked backward abruptly, caught by surprise. "You must be crazy," she said.

"Maybe I am."

"Doesn't my story disgust you?"

"It shocks me," he admitted. "You've been through hell, and I'm amazed that you held out this long before thinking of suicide. It shows that you've got guts."

"But what about all the things I've done—the whoring, the drinking—"

"You were off on a year-long spree. You were getting even with the world, weren't you?"

"You could call it that."

"I will. Look at it this way: you lived a good and virtuous life for seventeen years, and where did it get you? You landed up on a pile of straw in an old shack. So you drew the conclusion that it didn't pay to be good, and therefore you were going to be just as bad as you damned well could be. Am I right?"

"That's about the way I figured it, I suppose," Connie admitted.

"The only trouble was that you didn't take naturally to being bad. You faked it for a year—but what you wanted was really marriage, a home, security. So you jumped at the chance when your rich electronics man waved it at you. And you were so flattened to find out he was cheating you that you cut your wrists. And then tonight—you've been trying to live a decent life lately, only you don't know how to go about it. You haven't built up the kind of stability it takes for a girl your age to live alone. And so you backslid—and then remorse set in, and you thought of suicide again."

Connie said hoarsely, "Okay, Jack, you've analyzed me to a T. What now? Why don't you just shrug your shoulders and admit that you made a mistake—that you developed a crush on a patient because you thought she was a pretty little virgin, and instead she turned out to be a mixed-up whore. Why keep on talking about love?"

"Because I mean it, Connie."

"You don't want me. You want somebody pure."

"I can see *your* purity, Connie. Underneath that outer layer of grime, underneath the coating of the past year, is the you that once existed. And I'm in love with that girl. You need help, Connie. Real help, not just the fake sympathy or exploitation that other people gave you. And I want to give you that help."

"You're making a martyr out of yourself, Jack. I don't want you to think you have to."

"The past doesn't matter, Connie. The past can be locked up and put away. You're only eighteen. The best years of your life are still ahead of you. The things you've done in the past year aren't written on your forehead in scarlet letters. You were sick, confused, hurt. Why should you damn yourself forever?"

"Don't you want a virgin for a wife?"

Reynolds snorted. "This isn't 1875, Connie. I want a girl I can love. Period, end quote. Do I care whether I'm the first man in your life or not, so long as I'm the last?"

"But—it isn't right, Jack—"

"Who says so? I've listened to your little confession, and it hasn't changed my mind one bit. I want you to marry me, Connie. I've got a good practice under way, and a doctor always can use a pretty wife as an asset. And I'll help you all I can possibly help to forget last year. We'll wipe out the past with love. How about it? We can get married next week, privately. And then we can get in touch with your folks—they're probably worried sick about you—and after our honeymoon we can set up housekeeping here in L.A. What's the answer?"

Connie shook her head dazedly. "Jack—Jack, you madman—"

"Well?"

"Darling! Yes! You're crazy to do it, but—*yes!*"

The word seemed to set off a trigger reaction in her. She rose, flung herself at him, and felt her face go wet and hot with tears.

He held her tight, gripping her with strong arms, pressing her against him.

Connie murmured, "Jack?"

"Umm?"

"Love me. Love me right now."

"Before the wedding? Horrors!"

"This isn't 1875, Jack. You said so yourself."

"So I did. But I wouldn't want to take advantage of an innocent woman."

"I'm not very innocent."

"Yes, you are. Tonight you start all over again. As far as I'm concerned, that is."

"All right, then. Let's go to bed. It's too late for you to go home. And if you say I'm innocent, innocent I'll be. Only I command you to seduce me."

His deep laugh rang in her ears. "They say a gentleman should do whatever a lady wishes him to do. Your command will be honored, milady." He scooped her off her feet and carried her into the bedroom, depositing her gently on the bed.

"Set the alarm," she said. "You have to be at the hospital at six-thirty!"

"We won't need any alarm. I don't plan to do any sleeping tonight."

He peeled the robe off her. Connie waited, in the dark, listening to the sound of his clothing falling to the floor. Then she felt him against her, his body hard and muscular, his powerful arms cradling her, his big hands seeking for and finding her breasts. His lips grazed her nipples gently, and she flattened her body against his.

Slowly, tenderly, they entered into the rhythms of love. Connie held him tightly, supporting his weight as though it were nothing. As she stared at the ceiling she saw phantoms from her past—Dan Garfield, John Ludwig, Nick Tyler, Paul Henrichs, the gang boys. They wavered, became insubstantial, and vanished like puffs of smoke. The past was growing dimmer.

Now she could stop remembering. Now she could begin once again to look ahead.

"I love you," she whispered, and her future began.

THE END

MEG

Robert Silverberg

Writing as Loren Beauchamp

Prologue

There was a moon, and it was early spring, and they were together in a car parked in a dark lane bordered by bending elms, and she had had a little to drink after the movie. Not much. Just a couple of beers, and Jack had had a couple of beers, and then they had started to drive home, only Jack had driven into the secluded lane. She did not protest.

He said, "Let's sit in back, baby. There's lots more room there."

She did not protest that either.

They went into the back of the car, and she leaned back with her head limp and her feet thrust out against the seat in front of her, and suddenly she reminded herself that this was wrong, that she had never gone all the way before, that she hadn't wanted it to happen this way, in the back seat of a parked car on a lonely Idaho road with a couple of beers in her belly. And she hadn't wanted it to happen with Jack, not with any of the local boys. But it was happening.

She said, "Jack, I think we ought to—"

"Yeah, baby. Yeah." He put his big hand on the front of her blouse, and as if by magic the buttons parted, admitting the toil-thickened fingers, and before she could stop him he had found the clasp of her bra and was opening it with suspicious skill.

The bra fell away from the full peaks of her breasts. She felt a calloused palm against her flesh. No man had ever touched her bare breast before. Her bra, sometimes, but not the soft warm flesh within. She sucked in her breath sharply, feeling the stir of desire in her loins.

The big hand tightened. She shivered, thrusting the breasts harder against it.

All resistance melted away now. They squirmed for position in the car, on the worn seat of Jack's '47 Buick, and she felt his hand under her skirt, touching her knees, wriggling between them and up to her thighs, brushing the tender skin on the inside of her thighs. Then he was tugging on her panties and she made no attempt to stop him, and his fingers probed the secret places of her body, and then a zipper opened and he made another adjustment of position and she closed her eyes tight, digging her fingers into shoulders. Digging! Digging!

And then it was over. She felt wet and soiled and cheated. Reaching down, she found her panties on the floor of the car, and she thrust her feet into them and pulled them up around her hips, wondering as she did so if they were going to get stained.

"It was all right, wasn't it?" he asked.

"Sure," she said. Her voice seemed strange in her own ears, but she didn't want to hurt him. "Sure, Jack, it was okay."

"That's my baby. You're all right, you know?"

She clasped her bra. Jack looked at her anxiously.

She smiled without answering. Buttoning her blouse, she said softly, "I think we'd better go home now."

She said little as he drove her home. She was sober, now, and the full impact of the guilt was on her, and she felt the pain and the wetness in her loins, and wondered why she had let him do it to her.

Because I was liquored up, she thought. *Because he put his hands in my bra and it felt so good I didn't want him to stop. Because he probably would have done it anyway even if I said no.*

At her house, goodnights were brief. Jack didn't seem to show much interest in kissing her. Usually they stood in the shadows a half hour or more, body grinding against body—but tonight, for the first time, she had given him what he really wanted, and, satisfied, he had no present need for her. She kissed him lightly and ran into the house, upstairs, to her room.

Everyone was asleep. She undressed and examined her body critically. No, she didn't *look* any different. You couldn't tell that her status had changed. There was only the raw pain, dying away now, and the other pain, the inward pain of knowing that she had given herself away—

—and for what? For Jack? For a big farmer boy who smelled of sweat and had no future and would bang her every night and fill her up with children, if she gave him the chance?

I can do better than that, she thought.

I could be a beauty queen. A movie star. Everybody says so. They say I'm as sexy as Marilyn Monroe.

She stared in the mirror, at the big, full breasts, the sensuous hips and thighs. *I'm too good for this town*, she thought. *It's high time I tried to get somewhere in life.*

It was not the first time she had thought these thoughts. But tonight, with the rough touch of a man's hands still tingling on her ex-virgin breasts, she was able to carry her resolution through to its conclusion.

I'll go to New York, she thought. *Goodbye to Idaho. Goodbye to potato farmers. Jack doesn't know it yet, but he's had it from me. The first and last time.*

I'm not going to be his lifetime lay. I'm going to be famous. I'm going to be somebody big.

One

She was aware that every man she passed in the street turned around to take a second look at her. She didn't care. It was on old story with her—six years old. She had been fourteen when her beauty had flowered so astonishingly, and now she was practically twenty. For six years she had been stopping traffic in her home town of Harmons Glen, Idaho.

The difference was that this wasn't Harmons Glen. It was New York, and Meg Tandler was scared. She had been in Boise once, and that had seemed pretty big to her. But you could put all the people in Boise down in Times Square and lose them in half a minute. And there were ten times as many people on Manhattan Island right now than there were in the whole State of Idaho, Meg realized tensely.

She gripped the handle of her suitcase tightly, tried to blot the nervousness from her face, and kept on walking, straight toward the HOTEL sign blinking at her a couple of blocks to the north. She told herself that the way to keep from getting rattled by New York City was to do one thing at a time. First, get a hotel room; then, take a shower, freshen up, get the grime of travelling off her face. Next, put on the sexiest dress and start looking for the big break. After that, it would all have to be a matter of luck—luck, and the openings that her own sexiness could create for her.

She couldn't get used to the people streaming past her as she walked north on Eighth Avenue, past the bars and flophouses and souvenir shops toward that winking neon sign HOTEL. If any unescorted woman ever got off the bus in Harmons Falls and started to drag a heavy suitcase up Main Street, twenty men would surround her in an instant, like flies drawn to spilled honey, to offer to help her with her luggage. Not here. Not in New York. It didn't matter whether she was twenty or two hundred, whether she was pretty or a foul hag, whether she wore shapeless rags or a tight sweater or went stark naked down the street. Nobody approached her. Nobody tried to break through the barriers between one person and another. They just stared at her, ogled her breasts and hips, and moved on. Having moved on, they turned to study the voluptuous fullness of her buttocks, and then they were gone. The suitcase was heavy. Meg stopped for a moment, switched hands, and kept on going toward the sign.

The suitcase kept getting heavier. It contained just about all that she possessed, and she had toted it clear across the continent from Idaho.

The bus trip had been long and dreary, an endless jouncejounce-jounce through barren wastelands and dull cornfields. But it was the cheapest way of getting to New York, and every nickel counted. Meg had been saving for this trip a long, long time. She had piled up a thousand dollars, at last. That, and a one-way ticket to Harmons Glen, Idaho, were all she had. If the thousand ran out before she had made a start in New York, she would use the ticket. Otherwise, she would tear it up. She figured she could live for three or four months on that thousand dollars. After that—?

After that, defeat. Back to Harmons Glen. Back to home and family and friends and Jack. Back to all the people who had been horrified and angry and scornful when she announced she was going to New York to try to crash show business.

A whistle sounded behind her. Automatically, Meg turned. A boy was lounging against a lamppost, smiling at her. Slowly, boldly, his eyes travelled the length of her body, from her face past the thrusting mounds of her breasts, down to her belly, her hips, her legs, her ankles. Meg reddened. There were wolves in Harmons Glen, too—but they merely *undressed* a girl with their eyes; they didn't rape her with them too.

The hotel sign was only a block away, now. Meg thought her arm would drop from its socket. It would be awful, she thought, if the hotel were all filled up. She hadn't made any reservations anywhere. She was sure that there would be *someplace* in a city this big where she could rent a room for a while. The sign had been the first thing she had seen when she stepped out of the bus terminal at 41st Street.

Sweat poured down her body. It was the middle of April, but it felt like late June. She walked into the hotel lobby and gratefully dropped her suitcase just inside the door.

The lobby was poorly lit and not particularly clean. Meg tried not to notice. She wasn't exactly ready to move into the Waldorf, she knew.

"I'd—I'd like a room," she said. The words came out in a faint whisper.

The clerk was a faded old man in shirtsleeves, with a green eyeshade and a few iron-gray wisps of hair. He focused his eyes interestedly on Meg's sweater and said, "Single?"

"Yes, sir."

"Okay. Five with, four-and-a-quarter without. Which is it?"

"Pardon?"

"I said, five with, four-and-a-quarter without."

"Without what?" Meg said, perplexed.

"With or without private bath, of course."

"Oh." Meg's cheeks flamed. It seemed so obvious, now that it had been explained. "I'll take the one with the bath, thanks. Five dollars a night?"

"Not five a week, honey."

She opened her purse and started fumbling with her purse. The desk clerk shook his head. "You are a greenhorn, aren't you? Pay when you check out. Just sign this card, that's all."

Her hands shook as she signed in. When she had completed the card, he looked at it, nodded, and said, "Idaho, huh? First time in New York?"

"Yes, sir."

"Visiting relatives?" He frowned. "Sightseeing? No, I guess not. Your kind would come with a tour if you were sightseeing. You're here to make a million, aren't you."

Meg shrugged. "I think I've got some talent."

"There's only one talent that'll get you anywhere in this town. And that's the talent you've got inside your sweater." The clerk smiled at Meg's confusion. "I've seen so many of you, you know? We get them right up from the bus terminal. They come and they go, they come and they go. Got your return ticket?"

Meg nodded.

"Good," the clerk said. "Hang onto it. It's a nine to one shot that you'll be needing it before the summer's over."

"Not me," Meg said. "I'm going to make it. Right to the top."

"Okay, okay." The clerk sighed wistfully. "So you're the next Jayne Mansfield. Lord knows you've got the shape. But it takes more than shape, kid. The woods are full of girls with big headlights. You need the breaks, too. And I talk too goddam much. Front!" he yelled.

A bellhop appeared. Almost as a reflex, he gave Meg an eyeing. The clerk said, "Take Miss Tandler up to 301, Nick."

Meg followed the bellhop into the elevator. It creaked and wheezed up to the third floor, and he led her down a hall carpeted with threadbare rugs to a small, dingy room at the end of the corridor. He put her suitcase on the rack, opened the blinds, showed her where the bathroom was, and gave her the key. She handed him a quarter. He pocketed it with a grin and said, "Anything you want, Miss Tandler, just phone down to the lobby. It'll be a pleasure. A real pleasure." He started out. "And if you aren't doing anything tonight, I'm off duty at six."

"Sorry, no," she said, and closed the door. You didn't get to the top by dating bellhops, she thought.

She dropped down onto the dilapidated armchair and surveyed the room. It wasn't very much of a place, she admitted. But she wouldn't be staying here long. Just until she had her bearings and could find an apartment someplace in the area. In the meantime, five dollars a night wouldn't upset the budget too tremendously much, provided she didn't stay here more than a couple of days.

Rising, she peeled off her sweater and skirt. She had worn them all the way from Idaho, and they were filthy. A moment later she added her half-slip, bra, panties, and knee-length stockings to the heap of laundry. It felt good to be out of the sweaty things. On her way into the bathroom, she caught sight of her body down to the thighs, reflected in the mirror behind the dresser, and automatically she drew her belly in, squared her shoulders, thrust out her breasts.

She was a big girl, five feet seven, with a lustrous cascade of deep auburn hair mantling her shoulders and back. She had not cut her hair since she was fifteen, and when she let it all out it descended in a surprising mass. Her skin was fair, almost pale after the long winter, and the red circles of her nipples stood out strikingly on the big rounded globes of her breasts. Her body was lush, full in the breasts and hips, but her waist was narrow, her belly flat, her legs lean and tapering. If her figure had any flaw, it was a slight overabundance of rear—though so slight that she had never worn a corset in her life.

Fifteen minutes under a cold spray left her fresh and full of life again. Already the long, hot, dusty bus ride was blurring and fading from her mind; Harmons Glen seemed like a confused and jumbled dream. She was in New York. First thing in the morning she was going to make her initial assault on the entertainment world. For a moment, as she stood toweling her body dry, the old dizziness returned. She saw her name in lights, her face on a dozen magazine covers, handsome men with clipped mustaches bending to kiss her hand, an ermine wrap on her shoulders, diamonds sparkling, flashbulbs exploding, champagne, champagne, champagne... Then reality interposed. She was just a naked girl in a cheap hotel room.

She walked to the mirror again and surveyed herself critically. She had something extra. She knew it. It was in the way her breasts rose and jutted forward, not drooping the way breasts that size usually did. It was in the way little flecks of gold sparkled in the depths of her eyes. It was in the sensuous slash of her mouth, the perfection of her nose, the way she held her head, the breathtaking flare of her hips.

Those things hadn't been learned. She had been born with them—a gift, the way some people are given the gift of mathematics or poetry or opera singing. For the first twenty years of her life she hadn't added anything to her natural gifts. She had remained stuck away in a two-bit town in a three-bit state, being ogled by hicks and fending off propositions. A lot of people had told her she should go to Hollywood and try to break into the movies. But she had known instinctively that that would be a mistake, a mistake that all too many pretty young girls make. If you went to Hollywood, you were swallowed up at once. You had to compete for attention not only with hundreds of other girls just as eager as you, but with the pros, the Mansfields and Monroes, who weren't quite ready to move aside for their successors.

No, the way to do it was to go to New York, at the other end of the country. To work up the ladder, taking a year or two, suddenly blossoming into fame. Then let Hollywood beckon *you*, instead of spending years trying to crack the wall on your own. After that, you had it made. So Meg had come to New York.

After a moment she walked away from the mirror. Unpacking her suitcase, she found a simple blouse and skirt, and some fresh underwear. She dressed. Even in a plain loose blouse, her figure was attention-getting. She buttoned it all the way to her throat; experimentally, she opened the two top buttons, observing in the mirror the tempting way the soft white mounds of flesh glinted up from her collar. Then she buttoned up again. Her heart raced; the champagne dream seized her again.

She locked up and rang for the elevator. The elevator boy watched her out of the corner of his eye as they rode down. Meg smiled quietly. It was annoying, in a way, to have every male above the age of puberty pant at her—but, she admitted, it was wonderful to be able to attract that kind of attention. *I draw them like a magnet*, she thought. *A sex magnet.*

She ate in a diner on 43rd Street, sitting by herself in the far corner. Afterward, she strolled around Times Square, watching in awe as night descended and the bright lights went on. Broadway surged with life. Meg moved along in the crowd, eyes wide, mouth agape. Neither the newsreels nor the picture magazines had ever prepared her for the enormity of it. She remembered when her school had gone on a trip to the Grand Canyon, and how stunned she had been by the size of it. Well, Times Square was as overpowering as that, only in a different way. It was a Grand Canyon that was man-made, a Canyon of lights and buildings, people and cars and noise.

She walked up to 50th Street and turned back south again. She made the acquaintance of the New York crowd quickly: as she crossed 45th Street in a surging mob, a hand was drawn firmly across her buttocks, and, again, at 48th Street, someone squeezed her breasts. Neither time could she see who had done it. She clung tight to her pocketbook, feeling dizziness and shock. But then she reminded herself that this was New York.

Wearily, she returned to the hotel, stopping off at a newsstand to buy a copy of *Variety*. It was dark, now; the night staff had come on duty at the hotel. She smiled at the new elevator boy as she rode upstairs.

Bolting her door carefully, she donned her pajamas and got into bed to read. Words raced up at her—news of new plays and movies, of casting for shows, of chorus-girls wanted. New York seemed to be screaming for talent. Dancers, singers, actresses—anything.

After a while she put the paper away and shut off the lamp above her bed. Through the half-opened window came the sound of Times Square, a never-ending dissonant symphony of horns and voices.

It was dinnertime in Harmons Glen, she thought. Probably everyone in town was talking about her tonight. Well, let them talk. Ever since she was sixteen, she had had a bad reputation in town; everybody had assumed that a girl with her kind of body couldn't *possibly* be a good girl.

Well, they had been wrong almost up till the end. Meg had let the boys kiss her, she had let them fondle her breasts, she had sometimes even let them put their hands between her legs. But no further.

Until a month ago. That night with Jack, she thought. She had gone too far that night. Much too far. And so, finally, she had come to merit her reputation. It was one of the reasons why she had been able to make the break with Harmons Glen at last. Now that Jack had slept with her, he seemed to think he owned her—and, if she stayed there any longer, she would probably have come to think so too. And that would have been the end of her career, the end of her life; she would have married Jack and spent the rest of her years raising kids and potatoes, while her breasts grew flabby from nursing and her hands thick from toil, and by the time she was thirty she would be just another tired-out farm woman.

Not for me, she had decided.

So Jack had slept with her one night after a movie, getting what he wanted from her after chasing it for two years, and the next day he had come around and said, "We sort of jumped the gun last night, didn't we?"

"Yeah. We sure did."

"Well, don't let is upset you, honey. I'll make an honest woman out of you before the summer's out. How about June 23 for the date, and a honeymoon in Yellowstone Park?"

"No, Jack."

"Too soon? Don't you want to be a June bride, hon?"

"There isn't going to be any wedding, Jack."

"Huh? But—last night—"

"Last night you got my bra off before I knew what was going on, and I guess I couldn't stop myself after that. But you've had it, Jack. I'm going to New York City middle of April."

"New York City—?"

"I've got a thousand dollars saved, and nobody's going to stop me. You think I'm going to spend the rest of my life laying for a potato farmer, Jack? Uh-uh. Not this girl. Not little Meg."

Jack had left, hurt, bewildered. He had pestered her for days after that, but she had nothing more to say. She told her family, she bought her ticket, she left. Now Idaho was thousands of miles behind her.

Tomorrow, she thought. *Tomorrow I get my first step on the ladder. Tomorrow's a big day.*

She closed her eyes and was asleep almost instantly. She dreamed of champagne and glaring floodlights.

Two

The gold letters on the frosted glass door read,

MAX BONAVENTURA
Theatrical Agent
Walk in

Meg paused wearily outside. It was three in the afternoon; she had been tramping around all day. This was the sixth place she had tried. If she had expected to be welcomed with a contract the moment she stepped through the door of the first agency, she was getting rid of those delusions now. At the first place, there had been twenty other girls waiting ahead of her. For an hour and a half she had fidgeted in an anteroom, eyeing the other girls and mentally stacking herself up against them, only to be told by a lacquered receptionist that no apprentices were being considered—experienced girls only.

The second place had nothing for her; the third at least gave her a hearing and told her to get back on the bus for Idaho right away—"New York is loaded with kids who think they're it, Miss Tandler. You'll be wise to go home and marry some swell guy."

At the fourth, and at the fifth, no go. Now the sixth. Meg's legs ached. The fourth place was not seeing anyone except by appointment. The fifth told her to come back as a blonde. Now the sixth. *Max Bonaventura, Theatrical Agent. Walk in.* There were at least two hundred agencies listed in the telephone book. She hoped she wouldn't have to go to all two hundred of them before anything happened.

She opened the door.

There was a receptionist's cubicle, but no one was there. The door, in closing, tinkled a little bell, and a short, dark-complexioned man emerged from an inner office.

"I'm looking for Mr. Bonaventura," Meg said, stumbling over the unfamiliar Italian name.

"I'm he. My receptionist is—ah—out sick today. Won't you come in, Miss—Miss—"

"Tandler. Meg Tandler."

"Miss Tandler. Right this way."

He led her into the inner office and shut the door. It was a small room, cluttered with piles of papers, old newspapers, magazines, sheet music. There was a leather couch in one corner, a rickety-looking piano in another. He sat down back of the desk and gestured to Meg to take the seat facing him. The window behind him opened out onto Broadway, but all Meg could see was the tarred roof of a smaller building adjoining.

Bonaventura studied her out of large, liquid eyes. He was a lean little man, balding, big-nosed, olive-skinned. He said, "You're looking for work, Miss Tandler?"

"That's right."

"What can you do?"

"I can sing, dance, act a little. Or just stand around and look decorative."

"Professional experience?"

Meg drew a breath. "None, I'm afraid. Just local high school talent shows, I mean. And—"

"All right. All right. Where are you from, Meg?"

"Idaho."

"Just get to New York?"

"Yesterday."

"And you want to get into show business."

"Well, of course, Mr. Bonaventura—"

The little man leaned back, took out a cigarette case, and carefully extracted a cigarette without offering her one. He lit it and puffed for a moment. Meg took advantage of the silence to shove forward her little cardboard photograph folder.

"I've got some shots of myself here, Mr. Bonaventura. In bathing suits, evening gowns, you know—"

"Let's see."

She handed him the folder. He pulled the rubber band off with quick birdlike motions, opened the folder, leafed through the pictures. Jack had taken most of them. Meg waited, reddening a little when he came to the ones of her in that tight bathing suit.

He remained silent after he had closed the folder up. After a long moment he said, "Well, Meg, you're a good-looking girl."

"Thank you, sir."

"How old are you?"

"Almost twenty, sir."

"Cut out the *sir* business. I don't make enough to deserve it."

"Do you think I'll have a chance?" she asked.

"Sure. Sure. Matter of fact, I've got some work for you right now."

"Really?"

"Really. There's a convention going on at the Plaza, and they want a few pretty girls to serve as hostesses. You wear a low-cut dress, pour drinks, smile at the delegates. No sex stuff—you're just there as a decoration. Four hours, fifteen bucks. I get 25%. I can get you plenty of that stuff, Meg. You'll make seventy or eighty bucks a week."

"Just pouring drinks?"

"That's right."

"But I can sing and dance," she said feebly. "I can act."

"No, you can't. You can't act worth a damn. You can't dance. You can't sing."

Her eyes widened. "How do you know? You haven't even heard me!"

"I don't need to, girlie. You're green. You're an amateur. Maybe you can carry a tune, and maybe you were a smash hit in the high school play. But that's about it, Meg. Believe me—I can tell." Bonaventura grinned. "So we can skip the audition. Can I put you down for the convention job?"

"No."

"Don't be silly," he said, wheedling. "It's money, isn't it? What do you want—a lead in the next Rodgers & Hammerstein?"

"It isn't what I want to do."

"You've been tramping around all day, I bet. And getting nowhere. *'Don't call us, we'll call you,'* that kind of crap. And here I am offering you something solid, cash on the line, and you stick your nose up in the air."

"I've got talent, Mr. Bonaventura," Meg said icily. "Maybe you won't let me demonstrate it, but I've got it. And I'm damned if I'm going to take a quickie drink pouring job just because you're looking for a girl to fill a slot for somebody!" She stormed toward the door. "Good afternoon. And thanks for your time."

"Hold it!" Bonaventura snapped. *"Hold it!"*

Meg paused at the door, frowning. "What?"

The agent leaped out from behind his desk, crossing the room quickly arid closing the door, "Christ, that was something!"

"What was?"

"The temper. The eyes. The whole thing."

"I'm afraid I can't spend any more time—"

"Sit down," Bonaventura said. It was a command. His voice crackled. Surprised, Meg slumped back into the seat. Bonaventura remained at the door, leaning against it as if to prevent her from escaping. He said, "I spotted you the minute you walked in that door. I've been playing it cool ever since. I was just testing you, offering you that hostess job. I wanted to see if you had the stuff—the stuff of greatness. And you did. You turned it down. You didn't jump for the quick buck. You stuck to your goals. That's what I was waiting to see."

"I don't understand you."

"Sure you do. Listen, what do you want out of this career of yours? With your figure, you can get a job in any chorus line. For the next fifteen years you can make a guaranteed $7000 a year. Of course, then you're finished, and you're nowhere. But it's comfortable while you're going along. Is that what you want?"

"No"

"I didn't think so. You want the top. You've got legs and a pair of knockers, and you've got a devil inside you pushing you along. Right?"

Meg smiled. "Right."

"Okay, then. You saved your nickels and came to the Big City, and now you're making the rounds looking for an opening. With a little luck, you'd get that chorine job. And that would be the end of you. You get mixed up in a big agency and they find you work often enough to give you enough to eat, and that's as far as you get. With me it's different. I'm more than an agent. I'm a *manager*. A trainer. I'll build your career, Meg. It'll take hard work and sweat and tears, but before I'm through with you you'll be right up there on top."

The little man seemed to glow with enthusiasm. Nervously, Meg crossed and re-crossed her legs. "How did you know—what I wanted—?"

"Every girl who comes to New York wants to hit the big time. But it was written all over your face. You've got it bad. And, get this—when you want something in life really bad, you can get it. Every time. It's just a matter of putting your heart and mind to it."

"Do you really think so?"

"I know so," Bonaventura said. He lit another cigarette. "First thing is, you've got to trust me."

"I don't know you."

"You will," he said. "Starting now. I'm in lousy shape. My receptionist isn't sick. She's working for somebody else, because I can't afford her. I owe money. I'm going to have trouble paying my phone bill next month."

"That isn't very encouraging to me."

"It ought to be. A hungry agent's the best kind, kid. I'll be the kind who'll really get down there and work for you. I have to. I need the dough. I've been sitting here for years, waiting for something like you to come along. And I'm not going to miss the chance now."

"But are you sure you can help me, Mr. Bonaventura?"

"The name is Max. And yes, I'm sure. We'll start right now. Let's hear you sing, for a starter." He picked up a pile of sheet music and plopped it in front of her on the desk. "Here. Pick something out from here—something you know. Anything at all—Oldies, newies, anything."

She took the top song off the stack. It was from *Oklahoma*, and that had been the senior show at school. "Here. Let's try this one."

Bonaventura played, and she sang. She was nervous, and the voice wouldn't open up for her the right way, but the agent nodded when she was through.

"Okay," he said. "You can carry a tune. Your delivery is lousy, but that can be fixed. The important thing is that the raw talent is there. If you need to sing in a show, you'll be able to do it. We'll skip the dancing and acting for now. Stand up."

Too dazed to argue, Meg stood up. She began to realize that the brusqueness of the little man was his normal manner—that he never spoke gently. He stepped back, eyeing her. Then he pointed to her breasts.

"Is the bazoom real?"

"You mean my figure?"

"I mean the bazoom. The knockers, the knobs, the headlights, the—the whatever you call them in Idaho. Are they genuine?"

"Of course!"

"This I don't believe. Stacking like that gotta be supported with an affidavit. We gotta play it honest, both of us."

"I'm telling you the truth."

"Show me."

The two quiet words exploded like bombshells in Meg's ears. She felt her cheeks go hot, and she reached for her handbag. Bonaventura caught her wrist and pulled her back.

"Let go of me," she said. "Maybe I'm a greenhorn from the sticks, but I'm not dumb enough to go for the casting-couch routine."

Bonaventura beamed. "Listen to me, baby. To me you're so much meat. So much profitable meat, you get me. But meat all the same. Flesh. I got a motto, *Never crap where you eat*. You get me? You're my meal ticket. I can get a piece of ass anywhere, but I can't get the next Marilyn Monroe for a fiver."

"I'm not taking off my clothes."

Bonaventura's shoulders slumped. "Then you better get on the next train back to Idaho. This ain't any business for bluenoses, honey.

Between here and the gravy train you'll be taking off your clothes plenty, baby. You'll be undressing every time there's dough in it. Better get that idea through your head right now. I'm only the first. And me, I think of you like I think of a statue. I want to see the merchandise, I ain't going to risk getting taken in by a lot of foam rubber." He stubbed out his cigarette. "Make up your mind, Meg. Either you peel on demand, or you go home to the farm. Which is it?"

She was silent for a long moment. Butterflies were racing around in her stomach. She didn't like the idea of taking her clothes off for this rabbitty little man. There was something disgusting about undressing for appraisal, to be looked over like a heifer on the market. But yet—if he could steer her in the direction she wanted to go—

She moistened her lips. Then, with trembling hands, she reached for the first button of her blouse.

Bonaventura stepped back. His face became terribly pale, and Meg could see that the unveiling was having its effect on him. She finished taking off her blouse and hung it neatly over the back of her chair. Pausing for a moment to tighten the suspense, she reached around between her shoulder blades and unsnapped her bra. The tight-straining cups dropped away. She felt cool air blowing past her nipples. Her breasts thrust forward, high and firm, round and full. Blazing heat sprang out on her face and shoulders.

"Well?" she asked coldly.

"Christ," Bonaventura breathed. "Christ almighty everlasting."

"You believe they're real, now?"

"I see it, but I don't believe it," he whispered. "I see it, but I don't believe it."

"You want to see the rest?"

"Not if you're embarrassed."

"You said I'd be peeling. Okay, I'm willing to peel." She unsnapped her waistband and stepped out of skirt and half-slip simultaneously. She rolled her panties down over her hips to the floor. Proud and erect, naked and with lessening shame, she stood in the middle of the room, turning slowly to give Bonaventura the full view.

After a moment he walked toward the leather couch and sank down heavily on it. He put his face in his hands. "Okay," he said in a hoarse, hollow voice, "Put your clothes on. Fast. Before I lose control of myself, you hear?"

"You like it?"

"Christ," he said. "Christ almighty in heaven. I've never seen anything like it. A dumb little Idaho farm girl, and she radiates sex like crazy. Put the clothes back on, you hear me?"

Without hurrying, Meg bent over, retrieved the panties, pulled them up. She forced the heavy globes of her breasts back into the bra. She buttoned the blouse and put on the slip and skirt.

Bonaventura looked up. He was pale and shaky, and driblets of sweat glistened on his forehead. "You ever been married?" he asked.

"Never."

"You ever—been with a man? You know what I mean."

Meg felt the color return to her face. "Once."

"Just once?"

"That's all. Don't you believe me?"

"Baby, I believe anything you have to say. Who was the guy?"

"My boyfriend back home. We went to the movies and he got me a little tanked up afterward and he got inside my bra and I didn't stop him. That was about a month ago. That was the only time."

"Did you—enjoy it?"

Meg shrugged. "It didn't matter one way or the other, much. They say it never does, the first time."

"I guess so. Well, okay—look, Meg, is it a deal, you and me? I want a straight 25% interest. And I want you to give me absolute control over your career. That means no outsiders cutting in."

"How do you mean, absolute?"

"I'll tell you what to dress and how to look. I'll teach you to sing and act and dance. I'll tell you when to take your clothes off and when to put them on. I'll tell you when to go to bed with people. You're going to have to do some sleeping around, get me? Nobody gets to the top without paying for it. But you don't let anybody touch you who can't do you some good."

"Suppose—suppose I don't let *anybody* touch me."

"Back to Idaho."

"So I've got to be a whore, too."

"Listen, baby, what you've lost you can't ever get back. What does it matter if you crawl into a couple more sacks on the way up? It'll be worth your while. Believe me, it will."

She shrugged and said, "We'll see."

"Will you sign a contract now?"

"I want to think about it."

"Christ, baby, I'm *with* you! I'm not going to hurt you. I'm going to make millions for you—and twenty-five percent of millions for me. A nice shiny red Mercedes 300SL for you, and a Jag for me. Champagne for you, bourbon for me. But I don't want to lose you. We need each other, you and me. You've got the assets, I've got the know-how. And to-gether—"

"Straight to the top," Meg said.

"Straight to the top is right. Will you sign?"

He shoved the contract at her, along with a ballpoint pen. She read quickly through it, hardly caring. She had an intuitive belief that Bonaventura would not swindle her or take advantage of her, and that was enough. She signed her name, in her prim, school-girlish handwriting. Bonaventura gripped her hand.

"It's a deal, then."

"Right," she said. She felt dizzy again. It had been a long, hectic day—and, after only two days in New York, she was on her way. She had a manager who understood her goals and was determined to get her there. She was on her way.

"Let's drink to us," Bonaventura said. "I'll shut up the office and we'll go grab us some refreshment." He came around from behind the desk and stood next to her. She was an inch taller than he was. Playfully, he tapped her between the breasts. "Christ, but you're built. If I wasn't your manager, I'd proposition you myself. But I got a policy, and I gotta stick by it. Let's go get us some drinks."

Three

After an hour together in a booth at the back of a 55th Street bar, they had worked out a complete program for Meg's future. Bonaventura had done most of the talking.

"The raw material's pretty good," Bonaventura said. "And that's putting it mildly. You're a little pale, that's all. Couple of weeks under the sunlamp ought to do it. I want you tan *all* over, hear?" He clinked the ice cubes together in his drink. "We'll get you signed up for some massages, too. I'd like about half an inch paddled off your rear end."

Meg giggled. She had had two drinks, and they were going to her head. "I've always been too big there."

"Well, it doesn't hurt to be big there. But not *too* big, get me." Bonaventura grinned amiably. "I think we'll keep your hair the way it is. Short hair is the thing right now, but you've got such a swell head that maybe we can start a new thing. You know, once you make a big hit everybody will start growing their hair long again to imitate you."

"I wouldn't want to cut it."

"No, don't." He drummed on the tabletop and went on, "There's also the business of your name. Meg Tandler just won't do."

"But it's my name!"

"Sure it is. And Marilyn Monroe was once called Norma Something-

or-other, too. But we'll have to change it. Meg's too dinky, Tandler's too hard to say. We need something smoother. Ah—Meg. Meg Something. I need a last name."

"Meg Lawrence?" she suggested. "Lawrence is my father's first name."

Bonaventura shook his head emphatically. "Uh-uh. Lawrence is a man's name. Masculine connotations won't go. We've got to play this real smart, real Madison Avenue. Like I mean, you can't put a man's name on a girl and expect her to reach out and catch you. Get me?"

"I don't think so," Meg said doubtfully.

"Okay. It's probably a hogwash theory anyway. But Meg Lawrence is no good. We need something softer, more feminine. *Loring*. Yeah. That's it. You'll be Meg Loring."

Meg frowned. "Meg Loring," she said oddly, as though trying her new name on for size. "It sounds so strange."

"Don't fret about it," Bonaventura told her. "It takes time to get used to a new name. But Meg Loring's going to be a name that goes echoing through the universe, hear me!" He signaled to the waiter. "Two more bourbons, please."

"Meg Loring," Meg repeated. "Meg Loring. I'm starting to like it."

"It fits like a glove," Bonaventura assured her. "Now—the rest of this campaign comes off like clockwork. I'll get you hooked up with a voice coach, a dance-and-posture expert, the works. We'll enhance your natural sexiness with a little professional poise. But I don't want to overdo it, get me? You've got it, right now, and I don't want to mess it. Meg Loring, 1960's Goddess of Sex."

Meg laughed. "They'll be surprised back home, I'll bet."

"They'll be wowed." Bonaventura leaned forward. "Couple of months, we'll get you into a beauty contest. Miss Gowanus, something like that. You'll win it going away. We use that as a springboard for the Miss Galaxy contest in August. You win that too. That gives you a screen test in Hollywood. Nine out of ten Miss Galaxy dames fizzle the test. You won't. You'll get a contract and a big part. The studio press agents will go to town on you. You'll be on every magazine cover. Money will flow in."

Dizzy, Meg said, "But how can you be *sure* I'll win these contests? And get the movie part?"

"You'll win the local contest simply because you're a knockout," Bonaventura said. "You'll cop Miss Galaxy because I'll have dough spread all over the place, and because if necessary you'll lay half the judges."

"But—"

"I said you'll lay half the judges," Bonaventura whispered harshly.

"You'll lay them sideways and upside-down if that'll get your vote. If there are any lesbian judges, you'll lay them too." The agent's eyes had a feverish, almost demonic glint. "We aren't gonna do this by halves, honey. You're going right to the top—and you're getting there by every method in the book."

Confused, Meg looked down at her drink and bit her lip. She felt frightened by Bonaventura, frightened by the need to do the things he said she would have to. But, always driving her on, was the compulsion to be ahead, to shine in the firmament, to rise to glory. And if she had to use her body, she would, she told herself.

"So you'll win the beauty contest," Bonaventura said. "Then comes Hollywood. You'll get the contract. You'll sleep with the producer and you'll sleep with his twelve-year-old nephew, if that's what they want you to do. But you won't just be whoring around. You'll be sleeping only with people who can help you get ahead." He smiled and looked off into the distance. "Then, after you've made the movie, we can do the calendar stunt, and then—" He shrugged. "Hell, one thing at a time. If we sit here much longer I'll be planning your future clear into the 1980s. Let's get out of here."

Meg gulped what was left of her drink and stood up. Her legs felt wobbly.

"I—I think I had too much to drink," she said thickly.

Bonaventura frowned. "Can't hold the booze, eh?"

"I'm—not used to drinking."

"Get used to it, then. But one drink at a time, and never more than you can hold. I want you in absolute control of yourself all the time. You've *got* to be, if we're going to make the grade. No boozing past your limit, hear?"

"S-sure, Max."

"Okay. And no dating anybody without my approval. And no being seen in public in the wrong places. You've got to put your life into my hands, one hundred five percent."

"Okay, Max," Meg said woozily. She was feeling dizzier by the minute. The excitement of the agent's high-pressure talk, the drinks, the unseasonable heat, were all taking their effect. "I think I'd better go home, Max."

"Where's that?"

"Jenning Hotel. 44th Street."

"Christ, you're living in a *hotel?*"

"Just till I find a place."

"What are they soaking you?"

"Five dollars a night."

"A hundred fifty a month," Bonaventura said. "For one lousy room in a fleabag hotel. We can do you better than that. I'll get you a place in the morning. Two or three rooms, kitchen, bath, midtown Manhattan. And no more than a hundred twenty a month. How much dough do you have, anyway?"

"I came here with a thousand."

"If you need more, can you wire the folks in Idaho for it?"

"I don't think so. They don't have much—and they don't approve of my being here."

Bonaventura nibbled a cuticle. "A thousand won't last long here. And I don't have much loose cash myself." He shrugged. "But don't worry. I'll promote a deal. Let's get you taken home, first."

He hailed a cab and helped Meg into it. Almost before they had pulled away from the curb, they were coming to a halt in front of her hotel. Bonaventura gave the cabbie a dollar and they went in.

"Here," Meg said, as they reached her floor. "I don't think I could get the key into the hole. You better open the door."

He took the key from her. "Christ, alcohol really stones you, huh? Three lousy bourbon-and-gingers and you don't know which way is up. We've gotta watch that. It could be your Achilles heel."

Bonaventura opened the door. Meg tumbled past him into the room and sprawled out on the bed. She kicked off her shoes. Her skirt was up over her knees, and her legs were spread.

She felt Bonaventura pulling down her skirt. He murmured, "Don't make things hard for me, baby."

"Help me off with my clothes. I want to go to bed, Max."

"Listen, baby, don't tempt me. I want to keep this strictly business, and I mean strictly."

She opened her eyes. Bonaventura's pale, sweating face hovered above her. She smiled. "You're afraid of me, aren't you, Max?"

"What the hell do you mean, afraid of you?"

"Just what I said. You don't want to get too close to me. You're afraid you'll get burned."

His eyes narrowed. "Yeah," he said quietly. "Yeah, it's something like that. You're out of my class, Meg. *Meg.* I'd crawl right into bed with you now, only you're not for me, and I know it."

"Come on. Undress me and come to bed with me," she said coquettishly.

"Don't play games, Meg." Bonaventura's lips were trembling. "Don't mess."

"I mean it, Max."

"You're drunk. Stinking drunk. I'm gonna leave. You get undressed and get into bed and stay there. I'll call you first thing in the morning, hear?"

"You sure you don't wanta sleep over, Max?"

"I'm leaving. And heaven help you if you have any company in here tonight!"

He strode out, slamming the door loudly behind him. Meg giggled, the giggle rising to near-hysterical laugh. Abruptly she became quiet. She lay stretched out on the bed, listening to the booming of her own heart, and as the minutes passed the giddiness left her. She sat up. Her head was throbbing and she was drenched in perspiration. It was dinner time, but she had no appetite for food.

She undressed and went into the shower, standing under the spigot with the water as cold as she could bear it. *Meg Loring*, she thought over and over again. *Meg Loring, Goddess of Sex. I'm Meg Loring now.*

Stepping out of the shower, she toweled the lushness of her body dry. She was thinking about Bonaventura, thinking that he was a funny little character—so obviously anxious to go to bed with her, yet restraining himself because he was afraid it would somehow cheapen her, somehow tarnish her gleam to sleep with her own manager. It was like not mating a prize heifer with a scrawny bull. You didn't do it, because it would be an unworthy mating for the heifer.

She got into bed and lay there with her eyes closed, dreaming about the future Bonaventura had invented for her. She didn't like the idea of having to sleep with people to win prizes and contracts. She remembered the one sex experience she had had. There hadn't been any pleasure in it—only the sharp, savage pain of penetration, and the weight of Jack's grunting body on her own. But maybe she hadn't liked it because it was her first time. And most likely Jack wasn't as delicate as some men might be while making love. She couldn't judge sex by that one experience, she told herself. Maybe she would enjoy it. At least, it probably wouldn't hurt as much the next time. She could just lie back, blanking out her mind, letting the man do whatever he wanted with her, and telling herself that in the long run the few minutes of sweating and writhing would net her tremendous dividends in fame and fortune.

She daydreamed for an hour or two, picturing her name up in lights at all the big theaters, seeing her face smiling down from a thousand newsstands. Then she realized she was hungry. It was only nine o'clock, too early to go to sleep. But she didn't feel like going out again, not after her shower.

She picked up the telephone. The operator answered and Meg said, "Can I have some food sent up to my room?"

"Certainly, Miss. I'll take your order."

"Make it—oh, an open-faced hamburger sandwich and coca-cola."

"I'll have the boy bring it up in a few minutes," the operator said.

Meg put the phone back on the hook and relaxed again. Ten minutes passed, and then someone knocked. She opened her eyes, startled.

"Who is it?"

"Room Service, Ma'am."

She flew out of bed and hurriedly grabbed her robe. "Just a minute," she called, pulling the belt tight around her. It was a gauzy kind of robe, and you were supposed to wear something underneath it. But there wasn't time for that; she didn't want to keep the boy waiting out there. She went to the door.

The bellhop was about seventeen, and he nearly dropped the tray when he saw Meg. "W-where should I put it, Miss?"

"On the dresser, please."

He put the tray down and turned, slowly, his eyes widening enormously. His Adam's-apple moved in a visible gulp. Meg found a quarter and handed it to him, and he took it as though hypnotized, without removing his eyes from her.

"W-would you sign the check, Miss?"

She scribbled her name. He nodded and backed out of the room, looking dazed. When he was gone, Meg turned toward the mirror to see what sort of an appearance she had made. A broad grin came to her face. The robe was drawn tight against her bosom, revealing the upper halves of those twin snowy hills. The red buttons of her nipples showed plainly through the pale blue fabric of the gown. And the rest of her body was hidden as though only by fine smoke. She might just as well have answered the door in the nude. She chuckled at the impact she had had on the bellhop: the sight of her half-revealed body had turned him to mush!

And it's going to be like that all the way up the hill, she thought. *Max is right. I just have to flash my body and I can get anything I want. Anything in the whole universe. And I'm going to take it while I'm still good-looking enough to be able to get it.*

She devoured the hamburger, finding herself hungrier than she thought. For a moment she toyed with the notion of sending for another one and giving the bellhop a thrill, but she vetoed the notion. Max wouldn't approve. She had nothing to gain by showing herself off to hotel bellhops.

Instead, she went to sleep. This time, sleep came quickly, and it was dreamless. She was awakened by the harsh jangling of the telephone, seemingly only a few moments after closing her eyes, and she was surprised to realize it was morning. The wristwatch on the table next to the bed read half past nine.

"Hello?"

"Honey, this is Max. You up yet?"

"No."

"Well, rise and shine. Every minute counts between here and August, remember. Got a hangover?"

"I don't think so."

"Good. You go right to bed last night?"

"I had a hamburger sent up first."

"Did you fool around with the bellhop?"

"*Max!*"

"Don't Max me. Did you?"

"He was just a kid. He was so dazed he didn't know whether he was coming or going. He put the tray down and left, I swear it. If you're going to give me the third degree every time you leave me alone, I'm—"

"Okay, okay. Listen, how fast can you get dressed and out?"

"Twenty minutes. Why?"

"I've been busy, baby. You've got a date at the beauty parlor at noon, for sunlamp and rubdown. Meantime I've got someone I want you to meet. Or rather I want him to meet you. He's an angel."

"I don't get it."

"He's got dough, honeybun. I want him to lend me five thousand bucks to cover preliminary expenses of getting you going. The collateral is you. I arranged for him to meet you and inspect the merchandise."

"Another strip act?" Meg asked.

"Nah, nothing like that. This is business, straight business. He wants to look you over. In clothes."

"Where do I meet you?"

"We'll pick you up. Be down in front of the hotel at ten. We'll come by in a cab."

"Right."

"Oh—wear something low, like I mean *low*. Like showing everything but the nipples, if you've got something like that. Simple, wholesome sex—it hooks them every time. See you at ten, baby."

Meg checked through her skimpy wardrobe rapidly, and found something that seemed ideal. It was a half-bra that went with her low-cut evening gown. It hugged the lower halves of her breasts, pushing them upward and forward and just barely concealing the nipples. She donned it and put on over it a man-cut white blouse, leaving the first and third buttons open. That would give a pretty enticing view to a prospective backer, she decided.

She was five minutes late getting downstairs. The cab was waiting across the street from the hotel, and she came running out, doing the fastest trot she could considering that her skirt was so tight it kept her from doing more than a half-stride. She felt her breasts bouncing with each step she took.

Max was waiting in the cab with a long-legged, mustached man of about fifty, who looked well-dressed and well-heeled. She made sure to bend over as she entered the cab, giving the backer a good view through her open button.

"Jerry Marsh, I want you to meet Meg Loring. Meg, Jerry. Jerry's one of my oldest friends."

"Pleased," Meg said.

"More than pleased," Marsh replied. "Delighted." He winked. Without a cue from Bonaventura, Meg was uncertain whether or not a return wink would be appropriate. She decided against it. She merely smiled, and nestled down between the two men on the back seat.

"Hotel New Yorker," Bonaventura said.

Meg glanced to her left. Marsh's eyes were riveted on the bare patch of bosom. She looked away, to her right, at Bonaventura. The agent nudged her with his elbow and quickly gestured with one hand, forming a circle with finger and thumb. *Everything's fine*, he was telling her. *You did okay, baby*.

She relaxed. Jerry Marsh's thigh was pressed tight against hers, and his arm rested against the swelling side of her left breast. Everything was going to be easy, she realized. As easy as ABC.

Four

They had breakfast at the New Yorker coffee shop. Marsh sat opposite her, studying her intently out of pale blue eyes. Meg sat quietly, looking down at her food, while Bonaventura and Marsh reminisced. Abruptly, as coffee was being served, Marsh said, "This girl you've got here, Max. I like her."

"I knew you would."

"How much do you need?"

"Call it five thousand."

Marsh nodded, looking Meg over carefully. She met his gaze, but there was such naked desire in it that she had to turn away.

"Five thousand," Marsh said. "Okay. You can have it, Max."

"Terms?"

"Don't worry about that."

"Uh-uh, Jerry. Spell 'em out."

"I'd rather talk about it in private. Just the two of us, Max."

Bonaventura smiled and shook his head. "You got the wrong idea, Jerry. I'm not selling the girl."

"I never said—"

"I can read your mind."

Color rose in Marsh's face. He ran his fingers through his graying hair, drew a deep breath, and said, "You can have the five thousand for one year, no interest, if Miss Loring accompanies me to Connecticut for this coming weekend."

Meg burst out, "I wouldn't dream of—"

Bonaventura kicked her, hard, and she shut up. The agent said quickly, "Absolutely nix, Jerry. This girl isn't that kind at all. And I guess we'd better look elsewhere for our loan."

He started to rise, and Meg got up with him. Scowling, Marsh said, "If that's the final answer, I'll change my offer. You can have the five grand without interest, but I want a two percent interest in all of Miss Loring's future earnings."

"I'm not slicing the melon."

"One percent."

"Nix, Jerry."

"You'd think you were sitting on a gold mine, the way you talk," Marsh grunted, "Okay, you name the deal, then. I'll listen."

"Lend me the five G's for one year at five percent. No security except Miss Loring's potential earnings. Well?"

Marsh hesitated for a moment. Then he said, "All right, Max. You'll get your check in the morning. Only because you're an old friend—"

"Sure, Jerry. Sure. Thanks. Thanks a million."

Outside the hotel, after Marsh had paid the check and left them, Meg said, "Did you know that he was going to pull that Connecticut proposition?"

Bonaventura shrugged. "I guessed he might."

"It cost you $250 to turn him down," Meg said.

"That's good money for a weekend in Connecticut, isn't it?"

"Damned right it is. But Marsh isn't worth buttering up. I'd rather pay the five percent than let him be able to spread the word around that he slept with Meg Loring to pay the interest on a loan. When you start getting into the sack with people, it'll be for bigger prizes than a piddling two and a half bills." He looked at his watch. "Half past eleven already. I'm going to dump you off at the beauty parlor while I go hunt up an apartment for you. I'll pick you up again around one-thirty."

They taxied uptown to Fiftieth Street, and Bonaventura led her up two flights of stairs and into the waiting room of an expensive-looking place. A white-smocked fortyish woman with hard eyes and a grim professional smile came out.

"Hello, Max. This is the new sensation?"

"Edna Hayes, meet Meg Loring. How does she look, Edna?"

"She'll do," Edna Hayes said in her mannish voice. "She needs work, though."

"That's why I brought her here. Two weeks of sunlamp and massage. Just to round her into shape for the Miss Galaxy contest, you know."

"It'll cost you, Max. No more credit around here, no matter what kind of a knockout you've got."

Bonaventura flashed a chilly grin. "I just had breakfast with Jerry Marsh. He's staking me. Don't worry about the bill. Just do your best." He turned to Meg. "So long, chicken. I'll pick you up here at half past one, don't forget." He blew a kiss at both women and darted out the door.

Meg smiled uncertainly at Edna Hayes, who stepped back sizing her up. "Well," she said finally, "You've got a build. If it's real, anyway—and I'll be finding that out any minute. How'd you get mixed up with Max, anyway?"

Meg fidgeted. "Picked him out of the phone book, I guess."

"As good a way as any."

"Isn't he a good agent?" Meg asked.

"He's the best, girlie. All he's been missing is one really good property, and I think he's got that now. Come on inside."

Meg followed the older woman through a series of winding passageways. In rooms on either side of the passageway, Meg saw women of all ages and in every stage of undress being beautified—in steam rooms, mudpacks, massages, sunlamps, the works. Edna Hayes paused in front of an empty cubicle and pushed open the door.

"In here, honey."

Meg stepped in. The room was small and overheated. It contained a long upholstered table, a sink, a closet, a sunlamp. Edna Hayes pointed to the table. "Get your clothes off and lie down. We'll give you half an hour of the lamp, then the massage. Do you ever have trouble with sunburn?"

"Not really. I get red the first day, but it never hurts me. And then I get tan."

"Okay. I'd hate to give you blisters. Hang your stuff in the closet."

Meg undressed, and oddly she felt more self-conscious removing her clothing in front of Edna Hayes than she had before Max Bonaventura. Edna stood by, her arms folded, watching closely as Meg removed each article of clothing. At last she was completely nude. She turned toward Edna and was surprised to see a look of frank fascination in the older woman's eyes.

"You really *are* built," she murmured. "Well, old Max is in the dough this time."

Meg said nothing. She felt almost like curling up in a ball, pulling her knees up to her breasts to hide her nakedness from this strange woman's inquisitive gaze. Edna Hayes took a pair of goggles from the closet and handed them to Meg.

"Here. Put these things on and lie down on your back over there. Fifteen minutes on each side. I'll come back when the half hour's up, but in any case the timer will shut the lamp off. There'll be a gong after fifteen minutes, and you flip over."

Meg lay down on the table. Edna stood above her, adjusting her arms, and—accidentally, it seemed—managing to brush her hands over Meg's breasts while getting her into the proper position.

"Just lie still and don't look at the bulb, honey. And try not to move. We want a nice even tan, all over you. I'll be back in half an hour."

Meg closed her eyes. She heard the door shut, and she relaxed, letting her body go limp, feeling the delicious radiance streaming down over her. Light bathed her breasts, her hips; her thighs; the ultraviolet beams penetrated her loins, warming her, causing the secret hidden organs to unfold like flowers rising toward the sunlight. It was wonderful to lie there letting that incredible warmth caress her skin. Her nipples began to tingle; she had never exposed them to sunlight before, and they were particularly sensitive to the warm beams. She could almost feel her skin growing rosy, entering into the first stages of the tan.

The fifteen-minute bell sounded all too soon; Meg stirred reluctantly, turning over to present her back and buttocks to the glowing bulb. She lay quietly, becoming drowsy in the pleasant warmth. Abruptly the timer clicked; the bulb above her dimmed, and almost immediately the room seemed to grow cooler. Meg waited for Edna Hayes to return.

Perhaps five minutes went by. Then the door opened. Edna walked in—and, to Meg's amazement, there was a young man with her.

"Hey!" Meg yelled, reaching for a towel that hung nearby, and draping it over her bare body from breasts to mid-thigh. "Why didn't you warn me you were bringing company!"

"You don't have to worry about Joe," Edna said. "You're in no danger with him, believe me."

Meg eyed the young man uneasily. He was no more than twenty-five, slim, lithe, with a great mass of curly, glossy black hair. His eyes were soft, almost feminine. And there was a feminine quality about his smile, too, and about the way he walked as he advanced toward the table.

"If Miss Loring will please lie down on her stomach," he said, in a softly purring voice with just the hint of a foreign accent. "I will do my best to remove the unwanted flesh of mademoiselle's derriere."

"Don't be embarrassed, honey," Edna said. "Joe has paddled the rears of some of New York's fanciest society women. He won't be any threat to your virtue."

Meg dropped the towel and rolled over. The masseur leaned on the table above her, studying her body as though a diamond cutter planning his first stroke.

"I'll be back later, dearie," Edna Hayes said. "Just in case you have any complaints."

She left. Meg felt the masseur's fingers delicately touch the skin of her back and travel down her body, over her buttocks to the thighs.

"I am searching out the muscles," he explained softly. "Now we may begin."

His hands rested on her buttocks, one palm on each plump cheek. The feel of a man's hands against her buttocks sent a strange new tingle through Meg's body. He began to knead the flesh, grasping it with his fingers, twisting, squeezing. The kneading process continued for a few minutes. Meg felt all the muscles of her body loosening up. And the stimulation of the contact sent shivers of ecstasy through her loins, so intense that she had to clamp her thighs tight together.

"Relax, relax," the masseur murmured. He ceased kneading and began to pound the flesh of her buttocks lightly with the edge of his hands, and then to slap it, harder and harder, until every nerve-ending throbbed with excitement and her skin felt warm and raw. It was almost painful, but a delightful kind of pain, as his skilled hands travelled up and down, from the small of her back to the beginning of her thighs, kneading, pounding, paddling, kneading again. Meg closed her eyes tight, and her breath came in harsh thick bursts. The man above her seemed to take no notice. He went serenely ahead with the massage, while Meg approached an erotic peak.

Finally, he removed his hands. "That is all for now, Miss Loring," he said smoothly.

She pushed herself up on one elbow and looked at him. His face was calm, unruffled. "Is that all?"

"For now, Miss Loring," he repeated.

"You work me over for half an hour and you just leave?"

"Would you wish a complete massage?" he asked innocently.

Meg clenched her fists tensely. "You know what I want. I'm all worked up now. I—I—" She stopped.

What am I doing, she asked herself? *I'm asking a man to make love to me. Just a ladies' masseur, at that. Max would be furious.*

But the strange compulsion unleashed by the massage would not be mastered. She reached out, grabbed the masseur's hand, clapped it on the jutting ripeness of one breast. Her flesh, stiff and hard, bored into his palm. He drew the hand back, quickly, as though she had put it down on a hot stove.

"Please, Miss Loring," he mumbled, his face going crimson.

"I'm—I'm sorry," she said, equally confused.

"You must forgive me. I—I have perhaps handled you intimately. But it is the normal massage."

"You—don't like women, do you?"

He shrugged. "I am not responsible for the way I am. May I go, please, Miss Loring? And shall we forget this—or would you prefer a different masseur the next time?"

Meg forced a smile. "It's all my fault. I let myself get out of control. There won't be any need for a change."

"Mademoiselle is most kind," the masseur said, bowing gracefully. He smiled at her and left.

Alone, Meg sat up, feeling the tingling in her loins still. It had certainly been a dumb thing to do, making a pass at that poor queer masseur, she told herself. But it had been a sudden wild impulse that she could not control. The fingers touching the most secret parts of her body, the soft caressing hands alternately stroking and slapping her....

She was half-dressed when Edna Hayes returned. "Everything all right, dear?"

"Fine," Meg said.

"How does the backside feel? Any slimmer?"

"It was a wonderful massage," Meg said, buttoning her blouse.

"Joe is a fine artist with his hands," Edna agreed. "He's everyone's favorite here." She smiled. "Max is waiting for you outside."

Meg was conducted to the outer office again. Bonaventura met her there, and took her to the street.

"Well?" he asked, outside. "How was it?"

"The massage?"

"Everything."

"Swell," she said. "It's a little strange getting handled so intimately by a man, though." She decided not to say anything about her clumsy attempt to make love to the masseur.

"Handled by a *man?*" Bonaventura echoed. "Baby, a masseur at Edna's place isn't a man. He's an *it*. Your boy was as queer as a blue six-dollar bill. So is Edna herself, for that matter."

"Queer?"

"Didn't she make a pass?"

"She watched me awfully closely when I got undressed. And she kind of accidentally touched me while I was lying on the table."

Bonaventura nodded. "She's a les, all right. She doesn't mix business with pleasure. She knows it's worth her skin to fool around with the clients. I once met her at a show, though. Holding hands with the prettiest little seventeen-year-old you ever want to see. I almost threw up." He shook his head. "Well, queer or not, they know their trade at Edna's, and that's why I use 'em. Results is all that counts. Meantime, I rented a place for you this morning, while you were getting your fanny remodeled. Three rooms on West 56th Street, furnished, one-thirty a month. I laid out $260 for you—one month in advance, plus a month's guarantee, refundable when you move out. We'll call the outlay an advance against your earnings, huh?"

"But I've got some money—"

"Don't argue with me, baby. I've got five grand coming in from Marsh tomorrow, and I can afford to be magnanimous. You hang onto your money, and if old Uncle Max offers you an advance, you take it, hear?"

"If you insist."

"I indeed insist." He glanced at his watch. "You still have a pretty busy day ahead of you. We'll grab some lunch now. From three to three-thirty you've got a singing lesson on 57th Street. Every other day at the same time. Alternate days it's posture and grooming lessons."

"Who pays for all this?"

"I do, baby. At least, I lay it all out. If you ever earn any money out of this, I get it back out of your earnings."

"And if I don't?"

"If you don't," Bonaventura said, "I'm gonna get me a new pair of glasses, so I can see what a really sexy girl looks like." He grinned. "We've got it made, kiddo. It's a straight uphill climb. Anyway, let me go on with the schedule. At five o'clock we go over to the Plaza for cocktails with Roy Hammond."

"Who is—?"

"The big wheel of the Miss Five Boroughs contest. That's the local deal that we use as the springboard for Miss Galaxy. I want Hammond to get a look at you. Just a look, mind you. The week before the contest, he gets more than a look, if necessary."

"What do you mean, if necessary?" Meg asked.

"If it looks like being a tough contest, you sleep with Hammond. But if you're gonna be a shoo-in anyway, we play it pure. I'm not giving away anything I don't have to give away."

Meg looked down at the ground. For the hundredth time, she wondered whether it wouldn't be smarter to chuck everything and head back to Harmons Glen. Now, before she started bouncing in and out of bedrooms on the way to the top. Would it be worth it, using her body to get there?

She answered the question as soon as it raised itself in her mind. *Yes,* she thought. She knew what it was like to be poor—dirt poor. She knew what it meant to have to pinch pennies.

She had an asset. Her body. And she had a manager who was out for all he could get. Between the two, she could have millions. More money than she could count. Fame, glory, excitement.

She'd be a fool not to take the chance, she thought. *Sure, I'll sleep with Roy Hammond if I have to,* she decided firmly. *Max will call the turns, and I'll obey. Until I get to the top. But once I'm there, I'll pick my own bedmates from then on.*

Five

Getting Hammond interested in Meg was no difficult trick. He was eyeing her from the moment of introduction, and by the time the martinis arrived at their table he was watching her every motion with keen interest—and unconcealed desire.

The meeting broke up around seven. Before that, Meg had gone off to the ladies' room for a while, to give the two men a chance to discuss things privately, and the moment Hammond left Bonaventura said, "Okay, kid, we've got it made!"

"I'm in the contest?"

"Of course you're in the contest. I could have told you that the minute Hammond set eyes on you. But you're going to *win.* You're the next Miss Five Boroughs."

"Did he say so?" Meg asked naively.

Bonaventura shrugged. "He wanted to know whether you were available for socializing. Meaning he wants to go to bed with you. I told him it all depended. Meaning I'd wait and see how the contest shapes up."

Meg pursed her lips. Hammond wasn't bad-looking—a big, barrel-chested man of about thirty-five, with a thick mane of intensely black hair. But there was something offensively smug about him that Meg didn't care for. Still, if Max said so—

"How does he control the contest?" she asked. "Is he one of the judges?"

"Nah. He just tells the judges who to vote for. Listen, baby, this particular contest is pure Chamber of Commerce stuff. Roy Hammond gets paid to pick a sexy dame as Miss Five Boroughs—somebody who'll get her picture smeared around all over. Okay. So he gets together a bunch of girls, and he gets together some middle-sized big shots as judges, and he tells the judges who the winner is. If they want to be judges again, they listen to him. They're just flunkies. He's the coordinator."

Two days later, there was a letter from Roy Hammond inviting Miss Meg Loring to participate in the Miss Five Boroughs contest. A questionnaire was enclosed, asking for her measurements and vital statistics, place of birth, hobbies, talents. Bonaventura helped her fill it out. When they put down her age, Bonaventura peeled a year off, making her nineteen instead of twenty.

"How come?" she asked. "Twenty isn't very old, is it?"

"I know. But when you win this thing, your age is going to be tacked into every press release that goes out. Every morgue file on Meg Loring will begin with that clipping. I'm just thinking ahead, sweetie. The time is going to come when you'll want to slice a year off your age, and this takes care of it in advance."

The next few weeks were busy ones for the future Miss Five Boroughs. Bonaventura was a hard master. Dancing, singing, massaging, tanning—the remodeling process continued on all fronts. He made her read books, too—*Crime and Punishment, Point Counter Point, The Odyssey, Sons and Lovers*, and so on. He took her to plays and foreign movies and to concerts. "You're gonna be cultured on top of everything else," he told her grimly. "That's what'll make you a knockout. Sexy and innocent at the same time, and cultured besides."

Uncomplainingly, Meg waded through the books Bonaventura gave her. He quizzed her on them when she finished them, and studied his conversation with references to them until she knew the names of Raskolnikov and Agamemnon and Walter Bidlake as well as her own. "You'll really knock the reporters into the pond when you start talking about the slow movement of the *Eroica*, kiddo. Or casually mention that you're dabbling in Zen Buddhism just now. Tits and culture—what a combo!"

She read and she practiced singing and she learned poise. Bonaventura advanced her five hundred dollars for a wardrobe, and personally helped her pick everything she bought. It was a round-the-clock operation. Out of bed at eight in the morning, and on the go until midnight or sometimes later. Bonaventura was tireless. No matter what time he brought Meg home and departed for his bachelor apartment on the East Side, he was up and phoning her out of bed on the dot of eight.

She met people. She smiled graciously and pushed her bosom

unobtrusively forward. She began to attract attention, as they appeared together at shows, in nightclubs, in midtown restaurants. She got a line in a show business column in the *Mirror*: "Looks like Max Bonaventura has struck uranium this time. He's agenting beauteous Meg Loring, a belle from absolutely nowhere who's going to make big news this year, or we miss our guess—and we usually don't."

The time of the contest drew nearer. Bonaventura fidgeted, and some of his nervousness rubbed off on Meg. She found it hard to get to sleep, tired as she was at the end of each day. She lay awake, envisioning the contest, picturing herself coming in fifth or tenth, her career blighted at the start.

Bonaventura scouted the opposition. He didn't like what he saw. "There's a busty blonde named Lois Paulsen who stands a good chance. And there's another one I'm worried about too. Angela Martinez— Puerto Rican girl. Nice boobs and the sweetest pair of legs you want to see. Somebody may decide it's good publicity to elect a Puerto Rican girl Miss Five Boroughs."

"I thought you said Hammond named the winner himself."

"He does, he does. But there's pressure on him, sometimes. You can't always figure it. This Puerto Rican angle, now—that could queer everything. Or the blonde, if she comes on strong."

"But what if I lose, Max?"

"Don't worry, baby. You won't. I'll fix things up. Just you wait. I'll fix it all up."

Bonaventura fixed it. He reported back to Meg the next day—one week before the judging. "It's in the bag, kid."

"You sure?"

He nodded. "You gotta sleep with Hammond, though."

Meg bit her lip. "I was afraid of that."

"Don't mess things up now," he pleaded. "Hammond's okay. I mean, he don't have any perversions or stuff like that. I asked around first. The deal is this: Wednesday night you stay at his apartment. Friday is the judging, and you win. Sunday you sleep with him again."

"I have to do it twice?"

"Don't flip, baby. The second time is the icing. You don't deliver the goods unless you win—which gives Hammond an incentive to make *sure* you win. But he won't double-cross me."

"Unless he's sleeping with a few of the other girls," Meg said bitterly. "What's to stop him from promising the same thing to half a dozen of us?"

Bonaventura looked uncertain. "That's the chance you gotta take, baby. But I tell you, don't worry. Hammond won't pull a dirty on me. Old Max knows too much about him for that."

The weekend passed. Monday … Tuesday … Wednesday.

Meg went through her routine on Wednesday with her mind fixed stonily on the assignation scheduled for that evening. She kept remembering the episode in Jack's car—the harsh animal-like breathing, the fierce pain, the feeling of guilt and soiledness afterward. Was it worth it, going through all that again.

She told herself that it would all be different this time. This wouldn't be any back-seat coupling. This would be a shack-up in the grand style.

Hammond met her for dinner that evening at half past five, after her voice lesson. "You look magnificent," he told her, with a hungry twinkle in his eye.

"Thank you," she said, with a touch of irony in it. She was wearing one of her new dresses, a creamy beige affair with sparkling rhinestones embedded in the fabric. It was low-cut, and her breasts seemed about to spill out over the top. The skirt clung to her hips and buttocks like a second skin. On high heels, she was only one inch below Hammond's six-foot height. She was attention-getting, and she knew it.

They ate at a French restaurant on 57th Street—martinis first, then *escargot*, onion soup, *chateaubriand*, 1949 Burgundy, and all the trimmings. Hammond's credit card took care of the check, but Meg saw him leave a five-dollar tip. She was a little woozy as they left—the martinis and the wine had seen to that—but she didn't regret that; the only way she could deliver what she had promised this evening was to blur her conscience with alcohol.

They took a cab to Hammond's apartment. It was in a shiny new building on East 63rd Street, overlooking the river. Four rooms with terrace—a minimum of $400 a month rent, Meg thought, and probably a good deal more. Hammond ushered Meg in with a certain smug pride. The furniture, all of it Swedish Modern, reeked of money. Original abstract paintings decorated the wall. A vast high-fidelity rig dominated one entire room. Stereo, of course.

"How about some music?" Hammond suggested.

"Fine."

"You name it. Classical, pop, show tunes, folk songs—anything you like."

Meg grinned. "How about the *Eroica?* I think Beethoven's so divine—that slow movement just gives me *ecstasies!*"

Hammond looked momentarily baffled by her request. "I wouldn't have expected Beethoven," he said. "You've got hidden depths, I see." He went to the record rack. "Which performance do you want to hear? I've got Toscanini, Klemperer, Scherchen—"

"Oh, Toscanini," she said casually. "He does it better than anyone else."

"Toscanini coming up. It's a mono recording, of course, but I'll play it through both speakers." The sonorous opening chords of the *Eroica* boomed through the apartment. Hammond went to a sideboard and produced a squat liquor bottle. "What say to some cognac, just as a *digestif?*" he suggested. "Courvoisier VSOP?"

"Fine."

He poured out two snifters. They settled down on the couch, the music surrounding them, looking out across the terrace into Queens.

"You have a beautiful apartment, Roy. The public relations field must be very rewarding."

"It pays, yes. But I earn every cent. It's no cinch, promoting things."

No, she thought. *Look how hard it is to put on a simple beauty contest. You have to sleep with ugly females like Meg Loring—*

She imitated Hammond, breathing in the cognac fumes before drinking. The brandy gave her a warm glow, melting away her remaining inhibitions. Hammond's arm slipped round her shoulders. They nestled a little closer, and his hand suddenly but gently moved downward a few inches from her right shoulder to her right breast. It was a big hand, like Jack's, but a manicured, soft-fleshed, almost effeminate-textured hand. His fingers rested lightly on the upper curve of her bosom, then began to march down deeper into her neckline, until they were within her bra. He curved his fingers, scooping the breast up out of the cradling bra and out of the dress altogether. She heard him catch his breath sharply at the sight of the tanned, rounded perfection of her breast.

He turned to her, drawing the breast to his lips and gently kissing the flesh until it became stiff and tense. Lifting her other breast out of her bra, he buried his face between them, nestling in the warmth while continuing to gently rub her. She felt desire take hold of her, but she waited, letting him call the turns.

He toyed with her a long time, until she felt that she was on fire, and then, lifting her in his arms, he carried her into the bedroom. The bed was triple-sized, with a foam-rubber mattress that felt firm and yet yielding beneath her. Hammond undressed her with care, peeling the expensive dress from her, unfastening the bra that no longer contained her breasts, pulling down her panties and stockings and garter-belt. Bonaventura had told her not to wear underwear beneath the tight dress, but she had disobeyed him, feeling that it would be indecent to walk around without any panties on; leaving off the slip was the furthest she could go in that direction.

She was nude now. Hammond stepped back, admiring the flawless sensuality of her body. "You're incredible," he muttered. "Incredible!" She closed her eyes, lifted one knee, stretched out her arms, parted her lips. The lights went out. She sensed Hammond's burly body next to hers, stroking her thighs, cupping her breasts, murmuring sweet words of reassurance and affection.

She drew him to her. Desire exploded in her in one brilliant rush of colors.

Meg moaned in delight. Shivers of joy raced up her body. Her muscles contracted; sweat burst out all over her, and she went limp, knowing that she had experienced the act in its fullest.

It was not at all like the first time, she thought. Not at all like that clumsy, degrading session in the parked car.

They lay still for a while, and then Hammond turned on a lamp and offered her a robe, and they smiled at each other and went back into the living-room for more cognac. He put another record on, and they sat quietly in the darkened room until midnight. They went to bed then, kissing goodnight like husband and wife. Later, in the darkness, Meg was awakened by the touch of Hammond's hands at her breasts and thighs. He rolled over toward her, and, still half asleep, she let him take her again, lapsing off into sleep after the climax.

And then it was morning, and they were showering and getting dressed, and breakfasting together in a restaurant in a hotel across the street. They parted at half past nine, and Hammond smiled warmly at her and said, "See you Friday at the contest."

"Yes. And see you Sunday night, too."

He moistened his lips. "Yes. Sunday night, too."

She phoned Bonaventura as soon as she was alone, and reported to him, without going into excess details, that she was pretty sure it had been a successful evening.

Yet doubts remained, all during that day and the next. Hammond had seemed pleased—but suppose he had slept with other contestants, too? The busty blonde Max had talked about, or the fiery Puerto Rican?

Friday night came—the night of the contest. It was held in the main ballroom of the Hotel Norris on 56th Street; a big crowd was on hand, and dozens of photographers. Hammond had done his job well. Meg and Bonaventura arrived early and staked out a place in the big dressing room. The contest would have two parts: evening gown and bathing-suit appearance, evening gowns coming first.

The dressing room began to fill up with girls and their managers. There were thirty girls in the contest, and some had brought maids as well. The big room was hectic; a few of the girls objected to getting dressed and undressed in public, but their objections were overruled. Meg donned her gown and waited for the signal. She could hear music playing out front.

Hammond wandered by, looking impartial, and called out, "Five minutes, everybody!" The dawdlers screamed in dismay. Hammond circulated, telling the girls what order they were to appear in.

The minutes ticked by. Meg was the fourteenth in the procession. Some of the girls were going out, now. Meg spied the two nearest competitors: the blonde girl, with big pale breasts jiggling over the top of the gown, and the Puerto Rican, her skin a deep tan, looking like a lithe, sensuous panther. Meg wondered whether they, too, had given themselves to Roy Hammond.

But then she no longer had time to wonder. It was her turn. She felt an icy calmness come over her as she walked out of the wings. Footlights glared at her, and she could make out a sea of faces in the darkness. Cameras glared; television lenses peered at her. Moving gracefully, the way she had been so thoroughly taught, she advanced to stage left, smiled at the judges, curtseyed to display her bosom, and moved off again.

Backstage, everything was chaotic. The girls who had been out already were getting out of their gowns and into their bathing-suits. The more modest of them were trying to hide their nudity, but Meg did not bother with modesty now. Bonaventura helped her out of her gown. She peeled away her scanty underclothes. The agent was sweating at the sight of her bare breasts and buttocks, but he handed her the bathing suit. Regulations prescribed a one-piece suit; this one was skin-tight. As she got into it, she caught sight of her rivals getting out of their gowns. The big blonde was naked, and she was an imposing sight—breasts like basketballs, heavy quivering buttocks. She was too fat, Meg thought. She could never win. As for the Puerto Rican, she was the opposite. Her breasts were small and firm, her buttocks lean, her legs extraordinarily attractive. Her tan skin gleamed with perspiration.

Hammond stuck his head in. "Everybody ready?"

There were squeals again from girls who were either nude or had not yet pulled their suits all the way up. The music began again. The procession started.

Meg walked out, paraded around, displayed herself as proudly as she could, and walked off. The music continued. Some well-known singer was delivering a tune out front while the judges deliberated.

Then Hammond was appearing again; the judges had narrowed the field to ten. Would they please come out again?

Meg held her breath. The ten included the Puerto Rican, the blonde

… and herself. The ten girls paraded around stage and remained there, like a chorus line, while the judges conferred. Meg saw tuxedoed men in the front row whispering and handing a slip up to Hammond.

He grinned broadly. "Ladies and gentlemen, the judges have reached a decision. They have chosen, as your Miss Five Boroughs of 1960, a girl whose beauty and talent cannot fail to bring credit to the fair city of New York. Ladies and gentlemen, I give you Miss Five Boroughs of 1960. *Meg Loring!*"

Flashbulbs exploded. Meg felt dizzy. Waves of applause rolled up from the audience. The Puerto Rican and the blonde were hugging her, in the traditional congratulatory embrace of the losers.

This was it, she thought. The first big step on the ladder. Hammond had not double-crossed her after all. She was on her way. She was heading for the top.

Six

There was a victory party, held in a smaller ballroom of the same hotel. Plenty of champagne flowed, and Meg posed for dozens of pictures at almost every angle, first in her bathing-suit and then, after changing, in her gown. Bonaventura remained at her elbow constantly, advising her, introducing her to people, taking away her champagne glasses after she had had only a few sips of each. He didn't want her to get drunk or pass out or otherwise do something embarrassing. She was introduced to some important politician who hugged her and managed to grab himself a nice feel. She met big shot columnists and reporters. Plenty of important people had attended the judging, more to be seen than to see.

And then, finally, it was over. Exhausted, Meg let herself be led out of the hotel by Bonaventura and taxied the few blocks across town to her apartment. Her legs ached, her eyes were throbbing, and she just wanted to curl up and go to sleep.

"You were wonderful, kid," the agent told her in the cab. "And you must really have creamed Hammond. He's raving about you."

"Does that mean I have to become his mistress?"

"Nah. Sunday night you spend with Hammond, and that's it. He's small-time. We honor our agreement, but then we dump him in the ashcan. Subtly, mind you. We don't want to make any unnecessary enemies."

They reached the apartment. She invited Bonaventura in, and he reluctantly helped her undress. As she stood nude before him he muttered, "I can't get used to you. Most clients are just so much meat, but you're different. You give me the tingles every time I look at you."

She giggled, and flounced past him into the bathroom. She soaked in a hot tub for half an hour, while Bonaventura sat watching her in admiration. When she finally climbed out of the water, his eyes travelled the length of her nude body in awe once again.

She put on a gown. "You better not look at me so much, Max. It's bad for your blood pressure."

"Yeah. Yeah. Christ, what a build!"

"Why don't you sleep over, Max?"

He shook his head nervously. "Cut that stuff out, you hear me? You and me, it's strictly business."

She opened the gown wide enough to show one rosy nipple and a few curving inches of breast. "Does it have to be?"

"Christ, Meg, stop that!"

She laughed. "You're funny, Max. I like you. I think you're a prince."

"Yeah," he said. "Look, Meg, get yourself some sleep. I'll phone you around noon tomorrow. Goodnight, now."

He beat a hasty retreat. Still laughing, Meg shut off the light and got into bed. She wondered what Bonaventura would be like as a lover. He certainly tried hard enough to avoid going to bed with her....

She closed her eyes, but it was a long time before she could fall asleep. She kept seeing the exploding flashbulbs, and hearing the wild applause. *This was only a two-bit local shindig*, she told herself. *Just the beginning.*

Bonaventura called the next day with some good news. The thousand dollar check for winning was in the mails; he would have it on Monday. It represented the first income Meg Loring had earned. There was also a magazine cover deal: a hundred bucks for posing for a magazine called *Ambassador*, a sophisticated men's mag.

"Nude?" Meg wanted to know.

"Nah, you crazy? Not the first cover. This is just plain cheesecake, low-neckline stuff. Lots of bosom. They're using it in the issue on sale the month of the Miss Galaxy contest." He paused. "Oh, yeah. I almost forgot. There was a call from Las Vegas, too. Ned Myers of the Miss Galaxy shindig. You've got a bid."

"Max! That's great!"

"Don't go ape, honeybun. You gotta take these things more calmly."

"But the Miss Galaxy contest—!"

"Listen," he said, "I told you you're heading for the top. None of this oughta surprise you any. The *Ambassador* photog wants to see you

Tuesday morning at 11. I'll pick you up and take you over. And don't forget Hammond on Sunday night, neither."

"I won't."

"Take the day off and relax. Buy yourself some clothes, or something. I'll be over tonight and we'll do some celebrating at the Peacock Room or someplace."

She relaxed. They were spotted in the nightclub that evening by a gossip snooper previously tipped off by Bonaventura, and he agreed to give Miss Five Boroughs a little play in his column.

She slept late on Sunday. Roy Hammond phoned in early afternoon, and she went to his apartment around four. They ate by candlelight in a small restaurant two blocks away, and then returned to his place. The evening went much the way the previous Wednesday had. Meg thought she was better in bed, though; she knew what to expect, this time, and she able to put on a better performance. In the morning, as she was getting dressed, Hammond put his hands over her breasts from behind and said, "When am I going to see you again, darling?"

"Before very long. I'm so terribly busy these days, now that my career is launched—"

"Max really keeps you hopping, huh? But see if you can squeeze in some time for me. Maybe I can do you some good yet. And it's been grand so far, Meg."

She managed to escape without giving him any definite promise for another date. She rather liked Hammond, for all his smugness; he was good in bed, and he didn't mind lavishing cash on a girl. But Max had drummed it into her head that she always had to keep looking upward. There were bigger prizes than Miss Five Boroughs, and bigger publicity men than Roy Hammond.

The photography session on Tuesday went off smoothly. It lasted for two hours; they posed her from every conceivable angle, while Bonaventura stood by watchfully to make sure none of the shots went past the bounds of good taste. As he had explained to Meg earlier that day, it wasn't good sense to *begin* with nudes. That cheapened a girl. It was better to become known first, and *then* to peel in front of the camera.

She had brought a considerable wardrobe along. They shot her in a bathing suit, they shot her in a low-cut gown, and they shot her in a bath towel (covering all the vital areas adequately, though). The shot that satisfied them the most was a nipple shot—Meg wearing a tight cotton jersey and no bra underneath. The jersey was cut in a sharp V to reveal the cleavage and the circling hemispheres of her breasts, and the nipples jutted visibly but tastefully against the fabric.

Max collected the fee and they left. The proofs would be mailed out for approval in a few days, Meg would sign the release if Bonaventura okayed the pose, and the cover would go to the engraver. And, three months from now, she would find her picture on every newsstand in the country.

Bonaventura was busily preparing for the Miss Galaxy contest now. It was to be held in Las Vegas in the last weekend of August; there would be about ninety contestants, and the pot of gold for the winner was $7500 cash and a screen test. It was strictly a publicity brawl—unlike the Miss America contest, where purity and chastity were of the essence, Miss Galaxy was frankly intended to be a sex queen. Bonaventura set out to make certain Meg Loring would receive the acclaim she deserved.

The first step was a newspaper interview, nationally syndicated by a wire service. Roping in a reporter who owed him a favor, Bonaventura got broad coverage on the feature all over the country. Stressing the Cultured Sex Kitten approach, it highlighted Meg's interest in great books and art, offering a couple of choice quotations carefully concocted by Bonaventura. The accompanying photo showed Meg in her rhinestone-decked finery, a photo shrewdly designed to catch the eye and still be printable in most newspapers. The kicker on the story was that Meg Loring was a shoo-in for Miss Galaxy and for future fame.

It got spread everywhere. Overnight, Meg Loring's name was in front of the nation.

In mid-July came the second step. Bonaventura arranged an excursion to Coney Island for Meg, and passed the word along to an enterprising news photographer. Meg emerged on the beach clad in a bikini; the photographer stationed himself a few yards from the water; they waited half an hour for the beach to get really filled up, during which time half a dozen shots were taken by way of warmup. Finally Bonaventura said, "Okay, let's get it now." Meg waded out into the water until it was throat-high. Carefully she untied her halter. Then she began to run in toward shore, naked except for the strip of cloth around her loins. As planned, she stopped short with the water still swirling around her knees. Her jaw sagged and an expression of blank-faced horror came to her face, and she put her hands to her breasts. The photographer snapped the shot. Meg turned, diving into the surf, and remained there while Bonaventura came wading out with a towel to conceal her. It had all taken only a few seconds, and no more than a dozen people had had a clear view of it. What they had seen, though, would last them a lifetime—a radiantly lovely girl racing out of the water, her bare breasts bobbing with each step.

The shot appeared in the paper the next day. It was perfect. It showed

Meg frozen in shock, hands cupped to her breasts. Only her nipples were concealed, and the twin swelling mounds were otherwise bare, yet the shot was deemed printable. The caption read, "WASN'T HER FACE RED? *The surprised starlet, a victim of yesterday's Coney undertow, is none other than Miss Five Boroughs, 19-year-old Meg Loring. Powerful tides swept away the top half of her bikini just as lucky photog Charley Mueller happened by. Some guys get all the breaks!*"

The picture was picked up by the wire services and relayed all over the country. Some papers refused to run it, but others featured it delightedly.

Two weeks after it appeared, Meg was in Las Vegas, living in a $100-a-week hotel suite on the Strip, with Bonaventura inhabiting a cheaper room at a nearby motel. They held regular press conferences, at which Meg, rehearsed by Bonaventura, offered casual statements about the size of her bosom, the international situation, the relative merits of redheads and blondes, and the preludes and fugues of Johann Sebastian Bach. The newsmen gobbled it up. They sensed something big brewing, the crowning of the nation's next sex goddess.

"Start a feud," Bonaventura suggested next. Obligingly, Meg declared at her next press conference, "If there's one thing I can't stand, it's these Hollywood studios who bring in so-called sexy foreign females to pep up their films. Who needs them? There's plenty of American talent that isn't getting a fair break."

Only a month earlier, with fanfare and hoopla, MGM had announced the arrival of Italian starlet Maria Doman—a full-blown, busty creature whose figure was not unlike Meg's own. The Hollywood reporters played it up big—a feud between la Doman and Meg Loring, up-and-coming starlet! The Battle of the Bosoms, someone termed it. Bonaventura flew to Hollywood the next day for a hasty conference with Maria Doman's press agent, and phoned Meg to tell her, "Get on the next plane out here. You and Doman are going to meet face-to-face."

She took the next plane out, arriving in Hollywood late that afternoon. Bonaventura met her at the airport. "It's all set," he told her. "I've got you an invitation to a party in Doman's honor tonight in Pacific Palisades. Maria's going to play along."

The scheme was simple. The two rivals would vie with each other for maximum bosom display. Meg wore a low-cut gown with no bra; the Italian girl was dressed in an equally provocative outfit. They greeted each other coolly—and, as they shook hands, photographers clustered around. Maria Doman smiled, thrusting out her bosom; Meg inhaled, and her breasts came perilously close to escaping from the confines of her neckline. Bonaventura signaled and Meg bent forward just a bit *too* far; for a fraction of a second her nipples were on display, cameras clicked, onlookers oohed.

By two a.m. Meg was back in Las Vegas after her brief taste of Hollywood glamour. Bonaventura, grinning, said, "They'll probably kill the nipple shot and bootleg it to the girlie mags. But you'll be in the papers right along with her." He shrugged. "That Doman has a smart press agent. He didn't have to let you in on the act—you don't even have a contract with anybody. But he knows you're going to be somebody big in a few months, and he wants me to owe him a favor. Someday it may be handy for Maria Doman to be seen with Meg Loring, instead of vice versa."

And so it went, as the day of the contest drew near. Bonaventura eased up on the publicity barrage and cancelled all further Meg Loring press conferences; it was time to slow down, now, for fear of overdoing it.

"Won't I even have to sleep with anyone for this contest?" Meg asked.

Bonaventura chuckled. "This time we played it smart, honey. This town is full of girls sleeping with the judges. I made a better deal. I got you set up with Ned Myers himself."

"But the judging is tomorrow—"

Bonaventura winked and said, "Sleeping with judges is for the peasants. So is delivery in advance. If you win, you and Myers go off to Acapulco for a week right after the contest. If you don't win, Myers gets nothing. You're a big name now, kid. Big enough so I can dangle you like a carrot in front of Myers' nose."

The next morning there was a rehearsal for the judging. There was a bathing-suit parade and a talent display; each girl would have to sing, dance, play an instrument, anything at all. Ned Myers, a lean, keen-eyed man of formidable energy, buzzed all over the place, keeping the contestants under control. There were girls from all over—from Japan, from Korea, from Italy, Spain, and a dozen other countries besides the United States. Each of the girls seemed determined to display as much as possible of herself before the contest. But their antics were timed badly—for now they each competed with the others for attention, while Meg had had the field to herself for her bare-bosomed shot in July. Thus, when Miss Sweden did a high-dive at a Vegas swimming pool and bobbed up minus the top of her bathing suit, the resulting photo caused hardly a ripple. It was much the same when Miss Wyoming attended a burlesque show at one of the casinos and jumped on stage to provide an unrehearsed strip act herself, peeling to the buff and lacking even a G-string. It was too obvious a publicity pitch, coming as it did just before the contest.

Still, Meg had doubts—right up until the final moment. The field had been narrowed to a dozen girls, then to six. She had sung her song—not particularly well, she admitted, but then few of the other contestants had been singers.

Around the stage paraded the six survivors. Miss Barcelona, a raven-haired lovely with a Latin touch; Miss Iowa, sexy in a homespun Midwest way; Miss Detroit, a lush six-footer with astonishing legs; Miss Tokyo, petite, small of bosom yet oddly erotic; Miss London, a leggy blonde with heroic breasts; and Miss New York City, Meg Loring. They marched before the judges for what seemed like hours.

And, at last, the decision.

"Ladies and gentlemen," Ned Myers said, "it is my great pleasure to introduce you to the new Miss Galaxy—certainly one of the most attractive females of this or any other planet. Ladies and gentlemen, Miss Galaxy of 1961—I give you—Meg Loring!"

Seven

The victory celebrations were over; the flashbulb barrage had ended; the check was in the bank. The new Miss Galaxy was on a plane bound for Mexico with public-relations man Ned Myers, and, after the frantic weekend, Meg relished the chance to be free from reporters, up here at 18,000 feet. After this little interlude with Myers, the publicity wheels would begin turning again, as she moved on to Hollywood for her screen test.

Myers was stretched out with his long legs in the aisle, swirling a martini around. It was a first-class flight, with plenty of drinks for all. Myers said, "So you've never been in Acapulco, eh?"

"I told you, Ned. I'm just a simple little Idaho farm girl. I hadn't even ever been in an airplane until a month ago."

"Incredible. Utterly beyond belief. Do you mean to say that the sticks are full of girls like you, just waiting to be discovered by some shrewd cookie like Bonaventura?"

"Max didn't discover me. He stayed in New York and I discovered *him*. How about getting me another drink, Ned honey?"

Myers reached up to thumb the stewardess signal, and when the girl appeared he ordered refills for both of them.

"Certainly, Mr. Myers."

The girl scuttled away toward the galley. Looking after her trim rear as it retreated, Myers said, "You know, that girl could have possibilities. Put a pair of contact lenses on her and buy her a decent bra and she'd go big places. Good build, sweet face—"

"Maybe she doesn't *want* to go big places," Meg suggested. "Maybe she likes being sweet and demure. Or don't you ever think a girl ought to be anything but a glamor queen?"

"I hate to see her wasting herself."

"She enjoys it. We can't all be Miss Galaxy."

"I'd like to see them all try," Myers leered.

"So you could sleep with them all?"

"That's unkind."

"How many of the contestants *did* you sleep with, anyway? Promising them all that they'd win?"

"I decline to answer that question on the grounds that it would tend to incriminate me."

"Come on, tell me," Meg persisted. "If you don't, I'll turn around and get on the first plane out of Acapulco tonight."

"You can't do that!" Myers yelped. "We agreed—"

"Not in writing, we didn't. Anyway, I've won the contest, and you won't have a leg to stand on if I decide to welsh now. Come on, tell me. How many?"

"Six," Myers confessed.

"Six? And each one thought she had the contest sewed up. And you *didn't* sleep with me, but I won. How come?"

"You intrigued me. There's no fascination in climbing the same mountain twice. The only way I could get you was to make sure you won."

"That's blunt enough," Meg remarked. "So the contest is phony from the word *go*, every year."

"Sure it is. But don't get any ideas of publishing an expose," Myers warned. "You signed some papers prohibiting you from divulging the workings of the contest, don't forget. Anyway, why the hell should you rock the boat? You won, didn't you?"

"Yes. I won."

Myers snaked an arm around her. The stewardess appeared, bringing the martinis in little glass jugs that she inverted into their glasses. "We'll be landing in Acapulco in half an hour," she informed them.

Meg was not very sober as the plane touched down. A fog of martini-vapor hung about her brain as Myers helped her off, collected the baggage, and steered her to a waiting taxi. The air was warm but dry; the sun was bright, the sky extremely blue.

The hotel was an ultra-modern affair, built in a horse shoe around a huge outdoor swimming pool. Each room had its own terrace, glass-enclosed. Looking down, Meg said, "I'd like to take a swim right away. Then we can get dressed for dinner."

"Suits me," Myers said.

She began to undress, tossing her clothes into the chair next to her. She had her blouse and bra off and was unzipping her skirt when she realized that Myers was staring at her in awe.

"Something the matter?" she asked.

"No—go ahead. Finish undressing."

"You're impressed?"

"Stoned is the word. Lord, you're built! Come here."

Puzzled, Meg walked over to him. For the first time since embarking on this trip with Myers, she felt the strangeness of going off on a week's journey with a man she did not know, of standing here nude before him. How impossible this would have been six months ago, she thought! But, then, she had not been Miss Galaxy six months ago, either.

Myers reached out, cupping the undersides of her breasts as though weighing them. He tightened his grip, still maintaining the same amazed expression. He released her and stepped back for a perspective view.

It was the same story every time she showed her nude body to a man, Meg thought. There was something about the way her breasts rose like twin peaks, without the need of support; something about the sensuous line of her buttocks, curving gently into her thighs; something about the soft roundness of her hips. She *awed* men. Even coldblooded ones like Ned Myers, who slept with starlets every day of the week and twice on Sundays.

He peeled off his clothes and pulled her down to the bed, and they made love. He seemed distant, remote as he moved his body against hers; making love with him was like doing an exercise in geometry, she thought, except that suddenly the coldness was gone and her body was erupting with passion, and she panted wildly and shivered as Myers caressed her.

Afterward they went swimming, and dined in a crystal-and-ebony ballroom by the side of the pool, and in the evening they danced and sipped champagne and went to bed. It was that way for a week.

There were other Hollywood people there, and many of them knew Myers. He casually introduced her to them—"Meg Loring, the new Miss Galaxy"—and none of them seemed to take it at all amiss that the starlet and the press agent should be sharing a hotel room for the week.

During the day they rented a car and drove around town; Meg did some shopping, sent a postcard to Bonaventura, and saw the sights. And in the evening, the same routine, swimming, dancing, champagne, bed.

All very expensive. Thirty dollars a day for the hotel room, at least as much more for food and drink. Myers never blinked. Compared to him,

Roy Hammond was just small time. At the end of the week they flew back to Las Vegas, where Bonaventura was waiting to take Meg on to Hollywood for her screen test."

"It's been grand," she told him as the plane began to circle low over the Nevada desert.

"It's been more than grand," Myers said. "It's been magnificent. It's too bad it's all over."

"We'll keep in touch."

Myers smiled strangely. "No, we won't, Meg. We've touched like ships in the night, and now we're going to go our separate ways. Six months from now you wouldn't be caught dead sleeping with me. And six months from now I'll have next year's success-seekers to go to bed with. Not that any of them will get where you're heading."

"And where am I heading?" Meg asked.

He shrugged. "*Quien sabe?* As far as you want to go, my dear. You've got all the equipment. It's just a matter of how long it is before you get sick of success."

"How could anyone possibly get sick of success?"

"I won't answer that," Myers said gravely. "I'll let you puzzle it out yourself. In the meantime, thanks. You've given me a week for the memory book."

Bonaventura was waiting at the airport when the plane landed. Pecking her on the cheek in a brotherly fashion, Myers bid them both goodbye and slipped away, waving profusely every few steps.

Bonaventura looked nervous and tense. "Well? How was the week?"

"Divine."

"Everything was okay with Myers?"

"Sure. What do you mean?"

Bonaventure shrugged. "I've heard funny stories about that guy—that he sometimes makes love with a belt, that sort of stuff. He didn't lay a hand on you?"

"He was a perfect gentleman." Meg frowned. "Max, you *knew* this guy sometimes did oddball things, and you still let me go away for a week with him?"

The little man looked abashed. "It was a chance I took," he said bluntly. "We needed that contest. I made a deal."

"And if he had whipped me purple?"

"He didn't, did he?" Bonaventura barked. "Christ, girl, you gotta take *some* chances when you're shooting for the big prize. Come on, let's get a cab. I got all our stuff packed up and ready at the hotel. We're making a plane for Hollywood at six tonight."

"Seems like I'm always either getting on or getting off a plane, Max."

Bonaventura's jaw-muscles flickered irritably. "You're doing a lot of complaining today, kiddo. You're starting to get in the big money now. You have to work for it." He consulted his watch. "We'll be at the Beverly-Wilshire Hotel while you're in L.A. You've got a suite and I'm in the next room. $150 a week."

"Whew!"

"Sounds big, huh? But don't let it bug you. I've got a sheaf of photo assignments for you—a thousand bucks' worth of work, at least, for the next week alone. Plus the screen test."

"Which is when?"

"Thursday."

Meg nodded. She felt dizzy, being swept along on a torrent of publicity and hooplah. Screen tests, beauty contests, magazine covers, weekends in Acapulco—it was all unbelievable that this should be happening to her, to Meg Tandler of Harmons Glen, Idaho.

But she remembered what Bonaventura had told her, that first day in his office:

When you want something in life really bad, you can get it. Every time. It's just a matter of putting your heart and mind to it.

Well, she had put her heart and mind to it. As well as her breasts and thighs and loins and everything else she had. And she was getting there. She was climbing the rainbow straight to the pot of gold.

But she felt very tired, worn down by the steady demands of the publicity campaign. And that question of Ned Myers troubled her. *How long will it be before you get sick of success?*

She wondered about that for a while, aboard the plane out of Las Vegas. But once she landed in Los Angeles, there was no longer time to wonder about anything.

The suite at the Beverly Wilshire had a black and white marble floor, a Chinese bamboo bed with gold silk canopies, a private patio, and a closet almost as big as a room itself. Two hours after her arrival, Meg Loring was holding a press conference there, nude under a dress so tight it seemed to be sprayed on. She sat on a high table, legs crossed, leaning forward to give the newsmen the full benefit of her V neck and missing bra. She held forth on the Presidential elections a couple of months away, on the joys of unabashed sexuality ("not that I believe in absolute *immorality*, you understand"), on the works of Plato ("I've just been reading the most *fascinating* things"), and on feminine fashions ("If you ask me, I think we're in for greater uncovering in the future. It wouldn't surprise me at all if women started wearing bathing trunks on the beach, just like men. That's one fashion I'd like to help introduce.")

She delivered the lines, ghosted by Bonaventura, as glibly as though they were all spontaneous. The cocky, confident, dazzlingly beautiful starlet made tremendous copy. The next day, three local papers covered the interview. Naturally, the bathing-suit prediction got a big play in each story, and two of the papers dug up the July Coney Island shot to illustrate the possible new trend forecast by Miss Galaxy.

She spent that day in a photographic studio, doing a cover and interior pictorial spread for a big West Coast men's magazine. The cover was fairly chaste; for the centerfold spread, they photographed her in a nightgown that was opaque enough to hide her body while still giving the general idea. The cameramen were slightly incredulous when she stepped out from behind the screen; she was a lot more visible in the nightgown than she would be in the published picture, and the sight of her full breasts and lush buttocks startled even that jaded crew. When she was through with the stint—three hours, at $50 per—she went on a sightseeing tour of Hollywood and Los Angeles, and she and Bonaventura ate at a glossy-looking restaurant on La Cienega Boulevard before returning to the hotel. She spent the evening in the suite, exhausted, watching television, while Bonaventura made phone calls and drafted her next public statement.

On Thursday came the screen test. She was nervous and gloomy all morning; by the time Bonaventura and she went out to the lot, she was convinced that she would never be an actress.

They had given her two scripts to study—a comedy role and a dramatic one. There was perhaps ten minutes of dialogue in each sequence, and she had managed to get them down fairly pat. At the lot, Bonaventura jovially introduced her around. She met a producer, a producer's son, a director, several actors, an actress.

A makeup girl swept her away, and she returned twenty minutes later to face the cameras for the first time. They were beginning with the dramatic sequence. She was playing a young mother who had just discovered that her four-year-old son has disappeared. The director— an enormously tall, potbellied man named Fassett—stepped out onto the sound stage with her. The lights were fierce. One of the actors came out too, playing the role of the man whose task it is to inform her of the disappearance—and who was subsequently supposed to fall in love with her.

He delivered the first cue. Meg hesitated, then got the line off: "About Johnny, you say? Why—he's in the playground, isn't he?"

"Well, yes. That is, he—I mean—"

"Has anything happened to him! Tell me!"

And so on. They were only halfway through the scene when it was cut short, and the comedy sequence called for.

In this one, Meg was playing a beautiful-but-dumb maid being propositioned by her wolfish employer. She liked the scene better than the other, and had looked forward to playing it. But she fumbled a couple of lines badly.

"Okay, okay," the director called, again midway into the scene. "Now, Miss Loring, let's try some general shots. Smiling, frowning, all the rest."

For fifteen minutes more, she performed like a trained dog—terribly afraid, as the test went on, that she was bungling things. She did not know what to do with her hands, she could not find a comfortable standing posture, she was sure that her makeup was running.

Finally the director said, "Cut. That'll be all, Miss Loring."

She came off the stage. The officials were conferring. She ran up to Bonaventura.

"Well?" she said. "It was awful, wasn't it?"

"Now, Meg—"

"Don't try to jolly me. I bombed, didn't I? I was an all-time stinker."

"You should have seen some of the big stars when they took *their* tests."

"But that won't help me!"

"Sure it will," Bonaventura soothed her. "While you were taking your test, I did a little talking. You've got a date for tonight."

"What do you mean, a date?"

"You're going out with Arthur Fields. The producer's son. He and old Mack are co-producing their next film together. Young Arthur is very interested in you."

"Which means—?"

"Which means that you do what young Artie wants you to do tonight, sweetheart. And I can almost guarantee you a film contract in the morning."

Eight

"You want to be a big movie star?" Arthur Fields asked her. "You want to be the next Mansfield, huh?"

"What do you think?" Meg asked him.

It was two in the morning, and the scene was the junior Fields' sprawling bachelor home in Burbank. They had been out on the town since eight-thirty, pub-crawling, hitting the high and the low spots. Meg was about thirty percent drunk, now. Fields was a little bit higher.

He sat in a modernistic armchair, his arms and legs dangling in every direction. At twenty-seven, he had already begun to spread out flabbily. Put another thirty years on him and he would be a carbon copy of his father. He had the same look of having lived too well, the same bloated puffiness around the bloodshot eyes.

He said, "You were lousy this afternoon. I saw the rushes. They stank, in spades."

"So I won't get a contract."

"Nobody said that. There isn't a decent actress under thirty in this town, you know? They *all* stink. But they have homes with swimming pools, and a thousand bucks every Wednesday. No reason why you can't have the same. No reason at all."

"If someone gives me a contract."

Fields sniggered. "Dad and I are making a film next month. Comedy. There's a juicy role for a blonde with big tits. We were trying to borrow Mansfield. We could use you instead."

"I'm a redhead. And I'm staying that way."

"We could change the script. It's the tits that matter, not the color of the hair."

"Do you want a lousy actress in your movie?"

"We could train you," Fields said. "The raw material is there. Like I say, they're *all* lousy here. You can have the role, Meg. Just that it all depends."

"On what?"

"On how eager you are to get it." He rose, moving squishily over to the monstrous hi-fi set, and put a mambo on. "Let's dance for a while."

They danced until Fields was tired. He danced close to her, missing no opportunity to grind his gross, flabby body against hers. At the end of the record he said, "All right. Enough dancing. Why don't you be a good girl and take your clothes off, Meg? Do a little strip act for old Uncle Arthur?"

She cloaked her inner contempt behind a smooth smile. Fields put the other side of the mambo record on, and Meg began to move her hips rhythmically. She shimmied as she groped for the zipper of her dress and pulled it down. Without missing a beat, she stepped out of the dress, draping it over a chair. Fields caught his breath. She was wearing a half-bra, panties, a garter-belt, and sheer nylons. He watched, hungrily, as she unsnapped the bra and let it drop. He was practically drooling at the sight of her bare, rounded breasts.

She rolled the panties over her hips and kicked them off. As she started to unhook her stockings, Fields said, "No. Leave them and the garter-belt on. And come over here."

Clad only in the elastic belt and the stockings, she walked toward him. He reached out, catching her suddenly and yanking her down across his knees.

He gripped her tightly. Then, before she fully realized what he was up to, his hand descended smartly on the pink, quivering flesh of her buttocks!

A dozen times or more the hand fell. She felt the blood tingling in her buttocks and knew they were turning rosy from the spanking. Fields seemed to derive a perverse joy from striking her. His hand descended with stinging impact, until she wanted to cry out from the pain and the simultaneous erotic thrill. Fields' breathing was becoming harsh and irregular, like that of a man in an advanced state of asthma.

Then, abruptly, the spanking stopped. He pushed her away, down onto the carpeted floor, and ordered her to kneel. Puzzled, she knelt, heels against her tingling buttocks. Fields stood above her, bending to squeeze the swaying globes of her breasts. Then he began to open his clothes.

It almost made her sick, but she did as he wanted her to. And then, as soon as it was over, he seemed to lose all interest in her. He slumped back in the big chair, drowsy, sloppy, revolting-looking.

Feeling disgusted, Meg went into the bathroom. She took a mouthful of water, spat it out. She caught sight of herself in the mirror, clad in the belt and stockings. She had heard that for some men it was spicier to see a girl wearing stockings than one wearing nothing at all. And the spanking, and now this—Fields was just a mass of twisted lusts.

He was snoring contentedly when she returned from the bathroom. She dressed and woke him up, and he giggled foolishly and apologized for dozing off.

It was five in the morning when his Dual-Ghia sports car pulled up outside the Beverly Wilshire. He escorted Meg in, but did not ride upstairs with her. "I'll be seeing you," he told her at the elevator, grinning lewdly. "And don't worry about the screen test. The part is yours, and I'm not kidding."

Bonaventura was still awake, upstairs, pacing around the suite like a tense caged animal. He looked up guiltily as Meg entered.

"Of all the cruds," she said bitterly.

"I'm sorry. Honest, honey, I'm sorry—"

"You knew he was like that, didn't you? And yet you fixed me up with him."

"The screen test was a dud," Bonaventura said thinly. "I had to do something to save the situation. Was it that bad tonight? He didn't hurt you, did he?"

"Not really. He made me do a strip, everything but my garter-belt and nylons. And then he put me over his knee and spanked me. I bet I turn purple down there. And then, when he was good and heated up—" She scowled in disgust. "Ugh! I couldn't even tell you about it. But it was pretty awful."

"You poor kid. But what did he say about giving you a part?"

"He and the old man are making a comedy job, and they wanted Mansfield. It's a role for a blonde with big—with a big bust. He said I could have the part."

"Yippee!"

"But I'm not taking it," Meg said suddenly. "Not if it means amusing that pervert every night. And I suppose you'll pimp me off to the old man too. What funny little specialties does *he* have?"

"Now, hold on, Meg—"

"You heard me. I don't mind having to go through this once with Fields, but I'd hate to have to make a regular thing of it."

"You won't have to."

"Is that a promise?"

"We'll sign the contract. Then we'll lower the boom on Arthur. We'll keep you so busy dating Hollywood's eligible bachelors that Arthur won't be able to get his oar in. Don't worry about him."

As she undressed for bed, Meg wondered how much Bonaventura's promise was worth. No doubt the wily little agent meant well—but the only thing he was interested in was furthering the career of Meg Loring, and he didn't seem to care what sort of mud he dragged her through while advancing her career.

She dropped off to sleep. The next thing she knew the lights were on, and somebody was shaking her awake. She sat up groggily, the sheets dropping away from her nude body, and thumbed her eyes.

"Wake up!" Bonaventura was yelling. "And for God's sake cover yourself!"

She blinked at him, and sleepily pulled the sheet up over the steep peaks of her breasts. "What time is it? What's the matter?"

"It's two in the afternoon," Bonaventura said. "You can't sleep forever. Anyhow, I just got a call from Fields. The old man, not Arthur. They want you for *Sleepytime Gal*. He's talking contract, starting at $250."

"Great! Gosh, that's more than ten thousand a year—"

"It's crap," Bonaventura snapped. "I'd sooner sell you to a white slave ring than sign for that. Listen, baby, we've got 'em by the *cojones*, you hear me? I'm gonna hold them up for five hundred at minimum. Go take a shower and wake yourself up. We're due at the studio in an hour and a half for signing, but I'm going to talk to Fields again first."

Meg stumbled out of bed and groped her way to the shower. As Bonaventura scooted past her, she tripped, and stumbled over him. He caught her naked body, one hand clasping her breasts. The moment she was on her feet, he released her as though he had been touching a live electrical socket. She grinned at him and went on into the shower. *Poor Max*, she thought. *You'd think that after practically living with me for three months I'd be just a piece of furniture to him. But he's crazy to get into bed with me, and he doesn't have the guts. So it kills him when I keep waving my bare butt in front of him.*

She came out of the shower fifteen minutes later. Bonaventura was smiling.

"I got some nice terms, I think."

"Swell." She turned around. "You see any marks from last night's spanking on me, Max?"

"Not a one, baby. Your bottom's as flawless as ever. Be a good girl and get your ass covered now, and let's get over to the studio."

Meg signed her first motion-picture contract late that afternoon. It guaranteed her a salary of $325 a week for a minimum of thirteen weeks, plus a thousand-dollar bonus upon satisfactory completion of the film. The contract gave the Fields an option on her services—at a price to be decided—for their next production, whatever it might be, and required Meg to get their permission if someone else offered her a role before they were ready to use her again.

Meg was delighted with the contract, but Bonaventura did not regard it as anything worth getting excited over. "It's chicken feed, complete chicken feed. But you can't fight the system. Just wait. When this picture's done, get you $450 a week on the next contract, and no one shot movie deals either. By next year at this time you'll be pulling down a thousand a week and a percentage of the gross besides." Bonaventura's eyes took on a far-off, misty gleam. "I ain't gonna let you toss that money away, neither. Sure, you'll buy yourself a nice house like all the rest of them do. But you're gonna invest. Buy some good stocks and bonds. Buy an oil well. Because in another fifteen years there won't be any market for you as a sex queen, and that's when it's nice to have the stocks and bonds. It isn't everyone who can pull a Mae West and keep going for years and years. And *she's* got the stocks and bonds too, plenty!"

Despite Bonaventura's disclaimer, though, Meg was thrilled at the contract. $325 a week! Why, that was more than most people made in a month and a half, back in Harmons Glen! And, coming on top of her prize money and her posing fees, she was beginning to have some substantial wealth.

The next day, the script arrived. It was a dumb-blonde part, only it would be played by a redhead. The idea was a thin one—a sexy, big-busted girl who had somehow reached full-blown ripeness without ever learning about the birds and the bees, and who gets into all kinds of amusing scrapes because of her ignorance. The script-writer had milked the situation for all it was worth, and there were some pretty good lines in it. Meg's part was a big one, and it was studded with eye-catching sequences in nightgowns and chemises and even an outdoor nude bathing sequences that the Fieldses intended to make as risqué as possible.

Work began the following week. The director was Sid Fassett, and the film was starring David Hughes and Laura Wayne. According to the contract, Meg would not be starred, but would receive special treatment on the credits: "—*and introducing Meg Loring*." Bonaventura confidently assured her, though, that once the picture was complete old Mack Fields would see that the smart thing would be to build his advertising campaign around the new bosomy attraction.

The studio press-agentry corps went to work on Meg, always with Bonaventura sitting in to make sure nothing went amiss. A torrent of copy left the studio mimeograph machines—and an astonishing amount of it found its way into print. What had begun as a quick potboiling bit of fluff was turning, day by day, into a vehicle to launch a sensational new star.

Meg learned her lines diligently. At first, Fassett was blunt and unpleasant to her, but as she began to respond to his direction he warmed toward her. The part didn't call for any great subtlety of delivery—"As long as the camera stays on your tits, honey, you could be reciting the Gettysburg Address and the audience wouldn't mind," the older Fields assured her—and she managed to contribute some unexpectedly able bits of timing and motion.

The picture was taking shape. She was becoming a star. Every day, Meg Loring's name was in the paper. Every night, she was squired about town by some aspiring young actor—very rarely the same one twice. Bonaventura dug them up and discarded them with equal ease.

She never slept with them. It was orders from headquarters. "You let one of those monkeys make you and I'll personally horsewhip you," Bonaventura said. "You've got to play hard to make. Let the word get around that Meg Loring will sleep, but not for just anybody."

Three weeks went by. The picture was well along, and life was so hectic that Meg never had time even to stop and think, *This is it. I'm in Hollywood making a movie. I'm a star.* She was too busy being swept along by the stream of success.

People recognized her on the streets. They even asked for her autograph. Somehow, that was the biggest thrill of all—being spotted, being handed pens and autograph books.

Bonaventura was ever alive to publicity possibilities. The fourth week of shooting, they did the nude bathing scene, using a creek outside Pasadena. Both Fieldses were there, and a couple of cameramen, and the usual technicians and hangers-on, all of them drooling for a chance to see Meg Loring unveil. The sequence called for her to be hiking through the woods in a plaid blouse and tight blue jeans, for her to pull off her clothes impulsively and run down to the creek, while the male lead, all unknown to her, watched goggle-eyed from a rowboat.

She had to go through the sequence a dozen times before old Fields and Fassett were satisfied. Smile at the creek, unbutton the blouse, unzip the jeans, run down to the lake, with the camera getting a quick pan shot of jiggling buttocks as she ran. Then into the water, bobbing up, and the camera recording breasts and nipples. The nipples could be edited out later; the footage would probably be bootlegged around Hollywood.

Bonaventura had made arrangements of his own. A men's magazine photographer was on hand, stationed in a blind, and he snapped dozens of shots, Meg Loring peeling, Meg Loring running down to the bank, Meg Loring diving in. He took breast shots, buttock shots, profile shots, crotch shots. Fields and son had not objected; any publicity for the film was welcome, particularly when it played up the nude sequence.

"They'll be rushing those shots into print," Bonaventura told her later that afternoon, as she bundled into a warm robe and gulped brandy. "The first nude shots of Meg Loring, taken as she films a scene from her first movie. We get five hundred bucks, Fields gets publicity, the mag gets big sales. Everybody's happy."

"They won't print anything indecent, though, will they? I didn't have anything on."

"The mag has to go through the mails, honey. They won't run any raw stuff. A couple of tit shots and some backside stuff, and maybe a side view. The rest of the stills will get bootlegged around, same as the stuff cut from the rushes. So a lot of guys will find out that you're a real redhead. What of it? It's money in the bank, kiddo. You can afford to be modest in your old age, after you've made your pile."

Max's next brainstorm came the week before the film was to be brought in. "We'll do some nude art shots," he said. "The Meg Loring Calendar, we'll call it. Heck, so Monroe did it first. She didn't patent the idea."

He hired a photographer and they came up with four nude poses: a Spring pose, taken outdoors in a grassy meadow, Meg lying on her side with one leg drawn up, holding a greenhouse daffodil against her breasts. A Summer pose, indoors under bright lights, Meg lying on a beach blanket, face up, with a book opened to cover her loins. An

Autumn shot, Meg lying sprawled out dreamily on a pile of tinted leaves, with her backside to the camera. A Winter shot, Meg in red mittens, red boots, and a red cap, nothing else, standing in a fake snowstorm with one knee lifted to hide her loins, and her arms folded in a gesture that at the same time seemed to be a huddling against the cold and also thrust her breasts forward.

Plans were made to distribute the calendar a month before the release of the picture. The studio would then, of course, make a much-publicized attempt to suppress the calendar, and then bootlegged copies would "accidentally" leak from the publishers at three dollars apiece. Bonaventura had fifty thousand printed. He arranged distribution and sold three thousand at $1 apiece before the studio crackdown. It made headlines all over Los Angeles—STUDIO BUYS UP NUDE CALENDAR. The intimation was that they had snapped up the entire edition to protect their new star's reputation. Meg Loring issued a statement: "I'm sorry the whole mess happened. I needed the money and I posed for the shots. If I had it all to do over now, I'd know better."

A week later, a Hollywood box number offered "limited" quantities of the "suppressed" calendar at $2.98. Within a week, there were fifteen thousand orders. They were sold out two weeks later.

"We netted close to fifty thousand clams on that calendar shenanigan," Bonaventura told her proudly. "We're rolling in dough, now. *Rolling* in it."

Meg nodded distantly. It was seven months, now, since she had first walked into Max Bonaventura's office. She had slept with three men since that day, had been handled and ogled by countless others, and her breasts and thighs and buttocks had been displayed in a calendar and in greater or lesser degrees of bareness in dozens of magazines. And her gross earnings for the first seven months of her career were approaching $100,000.

The ceiling was unlimited. Her future was paved with gold. Yet there was lingering dissatisfaction. She was skyrocketing to glory, but something was missing. It all seemed so unreal, so tinselly and insubstantial.

She realized that hitting the big time wasn't as grand as she had dreamed. Not with men pinching and handling her, and sometimes going to bed with her. Not with photographers crowding around her, trying to get a real zorch tit shot to wow the editor. It was all tawdry and coarse, she thought.

Ned Myers' words nagged at her now. *How long will it be before you get sick of success?*

She was worried. She waited apprehensively for the first preview of her movie, and doubt and uncertainty preyed on her mind.

Nine

The movie opened at Grauman's Chinese on the first of March. The trade previews had already indicated that the film was going to do all right. The Fieldses were impressed, too. With only a little urging from Bonaventura, they had torn up Meg's limit contract and replaced it with one that called for her to continue receiving her $325 every week even while she wasn't working.

Radiant in evening-gown and orchids, Meg made a grand entrance to the theater on the arm of David Hughes, the suave veteran actor who had played the male lead. Bonaventura unobtrusively entered alone, but he took a seat down front on Meg's left. Meg closed her eyes, seeing again the brilliant lights on the theater's ornate front:

DAVID HUGHES   LAURA WAYNE

In

MACK AND ARTHUR FIELDS'

SLEEPYTIME GAL

introducing

MEG LORING

The audience was restless. Celebrities though they all were, they kept leaving their seats and roaming up front for a glimpse of Meg Loring in the flesh. Meg had taken care that plenty of flesh would be visible. She was wearing her most daring gown, with a slash front that sliced down to her navel. She had no bra on, and if she bent over her nipples would be visible.

Some of her thunder was stolen, though, ten minutes before show-time, when Maria Doman made her appearance. Her gown brought oohs of surprise from the usually blasé crowd. She wore an off-the-shoulder mink stole; she was bare above the waist except for a filmy bandanna that looped around her neck and covered her breasts without hiding them at all. She smiled sweetly at Meg, who repressed her first burst of anger and returned the smile. Meg told herself that she had no right to be angry with the Italian starlet. After all, she herself had made use of Maria's fame to boost her own career, and now Maria—already outpaced by the fast-rising Meg Loring—was continuing the unveiling feud.

The lights dimmed, and the credits appeared on the screen. Meg had seen the film half a dozen times already, but it was forever fascinating to watch herself in motion—laughing, dancing, talking, pouting, frowning. The bathing scene went off impressively; the producers had just barely skirted the borderline of decency, with one tremendously brief nipple shot, a fraction of a second that was over before the censors could scream.

There was a party after the premiere—plenty of champagne, and people weaving up to Meg to peer down her gown and tell her what a great career she had ahead of her. She smiled graciously, thanking everybody without seeming swell-headed. "You can't afford to go high-hat on one film," Bonaventura warned her. "There are going to be people trying to knife you in the back all the time, now. Don't make any unnecessary enemies."

The reviews the next day were all that she could have asked for.

"SLEEPYTIME GAL, *the latest offering of those master craftsmen Mack and Arthur Fields, provides ninety minutes of chucklesome film farce. Although David Hughes and Laura Wayne perform at their consistently high level, the flick is undoubtedly carried by the much-ballyhooed Meg Loring. In case you've been off in Siberia the past six months and haven't seen any of the numerous cheesecake shots of this new sexation, let us point out that Miss Loring is a stunningly endowed redhead with a voluptuous body and a wide-eyed, innocent face. Expectably enough, much of the camera action in* SLEEPYTIME GAL *is concerned with displaying Miss Loring's two most spectacular assets. But when she isn't bending over to show off her cleavage, going skinny-dipping (a most provocative scene!) or clambering into sudsy bathtubs, she demonstrates a genuine knack for deadpan comedy that makes her a delight to watch even with clothes on ...*"

Not one of the reviews failed to give Meg Loring a big spread. The day after, advantage was taken of this in the film's advertising. Every Los Angeles paper had a half-page ad whose headline screamed, A STAR IS BORN! Selected quotes on Meg Loring's performance were interspersed between nine stills from the picture.

The day after that, the ad was the same, only it spread over the entire page. And there was a new gimmick: a blank rectangle on the page, with the caption, "*Sorry—our ad would have been refused if we tried to publish this shot of Meg Loring. But you'll see it on the screen!*"

The theater reported record crowds, long lines for every show. National distribution was beginning, with the film placed in fifty first-run theaters. Two hundred other theaters round the country were clamoring for it. Bonaventura clipped out endless newspaper pages, pasting them all in a big scrapbook, muttering to himself, "If we were only getting a percentage of the gross! If we were only getting a percentage of the gross!"

The Legion of Decency gave the movie a *Condemned* rating. Attendance rocketed even higher. A police chief in Detroit tried to prevent the screening and failed. Billboards all over the country blossomed out with color shots of Meg Loring wearing practically nothing.

She was launched overnight.

This was it. This was the smash she had dreamed about—only it was even more spectacular than she had dared to envisage in her dreams.

It was strange, she thought. An entire nation going wild. About what? About a girl's breasts, nothing more. Two round, soft hillocks of flesh, tipped with red. Every woman has breasts. But Meg Loring's were a little rounder, a little fuller, than Everywoman's—and Meg Loring's breasts were up on the screen, on display to anyone who had good eyesight and the price of admission. That was the difference. A silly thing, Meg thought—but it was making her a wealthy woman.

Arthur Fields called at the height of the excitement. He and his father had plans for three Meg Loring films to be made in swift succession and released at six-month intervals starting in the fall. The first would be a Civil War story, with Meg playing the part of a Union Spy in South Carolina—a Perils-of-Pauline style epic, only done more seriously. The second would be a wild farce about Prohibition, with Meg in the role of a wide-eyed virgin who inherits a speakeasy from her uncle. And the third, Fields explained, would be a soap opera, Meg's first serious role, all about a beautiful movie star who cannot find love.

"Let's get together and talk contract on the whole package," Fields said. "Naturally, there'll be a hike in the girl's pay—"

"Naturally," Bonaventura said coolly. "Why don't you call back in a couple of weeks and we'll discuss terms. Meg wants a breather before she gets back into the whirl of things."

He hung up, and told Meg about the conversation. She said worriedly, "Why don't we grab the contract before he changes his mind?"

Bonaventura smiled patronizingly. "You'd sign for peanuts, too, I bet. Listen, kiddo: the box office on this first flick is going to be phenomenal. Fields will come crawling to us. I want to make him sweat it out. He'll offer you five hundred. I'll say no. He'll go to six. I'll ask for six and 10% of the gross. He'll get sore. Finally we'll settle for seven hundred a week and 5% of the gross. You know how much seven hundred a week is? That's $35,000 a year, just as your base pay. And from there it goes up and up. Two or three years from now, you form your own movie company. Then *you* hire Fields, instead of the other way around. And the net from the film is yours—at corporation tax rates, instead of personal. Sweetie, you'll be a millionaire before you're twenty-five, I promise you that!"

The excitement boiled on. Meg tried to keep out of the limelight. Through Bonaventura, she arranged to buy a house in Glendale. She was about to buy a car, too, but the Fieldses came through with a little token of their esteem, a cream-colored Mercedes-Benz 300SL. Bonaventura was ecstatic when he saw it.

"You know what that car costs?" he crowed. "Fourteen thousand bucks! Fields wants you so bad it hurts. He's itching for your name on a new contract."

"And Arthur's itching for something else, too," Meg said sourly. "Itching to paddle my butt again, and then to have me—"

"Don't worry, sweet. Old Arthur's gonna be frustrated, that's all. Six months ago he could get Meg Loring to cater to his little perversions, but not anymore! You're a hot property. You can thumb your nose to him and there's not a thing he can do about it, because he knows you're going to be his meal ticket for the next ten years."

The following week, Meg moved into the house. It had ten rooms and a swimming pool. She wandered through the bare rooms. The only furniture was a bedroom set, ordered on rush delivery. It would be months before the place would look like a home—and by that time, she thought, she would be moving on to an even more palatial place in Beverly Hills.

She offered to let Bonaventura move in with her, but the little man would not hear of it. He accepted one room to use as an office, but rented a suite in a nearby hotel to live in.

For the rest of that month Meg busied herself shopping for furniture, hugely enjoying driving around the sprawling city in her powerful racing car. Wherever she went, there were people pointing to her, even though she took the step of piling her hair into a bun and donning big black sunglasses. The disguise was ineffectual. She was rapidly finding out that there was no such thing as privacy for a film star.

And then, one day, she had a visitor.

By this time Meg Loring had a staff of four—a housekeeper, an engagements secretary, and a correspondence secretary, to handle fan mail, as well as her agent-manager. It was the engagements secretary who came to her one morning, looking perplexed, and said, "There's a man to see you, Miss Loring. He doesn't have an appointment."

"Let him make one, then. I think I have some time around next Wednesday. What does he want, anyway?"

"He says he's an old friend of yours."

Meg looked up, frowning. "Did he give you his name?"

The woman consulted a card. "Yes. Hazen, Mr. Jack Hazen."

The name cut through Meg's mind like a whirling sword. "*Jack*," she whispered. Her legs felt weak, and chills ran down her back.

"Should I make an appointment for him, Miss Loring? He looks like a pretty rough sort to me. Maybe I'd better tell him you're leaving for Mexico tomorrow, and—"

"No. No! Send him in!"

"But—without any appointment—!"

"*Send him in*," Meg snapped.

Shrugging, the secretary retreated. Meg glanced into a mirror. She was wearing an open-collared blouse that revealed the full globes of her bosom. Self-consciously, she buttoned all but the top button. There was a knock at the door.

"Come in," she said.

Jack pushed the door open and stood at the threshold. His face wore an odd expression, half awe-smitten, half contemptuous. He looked rougher and thicker and coarser than she remembered him. He was a big, burly man, six feet two and probably two hundred pounds, and he looked much older than his twenty-five years.

"Meg," he muttered.

"Hello, Jack," she said evenly, staring at this stranger who only a year ago had robbed her of her virginity and thus had helped to catapult her into her decision to leave Idaho. "I didn't expect any visits from you," she said. "What brings you to these parts?"

He put his hands in his pockets and lounged against the wall. "My Aunt Martha died. She lived in South Gate. I came down for the funeral. Then I figured I might as well look you up. The studio gave me your address when I said I was your ex-fiancé."

"We never were—"

"You slept for me, Meg," he said hoarsely. "In my book, when a good girl sleeps for a man, it means she wants to marry him. But I was wrong on two counts. You didn't want to marry me—and you weren't a good girl."

"It was my first time, with you!"

"Maybe so. But it wasn't your last!"

"Did you come here to boast about that grubby little scene in your back seat, Jack?"

He shook his head solemnly. "Nuh-uh. I just come here to get a look at the great Meg Loring in the flesh. You been showing a lot of your flesh around, too. That's okay. You're built. I never slept with a girl with better breasts than you—"

"Shut your filthy mouth! I'll have you thrown out!"

Jack smiled. "Yeah, you'd do that. You're a big wheel movie star, ain't you? We know all about it, back home. We been watching you. You got your picture in the Boise paper, did you know that? The one of you coming outta the water, without the top of your bathing suit. That was the first we knew what you were up to. Then we started watching. You were Miss Galaxy, or whatever. Then you made this movie. And you had those pictures in the magazines, showing your bare backside like the whore you are. I just thought I'd come tell you what the town thinks of you. Your picture's playing in Boise now. All the kids in town went to see it. It got them so hot up that they been running around like crazy for wimmen. You know what Dan Hymer said. He said he always knew you were a slut, and now you're proving it. So I told him—"

"Get out of here."

"I told him you were a lousy bed mate. But I guess you've improved in Hollywood. You must get plenty of practice." Jack smiled. "You ought to hear what your folks think about you, too. For a long time they were pretty sore because you never wrote to them. They ain't sore anymore. They say if they got a letter from you now, they'd tear it up without opening it."

Meg's lower lip trembled. She hadn't written home since she left, hadn't known how to write to her parents without telling them the truth. And that was impossible. To say that she was showing her breasts to men, going to Mexico with them, doing disgusting things to win a film contract—no. Silence was better. But somehow she had never realized the effect this might have on them.

Jack went on, "That's about all I got to say. I don't like this town and I ain't gonna stay here another half hour. But at least I saw you. At least I told you. Just one thing more that a lot of people are saying. They hope that you don't let anyone know you were born in Harmons Glen. It's bad for the town. We don't want people to think that all our girls are whores like you. We got some good girls too, who don't sell themselves to make a million bucks."

He glared at her for a moment. Then he spun around and left.

Meg felt stunned. She rose nervelessly and closed the door. Then, throwing herself down on the couch, she began to sob uncontrollably.

Whore. Slut. If they got a letter from you now, they'd tear it up without opening it. We don't want people to think that all our girls are whores like you.

A sudden wild notion seized her. She would go back to Harmons Falls, beg their forgiveness. She would give up this phony, high-pressure world and get back to decency. Marry Jack, have children, forget this nonsensical life of showing her body and making love to strangers for the sake of her career.

The moment the thought came, she knew it was absurd. She could never go back to the old life. There were too many fingerprints on her, too many soiled memories. There was no way she could unsleep with Roy Hammond, with Ned Myers, with the others. No way she could destroy the magazines that had run nude photographs of her. No way to call back the calendars, to unmake the movie. Idaho farm wives did not drive Mercedes 300-SLs. They did not have scrapbooks of their reviews. She moved in a different orbit, now, and there was no going back to the old, simple life. Skyrockets never re-turned to the launching site.

There was a knock at the door. Without waiting for a reply, Bonaventura walked in.

His eyes went wide. "Hey! What's the matter?"

"Max, I'm—I'm all mixed up."

He rushed over and sat down next to her. "Look, baby, you can't go crying your eyes all red! What's going on? Who was that character who just left? Joanie says it's an old friend of yours from Idaho."

She nodded dismally. "That's right. His name is Jack Hazen. I told you about him. He's the one who—in the back seat—"

"Christ almighty! He isn't trying to work a squeeze, is he? Selling his memoirs to a scandal mag if you don't buy him off?"

"No—nothing like that. He just came to tell me how the people in my home town are reacting. They know all about me. They think—they think I'm a whore, Max. A disgrace to the town. My own parents say they'll rip up any letters they get from me without opening them."

"Baby, who gives two craps what Harmons Falls Idaho thinks about—"

"No, Max. You don't understand. God, I almost wish I had stayed there and never gotten into this filthy business! Max, I want to go home!"

"You don't know what you're saying."

"Yes, Max. I want to give it all up. Go home, ask them to forgive me. Live a clean life."

"You're hysterical, baby. Just cry it all out. You'll calm down and see that you can't go back."

"I know that, too. But I wish—if there was only some way—oh, Max, I'm all balled up!"

The controls burst, and she threw herself onto Bonaventura's lap, sobbing wildly. He gripped her shoulders and held her tightly without saying anything. Meg cried until she could cry no more. She sat up, feeling suddenly foolish, and dabbed at her reddened eyes.

"Everything okay, now?"

She smiled weakly. "I guess I just had to blow off some steam. Jack's visit got me all twisted up inside."

"Sure, I understand. A face out of the past, that sort of stuff. You all calmed down, now? No more talk about breaking your contract and going home?"

She grinned. "No more. I must have been temporarily nuts to think of giving up all this just to go back to a whistle stop town. I wasn't thinking smart. I was forgetting how grubby and dull and petty the place is. I'd blow my brains out after a week there."

"That's my baby," Bonaventura said warmly. "I guess even a sensible girl like you gets her cockeyed moments. But now listen to me. I got a brainstorm. You *are* going back to Harmons Glen."

"Huh?"

"Sure. You're going to go back there for a two-day visit. You're going to consider retiring from the movies, get me? Only after a two-day retirement, the cries of your faithful fans will bring you back to Hollywood, full of a sense of obligation to them. It'll be a great publicity coup, honey. You're lucky you got a genius for a manager!"

Ten

She greeted Bonaventura's brainstorm with incredulity and derision. But he worked on her, wheedling, cajoling, persuading. And at last she gave in, as she always did when Bonaventura came up with a new gimmick.

Bonaventura arranged everything. He bought her a bus ticket to Harmons Glen. He tipped off Arthur Fields about the stunt, just so the producers wouldn't have apoplectic fits when the news of Meg Loring's "retirement" hit the papers. Finally, Bonaventura called in the reporters.

At eight-thirty on a Tuesday morning, Meg boarded a bus for Idaho. She was carrying a single small suitcase, and she was dressed chastely in a high-collar jersey and a flowing skirt. Sunglasses hid her face, and she had her hair done up in a ponytail. She took a seat in the back of the bus, hoping no one would recognize her.

That afternoon the L.A. papers carried the story on their front page.

"GLAMOUR QUEEN GOES HOME!

'SICK OF PUBLICITY,' SAYS MEG LORING

LEAVES H'WOOD WITHOUT WARNING

"The brief but spectacular film career of busty Meg Loring appears to have come to an unexpected finish. The well-stacked redhead, who scored smash hit in her first film, SLEEPYTIME GAL, *slipped unnoticed out of her Glendale home early this morning. A note found by her manager, Max Bonaventura, declared: 'I can't take it any longer. I'm sick of the publicity and the excitement. I'm leaving Hollywood for good and returning to a simpler way of life. I have nothing but affection for those people who helped me make the grade, but I don't feel that I'm cut out for the Hollywood way of life.'*

"Bonaventura, who noted that Miss Loring had taken virtually nothing with her, said he was 'Stunned' by the star's departure. Mack and Arthur Fields, co-producers of Miss Loring's first film, issued this statement: 'We are flabbergasted. She seemed like such a happy, well-adjusted girl. Meg Loring would have figured prominently in all our future plans, but naturally we will make no attempt to force her to reconsider. A movie star must be entitled to a life of her own, if such is her wish….'"

The town hadn't changed much, Meg thought, as she descended from the bus, suitcase in hand. She had been gone a year almost to the week, but everything looked the same, even the loungers in front of the bank on Main Street.

She had not come alone. Bonaventura had sent a photographer along with her on the bus. He crouched next to a telephone pole, out of sight, getting a shot of her as she stood, without makeup, her hair blowing in the breeze, looking around at the Main Street of her home town.

A moment later she began to walk north, toward Martin Street. As she expected, a few of the bank loungers came toward her. She recognized them, but they did not seem to see her.

"Carry your bag, Miss?"

She took the sunglasses off. "Don't I even get a hello, Tommy?"

The young man gasped. "Meg—"

"Surprised?"

"Yeah." There was awe on his face for a moment, and then sullen contempt veiled his eyes. "Why'd you come back here, anyway?"

"Don't I have a right to visit my home town?"

"This ain't your home town anymore."

They all recognized her, now. They were hanging back, whispering, nudging each other with elbows. Meg picked up her suitcase and started to walk. No one made any further offer to carry it for her. They drifted along some twenty feet behind her whispering. Meg hoped the photographer was getting it all recorded.

She felt apprehensive about this trip. Max had been glib, Max had oophed her into going. But now that she was here, she regretted it. They hated her. She wasn't the local girl who had made good. She was the local girl who had turned into a shameless hussy. These were small-town people, with small-town ideas. A girl could spread her legs for every boy in town, so long as she behaved decently in public. But to go make movies, and let magazines print pictures of her breasts and buttocks— that was against the grain.

She kept walking—up Main to Martin, then a left turn. Three blocks of frame houses down Martin was the house where she had been born. Her stomach felt queasy at the thought of ringing her own doorbell, coming home like a stranger.

The house hadn't changed much. It needed a new coat of paint, and the dog had been digging up the garden. She put her suitcase down and walked up the steps.

She rang the bell.

Silence. The kitchen curtain was pulled aside, and someone peeked out. Meg rang again. The door opened.

Her mother stood there, looking old and seamed and worn. Meg managed a tremulous smile.

"H-hello, Mom. Remember me? I came home to see how everybody was."

"I don't know you, young lady," her mother said in frigid tones.

Meg blinked. "Heck, Mom, don't be like that. I'm your daughter!"

"I've only got one daughter. She's inside."

Meg glanced past her mother. The rest of the family had gathered in the vestibule. Her father, stony-faced, grim. Her kid sister, fifteen, now, not going to be as pretty as her older sister Meg but already full in the bosom. Her brother Don, eighteen, lanky.

"Aren't you going to ask me in?" Meg said.

"You're no kin of ours."

"Don't say that, Mom!" Meg felt tears beginning to force their way into her eyes. But the faces before her were cold and tearless. "I—I told you all, I was going to go into show business. You ought to be proud of me. I'm a movie star. I'm famous, Mom."

"Infamous is the word. Letting men photograph your bare body— disgracing us so we hardly dare to go out on the streets here—and now you have the impudence to come home and expect a welcome! We've long since decided to forget you. You're not wanted here!"

Suddenly her father said, "Let her come in, Donna. There's someone across the street taking pictures of this. We don't want to make a public scene."

Meg picked up her suitcase and entered, surprised by the unexpected invitation. Once within the house, though, she felt no more comfortable.

The atmosphere was frosty. No one spoke.

"Well?" Meg said. "You invited me in. At least you can say something to me. Cuss me out. It's better than dead silence, anyway."

Her father said, "Jack Hazen told us he visited you in Hollywood. He said you lived in a house as big as the Town Hall."

"It's only middle-sized, Dad. But I make a lot of money. I'll be getting seven hundred dollars a week when I start my next movie."

"Seven hundred—" her father gasped.

"The devil's money," snapped her mother. "And how much do the magazines pay you to photograph your nakedness? A thousand dollars a picture?"

Meg smiled. "It isn't anywhere near that much, Mom. They pay well, but—listen." She turned to face her brother. "Don, are you still pining to go to that agricultural college?"

"Yeah, sis, but—"

"I'll pay for it. The whole four years. It wouldn't cost me more than a month's work."

Her brother's face lit up. "Gee, sis I—"

"No!" Mrs. Tandler thundered. "I won't hear of it."

"Please, Mom," Meg said. "He wants to go so bad—"

"I'll die before I let my son go to college on the earnings of a prostitute," her mother said coldly. "I'd rather see him stay here."

"Donna," Mr. Tandler began, "you mustn't carry this thing too far—"

Meg's lips were trembling again. "Don't call me that name, mother!"

"It's true, isn't it? You've sold your body for cash. That makes you a whore so far as I'm concerned—and so far as everyone else in Harmons Glen is concerned too. But at least your sister won't go the same way. She's getting married,"

"Katie? Married?" Meg exclaimed. "But she's only a kid!"

"She'll be sixteen when the ceremony's held, and that's old enough. She's marrying Sam Bryce soon as he graduates from high school this summer. It was my idea. She was soft in him anyway, and this way she won't have any chance to get fancy ideas about Hollywood. Or getting to do things with boys that she shouldn't be doing before she's married."

Meg stared incredulously at her younger sister. Kate blushed and looked at the floor. Meg suspected the real story—that Kate and Sam had been discovered in the pine grove with their pants down, and were being pressured into a quick marriage by Mrs. Tandler so at least one of the Tandler girls could claim a measure of respectability in the town.

After some discussion, Meg persuaded her mother to allow her to stay for dinner and to sleep over. The older woman's hatred seemed weakening, though there was no real warmth about her agreement. Next, she got permission for the photographer to come in and take some shots of the house. "Just so long as he doesn't photograph any of us," her mother declared stonily.

After she had left her suitcase in what had been her old room upstairs, she phoned the Harmony Hotel and reached her photographer.

"Looked like they were giving you a hard time," he said.

"They were. They're old fashioned people, Mike. But they're letting me sleep over, and they'll let you come in and take some shots of the house. But there's one catch. You can't photograph any of them."

"What kind of crap is that? I'm counting on a shot of you at the family dinner table—"

"Absolutely *verboten*."

"We've got to have it. Look, leave it to Mike. I'll take a sneak shot with a little Minox I've got. They'll never even know."

"Well—"

"We can't do without the shot. I'll be right over."

Dinner that night was conducted in stony silence. Meg sat at her old place, but the only conversation was "Pass the salt" and "I'd like the butter, please." The photographer had gone over the house completely just before dinner, snapping Meg in her bedroom, in the living room, on the front porch. Then, just as the family was sitting down for dinner, he excused himself, asking to be shown to the washroom to change his film.

He reappeared fifteen minutes later, just as the roast was being served. He stood in the doorway of the kitchen and said, "Thanks for your cooperation, everyone. You've all been swell."

Meg glanced at him. He made a quick finger-and-thumb gesture. Like a good sleight-of-hand artist, he had succeeded in taking a family shot unnoticed.

It was a long, dreary evening. Ten o'clock was the usual bedtime at the Tandler house, and the rule was not broken that evening. After changing into her pajamas, Meg went across the hall into her sister's room.

Kate was kneeling in the middle of the bed, combing out her long reddish-brown hair. She was wearing a pink shortie nightgown that revealed the rosy-tipped fullness of her young breasts. As Meg came in, the younger girl hastily snatched up a robe and held it to her bosom.

Meg grinned. "Don't jump, sis. It's only me. Mind if I come in?"

"No—of course not—"

"You don't hate me any?"

"Hate you? I—I feel like you're a stranger, Meg. Like I don't even know you. But I can't hate you. Mom hates you, but I don't."

Meg took a seat at the edge of the bed. "You've turned into quite a little woman since I was last here. When I went away you were flat as a board. Now you're almost as big upstairs as I am."

Color rose to the girl's cheeks. "I had to throw away all my old bras. But I'll never be as pretty as you, Meg. I'm big up here, but I won't be as tall, and I'm going to be plump. You're so lucky to look like you do, Meg!"

Meg ignored that. "Listen," she said. "What's this marrying business?"

"Just what Mom said. Sam and I are getting married in the summer."

"Whose idea was it?"

"Well, ours, of course. Only—"

"Only what?"

"Only Mom sort of suggested it. I mean—"

Meg's eyes narrowed. "You love Sam, don't you?"

"Sure. And he loves me."

"Let's hope it stays that way. You weren't figuring on getting married so young, though, I bet."

Kate shrugged. "When I was eighteen or so, I guess."

"But you're just going to be sixteen. That's too early for a girl like you to be settling down with a husband and all."

"We love each other," Kate repeated firmly.

"Sure you do. But when you're this young you can't really be certain. You can't *ever* be certain." Meg paused. "What's the real story, honey? Were you and Sam caught doing something wrong?"

Color blazed in Kate's face. "I don't understand—"

"Yes, you do. Come on. You can tell your sister the truth."

Kate stared down at her feet. In a hollow voice she said, "We had a real hot day about three weeks ago. Sam and I went for a walk, and we were down by the creek, and all of a sudden he said let's go swimming. We didn't have suits or anything, but we got undressed behind bushes and went into the water and we started fooling around a little. And then we got all wild and ran up on shore, and we sort of tripped and fell down and Sam fell on top of me, and I—and he—well, it happened. It was more the way we fell than anything else, and us not having clothes on, and it was sort of easier to do it than not to do it. And then just after we finished, Mrs. Brewster came along and saw us, with everything showing. She ran right over and told Mom. And then we had the explosion. I thought they were gonna kill us both, they were so sore. And then they decided I was going to marry Sam. Right now, instead of two years from now like we'd planned. Mom said a lot of nasty things about you, and how she didn't want me to become the same sort of—to become like you. So she was going to make sure I settled right down and became respectable."

"Good God. You aren't pregnant, are you?"

Kate shook her head. "No. I got my period last week right on time."

"Whew! All you need is a kid to saddle you down right now. Well, I think Mom's making a hell of a mistake, forcing you to get married like this. But I hope it all turns out okay."

"Sam and I still love each other," Kate said quietly. "We'll manage. He isn't angry about having to marry me, or anything. Meg?" she said suddenly.

"Hmm?"

"Meg, are you happy?"

The sudden thrust caught Meg off balance. She hesitated, then said, "Of course I'm happy! I'm making a fortune, people ask me for autographs—"

"But is it what you wanted? Really and truly? People around here talk about you a lot, Meg. And what they say isn't nice. Is it worth it, any amount of money, having people say things like that about you?"

Meg forced an insincere grin. "Believe me, baby, I'm happy. I'm doing what I want to be doing, and to hell with what people say or think. And I hope you and Sam are happy, too. As happy as—as happy as I am—"

She could go no further. There was a lump in her throat, and tears would be flowing from her eyes in another moment. She rose and left her sister's bedroom hurriedly.

Kate had hit the nail square on the head, Meg admitted. She saw right through the surface confidence to the misery beneath, the loneliness, the guilt.

It was a long time before Meg fell asleep that night, in the unfamiliar narrowness of her old bed.

She packed up and left right after breakfast. Goodbyes were restrained, and no one offered to kiss her, though Kate blew her a kiss when her mother was not looking. Meg met her photographer at the hotel, and they wandered around town together, ignoring the hostile stares of the locals. He took fifty or sixty shots of her—on the steps of the town school; in front of the town's one movie; out in the potato fields; down by the creek where she had spent many happy summer afternoons; and, finally, standing at the bus depot waiting for the California-bound bus that would take her forever out of Harmons Glen, Idaho.

She was glad to leave. The town's reception had been chilly, and everything about the visit depressed her. She sat quietly on the way back listening to the photographer criticize the town and her family. "That dinner-table shot came out swell—in focus and everything. But what a bunch of crocks they all were, not posing for me! And down at the hotel they talked about you like you were the Scarlet Woman of Babylon."

"It's a small town, Mike."

"They wanted to know whether I had ever taken any nude shots of you," he said.

"And what did you tell them?" Meg asked. The lensman was the same who had photographed the nude bathing sequence when she made her movie.

"I told them no, I hadn't," he said. "I figured they might lynch me if I told them the truth."

"Or try to buy unretouched prints from you," she said acidly. "These people have hidden depths."

"Boy," the photographer chuckled. "I wonder what they would have done if I showed them *this!*" He opened his wallet and dug into a secret compartment, producing a glossy three-by-four color print. It was a full-length nude of Meg Loring, taken during the filming. Unretouched, it showed the droplets of water forming at her nipples, showed the matted triangle of reddish hair at her loins.

Meg frowned. "You show this to many people?"

"Who, me? Violate professional ethics? This is strictly a private souvenir of a most enjoyable day."

Meg studied the revealing print of her nakedness and tried to be objective about it. But sudden shame overwhelmed her. There she was, in full color, every secret place of her body showing, and this man, this friendly stranger, carried it in his wallet. And, despite his claim of ethics, he had probably displayed it proudly to hundreds of friends. She felt self-loathing. It was as if she had coupled with this stranger at noontime at Hollywood and Vine. With a print like this in existence, she had no claim to her own body.

"Here," she said, handing it back to him. "Maybe someday I'll buy the negative from you."

"Not for a ton of gold, Miss Loring. Not for ton of gold."

It was eleven at night when the bus pulled into Glendale. She phoned Bonaventura immediately.

"I'm back," she said.

"Great! I'll phone the papers and we'll get it into the morning editions. How was it, going back to the old home town?"

"It was hell, Max. Don't ever make me do a thing like that again. Don't even *suggest* that I visit Harmons Glen again, or I'll get a new manager. You hear that? Don't even mention it to me, Max! I want to forget that place!"

Eleven

Before she went to sleep that night, Meg wrote a check for one thousand dollars, payable to Donald Tandler, and slipped it into an envelope along with a note that read, *This is for college, Don. Don't let them argue you out of it. I'm still your sister, whatever they say, and I'm damned if I'll let them ruin your life because they're too proud to accept my money. Please cash the check and use it. Yours with all my love, Meg.*

She sealed the envelope, addressed it to Don, and stuck an airmail stamp on it. Then she wrote a second thousand-dollar check, payable to Katherine Tandler, and enclosed a note that read, *This is my wedding present to you and Sam, darling. Use it for furniture or baby buggies or licorice sticks or anything else you please. Just remember that your sister loves you and wishes you all the luck in the world. Yours, Meg.*

Meg left the letters on the hall table for her secretary to send out in the morning. Both checks had, been signed "Meg Loring"—Meg was worth thousands, but Meg Tandler didn't even have her own checking account. She hoped her parents would not intercept the checks and louse things up in some way.

Meg slept soundly. At ten the next morning her secretary stuck her head in the bedroom door, saw that Meg was half awake, and said, "Mr. Bonaventura is outside, Miss Loring."

"Okay. Send him in."

Bonaventura entered, carrying a thick stack of Los Angeles newspapers. He was beaming broadly, obviously pleased with himself. Glaring sharply at Meg, he said, "You're showing, kiddo. Cover up."

Meg pouted and pulled the blanket up over her breasts. These days she tried to abide by Bonaventura's fetish for decency.

"You didn't come here to tell me that, Max. What's in the papers?"

"Stories about you." He tossed them down on the bed. "Every single one of them picked up the story. *Star Returns After Two Days of Retirement. Heeds Pleas from Fans, Manager, Film Makers.* That sort of stuff."

Meg picked up one of the newspapers at random. The story was on the front page, near the bottom. They had used one of her SLEEPYTIME GAL publicity stills with plenty of bosom emphasis. The gist of the story was that she had returned to her peaceful little hick home town with every intention of embracing a simple, bucolic way of life once again. But, though the people of her town had welcomed her back without fuss or hooplah, she had gone through an internal crisis and had come to the conclusion that her retirement was a mistake, that she had an obligation to the millions of people her first film had entertained, and that, furthermore, she believed that the only true fulfillment possible for her was the creative joy of acting—including some highly serious roles in adaptations of the classics she had always loved. Therefore, the article went on, she had left Harmons Glen as suddenly as she had come there, and was returning to Hollywood—and a big announcement about a forthcoming picture would be made in the very near future.

It was all very touching, very sincere, very moving. And one hundred five percent hokum. The article showed the master hand of Max Bonaventura.

The other newspapers had run virtually the same story—the double renunciation, first of Hollywood and then of Harmons Glen, being the big angle. From a Hollywood newspaper reader's viewpoint, of course, the really noble thing she had done was coming back. By leaving Hollywood for a sleepy small town, she was repudiating the values of existence that millions of Californians swore by. By coming back, she was affirming that the fraudulent and ersatz Hollywood way of life was true and good and worthy. It was just what the readers wanted to be told.

"You're the talk of the town, baby," Bonaventura assured her gleefully.

"You mean people are actually taken in by this phony deal?" Meg asked incredulously. "Can't they all smell how rotten it is? Don't they know it was all a publicity stunt, that nobody would give up a career and go back to a poky hole in nowhere—"

"Honey, they may *think* it's a publicity stunt, but nobody dares say it out loud. You're a Hollywood heroine, don't you see? You're the Girl Who Ran Away From It All and then came back—not because you were hungry for fame and fortune, but because you genuinely wanted to make your fans happy! Christ, Meg, nobody's going to question sentiment like that."

"It brings tears to my eyes."

"It brought tears to Mack Fields' eyes too," Bonaventura said. "While you were away we did some contract talking. You've got to sign the papers today."

"What kind of contract?"

"Three-picture package. You're guaranteed seven-fifty a week for two years, with renewal options on both sides. The base pay comes up for discussion every six months, and they have the option of revising it upward at any time they feel you're worth more. You also nick them for one percent of the gross in the first film, two percent on the second, and five percent on the third and any subsequent films you might make for them. Suppose that third film grosses five million. You know what five percent of that is, baby? It's a quarter of a million buckaroos. A quarter of a *million*."

Meg blinked. That much money was too much to understand. "But the taxes—" she said vaguely.

Bonaventura beamed. "There's a deferred payment kicker. If you make that quarter of a million, you'll get it spread out over ten or twenty or thirty years, like an annuity. It's a lot better to have ten or twenty grand coming in like clockwork every year than to make two hundred fifty G's in one lump and have the government grab three quarters of it right away."

"I don't know what I'd do without you, Max. I'd never be able to figure out these things for myself."

"That's what you got me for, hon. And don't think you're not paying me well to do your thinking for you, either. My share of that two hundred fifty grand works out to around sixty thousand. I'm closing my New York office, Meg. I only need but one client, because she's gonna make you and me both rich for life!"

Meg signed the contract that afternoon in Fields' office, in an appropriately low-cut dress and with appropriate publicity fanfare. Word went forth to the populace that the second Meg Loring film would begin shooting in two months. It was to be a Civil War film— everyone was making Civil War films, because of the centenary celebration, but this would be a unique Civil War film. It would be a *Meg Loring* Civil War film!

A week later, a messenger brought Meg a copy of the treatment for the new movie. In outline, it sounded pretty silly. She played a curvaceous Union belle, daughter of a noble northern statesman, who volunteers to go into Dixie on a spy mission. The actual mission was lifted vaguely from history—something to do with wheedling information about Rebel supply lines—but, of course, the plot called for her to fall in love (and vice versa) with a Confederate colonel. The colonel, however, is a staunch Jeff Davis man who despises damn Yankees, and who is able to love the pretty spy only because she fools him into thinking she is a Virginian. The truth, alas, is discovered, and the love-smitten colonel is forced to lead a spy hunt, the object of his quest being the girl he loves.

The main plot mechanism was the chase. Meg Loring would lead the Rebels a merry chase through woods and streams en route to the Mason-Dixon-line. The plot treatment abounded in specially concocted episodes designed to get maximum mileage from the Loring chassis. Escaping, she would run through a briar patch and emerge with her blouse shredded in all but a few strategic places. Obtaining a new blouse, she would be caught in torrential rains, and the flimsy material would cling to her skin (no bra). She would strip to the buff for a quick plunge in a secluded lake, in the interests of hygiene. Clothed again, she would be seized and stripped nearly nude by a sadistic farmhand minded toward rape. Rescued in the nick of time, she would be taken in for a day by a kindly Southern family, and she would take a bath in a low wooded tub with appropriate glimpses of cleavage and buttocks to titillate the audience. And, finally, captured by her Confederate lover, she would approach him in his tent and melt his hatred with a sensuous display of her irresistible breasts. For a moment he would hover, torn between loyalty to his cause and love for the beauteous spy with the ruby-nipples—and then, conveniently, the surrender at Appomattox would ring down the curtain and make it possible for the ex-foes to shack up permanently without a trace of guilt.

The scenario, Meg thought, was something less than a triumph of the artistic imagination. But it was sure-fire box-office. The sexy Civil War story was just the thing to send them jamming into the theaters—and one cent out of every dollar of admission money would go into Meg Loring's bank account.

She sent back the scenario with her okay on it. The next day, Fields Senior announced the rest of the cast. Co-starred with Meg, in the role of the Confederate colonel, would be none other than Brad Holman,

Despite her own considerable fame, Meg was impressed—jolted—by the news that she would be playing opposite Brad Holman. Brad Holman, who had been one of Hollywood's greatest stars for almost a quarter of a century, and was still going strong, as ruggedly handsome as ever, as thrillingly vital! Meg remembered having waited outside the theater for hours, ten years back, to see the latest Brad Holman movie. She had once made a special trip to Boise to see a Brad Holman revival, a picture he had made in 1939. And now—this man who had been a matinee idol before her parents had even been married was going to be her co-star in a movie! It was beyond all belief. It staggered her. It shattered her poise.

But bigger surprises were in store.

A week before filming was scheduled to begin, Bonaventura stopped over to see her.

"Congratulations," he said.

"Thanks. May I ask what for?"

"Sure you may."

She grinned. "Okay, What for?"

"On your impending marriage," Bonaventura said casually.

"Huh?"

"Sure. Didn't you know? You're all but wrapped up in a license."

Meg grinned. "And who am I marrying—or hasn't that been decided yet? Arthur Fields? Jeff Chandler? Herbert Hoover?"

Bonaventura said quietly, "You're marrying Brad Holman, darling."

"Max, are you drunk or are you just crazy?"

"Neither. I said you're marrying Brad Holman."

"But—just for item one—I don't even *know* Brad Holman. I've been dating half a dozen other guys, but not him. For item two, he's old enough to be my father. And for item three, who the hell said I was interested in getting married, anyway?"

Bonaventura folded his arms and ticked off the numbers with a scolding forefinger. "Item one, you're going to know Brad Holman. Shooting on the new flick starts Monday, and before you're through with it you'll know him all you need to know. Item two, Brad's only forty-six. And item three, you're going to get married because it's good publicity."

Meg shook her head. "No, Max. I absolutely draw the line here. God, to think I'd ever be refusing to marry Brad Holman! But it's inconceivable. It's one thing to spend a night in bed with a man to help your career; it's another to—to sign up for life!"

"Who said anything about for life? This is Hollywood, remember? You wouldn't have to stay married to him very long."

"Whose idea is this?" she asked coldly. "It gets lousier and lousier the more you tell me about it."

Bonaventura was perspiring heavily. "It was well, sort of a joint idea. Holman suggested it to old man Fields, and he liked it so they passed it on, to me. The gimmick is this: you and Brad will start dating as soon as filming begins. The gossip columns will begin whispering that you and he are *that* way about each other, that you feel you'd like to settle down with an older man, that Brad gives you the kind of thrills no one else ever has. Along around the time shooting finishes, you and Brad go off to Mexico and get married. You stay married for a while. You separate just before the premiere of the film—but you come to the premiere as man and wife anyway, a noble gesture for the sake of not washing dirty linen in public. Everyone knows you're separated, though. And right after the film is launched, you file for divorce. Mental cruelty. Filmgoers will mob the theaters, because filmgoers are ghouls who love to see a divorced couple together on the screen when they were still in love. You don't ask for alimony, because you don't need it and can afford to make the grand gesture, but Brad slips you ten grand privately for your troubles in all this. Then you go your separate ways, free as the birds."

"Whew!" Meg said solemnly, when Bonaventura was at last silent. "The whole marriage planned out—from the first to last. But why? Why go through with a silly farce like that?"

Bonaventura smiled. "Brad needs it. His career's in a lousy way. Sure, he won the Oscar in '39, and he's been making films since the Year Three. But he hasn't made a Grade A movie in five years. He hasn't even had a good-sized role in a B film in two and a half years. He's sagging. He needs a jolt."

"And I'm supposed to give it to him?"

"Precisely. You're red hot, publicity-wise. Anything you do gets into the papers. If Meg Loring has constipation, they print it. If she measures her bosom and finds she's now a 42 instead of a 41, they print that too. If Meg Loring gets married, you can bet it'll crowd Kennedy and the pennant race right off Page One. You'll be a transfusion for Brad—a publicity transfusion."

"I see," Meg said coldly.

"Besides perking up his sagging career, you'll also be putting money in your own pocket and his, since you'll be boosting the gross of the film and you're both cut in for slices of the gross. So you see it's a good deal all around, honey. I wouldn't steer you wrong. It'll all be over in a few months, and then everything will be as before—except you'll be a little richer, and Brad Holman will owe you a big favor. You can never tell when he may turn out to be a big help."

"And all I have to do is sleep with him for a few months? Nine girls out of ten would leap at the chance to sleep with Brad Holman. Me, too, except that I hate this business of having to marry him. Marriage shouldn't be taken lightly, this way. It—"

Bonaventura was laughing wildly.

"What's so funny?" Meg asked.

"Sleeping with Holman! Meg, baby, Brad is queer. Cue Doubleyou Ee Ee Are, QUEER. You'll be living with him, but I guarantee you won't be sleeping with him."

"What?" Meg said, aghast. "But he's been married four times—"

"Sure. And you'll be the fifth. But he didn't lay any of them, and he won't be laying you. I give you that as a fact. He may look rugged and masculine, and when he's in public he *acts* rugged and masculine. But that's only because he's a hell of a good actor. That boy hasn't had any tail since Hector was a pup. Give him a nice, lean teenage boy with a smooth backside, yeah. Not women. Oh, he could probably give you a ploughing if he wanted to, but he won't want to."

"That's the last straw," Meg snapped. "Marrying a man for publicity, and a homosexual at that—"

"That's all for the better!" Bonaventura cried. "You won't even have to worry that you're prostituting yourself! The man won't touch you. You could be married to him ten years and still be a virgin, if you were a virgin on your wedding night."

Meg refused angrily to continue the discussion. But Bonaventura ignored her. He wheedled and cajoled in his irresistible way. Meg weakened. Her arguments against the marriage grew more feeble. At length, she surrendered completely.

"All right," she muttered. "I'll go through with it. I'll marry him."

"There's a smart baby!"

"But I'm sore at you, Max. You're pushing me too far. You're getting me involved in one cruddy thing after another. One of these days I'll get tired of it. I'll decide I want to keep my breasts covered like a decent girl. I'll decide I want to marry someone I love, not a has-been fag you picked out for me. I'll decide—"

"Please, lover. Don't talk nasty to old Maxie. I got your interests at heart."

"You're just interested in your twenty-five percent," Meg snapped.

"Okay, then," Bonaventura blazed back. "I resign! You go be your own manager! I'm through, as of right now! Go back to Idaho and screw farmhands, if you like."

He didn't mean it, Meg knew. It was just another grandstand play. But she had no choice but to calm him down, to soothe his ruffled feelings. By the time he left her, he had her precisely where he wanted her—in the palm of his hand. She knew it was impossible for her to try to resist his plans for her.

Alone, she thought, *So now I'm going to marry Brad Holman. What a cockeyed life this is! It's like a dream—playing in a movie with him, marrying him. Queer or not. A wild dream. An opium dream.*

But someday I'm going to wake up.

What happens then?

Twelve

Filming the Civil War epic started soon afterward. A lot of it was going to be done on location in Oregon, but the studio scenes came first. Meg met Brad Holman officially, and tried her best to make the meeting a relaxed thing with no undercurrents of tension.

He was very courtly. In the flesh, he looked almost as rugged as he had in the movies, except that you could spot the gray at the roots of his hair, and you could see the little lines that makeup could wipe from his face, and you could detect the slight looseness around the throat that would turn into triple chins in another eight or ten years or so. He took to Meg immediately. By the third day of shooting, Holman was stopping by at her home each morning to pick her up in his long gray Bentley en route to the studio. On the fourth night, they went out together. On the fifth day, a carefully-planted item in a Hollywood gossip column tittered, *"Brad Holman and Meg Loring, co-starring in a forthcoming Mack and Arthur Fields blockbuster, are being seen around town together after hours. A little birdie tells us that wedding bells may be ringing before very long. Brad, terribly lonely since his divorce from Helen Clinton in 1955, may be just the right sort of man for the bosomy new star who is Hollywood's Number One Bachelor Girl today—and Meg may add new luster to the already fabulous Holman career."*

Holman took care never to let any hint slip to Meg that their romance was a synthetic fabrication. He dated her eagerly, lavished money on her, made sure they were seen together in the best spots. On the set, he developed the habit of staring at her fondly during moments when they were not performing.

He was the Brad Holman of the movies even off stage—hypnotically masculine, unfailingly gentlemanly. He held her hand, he kissed her good night romantically, he even lightly caressed her bosom once or twice. But that was all. Even after three weeks, he had made no serious advances, had not tried to seduce her or even hinted at it. Which was according to expectations. He went through all the motions of romance, right up to but not including the usual culmination.

And he had plenty of opportunity to view the Loring anatomy. The climactic tent scene was one of the first to be filmed; she began it in a tight blouse, changed to a filmy gown, and finally dropped the gown altogether. The camera cropped the view off midway down her breasts, but the few lucky ones on the sound stage had not such limitations; for eight retakes she stripped completely, standing nude in front of Holman nearly thirty seconds while the cameraman zeroed in at just the right height. Holman's face registered a good counterfeit of lust, as the script required him to, but Meg could tell he was faking. He didn't feel it. The director and the camera crew practically lit up when Meg dropped the gown and thrust her bosom forward, but Holman just went through the outward motions of being erotically excited.

She was up in Oregon for two weeks, filming sequences and discovering just how ingenious Hollywood could be when it wanted to display a star's body without getting into trouble with the police. Scene after scene—the briar patch, the tub bath, the skinny-dip—had her peel down to the minimum or less, for take after take. She became so accustomed to stripping before the crew that she hardly gave it a thought, and casually sat around nude for twenty minutes between takes while waiting for the outcome of a conference on lighting and camera angles.

Rumors of a Holman-Loring marriage became stronger and stronger as the shooting continued into its second month. Asked point blank, Meg declared (as coached by Bonaventura): "No, there's nothing serious between Brad and me right now. But that isn't to say I'm ruling out every possibility for the future. Let's just say we're very good friends, right now, and leave it at that."

A week later, to another interviewer, she amplified: "I've always felt that a girl shouldn't rush into marriage. I always planned to wait until I was twenty-four or twenty-five before marrying anyone. But I may just be changing my mind a little bit."

And four days after that: "Brad and I have had some very serious talks. We want to be absolutely sure we're right for each other."

And two days later: "You know, I think I'm just beginning to discover what love really is."

And, in the afternoon editions of the Los Angeles papers the next day:

"Film stars Brad Holman and Meg Loring were married today in a private ceremony at Miss Loring's home in Glendale. Less than a dozen close friends of the couple were invited to the surprise affair. It is the fifth marriage for veteran film star Holman, the first for the 20-year-old redhead sensation. The couple departed for a two-week honeymoon at an undisclosed resort in Mexico, after which they will return to complete the final scenes of their forthcoming Mack and Arthur Fields film, THE REBEL AND THE SPY."

At sundown that evening, the new Mr. and Mrs. Brad Holman were ensconced in a plush hotel suite at Cuernavaca, Mexico. All during the anonymous flight out of Los Angeles, Meg had incredulously revolved one thought in her mind: *I'm married to Brad Holman. Imagine—I'm married to Brad Holman!*

She was tired and sweaty after the flight. "I need a shower, darling," she told him. "Then we'll go down for dinner."

"All right."

She stripped off her travelling clothes and got under the needle spray. For five minutes she let the cold water play on her skin; then, invigorated, her blood pounding, her circulation stimulated, she stepped out of the shower, and, nude, into the living room of the suite. Holman was standing by the mirror, adjusting his four-in-hand.

"That was a wonderful shower," she said.

"I'm glad."

"Help me dry off, darling?"

He turned. "If you want."

He took the towel from her, and she presented her back. He toweled her dry as remotely as though he were drying off a statue. She dried her breasts and belly and wrapped herself against him.

"Love me?" she asked.

"Of course."

"Kiss?"

He kissed her.

"Brad, it's our wedding night, almost," she said huskily, deliberately baiting him to see what would happen. "Hold me tight. Touch me."

She took his hand and put it to her breasts. He left it there, but without enthusiasm. It might have been a California grapefruit in his hand, not a woman's firm stiff-nippled bosom. After a moment, Meg withdrew from him. She needed no further confirmation of what Bonaventura had told her about Holman's sexual proclivities. After all, never once during their much-publicized courtship had he shown any desire to sleep with her. And now, alone in this suite, naked against him, she could not rouse any hint of interest. Somehow, it was like the toppling of an idol, this definite proof of what Brad Holman was. The great lover, Brad Holman—a pansy!

They dined sumptuously, at an out-of-doors restaurant in the hotel courtyard. Half a dozen bowing waiters surrounded them, anticipating their every request. One of the waiters was a strikingly handsome Mexican boy who seemed to be about twenty. Meg was immediately taken by the boy's good looks—but so, too, was Holman. Brad could not take his eyes off the boy. Meg tried to ignore the open flirtation, but it sickened her so much she was unable to enjoy most of her meal.

They retired for the night about ten. Meg undressed first, bounding into the wide king-sized bed nude, as was her custom. Holman lingered in the bathroom a while, brushing his teeth for what seemed to be hours. He came in, finally, hanging up his dressing-gown, turning out the light, getting into bed. He wore a pair of ornately decorated silk pajamas.

"Good night, darling," he said calmly.

"Good night?" She echoed. She elbowed her way to a half-sitting position. "Brad, is that all you have to say to me? Just *good night?*"

"Meg—"

"I'm your wife. This is your wedding night, our wedding night, and I'm stark naked in bed next to you. And all you do is say good night."

"Please, darling. Don't—"

She took his hand and thrust it between her legs, tightening her thigh muscles to hold it there. She began to move rhythmically, stimulating herself, and at the same time she brought his other hand to her breasts. He tried to remove the hand locked between her thighs.

"Come on, Brad. Make love to me. I want you to, darling." She knew she was being cruel, that she was acting viciously, but she couldn't help herself. She wanted to revenge herself in some way for having been pitchforked into this mockery of a marriage. She began to pant in anxious urgency.

Holman managed to pull free. He sat up and turned on the light. He looked very middle-aged and weary, just now.

He said, "Haven't they told you, Meg? Didn't Max let you know the truth?"

"What do you mean?"

"About me. I haven't made love with a woman in thirty years. I'm—I'm homosexual, Meg. I asked Max to explain that to you, that this would be a marriage of companionship, that we would never actually have sexual intercourse."

She smiled crookedly. "Sure, he told me. But I didn't believe him. I couldn't believe that the great matinee idol Brad Holman was queer! And I'm still trying not to believe it. Make love to me, Brad. I promise you, you'll never go back to little boys."

"I couldn't."

"Sure you could!" She reached out, groping for his body. "You could get aroused. You could do it."

"But I don't *want* to," Holman protested weakly, running a hand through his hair. "Look—take Marilyn Monroe. A hell of a lot of people in this world would give almost anything to go to bed with Marilyn Monroe. How much would *you* give?"

"Why—nothing at all."

"Why not?"

"I don't want to sleep with her, that's all. Or with any woman."

"It's exactly the same with me," Holman said. "Women don't hold any more sexual interest for me than they do for you. Oh, I appreciate them abstractly—I know you have beautiful breasts, but they simply don't set me on fire. I could make love to you, I suppose. But I'd hate every minute of it. And so would you."

"All right," she said quietly. "I just wanted to make sure."

"And now you know. Don't torment me anymore, Meg. Let's just be good friends, yes?"

He kissed her goodnight, a brotherly peck. Within minutes, he seemed to be asleep. Meg remained awake much longer, pondering the disillusionment of Holman's homosexuality. Her loins throbbed with unfulfilled desire, all the more painfully frustrating because she was in bed with a handsome man who totally refused to gratify her.

She resolved to grin and bear it. It was only a marriage of convenience, that was all. For publicity's sake. It wasn't going to last forever.

The next day, they spent most of their time sunning and swimming in the huge hotel pool. But Holman disappeared for two hours, telling Meg he would "be right back," and at dinnertime that evening, when the handsome young Mexican favored Holman with a sly and knowing wink, Meg discovered where he had been. No doubt the young waiter was available to guests of either sex, for a price.

She had a measure of revenge the next day. It was a petty thing to do, she told herself—but she felt the need for a man, and the fact that Holman was getting his particular kind of sexual kicks seemed to give her equal license to prowl herself.

It was mid-afternoon, and they were at the pool. Holman had had a rendezvous with his Mexican in the morning, and now was relaxed and affable. They came out of the water and sprawled in the sun. Rising suddenly, Meg said, "I think I'll go back to the room and change into a dry bathing-suit. I'll put the bikini on instead of this one-piece thing. I'll be back in a little while."

Holman merely smiled. When she was in the room, she picked up the house phone and said, "Will you send a daiquiri up to me, please."

"Of course, Señora Holman."

The drink came ten minutes later. Still in her bathing suit, Meg answered the door, and was pleased to see that the bellhop was young and handsome, a good looking Mexican boy somewhat older than Holman's playmate.

"What do I owe you?" she asked.

"Ten pesos," he said, looking interestedly at the lushness of her body beneath the tight swimsuit.

She gave him an American dollar in payment. As he started toward the door, she said, "Just a minute."

"Señora?"

"I'm having some trouble unzipping my bathing suit. It seems to be stuck. Could you help me?"

He frowned, not knowing what to make of this. Meg's bathing suit unzipped down the back—a straight line down to mid-buttock. He grasped the zipper and easily opened it, pulling it down a few inches.

"There, señora."

"No—further."

The zipper went lower. Suddenly, he caught on, and pulled it down low enough to expose the creamy globes of her buttocks. She turned, the suit dropping away from her breasts, and put out her arms to him. He pulled the rest of the suit off and cautiously locked the door. Then she took him by the hand, and led him to the bed. He seemed astonished by the richness of her body, the flawless beauty of her breasts and thighs, the full curves of her buttocks. He was out of his uniform trousers in an instant, and she pulled his lean, hard body down on top of her, imprisoning his ready maleness in soft warmth.

When it was over, and she lay naked, satisfied, watching him dress, she said calmly, "That was very good. What is your name?"

"Ricardo."

"Ricardo. *Muy Bien*, Ricardo.   I'll be here for another ten days. I'd like to see you again—many times. Here." She handed him a fifty-peso note. "Are you married, Ricardo?"

"Sí, señora,"

"Then you can probably use the money. And your wife is a very lucky woman. Go, now. I'll call when I want you again."

She wanted him again four more times, before the "honeymoon" was up. Each time he came, and made love to her thrillingly but without emotion, as though this were all in his day's work. It was precisely what she wanted—physical relief without emotional entanglements. She gave her body to him, enfolding his lean slimness in her yielding flesh, and he satisfied her completely.

She knew that Holman was having a fine time with his Mexican, too. *A funny way to have a honeymoon*, she thought. *One for the books.*

When the two weeks were up, they returned to Los Angeles. Bonaventura met them at the airport terminal, drawing Meg aside anxiously, almost paternally, to find out how things had gone.

"It was wonderful, Max," she told him. "We did nothing but make love all the time."

"You're *kidding!*" Bonaventura gasped.

"Gospel truth. He found a nice Mex boy to make love with, and I found another one. And so we all screwed happily ever after." She glared at the little agent. "Max, there are times when I could gleefully take a knife to you for getting me into things like this."

"Please," he begged. "Just a couple of months, that's all it'll be."

It went on. They moved into Holman's enormous mansion in Pacific Palisades, although Meg kept up the payments on her Glendale home, holding it in reserve. The movie was nearly finished; they did the final few episodes, and then it was all in the hands of the cutting-room team. The premiere was tentatively scheduled for three months hence, which was all right with Meg.

She went on living as wife to Holman in name only. It was a steadily more depressing farce. They slept in separate beds, even in separate bedrooms. He was unfailingly polite to her, in a remote sort of way. They were seen frequently in public, and he took care to seem properly amorous, as the new husband of such a richly endowed female ought to seem.

He had two or three regular boyfriends—aspiring actors in their very early twenties—who visited him regularly. They were glacially polite to Meg, but it was obvious that they had nothing but loathing for her as a sexual object.

They annoyed her, with their giggles and their swishy ways. The whole relationship sickened her. But she stuck to it grimly, because Bonaventura begged her to. Even when one of Holman's former wives called up and said, "I guess you're finding out the truth about Lover Boy now, eh?" she managed to change the subject and keep from breaking down.

The weeks went by. The movie fan magazines were going to town on the romance, now. Interest in the forthcoming Holman-Loring movie was practically at fever pitch, thanks to the extra fillip provided by the romance.

But Meg could not hold out any longer. The savage mockery of a marriage that had never been a marriage, the constant irritation of finding Brad's effeminate young friends around the house at all times, the cool way they tolerated her—as though she were a maid, and not Holman's legal wife—finally exploded in her. One weekday afternoon she could no longer contain herself. Holman was in the salon, holding hands with his current flame, a gangling boy with long hair, gaunt cheekbones, and burning eyes. Two of Holman's former bedmates were on hand as chaperones. For an hour, Meg had been in the next room, listening to their catty chatter, their mincing giggles. Finally she broke loose.

Running upstairs, she stripped off her clothing and wrapped a flimsy gown around her. She took a hundred-dollar bill from her wallet. She went downstairs.

She walked into the salon. The four men looked up in surprise. Meg hurled the hundred dollar bill to the floor. Then, quickly, she whipped off the gown. She stood nude before them, legs spread wide, hands supporting her breasts and thrusting them lasciviously forward.

"Which one of you is man enough to win a hundred bucks?" she yelled. "There's a C-note there for any of you who'll sleep with me right here on this carpet. Come on, you fruits! Let's see some action!"

She was a little drunk. She sprawled on the carpet in an obscene pose. Holman loomed above her, his face dead white, his eyes hard with rage.

"Get up!" he bellowed. "Slut! Pig!"

He slapped her. She grabbed her robe and fled from the room. Upstairs, she phoned Bonaventura. "It's over, Max. I can't take it anymore. I'm moving out."

That night she slept in her own home again. The story was in the morning papers: "LORING, HOLMAN SEPARATE. *Summer long romance ends in quarrel.*"

Grimly, Meg thought that now she was at last a full-fledged Hollywood star. She was about to have her first divorce.

Thirteen

There were no complications attendant on ending the marriage. Meg suggested an annulment, on the very valid grounds that the marriage had never been consummated, but Holman would not hear of it. It had to be a divorce. She flew down to Mexico for a few days, while Bonaventura's lawyer conferred with Holman's lawyer and arranged matters amiably. It was agreed that Meg would not request alimony or support of any kind, and in return for this Holman would not contest the suit.

Things went smoothly. The decree was granted and the Los Angeles public was duly so informed. Meg moved back to her own home, and returned Holman's wedding band to him. By return mail the band came back, and with it Holman's check for ten thousand dollars, thanking her for her part in the farcical marriage.

Despite Bonaventura's near-apoplexy, Meg did not cash the check. She dropped a note to Holman telling him that she was keeping it "as a souvenir," and that he had better stop payment and cancel the check.

"But it's ten thousand crackers—" Bonaventura spluttered.

"I've got more money than I know how to spend right now," Meg told him firmly. "I don't mind cashing in on the publicity value of my marriage, but I'm not going to take Holman's money. It's a guilt-offering, that's what it is. And I'd feel dirty for the rest of my life if I cashed that check."

Three weeks after the decree became final, the grand premiere of THE REBEL AND THE SPY took place. Everyone who was anyone in Hollywood was there. Bonaventura arranged things so that Meg and Holman would arrive separately but at the same time, meeting outside the theater and entering together, Meg on Holman's arm as though for all the world they were still deep in love. It was the sort of grand gesture that made a big hit. They came down the center aisle of the theater, flashbulbs exploding all around, and took seats together in the roped-off area reserved for the stars and the studio bigwigs.

It was the first time she had seen him since the divorce. They said little to each other, maintaining tremendously polite attitudes. The picture went over well, even accounting for the traditional friendliness of an invited Hollywood audience; nobody in the theater could take the story as anything but preposterous, but everyone recognized the truly awesome box-office potential of the film. Civil War derring-do plus a staggering succession of strip-tease scenes with Meg Loring? Why, the combination was unbeatable.

There was a cast party after the premiere—no more than two hundred guests, so it was exclusive by Hollywood standards. Old man Fields had provided the champagne, not the ersatz California variety but genuine Piper Heidsieck *brut*, in quantity. Meg and Holman remained together for the first fifteen minutes of the party, as behooved them as co-stars, but after that they drifted apart and did not speak for the rest of the evening.

Meg found herself in a corner with Arthur Fields. The junior member of the producing team looked worn out; his little eyes were seamed with red, and broken capillaries distorted his nose and cheeks. He poured champagne for both of them, splashing it extravagantly, and, weaving unsteadily, muttered, "When am I gonna see you, Meg? It's been months. Christ, it must be almost a year since that night. And you've been ducking me ever since."

"Let's not talk about it here."

"I wanna talk about it. One thing when you were married to that fairy, but now you ain't. Come home to my place tonight."

"Please, Arthur. I don't want to."

"I disgust you, that it?"

"Arthur—"

"Come on, tell me! It was okay to do it with me before you had a contract, before you were anybody. Now you're a celebrity. Miss Bazoom of 1962. Who got you there, anyway? Who gave you that lousy contract? And now all I want is some thanks from you, a little bit of physical gratification, and you can spit at me because you don't need me anymore. You were just *using* me."

"We were using each other," Meg said.

"That night was one of the greatest of my life," Arthur said, and Meg was astonished to see his bloodshot eyes beginning to fill with tears. "You weren't just a starlet I had a lech for. You were *it*—the queen of sex, the all-time wonder. I had you once. Now you think you're too good for me. Listen," he said hoarsely, "you may think you're doing okay, but I can still make things worth your while. I got millions, Meg. And the old man is worth a hundred fifty million. I get it all when he kicks off. Marry me, Meg. We'll make a couple movies that'll wow the country, and then we'll take off and go on a cruise round the world, two years, a yacht big as the Queen Elizabeth, just you and me—"

"You're drunk."

"I'm askin' you to marry me."

"The answer's no, Arthur. I'll make films for you, but I won't marry you and I won't sleep with you."

The young producer's lip curled petulantly. "You listen to me, you tramp. You're nothing but a pair of big knockers on legs, and the woods are full of dames like you who could get the same buildup you got! I could break you just like *that!* I—"

A meaty hand descended on Arthur's shoulder, heavily. "Shut your mouth," Mack Fields ordered brusquely. The older man smiled at Meg. "Arthur has had too much to drink, my dear. I hope you'll forgive him."

"Of course, Mr. Fields."

"Don't take anything he might have said seriously," Mack Fields went on. He turned and muttered something sharply to his son in what sounded to Meg like German. Arthur nodded miserably, obviously cowed by his father's words. Shaking himself loose, he left the room quickly.

Mack Fields said, "He becomes unruly sometimes. But come—here is someone who wishes to meet you, Meg."

Fields gestured, and Meg found herself face-to-face with a tall, grinning, tousle-headed young man. She recognized him instantly: Brick Hyde, a juvenile lead who had been peeling potatoes on Olivera Street six years ago and now was in the $500,000-a-year bracket as Hollywood's Number One Glamor Boy. He was under contract to Fields. He stuck out his hand and said, "It was a great film, M.F. You ought to gross twenty million on it."

"Hardly, hardly. But maybe next time. And you two will have a lot to do with it, I hope. Meg, meet your next co-star, Brick Hyde."

Hyde widened the grin a little. Meg gave him a searching look and a smile. He was almost illegally handsome, she thought—his face had an awesome perfection that seemed unconvincing in its very flawlessness.

Fields bustled away, muttering something about leaving the two of them alone. Hyde said, "I've seen the treatment for our film. It's a riot."

"That's the Prohibition film, you mean?"

Hyde nodded. "You play a speakeasy owner, and I play a Federal agent who falls in love with you. Silliest damn picture. It ought to coin a mint."

"Let's hope so. I guess we're both in on the gross."

"I like you," Hyde said suddenly. "We've got a lot in common. We both came out of obscurity. We're both big stars now. We both got where we were because we're abnormally good-looking. I don't try to deny that I'm handsome. I don't believe in false modesty."

"You don't believe in wasting any time, do you?"

"I've wasted plenty. I've wasted almost a year before getting to meet you. Care for some champagne?"

"I've had some, thanks."

"Have some more. It's free."

"I've had enough," Meg said. "And I can afford my own, if I want any. So can you."

Hyde said, "I still remember when I was working for $31.50 a week. I make that much a minute, nowadays, but it's hard to break old habits. God, you're lovely. You're a poem in flesh. A symphony in pink."

Hyde was obviously phony, brash, cocky, egotistical. But he was handsome, and he had a good line. Meg let him talk her into having more champagne after all. And then, toward dawn, as the party began to break up, he said, "Hey, how about a swim?"

"Where?"

"Pacific. I've got my own private beach. You've never lived till you've seen the sun come up out of Nevada and light up the Pacific."

They hurried outside. Bonaventura, still on his feet, waved goodbye to them as they left. Meg had come in her Mercedes; Hyde's car was a Porsche RSK, sleek and powerful. He was off and running, and Meg had to pull out all the stops to keep from getting left behind. They zoomed down the freeways at 90 and 95, slicing through the dawn emptiness like a pair of jet-propelled eagles.

Hyde pulled up, finally, in Santa Monica. His home was a palace, virtually—a Frank Lloyd Wright-style ultra-modern cantilevered affair with artificial waterfall, glowing walls, towering eucalyptus trees to screen it from the public. He led her indoors and out the back way, down to the cabana. The house was breathtakingly beautiful, at least $150,000 worth of architecture.

Hyde's section of the beach, a hundred feet long, was walled off by opaque glass blocks. He began to peel off his clothes. Meg looked at him hesitantly for a moment, then started to strip out of her evening gown. There was no question of wearing bathing suits. Hyde would only laugh at the notion.

He gaped at her nakedness. "Jeez, but you're a knockout! You're the best-looking broad there is, you know that? I've seen a lot, and you take the gold-plated you-know-what."

She laughed, and they ran hand in hand down to the water. The water was cold, and darkness still hung over it. Hyde swam superbly, forcing her to exert herself to keep up with him. They came out of the water, tired and giddy, just as the sun was coming up. She had her arm slung around his shoulder, but as they emerged on shore she dropped away, sprawling down on her back and kicking her legs in the air. Hyde stood over her. He had an athlete's body, tapering, perfectly proportioned. And, suddenly, he began to desire her. She waited until he was fully ready, and then yanked his legs, tumbling him down on top of her. His hands sought the deep bowls of her breasts, and her legs scissored around him, and she felt the sand against her buttocks and their bodies locked together and she saw gulls wheeling and screaming high overhead, and then she screwed her eyes tight shut and saw nothing but fireworks.

When it was over, Hyde said suddenly, in a matter-of-fact tone of voice, "Do you think we might have made a baby?"

"I doubt it. This is the safest time of the month for me."

"That's too bad."

"For you, maybe. I'd just as soon prefer to have my babies *in* wedlock, thank you."

"But we ought to make a baby, you and me," Hyde exclaimed with sudden passion. "We owe it to the world. We have probably the most beautiful bodies in existence today. We should found a tribe of superchildren. Our babies would be Adonises, Aphrodites. We could have five or six, and they would breed only with each other—"

"That's against the law, buster."

"I've got a vision," Hyde exclaimed. "Our children multiplying, increasing from generation to generation, until all mankind recognizes their beauty, until they rule all nations—" He laughed harshly. "So I'm a crackpot. But we ought to make a baby."

"Is that a proposal of marriage?"

"I can't marry you. It would have to be a lovechild."

"What do you mean, can't marry me? Not that I'm sure I'd want to, but—"

"I'm married," he said. "I got married when I was a kid, seventeen. That was in Brooklyn. I left her to come to Hollywood. Haven't seen her in five years, her or the kids—"

"Kids?"

"Three. They look like her. Fat little pigs. I send her money. But there can't be a divorce. She's a Catholic, goes to church all the time, gives lots of my money to the priests. I'm a Catholic, too. I'm Italian—Tony Palladino, that's what I was before they christened me Brick Hyde. I don't go to church any. But I couldn't get a divorce. They'd excommunicate me, and my mother would kill herself if I married outside the church. But we could have a baby, all the same, a love-child—"

Meg blinked incredulously. "No deal. But I like you. Let's have fun instead of babies."

His hand went to her breast again, and instantly he was aroused, ready for another bout of love. His vitality was tremendous. He took her again and again, on the beach, until the sun was almost noon high, and they were both exhausted and sweaty and warm.

They swam again, and then went into the house for brunch. They made love one last time after eating, and then she dressed and drove home. She went straight to bed, leaving orders that she was not to be disturbed by anyone, not even Bonaventura.

The orders were obeyed. But when she woke, at ten the next morning, Bonaventura was waiting to see her.

"You and Hyde really hit it off last night, huh?"

She smiled dreamily. "Max, I've never had my ashes hauled so well or so frequently in one five-hour span before. He's remarkable."

"So I hear. But you're not going to marry him."

"I know that. He's got a wife in Brooklyn, and they won't get a divorce because they're Catholics," Meg said. "But—"

"I didn't know," Bonaventura said. "But it's just as well. Even if he was single I wouldn't let you marry him."

"Why not? And since when—"

"Since when do I run your life? Since the day I started managing you. And I'd frown on a marriage because it's bad for you to get the reputation of marrying all your leading men. Even in Hollywood you have to respect the proprieties. Sleep with your co-star, sure. But two quick marriages like this would put you in lousy with the public. I like this idea much better. You and Hyde make a classy twosome. Keep company. Let him rack you up five times a day. And in the background is the violins playing sad music, because these two perfect people are forever kept from wedlock by the evil wife in Brooklyn."

"Everything's a publicity gimmick with you, huh?"

"Baby, I got your interests at heart. I love you like my own daughter, and I should only have daughter stacked like you! I just wanted to tell you how this Hyde thing should be milked."

They milked it. The gossip columnists began prophesying a Hyde-Loring marriage, and every time the rumor arose it was promptly denied officially. After two months of this, a top fan magazine was allowed to publish for the first time the true Brick Hyde story, detailing lugubriously Brick's devotion to the church and the impossibility of his ever contracting a second marriage.

The sad news was a publicity miracle. Two star-crossed lovers unable to unite in wedlock because of religious affiliations—it made a perfect story.

Filming began on the third Meg Loring picture late that year. It continued, on and off, for most of the winter. In between, Meg and Hyde vacationed. Hyde had a tremendous love of the outdoors; they stole off to a hideaway he owned in Washington State, camping and fishing for two weeks. They spent a month in Yucatan together. They flew to the Caribbean for Christmas and went spear-fishing in the coral reefs.

And they made love. Two, three, four times a day—Hyde's virility was inexhaustible. He was, Meg realized, a true superman, physically. His degree of perfection made her realize, for the first time, how awesome her own endowment was. They were physically attuned to perfection. Their lovemaking was as harmonious as a Mozart duet. Time and again his body would seek hers, and they would scale the heights of ecstasy together, descending smoothly and without a jolt.

The idyll came to an end a month before the premiere of her third film. Hyde discovered, one day, that she had been taking precautions against getting pregnant, and the knowledge infuriated him. He had been serious about wanting to give the world a superchild—and, all these months of endless love, he had waited each day for the news that she was pregnant. Finding her diaphragm case sent him into towering frenzy of Latin rage.

"You've been cheating me!" he thundered. "Killing our babies before they could even be conceived!"

"I told you, Brick, I wasn't going to have any bastard children, no matter how handsome they'd be—"

He poured a torrent of abuse out on her. Then, ripping the diaphragm case from her numb hands, he hurled it out the window. He seized her roughly, threw her down on the bed, pulled off his clothing.

Without warning he was on top of her. He took her brutally, easily compelling her to yield to him, satisfying himself in no more than a few seconds. When he rose from her, she stared at him in bitter hatred, and rushed into the bathroom.

She did not become pregnant. But neither did she ever make love with Hyde again. She ignored all phone calls from him, all the abject attempts at apology. He bombarded her with flowers, wrote ornate letters of tragic tone, threatened to kill himself if she did not come back to him. She ignored everything. He had done the unforgivable. Other men had bought her; he had *taken* her.

He did not kill himself. Gradually, his passion subsided. At the premiere of their film, he was coldly cordial, strictly business. The love affair of the decade was over, no doubt about it.

It was announced that another Meg Loring film was in the works—this one starring both Hyde and Brad Holman. Bonaventura pressured Meg into signing for it, even though she insisted she did not want to act with them, did not want to have them kiss her before the cameras. Bonaventura won. Bonaventura always won.

The money rolled in. Her films were being shown abroad, now. Meg Loring was the toast of Europe. The studio was going to send her to the Continent on a good-will tour. She was a success.

She was miserable.

Fourteen

She was in Europe four months—lolling on the Riviera in a bikini that was daring even for the Riviera, just a bare G-string and an inch and a half of cloth over her nipples. She officiated at the premiere of THE REBEL AND THE SPY in London, she received orchids in Rome, she was cheered wildly in Paris.

And then back to Hollywood. Back to unreal reality.

They had a new movie for her, another comedy job with plenty of uncovering. It was filmed both in a domestic version (no bare breasts or buttocks) and a foreign version (in which the camera showed 100% of Meg Loring's anatomy, cuts to be left up to the discretion of overseas film distributors.) The uncensored version played in Switzerland and caused a sensation; people came from all over Europe to see it, and they did not go away disappointed.

Bonaventura had been busy with her finances, too. He had arranged her investments in such a way that she was guaranteed a minimum income of $25,000 a year for life, whether or not she ever worked another day—and this was merely from her investments, not from the percentage deals that were certain to bring her millions.

There were new lovers, too.

There was whirlwind romance with a young Spanish director, hired to make three movies in Hollywood. He was full of fire and passion and creative frenzy; he swept Meg off her feet, and for two months she kept company with him virtually around the clock. Then he left Hollywood, breaking his contract because they would not let him make the kind of films he wanted to make. The day he left, he urged Meg to return to Spain with him. "We will make films that will burn imperishably through the ages. I have a film planned for you, a film that no country will dare to present for a century. You will make love on the screen, in this film, and it will be such a scene as to drive the audience to frenzy."

She turned him down, though, at Bonaventura's advice. What seemed like art to the young Spaniard seemed perilously like sheer pornography to Bonaventura, and he refused to let Meg appear in what amounted to a stag film. Besides, she was under contract to Fields. The young Spaniard returned to his country alone. A month later, word came of his marriage to an Italian actress.

After him, there was a romance with Paul Greer, picked by many to be the next Brick Hyde. Like all her other love affairs, this one was conducted almost exclusively in public—all but the actual bedding. Every kiss, every quarrel, every reconciliation was mercilessly chronicled in the daily scandal columns, was mercilessly limned in photoflash light. It didn't last.

Nor did the next, or the next. Meg Loring had made five films, now. She was hailed everywhere as America's Goddess of Sex, eroticism incarnate. She was worth a fortune. Her every motion was print-worthy, now.

She was no longer the wide-eyed young greenhorn who had knocked on Max Bonaventura's office door so long ago, and who had been so queasy about displaying her breasts to him. She was almost twenty-five, wealthy, a hardheaded businesswoman who could drive a deal for herself almost as well as Bonaventura could.

She was lonely.

She used men to rid her of the loneliness. There were five or six major affairs—Brick Hyde, the Spaniard, Greer, a couple of others. The gossip columnists wondered each time, "Is this the one for Meg Loring? Will she at last find happiness with So-and-So? And if she marries, will it last or will it be another Brad Holman two-month fiasco?"

Bonaventura rationed out her love affairs—never too close together, and never anyone beneath her position. She couldn't afford to give the appearance of being a round heels who went with man after man. He created for her the image of the lonely beauty searching for her true love. For once, there was no fraud involved in Bonaventura's creation.

There were other men, one-nighters, bellhops, pickups, men who sometimes never even knew who it was they were sleeping with. She used them the way an addict used drugs—to calm her down, to put her to sleep.

She started drinking, too. With an income in six figures, she could afford the best. She bought the best. She used it.

The top blew off on a rainy night in March, her fourth March in Los Angeles.

She had been alone, that evening. She was between movies, and between love affairs. Bonaventura was in New York, lining up a possible Broadway appearance for her. She had been drinking heavily that evening.

It was a perfect night for suicide.

What's the use of it all? she kept asking herself. *I'm worth Christ knows how many hundred thousand bucks. I can have everything money can buy. I've slept with some of the most romantic men in the world. And really I've got nothing. Nada. Beans.*

My family pretends I don't exist. The man I married was a pansy. Nobody sleeps with me because they love me. Nobody even does it because I'm beautiful. They do it because it's good publicity. The public is interested in whichever lucky bastard is currently sleeping with Meg Loring, that's all. So they all try to make me.

The hell with 'em all.

The hell with the whole lousy world.

This is where I get off the treadmill, she thought.

She rose unsteadily and made her wobbly way through the enormous house, out to the garage. She touched a button and the garage door sprang up. Three cars were inside. A Rolls, a Mercedes 300SL, a convertible Aston-Martin. She bought cars the way other women bought handbags, to cheer herself up. She rarely kept them more than six months. This was the fifth 300SL she had owned, each one a different color.

She got into the Aston-Martin. The top was down, and rain pelted in, but she didn't care. She was wearing light clothes, a blouse, a skirt, no underclothes. She turned on the engine. It purred into life, and she pulled out, heading off into the night.

She was sober enough to drive, but not sober enough to drive very well. She did not care. She had no particular destination in mind. She let the car take her, down one boulevard, up another, roaring down the glistening, rain soaked streets at sixty and seventy miles an hour. She found herself on a freeway interchange, and drove on, streaking westward at eighty down the middle lane.

As the alcohol gradually burned out of her brain, a plan started to take shape. She decided that she would drive up to the canyon country north of the city. The roads were narrow and slippery, there. A twist of the wheel and you could plunge three hundred feet. It was a quick death, with practically no chance that you would survive, disfigured and maimed, to drag out a horrid existence. A twist of the wheel, a crash, the cleansing burst of flame to wipe away a thousand sins of the flesh, and it would be over. The bright bath of flame would at last eradicate the feel of men's paws, remove the indelible fingerprints from her breasts and thighs and buttocks. And in the morning they would find the ash-heap that would be all that remained, and someone would identify the charred corpse, and the news would rock the nation. MEG LORING DEAD IN CAR CRASH, and they would create a myth about her, they would inflate her into an image of self-destructive beauty, too glowingly voluptuous to survive.

A quick death, Meg thought.

And why not? Why bother to live? What for, just to go on piling up more money, more clippings, more applause, more lovers?

No point in it.

Her car weaved treacherously on the slick surface. *Uh-uh, be careful. Let's do this right. Death on a lonely canyon road. Not here in the middle of everywhere. They might save you, here. Rush you to the hospital and release you alive. No face left, but alive. I'd rather be sure. I want to do it right.*

A blurred interchanged sign loomed up. She flicked the wheel and shot off down the road, heading northwest now to the wild canyon country above the Palisades.

She laughed. It was good to laugh in the rain. She was soaked to the skin, and her blouse clung to her skin, transparent, her breasts and nipples showing plainly. The breasts that made a hundred million men hard, she thought. But they've had their last look.

Suddenly she became aware that somebody was following her.

Her eyes would not focus properly on it. Rain blurred her side mirror, but she saw the car, a sports car, red, with a man in it. Following her.

She kicked the speed up. Eighty, ninety, ninety-five. He kept right with her.

He was honking his horn.

She turned off another interchange. He turned too. She muttered a curse and jammed down as far as the accelerator would go. He dropped back, then started to pick up speed too. The rain became harder.

She realized that she was no longer heading for the canyons, that this last turn had swerved her off toward the ocean again. *Well, you can crack up there just as well*, she thought. *If only this guy wouldn't hang onto my tail like that.*

He was gaining, now. He was practically abreast of her. The freeway opened out, straight and smooth, ahead of them. Grimly, almost hypnotized, she clung to the wheel, driving straight on.

The bastard's passing me!

The little red racer was performing fantastically. At close to a hundred, it shot past Meg's car.

"Get out of my lane, you crud!" Meg screamed drunkenly, but her words were lost in the night. The red car was directly in front of her, now, matching speeds with her. It began to slow. Automatically, she slowed, then tried to spurt around at the left. The red car shifted lanes. It was impossible to pass him. She slowed some more, forced to. I ought to just ram into him, she thought. But suppose I don't get killed? Just get messed up?

Inexorably, he forced her speed down. Seventy… sixty … fifty …

At fifty, she pulled off the freeway suddenly. He went shooting past, but there was a second exit a hundred yards on, and he took that, curving down to meet her in the street. He blocked her off.

They came to a halt.

He left his car and ran over to her.

She was leaning against the wheel, dizzy, soaked with rain and sweat, close to hysteria. He had cut her off, whoever he was. He had halted her wild flight to self-destruction.

"Meg!" he was shouting. "Meg, what the hell was going on?"

She looked up. "You bassard," she muttered thickly.

"You're drunk!"

"Thassa lie." She slitted her eyes, trying to focus on him. She recognized him now. He was Ray Henrich, a new actor, a New Yorker, one of the Actor's Studio method actors who had just finished his second film. They had met at a couple of parties, but had had no real contact.

"Get into my car," he said. "I'll take you home."

"Got my own car."

"We'll come get it when you're sober. Come, Meg. Let's go."

He opened the car door and, reaching in, switched off the ignition and pocketed the key. Then, gently, he eased her out of her car and carried her over to his own. He was very strong, she thought. Not big, but strong.

"Why you doing this?" she asked. "Who asked you to butt in?"

"I was driving home from a party," he said, settling her like a bundle of rags next to him in his car. "And I saw you go shoot past me on the road like a bat out of hell. I got a glimpse of your face. You looked drunk. You looked hypnotized. So I followed you. You know you were doing better than a hundred, Meg? You could have cracked yourself up."

"Wanted to."

He started the car. "Just relax. Sleep on my shoulder. You've had a hard time tonight, I guess."

She slumped over immediately.

She woke up in bed. Alone in bed. She felt warm and dry. It was a strange apartment, a small place, prints on the walls, plenty of books. She was wearing a pair of pajamas, and the covers were pulled up to her throat. Henrich was sitting next to her, smiling.

"You said you were taking me home," she said.

"I don't know your address. I took you to my place. It's closer. You were soaked to the skin, Meg. You'll be lucky to get away without pneumonia."

She frowned. "I was going to kill myself. I remember. I was going to drive off a canyon road."

"For God's sake, why?" he asked, leaning forward, taking her cold hand between his own. "You're young, you're beautiful, you're successful—"

"And I'm miserable," she said.

She began to talk. She poured out the whole thing, her Idaho adolescence, her frantic desire for fame and fortune, her trip to New York. Her rise, masterminded by Bonaventura. And she told how, when she finally *had* attained the peak, the absolute top, she had realized that her triumph was hollow, unreal, empty. All that mattered was to find one human being you could genuinely love and be loved by—and in that she had failed.

She was silent, then, drained of energy, drained of words, having poured herself out to this virtual stranger as she had done to no man before.

Henrich said, "So behind the glittering facade you're just a mixed-up kid. Funny. All the time I was envying you, because you seemed so uncomplicated, so simple. A pair of breasts and a pair of legs and a lot of money, and the world was your oyster. How wrong I was!" He laughed mirthlessly. "I'm just the opposite. Mixed-up on the outside, simple inside. Just a simple kid who wants to be an actor and make a little money. And who thinks he's falling in love."

"Don't kid me. Next you'll tell me you love me for myself, not for my figure or my press clippings."

"You're too bitter, Meg."

"I come by it honestly."

"You don't have to be. Can't you believe that it's possible for a man to love you? *You*, not the money, not the bosom, but the Meg Loring inside?"

"I don't know," she said, "Christ, I don't know." And then she was crying again, and reaching out for him, and pulling away the pajamas he had put on her, baring her body to him, the breasts and thighs and all. He told her no, he tried to cover her, but she was insistent, she had a sudden, dreadful, unstoppable need to be loved, and the powerful magnetism of her body worked its magic on him and he climbed into the bed.

They made love, slowly, with mounting passion until she writhed wildly beneath him, gasping out her joy, and it was over. The first rays of sun were coming through the bedroom window.

They lay in each other's arms a long while. She took his hand, putting it on the steep rising curve of her bosom, and he stroked the silky skin. "Who would have believed it," he thought. "Meg Loring. Right here in my bed."

Later in the day they went back for the Aston-Martin, which was wet through and through. They drove to her place, and talked for a long while.

In mid-afternoon she phoned Bonaventura, in New York.

"I've got the part all lined up," Bonaventura bubbled, the moment they were connected. "Chicken feed money, of course, but tons of prestige, and—"

"I'm getting married, Max."

"You're *what?*"

"Married. Tomorrow or the next day. Civil ceremony, then we're going away somewhere for a while."

"For Juda's sake, what's this all about?" Bonaventura yelped. "Married? Who—"

"Ray Henrichs."

"Henrichs? The fellow who acts like Brando?"

"That's right. I met him last night. While I was—was out driving."

"Jesus, how come you picked *him?* He's got no reputation at all. He's just another actor who—"

"I love him, Max," she said firmly. "Do I need your permission to fall in love?"

"No, but—"

"Okay, then. I'm marrying Ray tomorrow."

Bonaventura was silent a few seconds. Then he said, "I don't get it, but okay. I'll get reservations right back. The moment you're away on your honeymoon, I'll spring the news. It'll be the making of that kid, marrying you. I bet we can get him some juicy parts. Christ, the town will rock when they hear it! They—"

"No," Meg said. "Please, Max?"

"Please what?"

"Don't meddle, this time. This is for real. This isn't any publicity gimmick. I'll explain when you get here."

She hung up. Henrichs was waiting, arms outstretched, a smile of love in his eyes.

"Come here," he said.

She went to him.

"I love you," he told her. "I love you for *you.*"

"I'll go to the plastic surgeon and have my bosom removed," she said. "Will you love me then?"

"I promise I will."

He wrapped his arms around her. As their lips met, as their tongues touched, she felt a shiver of apprehension. This was wonderful, now. They were new and they were still strangers, and they were more deeply in love than any couple since time began.

But this is Hollywood, she thought. *And Max will be coming back, and the flashbulbs will go off, and the gossip columnists will write us up. And there'll be new films, and two careers in the family, jealousy, arguments. Love withers under floodlights. How long can it last, this way, Ray and me, before it becomes a publicity gimmick instead of a love-match? A month? Two months? A year? And then the Hollywood people cheapen and ruin it all, and our love dies under the spotlight of publicity. And I go along, looking for a new love, getting older, and someday a new love goddess comes out of the hills.*

His hands tenderly cupped her breasts. Her body opened lovingly for him like a flower rising to the morning sun.

"Love me, Ray. Love me always."

"Always, darling."

"Not just words. Mean it."

"I do mean it."

Maybe he did, she thought. *Maybe he really did*. She clung tight to him, shivering with happiness, the first real happiness she had known. Maybe it wouldn't last—but right now, it was the real thing, the genuine article, Love. And that was all that mattered.

Or was it?

THE END

Bibliography

The Erotic Novels of Robert Silverberg

As by Loren Beauchamp
Love Nest (Midwood, 1958)
Another Night, Another Love (Midwood, 1959)
Connie (Midwood, 1959)
Unwilling Sinner (Midwood, 1959)
Meg (Midwood, 1960; reprinted as All the Best Beds as by Don Elliott, 1967)
Nurse Carolyn (Midwood, 1960; reprinted as Registered Nympho as by Don Elliott, 1967)
And When She Was Bad (Midwood, 1961)
Sin on Wheels (Midwood, 1961; reprinted as Orgy on Wheels as by Don Elliott, 1967)
The Fires Within (Midwood, 1961)
Campus Sex Club (Midwood, 1962)
Sin a la Carte (Midwood, 1962)
Strange Delights (Midwood, 1962)
Wayward Widow (Midwood, 1962; reprinted as Free Sample, 1968)
The Wife Traders (Boudoir, 1963)

As by Dr. Walter C. Brown
The Single Girl (Monarch, 1961)

As by David Challon
Campus Love Club (Bedside, 1959; reprinted as Campus Sex Club as by Loren Beauchamp, 1962)
French Sin Port (Bedside, 1959; reprinted as Rouge of the Riviera as by Don Elliott, 1967)
Suburban Sin Club (Bedside, 1959; abridged & reprinted as The Wife Traders as by Loren Beauchamp, 1963)
Thirst for Love (Bedside, 1959; reprinted as Wayward Widow as by Loren Beauchamp, 1962)
Man Mad (Chariot, 1960)
Suburban Affair (Bedside, 1960)
Campus Hellcat and Other Stories (Bedside, 1960)

As by John Dexter
Stripper! (Nightstand, 1960; reprinted as One Bed Too Many by Jeremy Dunn)
Sex Thieves (Nightstand, 1961; reprinted as Wife in Name Only by Jeremy Dunn, 1974)

Sin Festival (Nightstand, 1961; reprinted as The Goddess Makers by Jeremy
   Dunn, 1974)
The Bra Peddlers (Nightstand, 1961; reprinted as The Venus Affair by
   Jeremy Dunn, 1974)
The Lust Plotters (Nightstand, 1962)
Passion Bum (Nightstand, 1962)

As Walter Drummond
Philosopher of Evil: The Life & Works of the Marquis de Sade (nf; Regency,
   1962)
How to Spend Money (nf; Regency, 1963)

As by Dan Eliot
Dial O-R-G-Y (Ember, 1963)
Flesh Flames (Ember, 1963)
Lust Lover (Pillar, 1963)
Nympho (Ember, 1963)
Sin Doll (Ember, 1963)
Sin Hellion (Ember, 1963)
Sin Mates (Pillar, 1963)

Don Elliott (all published by Greenleaf under various imprints)
Love Addict (1959)
Gang Girl (1959)
Naked Holiday (1960)
The Flesh Peddlers (1960; reprinted as The Flesh Merchants, 1973)
The Lecher (1960)
Mistress of Sin (1960; reprinted as Depravity Town, 1973)
Party Girl (1960)
   Sin on Wheels (1960; reprinted as The Instructor, 1973)
Passion Trap (1960; reprinted as Carnal Cage, 1973)
Sex Jungle (1960; reprinted as Jungle Street, 1973)
Convention Girl (1960; reprinted as The Man Collector, 1973)
Summertime Affair (1960)
Woman Chaser (1960)
Backstreet Sinner (1961; reprinted as The Bed and the Beautiful, 1973)
Expense Account Sinners (1961; reprinted as Keep the Clients Happy, 1973)
Lust Goddess (1961; reprinted as The Temptress, 1973)
Lust Queen (1961; reprinted as The Decadent, 1974)
The Lust Seekers (1961; reprinted as Till Love Do Us Part, 1974)
Sin Club (1961; reprinted as The Lady from Soho, 1974)
Sin Cruise (1961; reprinted as Fifteen Nights of Love, 1973)
The Sinful Ones (1961; reprinted as Every Night in Rome, 1974)
Wild Divorcee (1961; reprinted as Nowhere Girl, 1973)
Streets of Sin (1961; reprinted as The Untamed, 1974)
Hotrod Sinners (1962)

Kept Man (1962)
Lust Captive (1962; reprinted as The Game Susan Played, 1974)
Lust Cat (1962)
Lust Cult (1962; reprinted as None But the Wicked, 1974)
Lust for Two (1962)
Lust Lord (1962)
Lust Market (1962)
No Lust Tonight (1962)
The Orgy Boys (1962)
Passion Thieves (1962)
Roadhouse Girl (1962; reprinted as No Pleasure So Painful, 1974)
Sex Fury (1962)
Sexteen (1962)
Shame House (1962)
Sin Bait (1962)
Sin Kin (1962)
Sin Quest (1962)
Sin Sick (1962)
Three Sinners (1962; reprinted as A Change for the Bedder, 1974)
Wild Flesh (1962)
Lust Crew (1963)
Passion Patsy (1963)
Sex Bait (1963)
Sex Bum (1963)
Sin Crazed (1963)
Sin Made (1963)
Sin Servant (1963)
Beatnik Wanton (1964)
Black Market Shame (1964)
Flesh Bride (1964)
Flesh Lesson (1964)
Flesh Melody (1964)
Flesh Pawns (1964)
Flesh Prize (1964)
The Flesh Seekers (1964)
Flesh Taker (1964)
Gutter Road (1964)
Lust Burns (1964)
Lust League (1964)
Lust Set (1964)
Lust Spree (1964)
Orgy Isle (1964)
Orgy Maid (1964)
Passion Pair (1964)
Passion Partners (1964)
Passion Trio (1964)

Pickup (1964)
Shameless (1964)
Sin Bin (1964)
Sin Circuit (1964)
Sin Partners (1964)
Sin Service (1964)
Sin Sold (1964)
Switch Trap (1964)
Wanton Web (1964)
Alternate Wife (1965)
Carnal Carnival (1965)
Escape to Sindom (1965)
Flesh Bigamist (1965)
Flesh Boarder (1965)
Flesh Cry (1965)
Flesh Man (1965)
Good Girl, Bad Girl (1965)
Lust Doomed (1965)
Lust Finale (1965)
Naked She Died (1965)
The Nite Lusters (1965)
Nudie Packet (1965)
Of Shame Reborn (1965)
Only the Depraved (1965)
Orgy Slaves (1965)
Passion Killer (1965)
Passion Peeper (1965)
Passion Pusher (1965; cover listed as by Don Holliday)
The Shame Protector (1965)
Shame Scheme (1965)
Sin for Solace (1965)
Sin Kill (1965)
Sin Spin (1965)
The Sin Switch (1965)
Sin Warped (1965)
The Sins of Seena (1965)
Teaser (1965)
Would-Be Sinner (1965)
The Young Wantons (1965)
All on Sunday (1966)
Big Blast (1966)
Campus Traders (1966)
Cousin Lover (1966)
Diary of Desire (1966)
Every Bed Her Own (1966)
The Gay Girls (1966)

Initiates (1966)
Lust Demon (1966)
One Night Stand (1966)
Pain Lusters (1966)
The Passion Barons (1966)
Take My Wife (1966)
The Virtuous Ones (1966)
All the Best Beds (1967)
Carnal Counselor (1967; ghost-written, author unknown)
Diary of a Dyke (1967)
Flesh Fever (1967)
Flesh Tryst (1967)
Orgy on Wheels (1967)
Registered Nympho (1967)
Rogue of the Riviera (1967)
Those Who Lust (1967)
The Wanton West (1967)

As by Marlene Longman
Sin Girls (Nightstand, 1960; reprinted as The Tormented, 1973)

As by Dan Malcolm
The Mystery of the Judge's Mistress (*Guilty*, March 1962)

As by Ray McKenzie
The Wild Party (Chariot, 1960)

As by Gordon Mitchell
Immoral Wife (Midwood, 1959; reprinted as Henry's Wife, 1961)

As by Mark Ryan
Company Girl (Bedside, 1959)
Streets of Sin (Bedside, 1959; reprinted as The Passion Barons as by Don
   Elliott, 1966)
Twisted Love, (Bedside, 1959; reprinted as Strange Delights as by Loren
   Beauchamp, 1962)
Savage Love (Bedside, 1960)
Illicit Affair and Other Stories (Bedside, 1961)

As by Stan Vincent
The Hot Beat (Magnet, 1960)

As by L. H. Walker
The Lascivious Abbott (Greenleaf, 1967; introduction by L. T. Woodward)

As by L. T. Woodward, M. D.

Sex Fiend (Monarch, 1961)
Sex and Hypnosis (Monarch, 1961)
Sex in Our Schools (Monarch, 1962)
Virgin Wives (Monarch, 1962)
The Deceivers (Beacon, 1962)
90% of What You Know About Sex is Wrong (Parliament, 1962)
Sex and the Armed Forces (Monarch, 1963)
The History of Surgery (Monarch, 1963)
You and Your Sex Life (Monarch, 1963)
Twilight Women (Lancer, 1963)
Masochism (Monarch, 1964)
Sex and the Divorced Woman (Lancer, 1964)
Sophisticated Sex Techniques in Marriage (Lancer, 1967)
I Am a Nymphomaniac (Belmont, 1967)

The Science Fiction Works of Robert Silverberg

Novels

Revolt on Alpha C (Thomas Crowell, 1955; Scholastic, 1959)
The 13th Immortal (Ace, 1956)
Master of Life and Death (Ace, 1957)
The Shrouded Planet (with Randall Garrett, as Robert Randall; Gnome.
   1957; Dell. 1963)
Invaders from Earth (Ace, 1958)
Lest We Forget Thee, Earth (as Calvin M. Knox; Ace, 1958)
Stepsons of Terra (Ace, 1958)
Aliens from Space (as David Osborne; Avalon, 1958)
Invisible Barriers (as David Osborne; Avalon, 1958)
Starhaven (as Ivar Jorgenson; Avalon, 1958; Ace, 1959)
Starman's Quest (Gnome, 1958)
The Plot Against Earth (as Calvin M. Knox; Ace, 1959)
The Dawning Light (with Randall Garrett, as Robert Randall; Gnome, 1959;
   Dell, 1963)
The Planet Killers (Ace, 1959)
Lost Race of Mars (Scholastic, 1960)
Collision Course (Avalon, 1961; Ace, 1961)
The Seed of Earth (Ace, 1962)
Recalled to Life (Lancer, 1962; revised version, Doubleday, 1972)
Blood on the Mink (written in 1959, first published in 1962 as "Too Much
   Blood on the Mink" in *Trapped* magazine, re-published by Hard Case
   Crime, 2012)
The Silent Invaders (Ace, 1963)
Time of the Great Freeze (Holt, Rinehart and Winston, 1964; Dell, 1966)

Regan's Planet (Pyramid, 1964)
One of Our Asteroids is Missing (as Calvin M. Knox; Ace, 1964)
Conquerors from the Darkness (Holt, Rinehart and Winston, 1965; Dell, 1968)
The Gate of Worlds (Holt, Rinehart and Winston, 1967; Magnum, 1980)
Planet of Death (Holt, Rinehart and Winston, 1967)
Thorns (Ballantine, 1967)
Those Who Watch (Signet, 1967)
The Time Hoppers (Doubleday, 1967; Avon, 1968)
To Open the Sky (Ballantine, 1967)
World's Fair 1992 (Follett, 1970; Ace, 1982)
The Man in the Maze (Avon, 1968)
Hawksbill Station (Doubleday, 1968; Avon, 1970)
The Masks of Time (Ballantine, 1968)
Nightwings (Avon, 1969)
Downward to the Earth (serialized in *Galaxy*, 1970; Signet, 1971)
Across a Billion Years (Dial, 1969; Magnum, 1979)
Three Survived (Holt, Rinehart and Winston, 1969)
To Live Again (Doubleday, 1969; Dell, 1971)
Up the Line (Ballantine, 1969)
Tower of Glass (serialized in *Galaxy*, 1970; Charles Scribner's Sons, 1970; Bantam, 1971)
Son of Man (Ballantine, 1971)
The Second Trip (Signet, 1971)
The World Inside (Doubleday, 1971; Signet, 1972)
A Time of Changes (serialized in *Galaxy*, 1971; Signet, 1971)
The Book of Skulls (Charles Scribner's Sons, 1971; Signet, 1972)
Dying Inside (serialized in *Galaxy*, 1972; Charles Scribner's Sons, 1972; Ballantine,
1972)
The Stochastic Man (Harper & Row, 1975; Fawcett, 1976)
Shadrach in the Furnace (Bobbs-Merrill, 1976; Pocket, 1978)
Homefaring (Phantasia, 1983)
Lord of Darkness (Arbor House, 1983; Bantam, 1984)
Gilgamesh the King (Arbor House, 1984; Bantam, 1985)
Sailing to Byzantium (Underwood-Miller, 1985; Tor, 1989)
Tom O'Bedlam (Donald I. Fine, 1985; Warner, 1986)
Star of Gypsies (Donald I. Fine, 1986; Popular Questar, 1988)
At Winter's End (Warner, 1988; Warner, 1989)
Project Pendulum (Walker, 1989; Bantam, 1989)
Letters From Atlantis (Atheneum, 1990; Popular Questar, 1992)
The New Springtime (Warner, 1990; Warner, 1991)
To the Land of the Living (Gollancz, 1989; Warner, 1990)
Nightfall (expansion of the 1941 novelette "Nightfall" by Isaac Asimov; Doubleday; 1990; Bantam, 1991)
Thebes of the Hundred Gates (Axolotl/Pulphouse, 1991; Bantam, 1992)

The Face of the Waters (Bantam, 1991; Bantam, 1992)

Child of Time (expansion and revision of the 1958 novelette "Lastborn" by Isaac Asimov; Gollancz, 1991; US edition, The Ugly Little Boy, Doubleday, 1992)

Kingdoms of the Wall (HarperCollins, 1992; Bantam, 1993)

The Positronic Man (based on the 1976 novelette The Bicentennial Man by Isaac Asimov; Gollancz, 1992)

Hot Sky at Midnight (Bantam, 1994; HarperCollins, 1994)

Starborne (Bantam, 1996; Voyager, 1996)

The Alien Years (HarperCollins, 1998; Harper Voyager, 1999)

The Longest Way Home (Gollancz, 2002; Harper Voyager, 2003)

Roma Eterna (Eos, 2003; Harper Voyager, 2004)

The Last Song of Orpheus (Subterranean, 2010)

Majipoor Chronicles

Lord Valentine's Castle (Harper & Row, 1980; Bantam, 1981)

Majipoor Chronicles (Arbor House, 1982; Bantam, 1983)

Valentine Pontifex (Arbor House, 1983; Bantam, 1984)

The Mountains of Majipoor (Bantam, 1995; Bantam, 1996)

Sorcerers of Majipoor (Macmillan UK, 1997; HarperPrism, 1997)

Lord Prestimion (Harper, 1999; Eos, 2000)

King of Dreams (Voyager, 2001; Eos, 2001)

Tales of Majipoor (Gollancz, 2013; Roc, 2013)

Short story collections

Next Stop, the Stars (Ace, 1962)

Godling, Go Home (Belmont, 1964)

Needle in a Timestack (Ballantine, 1966)

The Calibrated Alligator (Holt, Rinehart and Winston, 1969)

Dimension Thirteen (Ballantine, 1969)

The Cube Root of Uncertainty (Macmillan, 1970; Collier, 1971)

Parsecs and Parables (Doubleday, 1973)

Moonferns & Starsongs (Ballantine, 1971)

The Reality Trip and Other Implausibilities (Ballantine, 1972)

Valley Beyond Time (Dell, 1973)

Earth's Other Shadow (Signet, 1973)

Unfamiliar Territory (Charles Scribner's Sons, 1973; Berkley, 1978)

The Feast of St. Dionysus: Five Science Fiction Stories (Charles Scribner's Sons, 1975; Berkley, 1979)

Sunrise on Mercury (Thomas Nelson, 1975; Pan, 1986)

Capricorn Games (Random House, 1976; Starblaze, 1979)

The Best of Robert Silverberg (Pocket, 1976)

The Shores of Tomorrow (Thomas Nelson, 1976)

World of a Thousand Colors (Arbor House, 1982; Bantam, 1984)

The Conglomeroid Cocktail Party (Arbor House, 1984; Bantam, 1985)
Beyond the Safe Zone (Donald I. Fine, 1986; Warner, 1987)
The Collected Stories of Robert Silverberg Volume 1: Secret Sharers
    (Bantam, 1992)
Pluto in the Morning Light: The Collected Stories Volume 1 (Grafton, 1992)
The Secret Sharer: The Collected Stories Volume 2 (Grafton, 1993)
Beyond the Safe Zone: The Collected Stories Volume 3 (Grafton, 1994)
The Road to Nightfall: The Collected Stories Volume 4 (Grafton, 1996)
Ringing the Changes: The Collected Stories Volume 5 (Grafton, 1997)
Lion Time in Timbuctoo: The Collected Stories Volume 6 (Grafton, 2000)
Phases of the Moon (Subterranean Press, 2004),
In the Beginning: Tales from the Pulp Era (Subterranean Press, 2006)
To Be Continued: The Collected Stories Volume 1 (Subterranean Press, 2006)
To the Dark Star: The Collected Stories Volume 2 (Subterranean Press, 2007)
A Little Intelligence (with Randall Garrett; Crippen & Landru, 2009)
Something Wild Is Loose: The Collected Stories Volume 3 (Subterranean
    Press, 2008)
Trips: The Collected Stories Volume 4 (Subterranean Press, 2009)
The Palace at Midnight: The Collected Stories Volume 5 (Subterranean
    Press, 2010)
Multiples: The Collected Stories Volume 6 (Subterranean Press, 2011)
We Are for the Dark: The Collected Stories Volume 7 (Subterranean Press,
    2012)
Hot Times in Magma City: The Collected Stories Volume 8 (Subterranean
    Press, 2013)
The Millennium Express: The Collected Stories Volume 9 (Subterranean
    Press, 2014)

Wicked satires from the master of black humor.....

Barry N. Malzberg

Underlay
978-1-933586-85-4 $15.95
"A brilliant novel, wildly funny and surprisingly poignant in its deeply knowledgeable portrait of the obsessed world of the compulsive bettor. Malzberg understands the racetrack the way Hemingway understood the bullring."
—Robert Silverberg

Lady of a Thousand Sorrows/ Confessions of Westchester County
978-1-944520-61-8 $19.95
"Both novels are told through first person narration and effectively display Malzberg's uncanny insight into character and motivation. The dialogue is never less than convincing..."
—Alan Cranis, *Bookgasm*

The Spread/Horizontal Woman
978-1-944520-82-3 $15.95
"These tales are dark ... blackly comic... *The Spread* centres on pornography and its effect on people, *Horizontal Woman* on sexual liberation, vulnerability and social theory... they get under your skin."
—Paul Burke, *NB*

Screen/Cinema
978-1-951473-11-2 $15.95
"...the language of erotic literature repurposed for rather more disturbing ends—this is no paean to film, this is a lamentation, a demystification of the impossibility of it all that takes a hammer to cinematic illusions." —Joachim Boaz

Overlay/A Bed of Money/Underlay
978-1-951473-12-9 $19.95
The Horseplayer Trilogy in one volume.
"Barry Malzberg is a comic genius."
—Michael Hurd, *Review.*
"The ending is as absurd as the plot is strange and uncertain."—Paul F. Brooks.

Each book includes a new afterword by the author.

"There is no one, with the possible exception of Philip K. Dick, whose works, each one of them, are so unpredictable or so outrageous and outraged."
—Theodore Sturgeon, *Galaxy*

"Mr. Malzberg writes with cold stylishness about hot subjects."—*Detroit Free Press*

STARK HOUSE PRESS
1315 H Street, Eureka, CA 95501
griffinskye3@sbcglobal.net
www.StarkHousePress.com

Available from your local bookstore, or order direct or via our website.